DEDICATION

To Red:
My confidant, my partner in crime,
thank you for answering my random texts
and creeping Brian out by talking in unison.
I've known you longer than I've known these characters—and that's
saying something.

And for the One who's not finished with me yet:
Keep making me.

WILD MAGIC
CLEARWATER WITCHES #2

Madeline Freeman

ACKNOWLEDGMENTS

As always, thank you, Rachel Schurig for talking me off the ledge. I'm so thankful we can be that for each other.

Thanks to Janet at Dragonfly Editing for your editing services.

Thank you to Steven Novak for the beautiful artwork.

Chapter One

I'm still convinced it's a dream. Every time I look up and see her, I think I'm asleep, hallucinating. I've gone so far as to pinch myself in the twenty-four hours since I woke up to this new reality.

In my old reality, she was gone just a month. It's strange how many little things have already started to slip away. Like the way she sweeps her fingers over her brow as if to brush her bangs out of her vision, even though they aren't long enough to be in her eyes. Or how she almost never pushes the kitchen drawers closed with her hands, instead insisting on bumping them with her hip. Or the way she leaves the cupboard with the glasses in it ajar, like she's thinking about going back for another cup.

People used to tell me we looked alike, but I never saw it. Though we both have pin-straight hair, hers is chestnut brown where mine is pale blonde. We both have brown eyes, but hers are brighter, more luminous. But now, when I study her face, I see the similarities others always insisted on: the shape of our chins, the way our eyes squint when we laugh, the arch of our eyebrows, the shape of our mouths.

I do look like my mother. I don't know why it took her return from the dead for me to notice it.

From my spot against the door jamb between the kitchen and dining room, I shake my head. Saying she's back from the dead makes it sound like she's a zombie, but she's not. She's not so much back as she never left.

In this reality, she never died.

I've been watching her all day, so much that I know she noticed it. But I can't help it.

She hums as she makes dinner. I'd forgotten she did that, too. She catches my eye and I drop my gaze, crossing to the island where she set out several bowls full of different items: diced tomatoes, chopped lettuce, salsa, sour cream. The tune she hums is familiar as I collect the bowls, but by the time I exit the room, she's switched to something different, like the station in her head changed channels. I smile as I set the bowls on the dining room table. My aunt Jodi sits adjacent to me, sipping at her mug of tea almost absently as her keen blue eyes skim the newspaper.

It's the little things that stick out to me most. How I never saw Jodi read the newspaper before. During meals, Jodi would sip her tea and if she wasn't talking to me, she'd be doing something on her phone. But there are no phones at the table now. The addition of the newspaper makes Jodi look—well, not older, but more mature, maybe. Her wavy brown hair isn't loose around her shoulders like it usually is; instead, it's pulled back into a messy chignon. The effect is a gentle sharpening of her features, making the set of her jaw more pronounced. She still looks like the Jodi I grew to know—mostly. But I wonder if, under my mother's influence, she's sobered a bit. Like the cell phone thing: It never bothered her before if the two of us sat in silence at the table, eating and flicking through screens on our separate devices. But when I pulled my phone out yesterday to make sure the world at large was as I remember it, she stared at me like I'd lost my mind, like I should know better than to bring technology to the table.

It's not surprising, really. My mom always had that rule at our house.

But this is our house. And it has been for four years. Except it hasn't. I've only been here a month, and my mother wasn't with me.

I set down my glass, covering my eyes with my free hand as the conflicting realities battle themselves in my head. Two days ago, my mother was dead. Now she's making tacos. I don't remember the details of the life my mom and aunt are living, and they don't remember the details of mine. It's strange to hear my mother knocking around in the kitchen of a house that, to my knowledge, she'd never stepped foot in.

That doesn't stop her from bringing a plate of taco shells and a bowl of meat into the room and setting them on the table. "Eat up," she says, a smile stretched across her face.

Tears prickle in the corners of my eyes and I blink rapidly to clear them. Mom's eyebrows crease at the center and I come to my senses: I have to pretend. This isn't my reality, but I have to pretend it is.

Crystal Jamison told me I had to.

At the time, I agreed with her. Of course, it was better to pretend things were normal. How would the people in our lives react if we announced that this entire existence is a lie and not meant to be? How can I tell my mother she's supposed to be dead?

A fist tightens around my lungs and I struggle to breathe. How can I even think that? Maybe Crystal is right—I should just be happy about what's happened. I didn't intend to do it, but I got my mother back. I never thought I'd see her again, and now here she is. It's a miracle.

Except, it doesn't feel like one. Every time I allow the elation in, it's followed immediately by a sweeping guilt. I've cheated somehow. I messed with time and the consequences aren't entirely clear yet. Yes, my mother is back, and Jodi isn't sick—even Crystal's aunt, who died nearly twenty years ago—is actually alive. And these are all good things. But what are the negative things we set in motion by going back? I keep waiting for the other shoe to drop. And I have a feeling that when it does, it's going to destroy everything.

My fingers go to my neck, reaching for the ring I wear there. Or wore. I sigh, as I've done a dozen times already: In this timeline, I don't wear my father's ring. I don't even know if I ever found it. For some reason, having it would make me feel better. Perhaps it's because the one constant in all this change is his absence. He's gone, like he was in my real life. I need that ring to remind me of where I belong.

My mom's eyebrows scrunch as she chews her bite of taco. "Kristyl, what's bothering you?"

"Nothing." The truth is too complex even to begin to explain. But one look at her face tells me that she is going to require an answer, a real one. My mind flicks through the thoughts swirling around until it lands on the only one I can share: "I just... I'm thinking about Dad today."

Jodi looks up from her newspaper and exchanges a glance with my mom. I don't like it. Did I do something wrong? If events in this timeline are different, it stands to reason that I'm different, too. I've had different experiences. Do I not talk about my father?

"What is it?" I ask, unable to keep the question to myself. "Why are you guys looking at each other like that?"

My mom's mouth twitches before the corner pulls up in a half smile. "Nothing. It's just... It's been a long time since you've mentioned him."

Shit. I've already done something wrong. I need to control the damage. "I... I had a dream about him. Like, he just showed up, and suddenly... I was a little girl again and..." I grope for things to say that aren't too specific. I don't want to mention any memories just in case they didn't happen here.

But the bit of detail I've provided seems sufficient. Mom and Jodi exchange another glance, this one softer. Jodi folds her paper and sets it on the table in front of her. "I'm glad to see you can talk about him without... well, the usual drama."

I bite the inside of my cheek. How different am I here? Typically, I avoid drama like the plague. However, if what Crystal told me yesterday is true, she and I are besties here. And Crystal is something of a drama magnet. I force a smile. "Maybe I'm maturing."

Jodi grins. "We were hoping that'd happen one day."

My fingertips stroke my neck again and I decide to go for it: I need to know about the ring. "In the dream... Dad had this... ring. It was kind of heavy with a smoky stone."

My mom nods and a wave of relief comes over me. She knows what I'm talking about. "What about it?"

I take a breath. "Do... Do you know where it is?"

Mom squints at me and I know I'm missing something. "Of course. It's the same place it's been for the last—what?" She looks at Jodi as if expecting to read the answer in the lines of her face. "Two years? Three, maybe?"

I shift in my seat. "Oh?" My heart hammers in my chest. What does that mean? *Is it with my father? Did he take it with him when he left?* Or does she mean it's somewhere I should know, somewhere alternate-me put it? If that's the case, what if I can't find it?

"It's upstairs in my jewelry box. I put it there after you said you didn't want it."

Jodi laughs. "I'm pretty sure her exact words were closer to 'I never want to see that ugly piece of crap ever again.'"

I force a smile. "Yeah, I guess you're right. Maybe I... blocked it out or something. But... I think I've changed my mind."

Mom raises an eyebrow at me. "Are you saying you want it?"

I open my mouth to respond but stop short, realizing at the last second that my response will be a yell—yes! But that reaction doesn't seem very alternate-me, so I take a breath and relax my shoulders. "I at least want to look at it. To see if it's as ugly as I remember. It's just weird it showed up in my dreams after all this time, right? So... maybe I should give it another try."

Mom dabs the corners of her mouth with the cream-colored cloth napkin by her side before standing. "You finish eating; I'll go grab it."

Her footsteps creak against the wood floor and stairs. It seems a geologic age before I hear her returning. I try to eat in her absence, but I find it hard to focus. The ring. It's such a small thing, but it doesn't feel that way. In the past few weeks, I've felt like that ring was somehow a talisman of protection—a connection to my father. I need something of that last timeline, something from my reality, to make me feel better about this one.

I've only finished half of the taco in front of me by the time Mom returns, but it's all I'm going to eat. She holds the ring out to me and I snatch it before I can catch myself. I know she and Jodi are watching me as I study it, but I don't care. I can't care. It looks the same as I remember it—the same but for one detail: it seems smaller. Not the weighty setting or the stone, but the circumference of the ring itself. It looks like it might actually fit my finger. I poke my right ring finger through the center, but the ring doesn't make it past my first knuckle before I hesitate, pulling it off. The first time I put this ring on, in my reality, I had a vision and made everything in my room levitate. On the chance something like that happens again, I should wait until I'm alone before trying.

"Can I have it?" I ask, curling my fingers into a fist around the ring.

"Of course," Mom says, her tone dubious. "Your dad left it for you. You know that. He even had it sized so you could wear it."

I stand, picking up my plate and heading to the kitchen. "I think I'm finally ready for it."

Jodi nods appreciatively at me when I reenter the dining room. "I knew you'd come back to us eventually."

The skin at the back of my neck prickles. What could she mean by that? Does she know—does she remember my reality? Has this all been some sort of test? No, it's not possible that she knows the truth: Jodi's a witch, so she can do magic, but she doesn't have any special connection with time—that's a psychic's domain. I force a short laugh. "What, did I go somewhere?"

She shrugs. "Come on. I know Crystal and the girls are your friends, but let's not pretend their friendship didn't come at a price."

"Jodi." My mom's tone is light, but there's a hint of warning around the edges. The echoey sensation that accompanies the thoughts and feelings of other people fills my mind. It takes me a moment to interpret the impressions: They've had this conversation before and Mom is of the opinion I'm old enough to make my own choices about my friends; besides, telling me *not* to hang out with someone will only make that person more appealing.

Jodi crosses her arms over her chest and turns to my mom. "You know as well as I do they're the reason she stopped wearing Ben's ring to begin with."

My mom opens her mouth to respond, but I clear my throat. "Well, they won't make me stop wearing it again."

Jodi raises her mug. "I'll drink to that."

Chapter Two

My father's ring is warm and heavy in my hand and it tugs on my consciousness while I wait for Mom and Jodi to finish dinner. From where I set it in the living room, my phone trills. I tense but don't make a move for it. Jodi catches my eye, smiling, and I force a smile in return. Maybe she's more like the Jodi I know than I thought—maybe she's not as pro this no-electronic-devices mandate of my mom's as I originally thought.

When Mom finally takes her last bite, I clear the table quickly and load the dishwasher. My phone trills again before I get to it. Crystal Jamison has sent two messages:

The circle's meeting at Fox's house. I'll be by to pick you up in 20.

Are you ignoring me? I'll be there in 15 to get you.

I sigh. Even though it's evening, I'm still in my pajamas. This morning, before she left my house, Crystal alluded to the fact that the witches would be meeting today. With a quick glance toward the dining room, where Mom and Jodi are chatting about something, I steal away upstairs. I hope alternate-me didn't have any plans with either of them this evening: I don't think Crystal will take no for an answer.

At the top of the stairs that open up to my third story loft, I pause, uncurling my fingers and staring down at my father's ring. My ring. After a moment's hesitation, I slip it onto my right ring finger.

The flash overtakes me immediately, as if it has been waiting patiently in the wings for the go-ahead from me. My vision is overtaken by pure white light, followed by blackness that begins at my periphery and sweeps forward, plunging me into darkness. I don't fight it. I let the blackness wash over me and wait for it to abate and show me the scene.

When my vision clears and focuses, I'm not expecting the scene that greets my eyes. The first time I slipped this ring on, I was still in my room, just a past version of it, when my dad was just a few years older than I am. But the scene before me now is completely foreign. The walls and ceiling are constructed of heavy hewn timbers. Light spills in through small open windows on either side of the room, but the space still feels dim, like the sunlight isn't strong enough to dispel all the shadows. A man in his sixties sits in a rocking chair in front of a hearth smudged black with soot. His hands are folded atop the rough tan fabric of the shirt stretched across his ample belly and he stares toward the embers glowing in the hearth. Another man stands before the man in the chair, this one younger. Upon closer inspection, the second man doesn't look much older than me—perhaps in his early twenties. He wears a loose-fitting off-white shirt belted at the hips and simple brown pants tucked into a pair of high boots that tie at the calf.

"Grandfather, are you sure?" The younger man shifts his weight from one foot to the other as he examines the palm of his right hand.

The grandfather rocks gently in his chair, his eyes still on the hearth. "Am I not a trustworthy man, Eli? What in my character prompts you to believe a double-dealing on my part?"

"I did not mean to imply—" Eli plants his feet firmly, squaring his shoulders. "It is just that... When I spoke with—"

"I know to whom you refer." The elder man's voice is sharp, but not unkind. His gaze shifts to Eli. "The ring is mine to do with as I please. I know he believes he has claim to it because he is the eldest grandchild, but it is my wish that it remain in the Barnette line."

I gasp, immediately covering my mouth with my hand. My muscles tense as I wait for a reaction from either Eli or the old man, but they continue as though I'm not there. Because, I remind myself, I'm not. I'm merely witnessing an echo of a past event. I take in a breath and relax. They're talking about a ring and my family. Could they be referring to the ring I now possess? And if so, who is this other person who thinks it should be his? I tiptoe forward, not trusting myself not to make the boards beneath my feet creak, even though I know I *can't*—I'm not interacting with the world here. Eli's eyes are on his palm again, but as I near him, I see a heavy ring in it. I run my thumb over the ring on my finger. The two are too similar not to be the same piece of jewelry.

"He'll not be pleased," Eli says.

"I am too old to worry myself about pleasing everyone. I can only do what I believe is right. The ring passes to you, Eli. If your cousin finds fault with my decision, he is to see me."

Eli closes his fingers around the ring. "Yes, Grandfather."

The old man unfolds his hands and presses them to the armrests of the rocking chair. With effort, he stands. He is hunched with age and shorter than Eli by several inches. Eli holds out his hand to steady his grandfather, but the man doesn't accept his assistance. He straightens his spine as much as he can and takes Eli by the shoulders. "I know you wish to believe the best of him. The two of you have been inseparable your whole lives. And his motivations may seem pure—" He catches the look of surprise on Eli's face and nods knowingly. "Yes, Eli, I know. You are not the only ones who avail yourselves of the abilities of the town psychics. This path will lead to darkness, mark my words. He will listen to you, Eli. You must lead him away from this path."

Eli shakes his head. He attempts to take a step back, but his grandfather's grip is too strong. "He'll not listen to me, Grandfather—especially after he sees the ring. He already believes I wish to challenge him for power of the circle."

"His fear is his greatest weakness, yet he wears it like strength. We all fear something, Eli. It is a strong man who can see the difference between legitimate fears and baseless ones." Grandfather releases Eli's shoulder but takes up the hand holding the ring. He uncurls Eli's fingers and plucks the ring from his palm before straightening Eli's right ring finger and slipping the ring onto it. He doesn't push it past his second knuckle, but he doesn't need to. Eli buckles at the knees, tipping forward. His grandfather tries to arrest his descent, but he only delays the inevitable. His gnarled hands loop beneath Eli's armpits and slow him as his knees collide with the rough wooden floor.

Heat surges through me, followed by a sharp pain in my knees. The plank beneath me digs into my knees through the thick rough material of my pants. The old man's hands dig uncomfortably into the soft flesh of my armpits. My mind struggles to make sense of what's happening. I can see Eli in front of me, but I can also feel the sensations assailing him. A bright white light assaults my vision and I recognize it for what it is in the same instant it overtakes me: I'm experiencing another vision within this current one.

Fire. A barn is alight from within. Flames peek between the joints in the walls and erupt through the doors. Heat burns my cheeks and I raise my arm to cover my face. Screams rip through the air, high and terrified. Someone is in the barn, a girl. Shouts sound through the surrounding darkness. I pull my arm away from my face, but the barn is gone, replaced with darkness and murmured voices. Lights flicker into existence one at a time— candles, arranged in a circle, revealing a figure laid out in the center, covered in black and bound at the hands and feet. A robed figure enters the circle, a long knife clutched in the hand that hangs by his side. He crosses to the figure and raises the blade into the air, above where its heart would be—

A graveyard at dusk. Flowers adorn the headstone of a newly covered grave. White stones, each the size of a human head, encircle the freshly mounded earth. The robed figure approaches, dropping to its knees and clutching the gravestone.

A room, much like the one Eli and his grandfather stand in, with a low-hanging ceiling pressing oppressively over the heads of a couple of dozen people, both men and women, ranging in ages from around thirty to probably sixty. The old man is among them. In the center of the room is a younger man, who faces the far wall, his arms and legs bound to the chair he sits in. His head droops, his chin resting against his chest.

"There is only one solution," says Eli's grandfather, moving toward the bound man. In one hand, he holds up a fist-sized chunk of clear quartz crystal. "The evil must be contained."

The ring on my finger burns against my flesh, but, when I pull it off, the stone and metal are cool to my touch.

Darkness overtakes my vision again, plunging me into a black void.

I gasp, doubling over as I come back to the present. What just happened? Did the grandfather give that vision to Eli, and if so, why did I see it? Did it have something to do with the ring? And what was the evil he spoke of? Did he mean it needed to be contained inside the piece of quartz he held? There was something familiar about the piece of crystal in his wizened hand. It couldn't be *the* crystal, could it?

Yes. The answer bubbles to the surface of my consciousness immediately. The stone from my vision looked too much like the one Crystal and I brought back from the past not to be the same one. But if that's the case, what does it mean about the energy inside it?

Footfalls thunder behind me and I manage to stand as I turn toward the sound. Neither my mom nor Jodi takes stairs that quickly—but who else could be coming up toward by bedroom?

Crystal Jamison appears at the bottom of the landing on the second floor. Her blue eyes widen as she takes in my appearance. "You're not ready." It's not a question.

I look down. She's right. I'm still in my pajamas. Have I been standing here for the last ten minutes? I shake my head. "I'll be right down."

She doesn't take the hint. As I move toward my closet, I hear her feet creaking against the stairs. I grab the first shirt and pair of jeans my hands contact and move into the bathroom without looking back at her. How can I explain what happened, why I'm not ready? Crystal doesn't know about my psychic inclinations, and it's not something I particularly want to share with her. She's already the only other person who knows about things being different after our foray into the past. I don't like the idea of her being the keeper of all my secrets.

I pull on my clothes and run a brush through my pale blond hair. A quick scan of the vanity doesn't reveal a hair tie so I abandon any thoughts of pulling back my hair. In less than two minutes, I emerge from the bathroom. Crystal is circling the perimeter of my room. While she's not touching anything, I can't help feeling violated, like she's going through my things or reading my diary. Then again, it's difficult to be too offended when the room isn't exactly mine. There are several items that are familiar, but just as many things are alien to me. It's like I've been away so long I've forgotten all the details of the room. It feels like I *should* remember the pictures taped to the mirror above the dresser, but I don't. I can't. I didn't live those moments.

I clear my throat and Crystal turns, looking completely unabashed. She raises an eyebrow and although she doesn't say anything, I know she's judging my appearance. I roll my eyes. Meeting Crystal's stylistic expectations doesn't even register on my radar as anywhere near important.

"What's that on your finger?"

I glance down at my right hand even though I don't need to. My finger looks normal, despite having felt like it was burning just a few minutes ago. "It's a ring."

"An ugly ring."

I cross my arms over my chest, tucking my hand where she can't see it. "Are we going or not?"

Chapter Three

Crystal doesn't speak again until we're safely in her car, headed down the road. "You're going to have to try harder."

I throw up my hands. "I haven't *done* anything yet."

She sucks her teeth as she pulls up to a stop sign. There's no one else at the intersection and she takes a moment to turn to me. "What are you wearing?"

I rub my left hand over the knuckles of my right. "Enough about the ring already. It was my dad's okay?"

She shakes her head. "I'm not talking about that monstrosity, so you can dial it back. I'm talking about that *outfit*." Her lip curls as she looks me up and down.

I pulled on an oversize navy hoodie on my way out the door when I couldn't find a jacket that looked familiar. My jeans are dark and flare at the ankles. The only shoes I could find at the front door that looked even remotely like something I might wear were a pair of black Converse, though they're a bit loose and might actually belong to Jodi. "What's wrong with it?"

Crystal rolls her eyes before refocusing her attention on the road and proceeding through the intersection. "Didn't you pay attention to the yearbooks I showed you last night? So far as everyone knows, you and I are best friends."

From the way she says it, her meaning is clear. How is anyone going to believe someone like Crystal—in her painted-on skinny jeans, low-cut red sweater that flares in ruffles around the hips, and seasonally-inappropriate tan corduroy jacket—would willingly hang around with someone dressed like me? I consider mentioning that people might assume we're friends because of my personality but quickly change my mind. "Just tell everyone I'm still not feeling well after the spell last night."

She flicks her chestnut hair over her shoulder. "Like they'll buy that. Clearly I feel fine."

I don't bother reminding her that I'm the one who brought us back from the past, and I don't mention at all that my psychic abilities are the reason we were able to travel through time to begin with. I know Crystal well enough to be sure inferring I did all the heavy lifting would not be received well. Instead, I tell her what she wants to hear. "I'll try harder."

"Good. Because no one can know we went back and changed things. So far as everyone's concerned, we're exactly the same people we've always been, and everything is as it should be." She gives me side-eye and I nod.

It's what we decided last night after realizing the world wasn't the same as we left it. At the time, it seemed logical—after all, if we start announcing from the rooftop that we're living in an alternate reality, people will probably think we've gone a bit crazy. Still, I don't know if I can pretend that everything is as it should be.

But maybe it is. I can't lie—having my mom back in my life is more amazing than I could have imagined. And the fact that Jodi isn't sick, that she never was, that she never had to deal with the knowledge that the candle of her life was about to burn out, is incredible. Still, a weight sits in the pit of my stomach, like we've cheated somehow.

But Crystal doesn't want to hear that.

She pulls her car to a stop in front of Fox and Griffin Holloway's house. Everything is the same—down to the garden gnome leaning against the porch—and it comforts me. Maybe things aren't quite as different as I imagined.

We're clearly not the first to arrive: Parked in the street nearby are a red SUV and a motorcycle, and in the driveway there's an old but lovingly detailed dark blue Mustang behind what looks like a monster truck. I wrinkle my nose at the truck. Whose could that be? Zane's, maybe?

Crystal leads the way to the front door and lets herself in. The inside of the house is not like I remember it. Before it was very much a bachelor pad, with laundry strewn around the room and old take out containers on the table. Now it's downright tidy. The pulled back curtains allow the last rays of sunlight to spill into the space. The video game controllers are still visible, but placed in a cubby on the entertainment center. There's a vase of fake flowers in the center of the coffee table.

Crystal whistles as she closes the door behind us. "Well, this is an interesting twist."

Voices float up from the basement and before I can ask Crystal what she means, she heads through the dining room toward the stairs.

As I descend to the basement, my heartbeat increases. For all the differences between this reality and my own, the one I'm least happy about is waiting for me at the bottom of the stairs. So far as my memories are concerned, two days ago, I was just beginning my first serious relationship—with Owen Marsh. However, according to what everyone here remembers, Fox Holloway and I are together, and from the brief yearbook research I engaged in last night, Owen and I might not even be friends.

A swell of greeting resounds as Crystal reaches the bottom stairs, but I can't distinguish what's being said. My head is too full of buzzing to differentiate between voices. What am I supposed to do if Fox tries to kiss me again? I didn't react when it happened last night, but only because it was so unexpected. But what about now? I'm not sure if I can kiss him back—even if it's just pretending.

Crystal crosses the floor toward the crude sitting area that takes up the bulk of the room. Griffin lounges in his usual arm chair at the far left, looking both haughty and bored, as usual. He chats with Zane Ross, who looks as relaxed and at ease as ever. Two girls stand from the couch to greet Crystal and the surprise of this fact jerks me from my own thoughts. Besides Crystal and me, there should only be *one* other girl here—Bridget Burke, Crystal's darker hair and skinned double, whose hair, makeup, and clothing choices are typically slightly sluttier versions of Crystal's. But beside Bridget stands a tall girl whose tight jeans and tan jacket match Crystal's and Bridget's nearly perfectly. The thing that distinguishes her is her hair—it's red, not brown like Crystal's and Bridget's.

Red hair. No, it can't be—she and Crystal haven't been friends for years, not since Crystal first started exploring her magical abilities. She thought Crystal was messing with something dangerous, something that could get her killed. Then again, she doesn't have the same experiences as the girl I knew because her aunt didn't die that night nearly twenty years ago. Something Crystal and I did affected that.

Lexie Taylor raises an eyebrow. "Stare much, Kristyl?"

The sound of my given name is jarring coming from her mouth. Lexie has only ever called me *Krissa*, the nickname Owen gave me my first day at Clearwater High. But things didn't happen that way here. Now I wish I'd taken yearbook research a little more seriously last night. I recall the pictures I saw of Owen and try to remember if I saw Lexie in any of them. I don't think she was. Are the two of them even friends now?

I force a smile and start across the room to her. "Sorry—I'm a bit out of it still."

Crystal crosses her arms over her chest and peers at me. "Yeah, that spell took a lot out of you, didn't it?" She shrugs. "I feel fine, though."

"You are *so* amazing, Crystal," Bridget gushes. "That retrieval spell was *way* harder than anything we've ever tried. I still can't believe it worked. After all this time, we finally have the crystal."

Bridget's words stick in my mind. Retrieval spell? That's not what we did—it was a time travel spell. But as the memory forms, another edges it out: Last night, during Crystal's litany of differences between our old reality and this one, she mentioned even the quartz's history had changed. Before, the stone had been all but destroyed in a fire, but here, it had merely disappeared on that night. Instead of passing through time to acquire it, our alternate selves *retrieved* it from some kind of magical limbo. The crystal disappearing the night of the fire makes some sense, I guess—since we took it back to the present with us. But thinking how it changed things in this reality makes my brain throb.

"Yeah—let me see it," Lexie says, holding her hand out toward her cousin. "I've been patient enough waiting for *my* turn." She gives a pointed glance in my direction and I bite my lower lip. I ran off with the crystal last night, thinking I needed it to save Jodi.

"Chill out," Crystal says, knocking Lexie's hand away from her. She pushes past the girls so she can sit on the couch. I move to sit next to her, but arms encircle my middle, pulling me backward. Before I can react, I'm on Fox's lap on the couch adjacent to Crystal's. He must have come downstairs when I was talking with the girls. He lands a loud kiss on my cheek.

"You snuck in," he says, his lips close to my ear. "I wanted to ask how you're doing. You didn't return my calls."

His tone is easy, casual, but a sensation creeps over me—an emotion that's not mine. He's hurt, worried. I tamp down my guilt and twist to face him. "I texted." The defense sounds thin even to me so I try again. "I've been kind of out of it all day. But I'm feeling better now."

Something flickers in Fox's gray eyes but he blinks and it's gone. He smiles and reaches forward to tuck a strand of hair behind my ear. "I forgot how nice your hair looks like this."

I run my hand over the ends self-consciously. Is this not how my alternate self wears it? "Like what?"

"All straight. And down. You've usually got it up or all wavy. But I like it like this." He runs his fingers through the length of it for emphasis.

I glance at the adjacent couch. Crystal, Bridget, and Lexie all have wavy hair. Am I expected to do up my hair to match theirs? Or do I do it because I want to? Just how different am I from this alternate version of myself?

Before I can consider the question too deeply, a scuffle breaks out on the next couch over. Lexie has thrown herself across Crystal, who is leaning as far away from her cousin as possible, her right arm outstretched to its farthest extent.

"Cat fight!" calls Zane enthusiastically. "My money's on Lexie!"

Griffin tips his head back, laughing. "I'll take that bet."

"Just hand it over!" Lexie's voice is shrill. "You've had it almost a whole day. It's not *yours*! That crystal's been passed down in the Taylor line. It's as much mine as it is yours!"

"Get off me!" Crystal yells. "You'll get your turn—"

"I don't want a *turn*, I want—"

What Lexie wants is cut off by a small explosion. Lexie screams as she sails backward, colliding with the wall adjacent to the stairwell. Bridget leaps off the couch like she's been jolted with electricity. Fox's grip around my waist grows firmer as he pulls me toward his torso protectively. Zane and Griffin stare open-mouthed at Lexie's crumpled form. Crystal's eyes are wide, afraid, her posture rigid. Zane comes to his senses first, launching himself out of his chair and moving to Lexie's side. She gets up slowly, leaning heavily on his arm. When she fixes her gaze on Crystal, Crystal's stance relaxes and her eyebrow arches.

"I *said* you'd get a turn," she murmurs.

Lexie charges at Crystal, fire in her eyes, but Zane catches her around the middle, restraining her. Crystal stands, a smile curling at the corners of her mouth. Her meaning is clear: *I dare you.* Lexie only fights harder to get away from Zane.

This is quickly getting out of hand. I don't know what my role in the group is, but I can't sit back while Crystal taunts her cousin, or while Lexie's eyes are so full of malice. I extricate myself from the circle of Fox's arms and move between the cousins, one arm up toward each of them. "Okay, let's just calm down."

"Calm down?" Griffin blinks a few times, shaking his head. "That was *awesome.*" He stands and edges toward Crystal, his hand out, his palm up. "Let's see it, then."

"No way," Lexie growls. "*He* doesn't get it before I've had a chance to see it. Let *go* of me, Zane!" She struggles against his arms but makes no forward progress.

Griffin takes another step toward Crystal, whose eyes narrow. "Keep coming, Griffin. I'll do to you what I did to Lexie."

Fox stands. "Come on, Crystal. You made your point. You don't have to throw us all across the room now, do you? It seems like overkill."

"I'll decide what's overkill." Crystal's eyes slide from Griffin to Fox.

I can't figure out what she's trying to prove here. If everyone's going to get a turn, why can't we just get started? My experience with the circle until this point has been limited, but I can't imagine Crystal's been like this all along—why would everyone put up with her? One thing's certain: If *I* have to pretend to be part of this circle, I'm going to actually be a part of it, not just a bystander. I step closer to Crystal—nearly an arm's length away. Her muscles coil, ready to spring. I sigh. "Enough. You called this meeting because we've finally got that stone. If you're not gonna share, I'd like to go home."

Crystal's face tightens. She points at me with the crystal, like it's an extension of her hand. "*You* don't get to say how things—"

She's cut off as the quartz slips from her grip and flies straight to my hand. I catch it reflexively and stare down at it, dumbfounded. I barely formed the thought that things would be so much easier if she'd just hand the stone over, and now here it is in my possession. Did I just do a spell? My experience with magic is limited at best. In my reality, Crystal taught me how to light a candle, and the surge of energy that accompanied it was enough to scare me. The only other spell I've done—on purpose—is the one that moved us through time.

I held this crystal last night. I took it from the clearing by the river where we did the spell, back to Jodi's house, convinced I needed its power to cure her of a curse. I sensed the magic in it then, but I was too distracted, too hopped up on adrenaline to focus on it. Now the energy fills me, moving like wildfire from my right palm to every other part of my body, making my skin tingle and my hairs stand up on end. I can do anything with this much power. No wonder Crystal didn't want to give it up. Possibilities open themselves up to me—everything I could accomplish with this much magic. I could set things right—to the way they're supposed to be. I could make Owen remember the two of us together, make Lexie remember that she and Crystal *aren't* friends—*and* I could make sure Jodi remains uncursed and my mom stays alive. I can have everything.

But to do those things, *I* need this power. Not the others. What would they even do with magic like this? They don't *deserve* this magic, this power. No. I'm the one who needs to control it.

My ring warms around my finger. My vision clouds and the

flash overtakes me so quickly I'm not able to prepare for it. I can't see anything, just a soft and milky nothingness. I'm pressed in on all sides, surrounded by something cold and hard. A hot wave of pain tears through my body and I try to scream, but no sound comes out. Cool air brushes my skin—I'm free of my prison. But I'm empty; I've lost something, something important. And I need it. Rage boils in my stomach. I will reclaim it.

The skin of my ring finger is burning, I'm sure of it. The heat of the ring is overwhelming, cutting through the vision, pulling me back to present. I blink rapidly and the room comes back into view. I still clutch the crystal in my hand, and although I could swear there were flames dancing around my father's ring seconds ago, the area looks completely normal. In fact, the skin under the ring is cool again, like nothing has happened.

"Give it back," Crystal snaps, holding her hand out to me.

Has no time passed? Fox's face is unconcerned, not like it would be if I'd been unresponsive for any length of time. I stare at the quartz in my hand. The energy is still there, but it's contained within the stone again, not filling me the way it did. I hold it out toward Crystal but hesitate. Did she experience the same thoughts that went through my head—the certainty that no one else should be able to wield the magic within? A look in her eyes is all I need to confirm the suspicion. I can't give it back to her, not if it'll bring on another episode of throwing people across the room. Instead, I place the quartz in Fox's hand, watching his face for a reaction.

Besides surprise, I don't see a change behind Fox's eyes. I allow my fingers to linger on his hand, reaching out with my psychic abilities the way I used to with Owen. As psychics, Owen and I would practice sending thoughts to each other, but a person doesn't have to be psychic for me to pick up on his thoughts or feelings—I've been doing it accidentally for years. Slowly, a faint echo builds in my brain. I sift through the noise to decipher what's going on in Fox's head. He's curious, confused, but not filled with desire for magic or plans for the power within the crystal. Removing my fingers, I sigh. It's not affecting him the way it affected me.

"Why don't you guys take turns trying a spell with the crystal?"

I smile encouragingly at Fox.

Crystal releases an exasperated sigh but I catch her eye, raising my eyebrows. She and I need to talk, but not here in front of everyone else. I hope she gets my meaning.

Fox grins as he stares down at the stone. He squares his shoulders and takes in a breath before turning to Lexie and holding it out to her. "Ladies first. You did, after all, suffer bodily harm for a chance to hold this thing."

Lexie hesitates before taking the crystal and smiling. "Thanks, Fox." She sounds surprised.

As she moves toward the center of the seating area, I grab Crystal's arm and tug her toward the stairs. "We need to talk," I mutter.

She fights for only a moment before letting out a sigh. "Fine. I don't want to watch this anyway." Over her shoulder, she calls, "Don't light anything on fire."

Lexie's sarcastic *ha ha* follows us as we ascend the stairs. I don't release Crystal's arm until we're safely in the living room. I cross to the couch but don't sit: Crystal lingers in the archway between the living room and dining room.

"What is it?" She rests her left hand in the crook of her right arm and examines the nail beds of her free hand.

"Come on. You can't tell me you didn't feel it." I cross my arms over my chest.

She glances up only momentarily before resuming her study of her fingertips. "Feel *what*? Besides pissed that Lexie tried to grab the crystal from me. I thought she was bad *before*. And now, apparently, I have to deal with her because she's in the circle." She rolls her eyes for effect. "Make that one mark against this reality."

My mouth drops open. "That's not what I'm talking about—"

"Oh, I suppose you thought it was fine for her to take it from me. Clearly. I can't believe you used magic to take it from me. That was kind of a bitch thing to do, you know."

"I didn't *mean* to. It just kind of happened—"

The look on her face silences me. She doesn't believe me. "Does this conversation have a point? Because I'd like to get back downstairs."

"Can you even hear yourself right now? If anyone's being a bitch, it's you."

Crystal closes the space between us in three strides. She stands so close I can see the faint sprinkle of freckles across her cheeks. "Have you got something to say?"

I fight the urge to take a step back. "I think there's something wrong with the crystal. I— I *felt* something when it was in my hand. It was an overpowering desire to keep all the magic for myself, to not let anyone else touch it."

Her eyebrow hitches upward. "Well, maybe you shouldn't touch it anymore."

"You shouldn't either."

She snorts. "What?"

"Are you honestly gonna tell me you didn't have the same feeling when you had it? That it's not the reason you didn't want to hand it over to Lexie?"

"I didn't want to give it to Lexie because I wanted to discuss the anchoring spell before everyone got carried away messing around with magic."

As if on cue, cheers sound from the basement. Crystal holds up her hands as if to say *see what I mean?*

She has a point; still, I can't believe her motives were that pure. "You knocked Lexie across the room."

She shrugs. "She was climbing on me. Tell me you wouldn't do the same thing."

The fact that I *wouldn't* is clouded by my memory of holding the crystal in my hand. If someone had tried to take it from me while those emotions coursed through my body, I may have. "There's something wrong with the crystal. I don't think— You shouldn't anchor the circle to it."

Her eyes go round. "Are you on crack? Of course we're gonna anchor to it. I understand you're new to all this, but we've been looking for this thing for *years*. The crystal will focus our magic so we can channel it better, use it better. Without an anchor, the magic is sporadic and unpredictable. Now, if memory serves, that's *exactly* what scared you about learning to use your own abilities."

I press my lips together. She's right about that. "I get that you've been looking for this thing forever. I'm the one who helped you find it, remember?"

"Yeah, but only because you wanted it for something." Her eyes narrow. "That's what this is about, isn't it? You don't want us to anchor to it because *you* want it. You want all that magic for yourself."

An echo of the desire that coursed through me minutes earlier returns, but I tamp it down. "That's not it. I'm serious, Crystal. There's something—" The word *evil* bubbles to my lips, but I don't say it. "There's something dark about it."

She rolls her eyes. "You're being paranoid. It's just magic. And, loath as I am to admit it, you're the one with the most magic in you. You should know better than anyone that it isn't bad on its own. It's just... natural."

Although her tone doesn't suggest jealousy, she can't hide her true feelings from me. I'm the one with the most ability—even if I'm not the most experienced. What the circle wants most of all is more access to abilities. If that's the case, maybe there's something Crystal's overlooking. "What about me?" I ask as the thought takes shape. "Instead of anchoring to the crystal, could you—I don't know—anchor to *me*? Then you could use my magic and—"

She shakes her head. "You mean a binding spell?"

"Sure—what's that?"

Another eye roll. "It's a way to link people together. The circle looked into it years ago. It's not the same as anchoring to something like the crystal. If we bind together, one of us could have more power—sure—but at the expense of everyone else. It's just a way to pool energy, not give everyone access to more."

"I wouldn't mind," I insist. "Why don't we try a binding spell first, and if—"

"No. We're anchoring to the crystal. That's final."

Another exuberant shout sounds in the basement and Crystal shifts, easing backward. I'm losing her—she wants to get back downstairs. Panic floods me. The anchoring spell—that's why we're here. "Are you doing the spell tonight?"

She shakes her head. "It has to be done on the full moon. The next one's Tuesday night. There's some prep work we've got to do first, but I'm pretty sure we can be ready by then."

A shiver courses through me. *Two days.* "Look, promise me something: If I can prove to you that there's something wrong with that crystal, you won't anchor to it." When she just stares at me, I grab her arm and give her a shake. "Crystal."

She pulls out of my grip. "Okay, whatever. But you're wrong. The crystal's perfectly fine. You're just being paranoid."

Another cheer rises from the basement and Crystal pivots on her heel and heads for the stairs without a backward glance. As I watch her, I twist my ring around my finger, gasping as a sharp pain ricochets up my arm. With the thumb and forefinger of my left hand, I wiggle the ring from its resting place. Beneath the band is a shiny red strip of skin, like a burn.

Chapter Four

Nerves knot my stomach Monday morning. I'm not at all prepared to go to school. What if someone there can tell I'm not the girl I'm pretending to be? Before I get out of bed, I consider pretending I'm sick but quickly abandon the idea: My mom has always been of the if-you-don't-have-a-temperature-you're-not-sick school of thought and I don't want to lose the gamble she's different on the point in this reality.

I take extra care selecting my outfit, not wanting another lecture from Crystal about not trying hard enough. I leave my hair straight and down, though. In addition to not having the faintest idea how to get it all wavy, keeping my hair down has been my default for most of my life. I used to use my hair as a curtain to hide behind, and I might need that security today.

I sit patiently in the living room after breakfast, waiting for someone to take me to school, but neither Jodi nor my mom seem like they're planning to do so. Their voices float to me from the kitchen; their easy banter is a weight in my stomach. They're friends here. I've never known them as friends. But if we've been living here for years, it makes sense that they would have built a rapport in that time.

An engine rumbles and I peek out the window. A large black truck sits in the driveway. It's the same truck I saw at Fox's house yesterday and I sigh. Of course, it's his.

My mom emerges from the dining room and peeks out the window above my head. A smile touches her lips. "You and Fox aren't in a fight, are you?"

I force a smile and shake my head. "No, we're not fighting. I'm just... lost in thought."

Fox taps on the horn again—an almost polite beep—and I sigh. "I should go." I wrap my arms around my mom, pulling her tight against my body. She stiffens for an instant before returning the embrace, rubbing my back with one hand and cradling my head with the other. I hold on a beat too long and she takes the opportunity to plant a kiss on the top of my head. A prickling sensation gathers in the corners of my eyes and I pull away quickly, not wanting to tear up in front of her. How would I explain my reaction? There's no way she'll believe there isn't something wrong with me and Fox, and there's no way I can tell her the real truth, that I never thought I'd be able to hug her again. Instead, I duck away and grab my backpack off the couch.

Mom sniffs and shakes her head. "You must be having a weird day."

I rub my eyes as I rush out the door. When I get to the passenger side door of Fox's truck, I stare at it in wonder. How am I supposed to get into this thing? The underside of the truck has to be at least two feet off the ground. I pull open the door and take in a breath. I have to pretend like I've done this before—like I've done this every day since Fox bought this ridiculous thing. I place one hand on the open door and the other on the truck's frame and hike my foot onto the step before trying to hoist myself into the cab. It takes me several tries and by the time I make it into the passenger seat, Fox is shaking with barely-suppressed laughter.

I glare at him as I swing the door closed. "Something amusing?"

He presses his lips together as he puts the car into gear and backs out of the driveway. It's not until he's heading down the street that he looks at me, his gray eyes dancing. "Nothing. I just forgot how much I enjoyed watching you struggle to climb into this thing."

Heat rises in my cheeks. "Well, it's ridiculous."

He laughs. "Thus the basis of its appeal." He reaches over and places his hand on my leg, squeezing above the knee. On instinct I put my hand atop his, prepared to push it off, but I stop at the last second; I have to pretend. I settle for patting Fox's hand twice before pulling mine away. "Don't tell me you like Griffin's Mustang better? You complained all last week when he was working on the truck that you couldn't wait till I got it back. Did it finally win you over?" He pulls up to a stop sign and studies me before continuing. "Don't worry. You'll get the hang of climbing in again, just like you did before. Don't forget who wanted me to get this thing in the first place."

Fox laughs but I flush. Is he implying that I'm the reason he drives this monstrosity? No, he can't be. No matter what reality, there's no way I'd support him in buying something so giant and unnecessary.

When we get to the school, Fox offers to help me out of the truck. I decline. It's far from a graceful descent, but I manage to get onto the pavement without injuring myself. The corners of Fox's mouth twitch as I approach and I give him a gentle shove. "Shut up."

He smiles at me, his gray eyes twinkling. His brown hair is mostly pushed back, but a few strands fall onto his forehead. I have the impulse to push the hairs back but stop myself. This is the danger of Fox. When I first met him, in my reality, he used an attraction charm that amplified his natural good looks—and my desire to be near him, to touch him. He's not using the charm now, but the ghost of those memories grips me. It would be so easy to pretend Fox means something to me. Before things changed, we didn't know each other well, but he told me once he wanted to be the kind of person I could trust. He was one of the few people who knew about my mom's death—and the only one who knew the reason I chose to help the circle locate the crystal. He was kind to me when I needed it. Despite his flaws, there was good in that Fox, and that good only seems amplified in this version of him. It's difficult not to get caught up in the possibility of him.

Fox cups the side of my face with his hand and my breath catches. His eyes smolder as he leans in toward me. My heartbeat thunders in my ears. He's going to kiss me, right here in the parking lot, like he's done it a thousand times before. Except he hasn't—not really. No matter how many times he kissed *her*, he's only kissed me once, when I was too shocked to do anything about it.

Crystal would tell me to let him do it—to pretend. I can't do anything out of the ordinary that could cause people to start asking tricky questions. Still, I don't want him to kiss me—not here, not where anyone could see us.

Not where Owen could see us.

Someone calls Fox's name and he turns away just before his lips connect with mine. I take a step back, removing his hand from my face. He murmurs something about catching up with me inside before heading off toward a knot of guys standing by a red car. I don't really hear him. Adrenaline courses through my veins and I walk faster than I should toward the school building. I need to put space between me and Fox.

Owen. He's the one I want to be kissing—the one I *should* be kissing. He was my choice before and he still is, no matter what my alternate-self decided. But the fact is he and I are not together. My stomach twists. How can I pull this off? How can I pretend to be happy with Fox when he's not the one I want?

I'm only feet from the school's door when Lexie calls my name. "Hey, wait up!" She walks between Crystal and Bridget in tight formation. I curse silently as I take in their appearance. It looks like all three girls consulted each other on the day's outfits: They're each wearing a baby-doll dress, even though the weather is turning cooler. The cut of the dresses are identical, although the patterns differ: They all wear blue, but Crystal's dress has a floral print, Bridget's has a spotty pattern, and Lexie's is solid. They walk in unison, their high heels clicking against the asphalt of the parking lot. The only thing that makes Lexie stand out from the others is that she wears a pair of shimmery cream leggings whereas the others are bare-legged, and Lexie's curly red hair is piled at the crown of her head in a messy bun, not in loose waves around her face like Crystal's and Bridget's. I take the tiniest bit of solace in the fact that the Lexie I knew might be somewhere inside the one before me.

Bridget's eyes flick down at my outfit—skinny jeans and a long, belted sweater—and she rolls her eyes in disapproval. The group doesn't slow as it approaches and I know without being told that I'm expected to fall into step with them. Unsure what else to do, I submit, walking beside Crystal.

Lexie peeks around Crystal as we enter the building. "Didn't you get that sweater last year?"

I tug at the cowl at my neck, my fingers tingling. The tone of Lexie's voice indicates that I've committed some kind of fashion faux pas, something I have honestly never worried about before. But alternate-me must be aware of this rule, and I have to give a reason for breaking it. My eyes find Crystal's for the briefest moment, hoping she'll say something to save me, but the slightest arch in her eyebrow is the only response she gives. "It worked so well last year, I thought I'd bring it back for an encore." Lexie's gaze remains dubious, so I add, "Fox mentioned it the other day and I decided to wear it for him."

After a beat, Lexie rolls her eyes. But the smile that curls the edges of her lips tells me the lie was a smart one.

Bridget sniffs and murmurs something about today being the day to wear our dresses, but Lexie swats her in the arm.

"No worries," Crystal says. She lifts her chin in the direction of a bathroom and, as one, the three of them head toward it. A half-second late, I follow.

Bridget checks the stalls and nods at Crystal when she's verified they're all empty. Crystal snaps her fingers and the key-operated lock on the main door clicks. Lexie crosses to the mirror, checking her lipstick. Crystal digs through her purse for a few moments before pulling out a small drawstring bag. Before she opens it, I know what it contains.

"You brought it to school?" I ask.

She tips the crystal into her palm and raises an eyebrow at me. "What do you expect me to do with it? Hide it in my underwear drawer?" I open my mouth and she rolls her eyes, effectively cutting me off. "I'm gonna do a glamor on you so you match us."

My skin prickles. "You're gonna *what*?"

Crystal tilts her head ever so slightly—a warning. "You *know*. A spell to change your appearance?"

I hold my hands up. "Um, no you're not."

She narrows her eyes. "Excuse me?"

Lexie releases an exasperated sigh. "Isn't it obvious? She wants to do it herself."

Bridget edges closer to us. "She *is* the best at glamors," she admits tentatively. She meets my eyes, a flash of expectation crossing her face. "I'm kind of curious what she can do with the crystal's help."

Crystal's lips twitch for a moment before she holds the quartz out. I hesitate before reaching for it. I haven't the foggiest idea how to cast a glamor spell. Trying to do one for the first time with an audience seems like a recipe for disaster. But what option do I have? If I refuse or insist Crystal do it for me, Bridget and Lexie would be suspicious.

I close my fingers around the stone and a spasm crosses Crystal's face when I pull it from her hand. An emotion sparks through me: reluctance. She doesn't want to give it over, but she's trying to prove me wrong about the crystal, about its effect on her.

The overwhelming emotions that accompanied my touching the crystal yesterday don't flood through me today and I'm relieved. Maybe Crystal's right and there's nothing wrong with the stone. Maybe yesterday was just a fluke. The energy in the quartz thrums through my hand, but no sinister feelings.

Now for the hard part.

I study the dresses worn by the girls and imagine something in the same style for myself. When Crystal taught me how to light a candle, she directed me to imagine a flame and touch that imaginary flame to the real life candle. I hope casting a glamor is a similar process. In my mind's eye, I call up the image of a dress like theirs, then I see myself wearing it—along with leggings like Lexie's and the same kind of shoes they all have on.

I close my eyes. Warmth floods over my body, starting at my head and ending at the tips of my toes.

Bridget squeals and claps her hands together. I open my eyes and look down. No longer do I wear the jeans-and-sweater combo—I'm in a blue-and-white baby doll dress with cap sleeves, shimmery white leggings, and blue high heels. Surprise and relief mingle in my chest. I did it. I spin around, getting a feel for the shoes I now wear.

"Wow! I think that's a speed record." Bridget nods

encouragingly.

Lexie's eyes flick from my feet to my face. "You didn't do your hair."

I tug at the ends of my still-straight hair. "It's the way I want it."

She rolls her eyes and I bristle. How can this Lexie be so different from the one I knew?

The warning bell sounds and Crystal holds her hand out expectantly. I hand the stone to her and she packs it back in her purse. With another click of her fingers, the door unlocks and the four of us head into the hallway.

Our group's unified line breaks apart when we enter the stairwell and I'm relieved. I want to get away from Crystal and Bridget and from this altered version of Lexie. It's all too much change for me to take in all at once. Not for the first time, I'm looking forward to the monotony of a school day, the easy, familiar rhythm of instruction and assignments. Unless the world has *really* changed, that, at least, should be the same.

When we get to the second floor, I break off from the group and head down the hall toward my locker. As I approach, a weight presses on my shoulders. What if it's not my locker anymore? Something so simple should be the same, even though it seems like nothing else is. But the only way to know is to try; I can deal with odd looks and confused questions later if I'm wrong.

I say a silent prayer as I dial in the combination and tug on the lock, relief swelling in me when it opens. The relief is replaced immediately when I open the door. I didn't realize I was looking forward to seeing Owen's sweatshirt until it's not there. The sweatshirt Owen wore the day we met remained in my locker since my second day here. I kept meaning to give it back to him, but it kept slipping my mind. Once or twice, I tried to give it to him between classes, but he claimed he couldn't hold it or he'd just get it later. And he never did. Having his sweatshirt in my locker had imbued it with his scent; now, it smells vaguely of flowers and I notice a satchel of herbs on the top shelf.

Tamping down my disappointment, I grab the books I need for my first few classes, hoping against hope that since my locker is the same so is my class schedule.

A whistle sounds behind me and I don't have to turn to know it's Fox. "Quick wardrobe change," he says as I slam the locker closed. "So fast one could call it *magical*." He winks.

Glancing around to make sure no one overheard him, I tug at his sleeve. "Fox, shush."

He makes a face as he reaches forward to sweep my hair over my shoulders. "I'm glad you left the hair straight." He rubs the pads of his thumbs over my cheeks and my breath hitches. He *is* good-looking—there's no use denying it. Objectively, I can see why a girl might want to be with him. I can see why *I* might want to be with him. If Crystal's right and we've set things on the course they were always supposed to take, does that mean that I'm with the person I'm supposed to be with? I'm not sure I can accept that.

"Fox, you got a second?"

Fox turns toward the speaker and my heart begins to pound. Owen is standing in front of us. My stomach twists as I take in the perfect lines of his jaw, the curve of his lips, the deep, sparkling blue of his eyes. Of course Fox isn't who I'm supposed to be with. How could I even think that? I've had a connection with Owen from the moment we met. But here that moment never happened. He doesn't even look at me. His gaze is turned to Fox, who engages him in conversation about some class assignment.

While Fox talks, he slips his arm around my waist, pulling me close to him. I feel a rush of embarrassment, but Owen doesn't even seem to notice.

We're nothing to each other here. The realization washes over me and I struggle to take in breath. Owen and I had been at the start of a relationship just days ago; he kissed me on my front porch and before we separated for the night, he begged me not to change my mind about him—about us. And now that had never happened. I'm with Fox and Owen couldn't seem to care less.

Chapter Five

I make it through the first three hours of the day without much of an incident. But I can't help cataloging subtle differences. Lexie and I still sit together in first hour English, but West Harmon sits on the other side of the room with some guys I don't really know. When Lexie catches me staring in his direction, I can't even come up with a lie about why I'm watching him. She raises an eyebrow and glances at me for the rest of the hour, making sure I'm not paying undue attention to a guy who's not my boyfriend.

Is West still friends with Owen? It's clear that Lexie doesn't think much of West, but she and Owen aren't friends here, so that might not affect Owen's opinion. And what about Bria Tate? A plump girl with black hair and a penchant for heavy eyeliner, she's not exactly the kind of person who would be accepted into Crystal Jamison's inner circle. I never asked, but it seems likely that Bria and Lexie became friends after Crystal and Lexie cut ties before ninth grade. Since that break never happened here, there would be no reason for Bria to enter the equation.

In second hour, it's hard to pay attention to Mrs. Bates, the science teacher, because my eyes keep straying to Owen. He sits several seats in front of me and doesn't turn to look back once. I can't decide whether that's good or bad. I don't know if I could handle him looking *through* me the way he did at my locker when he spoke to Fox. I don't want to deal with the fact that I don't mean anything to him anymore.

West is in my third hour, along with Felix Wolfe. Though I wasn't particularly close with Felix, he was a member of my old group of friends—Lexie, Owen, Bria, and West. He and West sit together and I take comfort in the fact that, at the very least, the two of them are friends.

Mrs. Ortiz has already begun the day's lesson when a student arrives late. My breath catches when I see who's walking into class: Tucker Ingram. Mrs. Ortiz admonishes him briefly before allowing him passage into the room. He takes his time walking across the room to the last row—my row. He grins easily at anyone who will make eye contact with him. A few girls titter as his gaze rakes across them and my stomach twists. Objectively, I suppose, I can understand their reaction. Tucker's shaggy brown hair is mussed just enough to give him an I-just-climbed-off-a-motorcycle look, and his blue eyes are surrounded by thick, dark eyelashes. The barest hint of stubble on his jaw and his black leather jacket give him the bad-boy look so many girls are drawn to. But I can't see him as attractive. I can't be objective when I look at him, because all that flashes through my mind is our last encounter, before I found myself in this reality: After a movie night at the bookstore downtown, an intoxicated Tucker tried to attack me. When I look at him, I can smell the sweet alcohol on him and feel his warm breath on my face, my neck.

Tucker continues on his journey across the classroom and heads up my aisle. My muscles tense as he settles into the empty desk behind me. Mrs. Ortiz continues her lesson and I attempt to focus on her words, but the skin on my back crawls; I can feel his eyes on me.

When Mrs. Ortiz turns to write something on the board, fingers tap on my shoulder and I jump. Tucker snorts as I turn to face him.

"What?" I snap.

He leans across his desk and it takes everything in me not to leap from my seat. "Can I borrow a pencil?"

"No." I turn forward and scribble down the notes Mrs. Ortiz has written. Tucker hasn't moved: I can feel the heat radiating off his body.

"Come on," he breathes, his voice low. "We both know you're like an office supply store. Give me a pencil."

The hairs on the back of my neck stand at attention and I

clench my jaw. Without looking back, I hold my pencil over my shoulder. After a second, he pulls it from my fingers. I pull my backpack onto my lap and dig through the front pocket for another pencil.

No sooner do I put my backpack back under my desk than Tucker taps me again. "Can I get some paper?"

I stifle a groan, making a mental note to ask the teacher to move my seat. I rip out a couple of sheets from my notebook and turn. "You've got a pencil and paper. Now leave me alone."

Tucker sneers as he pulls the paper toward him. "No need to be a bitch about it. What'd I do to you?"

"Silencio, por favor, senor Ingram," Mrs. Ortiz says from the front of the room. "Escuchen, por favor, senorita Barnette."

I turn my attention back to the front of the room, grateful for a reason not to continue a conversation with Tucker. He doesn't bother me for the rest of Spanish, and after third hour, I stop by my locker for my lunch before heading down to the cafeteria. I bypass the lunch line, my chest aching as I remember my first day here. Owen and I stood in that line, and I thought about how I never bought lunch at my old school, how my mom was too proud to admit we needed help and always sent me to school with a lunch packed from home. As I hold the brown paper bag in my hand, I can't help smiling. At least not everything has changed.

It's not until I walk into the cafeteria proper that my pace slows. On Friday, I knew exactly where my place in the room was: at the table in the center of the room on the right side, with Owen, Lexie, Bria, West, Felix. But there's no way that's where I sit now.

I don't even realize I've stopped in the center of the room until Lexie nudges me with her elbow. "Get lost?"

I force a laugh, though what she's suggesting is pretty accurate. "Sorry. I just... I got lost in thought."

She raises an eyebrow before surveying the immediate vicinity. It takes a second for me to realize she's checking for West. I curse myself silently. I have to be more careful. The last thing I want to do is start some kind of rumor that I'm interested in West, and while the Lexie I knew wouldn't do something like that, I'm pretty sure this one would.

When her scan comes up empty, Lexie heads toward a table near the back of the cafeteria. I recognize it instantly as the table where Crystal and her friends always sat. Lexie settles down at Crystal's right side. Bridget is already sitting at Crystal's left. I'd be concerned about selecting the right spot for myself except that Fox is already seated across from Bridget. I don't need the warning look Crystal is giving me to know I'm supposed to sit beside him. I take the seat and Fox immediately slips his arm around my waist. I fight the urge to shift under his touch. Crystal's eyes are on me.

As I eat my tuna sandwich, Bridget reaches across the table and grabs my right hand. I have to be quick to keep my sandwich from falling. "Hey!"

Bridget pulls my hand up to her face and squints. "Gah, Kristyl, what are you wearing?" She studies my father's ring.

Before I can respond, Lexie pulls my hand from Bridget so she can perform her own inspection. "Isn't that your dad's ring?" She presses her lips together thoughtfully. "Yeah. I'd recognize that ugly thing anywhere." She raises her eyebrows before taking a bite of her apple.

Bridget wrinkles her nose. "Oh, yeah. I remember it now. Crystal, didn't you say it was the ugliest piece of jewelry you'd ever seen?"

Although I already knew a bit of my alternate-self's history with this ring, hearing it repeated irks me. I cock my head at Crystal, waiting for her to say something.

It takes a beat before she sighs. "It's *still* the ugliest piece of jewelry I've ever seen. Why would you willingly wear something that hideous?"

I narrow my eyes. "Maybe you didn't hear Lexie. This ring belonged to my dad."

Her dark blue eyes fix on mine. "Oh, I heard her. It still doesn't answer my question."

I pull my hand from her grip and settle it on the table, not breaking eye contact. "Yes, it does. I don't care if you don't like it. This ring makes me think of my dad, and I want to wear it. I want to feel close to him. If you don't like it, don't look at it."

She stares, mouth twitching like she's got too many things to say and is sorting through which comments should go first. Her lips part, but before she speaks, Lexie points across the lunch table toward the wall by the courtyard.

"What do we have here?" A cruel smile curls the corners of her mouth and she holds her hand out toward Crystal, opening and closing her fist. "Give it."

Crystal's eyes flash to mine for a second before we both follow Lexie's gaze. My heart sinks. Bria Tate is sitting on the floor, her back against the courtyard windows, large headphones covering her ears, her head down. No one sits near her. Doesn't she have friends? Sure, she and Lexie aren't friends anymore for obvious reasons, but it's hard to believe someone as vivacious, as sweet as Bria wouldn't find a new group to be with.

Lexie knocks on the table impatiently. "Come on, Crystal. Give it to me."

After a beat, Crystal opens her purse and pulls the drawstring bag out of it. She glances around the cafeteria before handing it to her cousin.

My blood runs cold. What is Lexie planning?

Bridget is watching with interest, leaning forward so far that her cleavage appears to expand exponentially, spilling out over the top of her dress. She's not doing it on purpose—well, I don't think she is—but that doesn't mean that the guys around the table haven't taken notice. To his credit, Fox turns to the table behind us and strikes up a conversation with some guys sitting there.

Lexie rubs the pads of her fingers over the bumps and ridges of the crystal for a few moments, her eyes closing in concentration. My whole body tenses. When Lexie opens her eyes, they're narrowed intently. I turn just in time to see several lunch trays launch themselves at Bria from nearby tables. Bria screams as she's splattered with french fries and ketchup, milk, and lettuce dripping with dressing. She covers her head with her arms, pulling her legs up toward her torso. Lexie lets out a cackle and a second barrage of food flies at Bria.

Kids at the tables nearest Bria jump up, looking around for something to explain why their trays are sliding away from them. Just as eyes flicker in our direction, the bell rings and in a flash, everyone is standing. Crystal closes her hand over Lexie's, pulling the stone from her grasp. Lexie gives it up without a fight, still laughing. She and Bridget link arms and head into the swelling stream of bodies. I peer toward the courtyard but can only catch glimpses of Bria between people. Everything in me wants to go to her, to help her get cleaned up, but I know I can't.

Crystal tucks the pouch containing the quartz back into her purse and merges into the mass of students heading for their next class. With one last glance at Bria, I start for her. How can she be so nonchalant about what Lexie did?

I don't get more than a few steps before Fox catches my hand. A scan of the vicinity doesn't reveal Crystal: She's been swallowed by the crowd. I allow Fox to lead me toward the nearest stairwell. Zane is on Fox's other side, going on about Lexie's display. I do my best not to listen.

I need to talk to Crystal. Is this what the circle is all about? Picking on other people? And this is the way Crystal thinks things are supposed to be? I don't know what kinds of magic the circle has been practicing until now, but I can't be part of a group like this. And I would hope Crystal wouldn't want to be either.

Chapter Six

Zane doesn't stop talking about what happened at lunch until we're all seated in math. I'm distracted all hour.

Bria's supposed to be in this class.

Agitation grows with every minute Bria's absent. Is she in a bathroom somewhere, trying to clean up? I should get the pass and go find her. Maybe I could help get the food off her clothes. Or maybe I could do a glamor like I did this morning.

No. I can't do magic. I have no idea if she even suspects witchcraft. Before, it was Lexie who proposed the theory, based on what she knew about her late aunt, Crystal Taylor. But since Lexie's one of the witches now, who would even come up with the idea of magic?

As hard it is to get through math, health class is worse. Last time I was in health class, Lexie, Owen, Felix and I all sat together in one often-chatty group. The teacher, Mrs. Stanton, threatened to break us up several times—sometimes more than once a day—though she never made good on the promise because we always got our work done. But now, Lexie and I share a table with a girl named Heidi who seems desperate to be accepted by the two of us; she keeps offering us things—to give us the answers or to get us a special at the salon her mom works at. Owen and Felix sit on the other side of the room, but not together.

I do my best to be polite to Lexie, even though I want nothing more than to yell at her for what she did to Bria. Heidi, while annoying, is perfect for running interference.

I count down the minutes until the end of fifth hour. Crystal is in my last class of the day and I want to catch her before she makes it there. We need to talk and I'd like to do it before we get to Mr. Martin's history class. I swing my backpack over my shoulder and head out of health as soon as the bell rings. If Lexie calls after me, I don't hear her. I'm the first one in the hallway and I start for the nearest stairwell.

Crystal's not at her locker and I hesitate in front of it before going to my own. So far, all my teachers' personalities have been intact and I don't want to be caught in Mr. Martin's class unprepared. I keep one eye on Crystal's locker as I change out my books, but she doesn't show up. Maybe her fifth hour teacher held her back? I'm not sure what class she has fifth hour, but she always approaches her locker from the same way. Pulling my backpack back on my shoulders, I head down the hallway past her locker, toward a stairwell I've never used. There are fewer people at lockers in this area of the hall and half of the classroom doors are closed, like they're not even in use. I'm a few feet from the stairwell doors when I stop. There's no reason she'd come from down here. Maybe I'm remembering things wrong.

I'm about to turn when I hear a raised female voice. A muffled male voice follows it immediately. My skin prickles. The voices are coming from the stairwell. I shift on the balls of my feet, unsure whether I should investigate. There's no further sound for a few seconds and my body relaxes. I must be hearing things.

But then a shriek turns my blood cold. I run at the stairwell door and push it open so hard it bangs against the adjacent wall. A guy with short dark brown hair presses a girl into the corner of the stairwell, pinning her arms against the walls on either side of her head. The black leather jacket he wears is unmistakable. Tucker. Sense memory overwhelms me—I feel the rough chill of the brick wall outside the book store against my back, the warmth of his body pressing against mine.

Although I can't see the girl's face, the pattern on her blue baby-doll dress tells me all I need to know.

Crystal.

Heat builds in my center and before I can direct it, it flashes outward. Tucker flails as he's blasted backward, away from Crystal. He stumbles, landing on his back just a few inches from my feet. He groans, but I ignore him, rushing to Crystal's side. Her eyes are wide, shocked, as I approach.

"Are you okay?" I scan her body, but everything appears to be in place. Even her hair is unmussed.

"The *hell*, Barnette!" Tucker pushes himself to his feet, glaring. "What's your problem today?"

I stare at him, incredulous. "What's *my* problem? I could ask you the same thing!"

The warning bell sounds and Tucker shakes his head. "Jealous much? It's not my fault if you're bored with your boyfriend." He raises his chin in Crystal's direction. "Later."

He exits the stairwell and Crystal hits me in the arm. "What's wrong with you?"

The adrenaline in my system ebbs and I release a shaky breath. "I thought he was... He wasn't attacking you?"

She gapes. "No. Why would you think that?"

I replay the scene in my head—the sounds of their voices, the way he had her pinned against the wall. Even now, I can't compute that Crystal was a willing participant. "You—you shrieked."

She cocks her head to the side and rolls her eyes like I'm hopelessly infantile.

"What, are you guys, like, *together* or something?"

She shrugs, a grin spreading across her face. "I have *no* idea. But he seemed to be expecting me."

A memory floats to the surface of my mind: In the other timeline, Crystal and Zane Ross hooked up on a few occasions. She has a thing for bad-boys. She's probably pleased to find out her alternate-self is together with Tucker.

I shake my head to clear it of the image of the two of them making out. "Whatever. I'm sorry I interrupted. Now, let's get to history before Mr. Martin kills us."

The two of us emerge from the stairwell and make our way through the progressively emptying hallway toward Mr. Martin's class. A couple of freshman girls dawdle by a freshman boy's locker, but all three scatter when a friend hurries by whispering, "Better move, Mrs. Cole's coming."

I freeze and so does Crystal. When her eyes meet mine, they're round and wide; this is news to her, too.

"Mrs. Cole's alive?" I whisper. In our other reality, our principal died on the night of the harvest dance. It was some kind of curse that killed her; the same curse was affecting Jodi before I decided to help Crystal and the circle go back in time. But when I got back, Jodi was fine—nothing had ever been wrong with her. Maybe nothing happened to Mrs. Cole either.

Crystal tugs on my arm. "Looks like it," she says, her voice quiet. "And we'd better move or she'll give us detention for being late."

I think it's safe to say that this is the first time anyone has ever been elated to be threatened with detention. I didn't know Mrs. Cole terribly well, but she'd been nice to me, even though my school record gave her no reason to be. She was friends with Jodi, but I know that wasn't the reason she gave me a chance here; she really believed I could do better here, I could *be* better here.

Crystal and I ease into Mr. Martin's class just as the tardy bell rings, but it's not Mr. Martin behind the teacher's desk. A woman with short, dark hair is bent over the desk, peering at something written on a piece of paper. Her face is obscured by her hair, but there's something familiar about her. She must be a substitute in for Mr. Martin today; I've probably seen her around school before.

Someone taps at the still-open classroom door behind us as Crystal and I head toward the empty desks by Bridget. "Miss Tanner?" calls a woman's voice.

The woman behind the desk looks up, and, in front of me, Crystal lets out an audible gasp. She's our principal, Mrs. Shelly Cole. But that doesn't make any sense—the freshman in the hallway said she was behind us. Besides, the woman in the door called her Miss Tanner. The name Tanner sticks in my mind, but I don't know why.

Crystal has turned toward the person in the doorway and is staring open-mouthed. I follow her gaze. The woman standing there is familiar; I know I've seen her before, but I can't place where. Her straight, light-brown hair is pulled into a chignon at the base of her neck, accentuating her pointed chin and almost elfin features.

"Yes, Mrs. Cole?" asks the woman I thought answered to that name. I look to Crystal to see if she knows what's happening, but she seems incapable of speech.

The elfin woman smiles and nods in my direction. "Could I see Miss Taylor and Miss Barnette for a moment?"

"Sure." The darker-haired woman makes a sweeping motion with her hand and I have to tug on Crystal's arm to get her to follow me.

The woman called Mrs. Cole closes the door after Crystal and I follow her into the hallway. She crosses her arms over her chest and shakes her head at us. "Have you been using the bathroom as your private office again? There was a complaint earlier about how a bathroom door wouldn't open after you two and Lexie and Bridget walked in."

I wait for Crystal to respond, but she doesn't. I clear my throat. "We had to talk about something."

The woman bites back a smile. "While I'm sure it was very important, that still doesn't give you the right to commandeer the lavatory. It's not your personal meeting room."

I nod. "We won't do it again." I look to Crystal, waiting for her echo of my assurance, but she doesn't speak. I nudge her with my elbow and she blinks heavily.

"Yeah, of course not. We won't do it again, Aunt Crystal."

I gasp. That's where I know this woman from—*when* I know her from. Crystal told me this the day after we got back from our excursion in the past, but it's still a shock to see it with my own eyes. Crystal Taylor didn't die in a house fire the way she did in our reality. Somehow we changed that by going back.

Crystal Taylor smiles at her niece. "What have I told you? At school, you've got to call me Mrs. Cole, just like Lexie."

Crystal Jamison nods numbly and her aunt opens the classroom door. Our business is done. As we take our seats by Bridget, I try to piece everything together. Crystal Taylor is now Crystal Cole, and she's the principal of Clearwater High. It makes sense, I suppose—I had a vision of the past before going there, and Crystal Taylor's mother mentioned something about her hanging out with David Cole—the man who, in my reality, was married to

Clearwater High's principal—Shelly. Now I remember why the name *Tanner* sounded so familiar: It's Shelly's maiden name. Apparently since Crystal Taylor lived, Shelly Tanner and David Cole never married. And now Crystal Taylor-Cole is the principal of my school and Shelly Tanner is my history teacher.

By the end of class, I'm massaging my temples to stave off the ache gathering in my head from doing so much thinking. Beside me, Crystal Jamison doesn't look like she's doing much better. When the bell rings, the two of us are out of the room as quickly as possible, leaving Bridget behind. Once we merge with the groups of students already pouring into the hallway, she shakes her head. "I think my brain just exploded."

I nod. "Me, too."

We're almost to my locker when she tugs on my arm. "Are you working at Jodi's shop today?"

I bite my lower lip. "I have no idea. I mean, before I worked there after school every day—"

"I know." She shakes her head. "Doesn't matter. It closes at six, right?"

I nod. "I mean—it *did*. I don't see why it wouldn't be the same."

She glances down the hall like she's making sure no one's listening to us. "At seven, the circle's meeting at Fox's place. It's important for you to be there."

I press my lips together. If the circle's meeting again, it's probably about the anchoring spell. I should go—it might give me more opportunity to convince Crystal and the others there's something wrong with the stone. Or maybe it'll convince *me* that everything's okay. "I think I can make it."

"Good." She glances over my shoulder and nods a greeting. "I'll see you at seven." She turns and calls over her shoulder, "See you later, Fox."

I'm thankful for Crystal's warning as it's the only thing that keeps me from jumping when Fox slides his hands over my hips. "You ready to get out of here?"

Fox's lips are close to my ear and I squeeze my eyes closed, willing myself not to pull away. I take in a breath before turning to face him. "I just have to stop and get my stuff," I say, forcing brightness into my words.

He nods. "I've gotta stop in to see Miss Tanner. I'll meet you at your locker."

I smile and pivot, heading down the hall. I take two steps before colliding with someone. He grunts and his books slip from his hands, clattering on the floor.

"I'm sorry!" I crouch down and begin collecting the belongings without thinking.

"It's okay."

I freeze as Owen's hand brushes mine as he reaches for his notebook. I meet his eyes for the first time today and immediately wish I hadn't. There's a barrier up behind his eyes, like he's uncomfortable around me. I bite my lower lip and hand him his textbook. He takes it and nods a thank you as he presses himself to standing. I stand too and, not wanting our interaction to end quite yet, grope for something to say. "Yeah—I'm sorry about that. I should've been watching where I was going."

He shrugs. "It happens." His eyes dart down the hallway and a muscle in his jaw jumps. "See you, Kristyl."

Owen starts down the hall and my stomach sinks with every step he takes.

Chapter Seven

Tuesday morning dawns crisp and cold, and I groan when my alarm goes off. Crystal called an emergency circle meeting last night to prep for the anchoring spell. I was stuck in the Holloways' basement until after eleven—a fact that earned me a lecture about appropriate hours on school nights when I got home. Sleep was fitful at best. Although I handled the crystal as much as possible last night and didn't sense anything dark or ominous about it, a sense of dread lurks at the edges of my mind. I'm still not convinced anchoring to it is the best idea.

The display on my cell announces I've missed several texts from Crystal. I blink a few times to clear my vision enough to read them. They're all about clothes, including a schedule of the types of outfits appropriate for each day of the week as well as a few suggestions about what I should wear today. I roll my eyes.

After searching through my closet for a few minutes, I select an outfit that might meet Crystal's criteria, but when I get to my bathroom, I just stare down at it. I have no interest in putting as much effort into my appearance as Crystal seems to think I require. I catch the eyes of my reflection and an idea flashes in my head: I could do another glamor spell. I laugh at the thought. Wouldn't that be amazing—not having to worry about doing my hair or makeup or picking the right outfit from my closet, just using magic to make it so? I bite my lower lip. It might be worth it.

In my mind's eye, I conjure an image of how I want to look today. I close my eyes and wait for the feeling of warmth to course through me, but it doesn't happen. I take in a breath and try again. I reach out and connect with the thrum of energy in the things around me—the air, the wind whistling against the windows, the trees in the yard. A tingle begins at the crown of my head and slowly creeps downward. After what feels like minutes, my entire body buzzes with energy and I open my eyes. A giddy bubble rises in my chest. *I did it.* I spin, admiring the fit of my jeans and the cut of the purple top that hugs my body.

"I'm never gonna have to buy clothes again," I murmur.

By the time I make it to the dining room for breakfast, I'm grinning from ear to ear. Sounds in the kitchen tell me my mom is in there, making breakfast, and the need to see her floods through me. In my head, I've accepted she's here now, part of this reality, but my heart keeps expecting her to disappear. I lean in the doorway, watching as she scrambles eggs. She glances up at me, raising an eyebrow.

"What?" Heat rushes to my cheeks. I'm staring too much, I know I am. But I can't help it.

Mom shakes her head. "Nothing. Just usually you're dressed before you come downstairs."

Confused, I look down. I'm still in my pajamas. Somehow, the glamor I cast wore off between my bathroom and the kitchen. The skin on the back of my neck prickles and I look around, grasping for an excuse for my appearance. My eyes land on a pile of shoes by the front door and I cross to them. "I, uh, just wanted to make sure the shoes I wanted to wear were down here," I say, scanning the pile for a pair that might fit my feet. "I didn't see them upstairs and—ah." I rush to the end of the hall and select a pair of ankle-high brown leather boots, setting them off to the side. "Found them. Didn't want to get dressed and then not be able to find the right shoes."

Mom grins from the kitchen doorway. "The horror."

I rush back upstairs and pull on the outfit I chose earlier. Why didn't the glamor hold? I did exactly the same thing I did yesterday, and that spell held until I got home.

Of course, I know exactly what the difference is: the crystal. I used its energy to cast the spell yesterday. That's why it was so much easier to cast—and hold—the illusion. It really does make magic easier. Maybe there's something to the circle's desire to anchor to it.

No. Just because I didn't feel anything last night doesn't mean I think it would be a good idea to anchor myself to it. What if the power-hungry feelings I had Sunday evening return when I'm linked to the stone—and I can't turn them off? What if the whole circle feels the same way? We would tear each other apart. It's not worth the risk.

It's clear the others don't share my opinion. At school, all Crystal, Lexie, and Bridget can talk about is the ceremony tonight. Fox brings it up to me once, but when my response doesn't match his exuberance, he drops the subject.

The first few hours of the day pass in a haze. At lunch, Fox's cell buzzes every few minutes, and each time, he picks it up, grins, and replies. A few times, he shows the message to Zane. After about a dozen times, I can't curb my curiosity. "What's so funny?"

He shakes his head, his eyes on the screen as he taps out a reply. "Nothing—it's just Griffin." He fixes me with his gaze as he tucks the cell into his back pocket. "It's slow at the garage and he keeps sending ideas of all the things he won't ever do again once we anchor to the crystal."

"What do you mean?"

He smiles and I find myself smiling back. I bite the inside of my cheek, dropping my gaze to the lunch table. He is *not* my boyfriend. He might think he is, but that doesn't make it so.

"Just simple stuff," Fox says, his tone still as light as before. "Like he'll never have to search for the right size wrench—he'll just use magic to twist off bolts. And he'll have a never-ending supply of Mountain Dew."

I shift on the hard plastic seat. "Can't he do those things now?"

Fox's eyebrows cinch. "You know how much concentration it takes for him to do spells—even simple ones. There's no way he can focus enough to loosen bolts at work—not with all the noise and stuff around. And, in case you forgot, you're the only one who's been able to do a multiplication spell."

His cell buzzes again and it's in his hand in a second. I'm glad for the interruption since I'm not entirely sure how to respond to him. I don't know exactly what a multiplication spell is, but it probably has nothing to do with math. Could I really make more of something out of thin air, just with magic? And why would I be the only one in the circle who's been able to do it? Yesterday in the bathroom, Bridget said I was the best at glamors. Am I the best at *all* magic?

The first time I did magic with Crystal, she said she'd never felt power like mine before. Is the same thing true in this reality? Am I the most powerful member of the circle? How am I supposed to play along with that? What if someone asks me to do a spell and I can't do it?

It won't be a problem if you anchor to the crystal. The solution is so simple. I did the glamor without any problem yesterday—*because* I was using the crystal. If I anchor myself with the rest of the circle, I won't have to worry they'll realize I'm not the girl I'm pretending to be. I'll be able to do magic the way they think I've always been able to do. Better, even.

These thoughts swirl in my head for the remainder of the school day. It's a mark of how excited everyone is about tonight that no one notices I'm not saying much. Fox drops me off at home with a promise to pick me up at seven for the circle's meeting. I'm so distracted I don't put up a fight when he leans across the center console to kiss me—and he's so caught up in the idea of tonight that he doesn't notice I don't kiss him back.

The house is empty and, while I'm thankful for it, I almost long for the presence of Jodi or my mom—just to distract me. I try to lose myself in homework, but my attention wanes. I reread the same line of the short story from English class a dozen times without gleaning any information from it before giving up.

Lying on my bed, staring at the sloping ceiling above, I slip my ring on and off, trying it on each of my fingers and my thumbs, willing a vision to come. I need direction about the anchoring spell tonight. Sunday, I was convinced the crystal was dark and evil, but now I'm not so sure. What if the sensations that overtook me when I held it had nothing to do with the stone itself? I haven't experienced anything like it since.

Crystal expects me to anchor to the stone with the rest of the circle: She didn't have to say it out loud for me to know it. I'm one of them now. But what happens if I don't go through with the spell? Am I out of the circle? My stomach flutters at the prospect. Could it be that easy to break away from them? Despite what they think, they're not my friends. Maybe cutting ties with them would be the first step in reclaiming the life I used to have.

***

The full moon hangs low on the horizon. I can just make it out through the branches of the trees outside Fox's house. It looks enormous—double its normal size, like it's closer than usual, somehow. Like it knows what the circle plans to do tonight and is ready to play its part.

Fox pulls his truck into the driveway, behind Griffin's Mustang. Crystal's car—a bright green Spark—is parked in front of the house, along with Zane's motorcycle. Assuming Crystal picked up Lexie and Bridget, everyone's here.

The overhead light comes on as Fox opens his door. "You coming?"

I follow him up the driveway, apprehension building with each step. Instead of heading to the front door, he leads me to the back yard. Murmuring voices greet my ears even before we turn the corner of the house, and the other members of the circle are revealed, faces lit by flickering firelight. In the center of a ring of white stones the size of Chihuahuas is a small fire. To the casual passerby, it might look like the seven of us are making the most of this autumn evening, probably one of the last mild nights we'll have as we head into November. But we'll not be roasting marshmallows or sipping pilfered alcohol tonight. Although it's difficult to see in the darkness, there's a ring of herbs spread out just beyond the white rocks, and another of salt a few feet beyond that—just inside the ring of canvas camp chairs Crystal and the others sit in. I'm sure I wouldn't have been able to pick up on either of these things if I didn't know they'd be there: We spent several hours last night spelling the herbs and salt to prepare it for the ceremony.

Griffin rubs his hands together when he catches a glimpse of us and stands, kicking his chair out of the way. "Finally. Let's get started."

Zane and Bridget sit at attention, but Crystal merely tips her head backward. "It's still too early. The moon's gotta be higher."

Griffin curses and mutters something about being right back before wandering into the house. Fox settles in the empty chair beside Zane, leaving me to the chair on Crystal's left. She nods a hello before turning her attention back to the large, leather-bound book in her lap—Crystal Taylor's book of shadows. Bridget offers a smile, but Lexie doesn't even glance up. A week ago, I would have been sitting beside her, but this girl is not much like the Lexie who was my friend. She stares at the illuminated screen of her cell, not even acknowledging my presence. That this doesn't bother me is unsettling.

These people aren't my friends, but it's naive to think that by *not* being a part of the circle will somehow transform things back to the way they used to be. Even if I could befriend Bria and Owen and West and Felix again, it wouldn't be the same because we wouldn't have Lexie—not the way she was.

No, that life is gone. All I can do now is make the best of *this* life, of these circumstances. And why shouldn't that mean making the most of my magical potential?

I twist my ring around my finger and stare into the fire, watching as the orange tongues of flame twist around each other and lap against the air. This is my life now, and I need to take control of it.

I'm not sure how much time passes before Fox gives my shoulder a gentle shake. I blink a few times. Griffin has emerged from the house and the rest of the circle's members are standing, their chairs positioned several feet behind them. I stand, too, and Fox moves my chair back.

Crystal kneels, holding her phone up like a flashlight above the yellowing pages of the large book on the ground. Lexie clicks her tongue impatiently. "Come on, Crystal. If you don't know the spell by now, you never will."

Crystal glares at her. "I just want to be sure. This is possibly the most important spell we'll ever cast. Excuse me if I want to make sure I get it right."

"Well, maybe if you'd let anyone *help* you." Lexie casts a reluctant glance in my direction and I shift. An echo builds in my mind as thoughts that aren't mine fill my head. I sift through the noise until impressions clarify themselves: Lexie thinks I should be the one leading the ceremony. It irks her, but she knows I'm the most naturally gifted of the group.

I suck in a breath, rolling my shoulders. No matter how many times it happens, it's still awkward when I hear what someone else is thinking. I can't help feeling the tiniest bit guilty. A person should be safe in her own mind and not have to worry about someone overhearing her. But, it's not like I'm *trying* to read her thoughts. It's a small consolation.

"I don't *need* help," Crystal says, slamming the book closed and placing it behind her. She stands and pulls something out of her jacket pocket. I don't have to see it to know what it is. "I'll recite the spell. I'll pass the crystal to Bridget and she'll pass it to Lexie and so on until it gets back to me. Make sure you take it with your left hand and pass it to your right hand to give it to the next person—"

"We *know*," Griffin says, his tone impatient. "We've only been over this a *hundred* times."

Crystal doesn't look at him. "When it gets back to me, follow my lead for the last part of the incantation. Do your best not to move—you might mess something up. And whatever you do, *don't* cross the salt line."

Bridget bites her lower lip. "What happens if we do?"

Crystal rolls her eyes, adding an exasperated sigh for effect. "You break your link to the spell. So, feel free to cross the line if you want, but you won't be connected to the crystal."

Bridget tugs at her jacket, muttering under her breath. Zane snorts.

"Now, if there are no more questions..." Crystal's eyes linger on Bridget, who stares resolutely at the fire. "Then let's get started."

"Finally." Griffin is the first to cross into the salt circle. He rakes his upper teeth over his lower lip, his eyes fixed on the stone in Crystal's hand. The eagerness radiating off him hits me like a wave, like the heat of the fire. He's been waiting a long time for this—they all have been.

I'm the last to step into the circle. Crystal surveys us before holding the quartz out in front of her. She lifts it, cradled in her palms, toward the moon and begins murmuring an incantation in a language I don't recognize. As she speaks, the air around us becomes charged with electricity.

The words she chants begin to sound familiar and I realize she's repeating the incantation. She brings her arms back down and passes the stone to Lexie with her right hand. As directed, Lexie takes it with her left hand and passes it to her right before giving it to Bridget. I follow the crystal's progress around the circle, from Griffin to Zane to Fox. I reach my left hand out toward Fox, my skin tingling with anticipation. As my fingers close around the chunk of quartz, I brace for a thrum of energy, a flash of feeling—anything—but nothing happens.

I've made the right decision. The firelight glints off the rough edges and ridges of the stone, amplifying its natural beauty. I was foolish to think there was something dark hiding inside something so pure, so lovely. I pass the crystal across my body to my right hand.

It happens as soon as the stone touches the band of my ring. My body goes rigid as icy jets shoot through my right arm, straight at my heart.

The blinding white light and plunge into blackness pass in seconds, flooding my mind with an onslaught of images. The pictures flick past so quickly I can't decipher them, but the accompanying emotions are unmistakable. Fear grips my heart, constricting my chest and making it difficult to draw breath. My body goes icy before heating to boiling—a simmering rage ready to explode. I don't care who gets hurt—someone needs to pay for what's happened. *Everyone* needs to pay. And I have the power to make them regret having been born. I will kill them all and feel no remorse. After all, if they were as strong as I, they could stop me. The fact they can't means they don't really matter—

"Kristyl! Kristyl!"

Crystal's voice comes to me as if from a great distance. My vision returns by degrees. Six sets of wide eyes stare in my direction. Fox's body is coiled like he's ready to leap to my side. The only thing keeping him from me is Crystal's outstretched hand.

I blink heavily. "We can't do this."

Crystal holds her left hand out, opening and closing her fist. "Give it to me."

I pull the stone toward my chest. "No. We *can't*." The emotions from my vision reverberate within me and I shiver. "There's power inside this thing, all right, but it's *dark*. We can't anchor to it."

She shakes her head, her fingertips stroking her chest where the shard of this stone she used to wear as a pendant rested. "No. We were *supposed* to find this crystal. It's meant to be part of us."

"What the hell?" Griffin calls. "After all the time we spent looking for this thing, there's no way we're *not* anchoring to it. Now give it to her."

"I'm with Griffin," Zane says. "Hand that thing to Crystal so we can finish this spell or I'll come over there and *make* you hand it to her."

Fox points at Zane, narrowing his eyes. "You even think about touching her and I'll kick your ass, Zane."

"Shut *up*," Crystal snaps. When she turns back to me, her eyes are soft. "It's okay. There's nothing dark about the crystal. Of all people, I think *I'd* know."

"No—no, you wouldn't." Is it possible she *can't* feel the energy inside it because she's not psychic? I squeeze my eyes closed. As much as I want to keep my visions a secret, I have to tell them. "I... I felt something when I held it in the basement—this overpowering jealousy and rage. And just now—when it touched my ring—I saw..." I shake my head, not wanting to describe the images that passed through my mind. "It's dark, Crystal."

"How do you know it's not your ring that's dark?" Lexie asks. "We've all held that stone and none of us felt anything bad." She crosses her arms over her chest as the others murmur agreements. Her eyes narrow. "Unless... unless you're not having any mystical feelings at all. That's it, isn't it? I bet you felt jealousy when you held the crystal—you were jealous because we'd all finally have the same kind of power that you have. Don't pretend you don't like being the best at magic. You're afraid that once we anchor ourselves we'll *all* be just as good as you—or better—and you won't be special anymore."

My jaw drops. How can she think that? Is that really the kind of person my alternate self is? "I don't care who's best at magic—I care about us *not* being connected to something evil—"

"It's not *evil*." Crystal stares at me like she's seeing me clearly for the first time. "The only reason you helped me get the crystal to begin with was because you wanted to use it."

An echo builds in my mind as her thoughts filter in. She thinks Lexie's right, that I want all the magic for myself. She thinks I'll find a way to anchor myself to the stone without the rest of them. "Crystal—no. I don't want to anchor to this thing—I don't want *any* of us to!" I pull my arm back and launch the chunk of quartz toward the fire.

Crystal screams, her left arm outstretched. The stone freezes in midair, just inches from the greedy fingers of the fire. It begins creeping backward, toward her hand, and I reach for it. When I take a step forward, I'm knocked backward by an unseen force. Beside Crystal, Lexie's arm is outstretched and I know the source of the energy. She sends another shock wave at me and I reel backward. I land hard on my butt, just outside the salt circle.

The quartz reaches Crystal's hand just as I get my feet under me. I have to stop her—I need to get the crystal and destroy it before they can anchor themselves to it. I lunge at her, but a milky blue light flashes between us, knocking me off to the side. I stumble but manage not to fall over again. I rush toward Crystal again, but when I come to the salt circle, I can't move any farther. A force stops my progress. She must have cast some kind of protective spell around them. I bang my fist against the thickened air surrounding them, but it does nothing but cause another milky blue flash, followed by ripples like a disturbed puddle. A muffled murmur reaches me through the shield: They're continuing the spell. Crystal lifts her hands skyward again and the stone floats from her palms, moving until it hovers directly over the fire.

Everyone's eyes are fixed on the crystal—except Fox's. He stares at me, his mouth agape. Above the fire, the crystal begins to give off a silvery glow. Thin filament-like threads of energy unfurl from it and inch toward the members of the circle. Each strand reaches its target at the same instant, and the six people within the salt circle seem, for an instant, to be cloaked in the same silver light emanating from the crystal.

The bonfire blinks out in an instant and the crystal drops into the smoking embers. But for the light of the full moon above, the yard is dark.

The anchoring spell is complete.

Chapter Eight

The anchoring ceremony replays over and over again in my dreams. Sometimes, after the flash of silvery light surrounds the members of the circle, they fly into the sky, sprouting ragged black wings and eclipsing the moon. Others, they burst into flames. Each time, I wake gasping.

Fox drove me home right after the ceremony ended, apologizing profusely for what Lexie did, promising he'd figure out a way to fix things, to link me with the crystal, too. Regret and fear filled the cab of his truck; no matter how many times I tried to tell him I didn't *want* to be anchored, he didn't listen. I allowed him to hold my hand and I reached out with my psychic abilities to see if I could sense anything off about him, but he didn't seem changed. Still, I can't help worrying. No matter what they think, there's something dark about the energy they're now linked to.

My stomach knots as I dress for school, and I can't eat more than a few bites of breakfast. After trying to strike up a conversation several times, my mom and Jodi give up, allowing me to eat in peace.

I'm already waiting on the porch when Fox pulls into the driveway. Frost glitters in the early morning light as I rush to his truck. As he pulls back onto the street and heads for school, I watch him—the set of his jaw, the lines of his neck. He doesn't *look* any different than yesterday.

We're nearly to the school when he turns to me while stopped at a sign. "What? You're creeping me out." He doesn't sound mad, but, although his tone is playful, there's a flatness to it.

"How do you feel?"

He shrugs. "Only mildly evil."

His taunting grin doesn't stop me from swatting his arm. "Fox. Come on, really. Do you feel any different from yesterday?"

A horn sounds behind us and he turns his eyes back to the road. "Yeah, I feel different. But, it's a good different. It's like—it's like when you're right in the middle of a spell and everything is going right and the energy is flowing through you—you know? Only it's like that all the time. I feel—I don't know... Like I could do anything."

He pulls into the school's parking lot and I catch a glimpse of Crystal's car. "Are the others all pissed at me?"

"Nah." He parks the car and cuts the ignition. The way he says it indicates there's more to the story, but he doesn't volunteer any information. I don't ask: I'll find out soon enough.

Fox holds my hand as we walk into the school, and again I take stock of him, his energy. There isn't the barest echo of the sensations I received from the crystal, even when I touch my ring to his skin. Maybe I was wrong.

I *hope* I was wrong.

Crystal, Bridget, and Lexie are at Crystal's locker when I get upstairs. Crystal's eyes flick in my direction momentarily but she doesn't wave me over. I'm not sure whether or not I'm upset by this.

The girls all look like they always do, coordinated today in purples and blues. I'm wearing a black sweater and jeans, but something tells me no one will demand I do a glamor to match today.

Fox squeezes my hand as we walk past them to my first hour class. "Don't worry. Things'll be fine, you'll see."

I force a smile to match his, even though I'm not sure he's right. I tried to stop them last night. They could look at that as betrayal. Icy dread knots my stomach. Will they try to retaliate against me? I press the idea from my head. No, they got what they wanted—I didn't *actually* stop them. Maybe I'll be lucky and they'll just ignore me. I've dealt with that enough in my life to be able to deal.

Gratitude for Fox wells inside me. He, at least, doesn't seem upset with me. Although he's not who I would have chosen to be with, he's chosen *me*, and he's standing by me now, even though I'm sure it'll cause stress between him and the other circle members.

When we stop outside Miss Buchanan's English class and he leans in for a kiss, I pull him to me in a tight hug instead. He stiffens, surprised, but quickly relaxes into my arms. His disappointment flashes through me, and I wish I could explain how much more this hug means for me than would a simple acceptance of his kiss. When he kisses me, I pretend, but this embrace is my choice, my thanks, my acceptance of him as a part of my life. I still don't want Fox to be my boyfriend, but I'm glad to have him as a friend. There will be a time to tell him all this, but now is not it.

Fox squints when I release him, his eyebrow raised slightly. "You gonna be okay?"

I smile, and this time it's genuine. "Yeah. I'll see you after class."

I hesitate before making my way toward my regular seat. Lexie isn't there yet. If she doesn't want to sit by me, she can choose another seat. I spent too much time being afraid of what my classmates thought about me to allow myself to slip back into those thoughts. After all, maybe she's not mad at me for last night. I don't want to make her think *I'm* mad. Although I can't sense anything off about Fox's energy, I'm still not convinced last night's ceremony won't have consequences. The best way to help the circle is to stay connected to it.

Lexie slides into the room just before the late bell and I do a double take. At Crystal's locker, she was in jeans and a purple-and-blue checked baby doll top, but now she's in knee-high black leather boots over tight tan pants and a billowing red-checked top. I catch her eye as she takes her seat behind me. "Nice look."

She meets my eyes just long enough to roll hers before focusing on the front of the room. I sigh. So much for the circle not being mad. Still, eye contact is better than complete ignoring. Things could be worse.

Fox is outside the door after class, his face tight with tension. I link my arm through his and start toward my locker. "How long do you think it'll take her to cool down?"

He exhales noisily. "You know Lexie. Either by the end of the day or sometime next year."

We arrive at my locker and I spin the dial. "Okay, time for honesty. Are they all mad at me?"

"No," he says too quickly.

I change out my English novel for my science book. "Fox."

"Griffin couldn't care less. He figures with you not anchored it means more for him. Zane hasn't said anything, but I'd bet he feels the same way. Lexie's always been jealous of you—you know that. My guess is she's gonna want to rub it in for a while that she's finally better at magic than you. And when she gets bored, she'll be back to the same old Lexie."

My heart clenches at his words. If only she could be the same old Lexie.

"Crystal's a bit harder to read. I don't think she's mad, though."

"And Bridget?"

Fox snorts. "She does whatever Crystal and Lexie do."

The next two classes pass without incident, but no one from the circle is in either of them. In science, Owen ignores me the same way he's done the last two days. At first, I thought perhaps Owen was just not paying attention to me, but today it's clear he goes out of his way not to look in my direction: When the girl at the front of my row passes the day's assignment behind her, there's a connection error and the papers spill out into the aisle. Owen stoops to help pick them up and when he hands the assignment to the girl in front of me, his eyes graze mine for the briefest of seconds before he drops his gaze and turns hurriedly forward—almost like he's guilty. But why should he feel guilty for looking at me? The question rattles around my head for the rest of the period and into the next, causing me to mess up an answer during my Spanish skit, asking the boy pretending to be my waiter for *un taco de pecado* instead of *un taco de pescado*—a sin taco instead of a fish taco.

Felix and West, at least, find my error *hilarious* and snicker about it for the remainder of the hour.

At lunch, I sit beside Fox like I've done since Monday, and

while no one says anything about it, no one says anything to me either. Fox keeps up a steady stream of chatter to make up for it, but he can't cover the fact that Bridget, Crystal, and Lexie—who now wears a boat-neck leopard print dress cinched at the waist with a skinny black belt—are pretending I don't exist.

Class never actually begins in math fourth hour, and it has everything to do with Zane. Mrs. Hill keeps walking to the chalkboard, scratching her head, and backing away to consult her textbook or her notes. A few students in the front of the room try calling things out to get her on track, but nothing helps. After about ten minutes, the majority of the class stops trying to be quiet and talks at full volume. Several people move from their desks to sit closer to friends, and a couple of guys start fashioning and flying paper air planes. A handful of girls pull out their cell phones. Zane just sits back in his desk with his arms crossed over his chest, a smug smile playing about the corners of his mouth.

"Having fun?" I ask.

His eyebrows draw together and the corners of his mouth turn down. "I have no idea what you're talking about."

"You know exactly what I'm talking about. Seriously, this is how you're gonna use your magic? To get out of schoolwork? Why not just do a spell to do the work for you or something?"

Fox places a hand on my shoulder. "Just let him have his fun," he murmurs.

I want to argue but think better of it. I don't want Fox to be mad at me. If I have to deal with an hour of downtime, so be it. Math isn't exactly my favorite subject anyway.

By the time I get to health, Lexie—wearing a cap sleeve dress in blue camouflage—has filled our regular table. She offers me the barest smirk as I pass by. I roll my eyes in response. If she thinks she's punishing me by not letting me sit with her, she's wrong.

There's an empty spot at Felix's table and I sit before it occurs to me how out of character it is for my alternate-self. Felix raises an eyebrow but says nothing as I pull my textbook out of my backpack. I offer a smile, hitching my thumb in Lexie's direction. "Do you mind? My usual spot's taken."

He holds up his hands. "By all means." His eyes remain on me as I open my notebook to a fresh page. I shift under the weight of his gaze but say nothing.

Mrs. Stanton is absent today, and the substitute puts on a video about the effects of drugs that looks like it was filmed about thirty years ago. After pressing play and turning off the lights, the sub settles behind the teacher's desk and opens a novel. Every two or three minutes, she shushes us, but the low murmur of voices never actually ceases.

As I watch, I try my best to pay attention and fill out the guided viewing worksheet, but Felix's eyes remain on me. About ten minutes in, I can't stand it anymore. "Why are you staring at me?"

One corner of Felix's mouth upturns and he cocks his head to the side. "You know, I think this is the most you've said to me since seventh grade."

I open my mouth, ready to say I didn't even know him in seventh grade, but stop myself just in time. "Sorry," I say because I can't think of anything else *to* say.

He shrugs. "I get it. You chose your path, right? And it's not like I can blame you. Once you and Fox got together, it wouldn't really be fair to him to still be friends with me."

I stare at him, not sure what he means. To buy time, I scribble *marijuana* on the next blank, even though I'm sure it's not the answer to the question.

"After all, you heard what Mrs. Stanton said last week—there's always a special place in your heart for your first kiss."

I snort at his implication. Felix, my first kiss? No. My first kiss was Owen...

Felix leans back in his chair, crossing his arms over his chest. "Oh, what? So you're gonna pretend it didn't happen?"

Guilt bubbles in my stomach. He's being serious, and from the look in his hazel eyes, he's hurt. I appraise him quickly through the eyes of my seventh-grade self. The last part of sixth grade wasn't good for me: After a crazy explosion of my burgeoning abilities at a friend's birthday party, not only did I become a social pariah, but my dad took off without an explanation. In this timeline, I came to Clearwater just before I started seventh grade. Although I didn't know Felix particularly well in my old life, he was always funny and kind—the type of person I could feel safe and accepted with. And while with his longish brown hair brushing his shoulders isn't a style that appeals to me, Felix does have a sort of rugged handsomeness. Maybe my alternate-self having kissed him isn't entirely outside the realm of possibility.

I force a smile to cover my error. This is Felix, no matter whether I know this version or not, and I know how to talk to him. "What, Felix? You're not still carrying a torch for me after all these years, are you? I think you're the one still hung up on your first kiss."

It's his turn to snort. "Yeah, right. Like you were my first."

He smiles and I can't help smiling back—a genuine one this time.

At the end of the hour, I head straight for history. I want to catch Crystal without her usual entourage and figure this is my best chance. I linger in the hallway by the door, waiting for her to emerge from a clandestine stairwell makeout session with Tucker. Bridget passes me on her way into the room, smiling for an instant before pursing her lips, pulling her eyebrows together, like she's not sure whether she should smile at me or not. This is good news: Maybe Crystal hasn't assigned me status as Public Enemy Number One yet.

Miss Tanner exits the room and heads down the hallway. She's no more than two doors down when a vaguely familiar brunette darts into the room. She's in one of my classes, I'm sure of it, but it's not this one. She wears a pair of skinny black pants and a purple shirt that doesn't quite cover her stomach. Something snaps in my head and it comes to me: Dana Crawford. She was West Harmon's date to the Harvest Dance, and Lexie and Bria called her a hussy.

Now, Dana approaches Bridget and clamps a hand down on her shoulder, spinning the slightly shorter girl to face her. Bridget's face registers surprise for a split second before switching to defense and then anger.

"What?" she snaps, pushing Dana's hand from her shoulder.

"You *know* what," Dana growls. "I'm only gonna say this once, so you better listen. Stay *away* from Marcus. He's mine."

A smile creeps across Bridget's lips and she crosses her arms over her chest. "Oh. *That*."

"I'm about to smack that smile off your face. Stay away from him."

Bridget sighs. "Look, I can't help if he likes me. You know, you should really be having this talk with him, because *he's* the one who can't seem to stay away from *me*."

I haven't noticed any guy hanging around Bridget today, but I know enough to guess what's going on: While Lexie is using her connection to the crystal to do a new glamor every hour and Zane is making his teachers forget their lesson plans, Bridget is casting an attraction charm of some kind.

Dana lunges toward Bridget and Bridget flinches. Dana laughs, easing back a step. "Don't say I didn't warn you." She takes a few more steps backward, keeping her eyes trained on Bridget, before turning and stalking toward the door. When she's almost to the threshold, she stumbles as though she's tripped over something, although nothing is in her path. She careens toward the floor, her arms outstretched to break the fall, but at the last second, her arms fly outward and she crashes face-first into the cream-colored linoleum. An audible gasp sounds through the classroom as Dana lets out a sharp yelp. The tardy bell sounds and Miss Tanner appears in the doorway, freezing at the scene before her. She's at Dana's side in an instant, helping her up. A smear of blood remains on the tile where Dana's nose hit. Miss Tanner supports Dana and heads out of the room, instructing the class to keep away from the blood, that she'll send the custodian to clean it up.

While half the class snickers about what kinds of diseases they might catch off Dana's blood, I cross to Bridget, whose eyes are wide and whose complexion is several shades paler than usual. "I just wanted her to trip," she murmurs. "I didn't mean..."

I slip my arm over her shoulders and lead her to her desk. "I know you didn't mean to."

It was the crystal, I know it.

Chapter Nine

Fox parks behind Jodi's shop and stares at me for a long moment. He doesn't have to say anything for me to know what's on his mind.

"You don't believe me," I say.

He shakes his head. "Kristyl, it's not that I don't believe you. It's that... I just... I think you're..."

"Wrong?" I throw up my hands. "You didn't see it, Fox. The way Bridget took Dana down? It was violent. I heard Dana's nose might be broken, and she's definitely got a black eye."

Fox shrugs. "So, Bridget's got some pent-up rage. You've seen the way Crystal and Lexie treat her. Can you really blame her?"

I shake my head. "You're wrong. The look on her face afterward—she was *scared*. She didn't mean to hurt Dana like that, I'm sure of it."

"And she probably didn't. You know what most likely happened? She's not used to the magic coming so easily and she overshot. It happens to the best of us. Remember the first time you tried to light a candle? The flame shot up like three feet in the air. Is it because you're secretly a pyromaniac? No. You just gave the spell a little too much oomph. But you learned, and so will Bridget."

I sigh, frustration rising. There's nothing I can tell him that will convince him I'm right. I don't even know why I'm trying. I already told Crystal, and she waved me off, just like Fox is doing now. "Fine. Whatever. I'd better get in there." I push open the truck's door and Fox's hand closes around my wrist.

He offers the smallest half smile. "What? No kiss?"

I pull my hand from his grip. "No. I'm mad at you."

His shoulders sag. "Don't be like this."

I jump out of the cab and consider slamming the door without looking back, but it seems too childish. "I'll see you tomorrow."

After a beat, Fox nods. I close the door and head into Hannah's Herbs.

Relief washes over me when I pass through the door. The store smells exactly the way I remember: a mix of sweet and savory herbs and the subtle waxy aroma of candles. The banks of tall shelves running perpendicular to the walls are filled with the items in the same places as I remember. The books are still along the wall between the front door and cash register, and the glass case displaying the different stones and crystals still sends a cascade of rainbows across the carpet. After everything that happened at school today, I'm glad for the normalcy of a day at work.

Jodi's voice comes from the break room and I head for it, figuring she's on the phone with a supplier. I stop short when I turn the corner and see she's talking to a person. He stands with his back to me, his arms stretched above his head to pull a box off the top of a metal shelving unit. I've told her before that putting things up that high is an accident waiting to happen and she's joked that she just waits until tall customers come in to get things down. Is that what she's doing now? The guy's fingers gain purchase on the box and he pulls it down. The muscles beneath his long sleeved shirt tense as he pulls. He's tall, of course, with broad shoulders and strong arms. Besides that, all I can see of his appearance is he's got short brown hair.

Jodi edges toward the guy and pulls open the folded-over edges of the box. "Excellent. I knew this was the right one."

I clear my throat and Jodi jumps, clutching at her heart. She turns and lets out a laugh, running her hand through her hair. "Kristyl. You scared me."

I nod. "Clearly." I almost ask who the guy is but stop myself. Maybe he works here, like Devin did in my reality. Not sure how to greet him, I spin to the time clock and punch in.

"The day's gone by so fast, I didn't realize school ended already." Paper rustles as Jodi sifts through the box's contents. She pulls a smaller box from within, this one filled with tubes of lip balm. She straightens and holds a hand out toward the guy. "I bet you're wondering who our tall assistant is. *This* is Seth. He works here now." She points a finger at me, narrowing her eyes. "Now, don't let it go to your head that you've finally got seniority over someone."

I relax. It's good news that Seth is new—I don't have to blunder through pretending to already know all about him. "It's nice to meet you, Seth," I say as I turn to him. When he faces me, I'm caught by his eyes. They're green and there's something so familiar about them. Like they belong to a long-lost friend.

It feels like my body has been doused in cold water when I realize *where* I've seen his eyes before: I used to see flashes of them when I touched Crystal Jamison. I never knew why I saw them when I touched her, but there's no denying that these are the same eyes. Is he connected to her in some way? Have I seen him around town somewhere? No, that's not possible—I would have realized that when I first had the visions.

He closes the distance between us, holding his hand out. He's standing right in front of me before I manage to move.

"Hi." I take his hand, expecting something to happen—some flash or echo to appear in my head—but nothing does.

Seth smiles, revealing straight teeth with a friendly gap between the front two. On most people, it might look weird, but on him, it fits. It's charming, even. A shadow of dark stubble colors his jaw and upper lip, contrasting nicely with the just-cut look of his hair. "So, you're the Kristyl I keep hearing so much about." He nods at Jodi. "She's comparing everything I do to the way you did it when you were learning."

Heat rises in my cheeks. "I'm sorry."

He shakes his head. "No need. It's clear how much she cares for you. It's sweet that you're on her mind so often, actually."

Jodi rolls her eyes good-naturedly as she heads back into the store. Seth and I follow. "Well, Kristyl, now that you're here to hold down the fort, I'm heading over to the coffee shop. Can I get anything for either of you?"

Seth shakes his head; I order a frozen coffee drink—mostly because I know Jodi will think I'm crazy for doing it, since today is decidedly *not* frozen drink weather. She raises an eyebrow as she heads toward the door, murmuring, "Crazy," as she exits.

I wait until the bells tinkle as the door closes before turning back to Seth. His gaze rests on me already, and I shift. I know he shouldn't make me nervous—after all, Jodi seems enough at ease with him to have given him a job—but I can't get past the fact that I've seen him—his *eyes*—in visions before. It's unsettling. Why would I have seen him when I touched Crystal? If he's new to Clearwater, it's not like their paths have crossed. Could the two of them be connected somehow? I should ask Jodi later—maybe she'll know something about it.

For now, I tamp down my discomfort. "So, how're you liking the store?"

A smile tugs at the corner of his mouth. "It's very... interesting."

I can't help grinning. "Right? You get used to it, though. Believe me, in just a couple weeks, you'll think it's crazy that there was a time when you didn't know what bloodwort was used for."

An expression flickers across his face, but it's gone before I can interpret it. "To be honest, I'm just glad for the job. I don't know what I'd be doing if not for Jodi's kindness."

I nod and head over toward the row of dried herbs in decorative metal planters. I pass my fingers along the edge of the table where they sit, willing myself to relax, when another thought tugs at the edge of my mind: There's something oddly formal in the way Seth speaks, and it reminds me of something, but exactly *what* is eluding me.

Eyes prickle the back of my neck. Seth is watching me. Self-consciousness overtakes me. Can he sense my discomfort? I'm acting strange, I know it, but I can't help it. I've seen his eyes in my mind, and now he's here, working at Jodi's shop.

The silence in the store is oppressive. I clear my throat. "So, do you live here in Clearwater? I've never seen you around."

"I'm new to town. My family's from out east. Massachusetts."

"They didn't come with you?" Despite my attempts to not look at him, it's obvious Seth isn't too much older than I am—two or three years at most.

His face tightens for a moment. "My parents and I... We had a...

difference of opinion."

"Oh. I'm sorry to hear that." I catch myself staring and blink heavily before crossing from the herbs to the shelves of stones and crystals on the other side of the store. I move each one by about a centimeter, just for something to do—something to keep me from looking into his eyes. "So, how'd you decide to come to Michigan?"

He shrugs. "I took up an interest in genealogy. When I learned some ancestors were responsible for founding a town, I had to come see it."

I tense, turning slowly to face him. "You're from a founding family?"

The corners of his mouth quirk upward. "Yes. It's partially why your aunt was so quick to give me a job, I would think. Some of my family stems from the Barnette line."

"Really?" Forgetting my desire to not stare, I step closer, my eyes poring over the lines of his face, looking for a resemblance. Besides Jodi, I always thought I had no extended family. And while I suppose that after several generations, Seth and I aren't closely related, it doesn't matter. I've always been jealous of other people when they've talked of their brothers and sisters and cousins because I've never had that. And now, suddenly, I do.

Seth grins broadly, revealing the gap between his front teeth. "This pleases you."

I return his smile. All my former apprehension about seeing his eyes in visions evaporates. Maybe I saw him because we're related, because on some level I knew he was coming. "Yeah. It does."

The bells above the front door tinkle and Jodi enters the store, along with a strong gust of wind that makes the informational leaflets on the far wall flap like dozens of brightly-colored birds. One hand clutches a cardboard cup caddy while she struggles with the other to pull the door closed behind her. The bells chime frantically and Seth darts to her side, grabbing the door's handle and yanking it shut. I cross to the front window and peer at the sky. When Fox dropped me off, it was blue with a few stray white clouds, but now it's filled with dark gray clouds. Winds rip through the bare trees, causing the limbs to bend and twist.

"Yikes," I murmur as Jodi presses a cold plastic cup into my hand.

"Yikes is right," she agrees, attempting to straighten her hair. "It wasn't like that when I walked down there, but by the time I got out of the coffee shop, it was insane." Giving up on her hair, she pulls the two remaining cups from the caddy and holds one out to Seth.

"I placed no order," he says.

"Take it. Millie wouldn't give me a cup carrier unless I ordered three drinks." She pushes the cup closer to him, waggling her eyebrow at me. She's lying, of course—Millie, the owner of the coffee shop, is Jodi's good friend, and there's no way she'd deny a cup carrier if one was requested. Jodi just wants Seth to feel accepted.

He finally takes the cup, ducking his head. "Thank you very much."

The three of us stand in silence for a few moments, sipping our various drinks, before Jodi speaks again. "It's weird. I just checked the weather this morning and it said it was supposed to be clear the next few days."

Weather reports are notoriously incorrect; then why does my skin prickle at what Jodi says?

The overhead lights go out and the shop is plunged into darkness. Even the front window and glass door don't provide enough light to see more than a few feet into the store. Jodi hands me her coffee and goes to the front door, squinting as she looks across the street. "Looks like the whole street might be out."

***

We wait for the power to return for nearly half an hour before Jodi decides to close the store. After locking up and taping signs up in the front and back doors, she, Seth, and I leave. She offers to give Seth a ride home, but he insists he can walk—he lives in an apartment above the bookstore just blocks away.

My hands tremble as Jodi drives home at five miles an hour. Her windshield wipers are going at full speed, but the road ahead is still barely visible. Every few minutes she murmurs something about how the turn in the weather is so crazy, and while I grunt agreements, I'm not really listening to her. With every block we travel, the muscles in my body tense and icy dread fills my core. Downed tree limbs are everywhere—including atop cars parked in driveways and sticking out of roofs at odd angles. At one point, Jodi has to turn around and take another street because a whole tree has fallen, blocking the road.

The weather isn't crazy. It's not random. It's calculated. It's on purpose. By the time we finally make it to the house, I'm convinced of it.

The circle is behind the storm. I don't know how I know, but I do. There's something about the storm—a *feeling*. The air thrums, not with electricity, but with magic. I've felt it before, most recently when I used the crystal to cast the glamor to change my appearance.

Mom's car isn't in the driveway and an ache builds in the back of my throat. I swallow in an attempt to clear it. *She's fine. She'll be home soon.* I repeat the words over and over in my mind, but they're no comfort. In my reality, my mom died in a car accident on a perfectly normal day. What might happen when the weather is as bad as this? I couldn't handle losing her—not again.

I shake my head. I can't obsess about it. She *will* be fine. And there's nothing I can do right now, anyway. I open the car door and start running for the house. Jodi is several feet ahead of me and I can barely make out her figure through the sheets of rain falling between us. Why would the circle want to cause a storm? The answer comes to me when I get to the top of the porch stairs.

Because they can.

I shiver as I cross the threshold into the house, but it has nothing to do with the chill of the rain.

Jodi flips the light switch in the hallway but nothing happens. She sighs. "Good thing we've got candles."

We spend the next several minutes placing candles strategically around the house. By the time the sizable supply is diminished, I'm pretty sure the power will be back on by the time we can light them all.

A car door thuds closed in the driveway and I peer out the front window, releasing a sigh of relief when I recognize my mom's car.

Jodi joins me at the window, but instead of being pleased, she clucks her tongue. "Better make this fast."

Before I can ask what she's talking about, Jodi turns and closes her eyes, raising her hands, palm up, toward the ceiling. I gasp as the dozen candles spread throughout the living room spring to life. A quick glance toward the dining room confirms my suspicion that all the candles are now lit.

Jodi raises an eyebrow. "What's that face for? It's not like you've never seen me do that before."

I open my mouth to disagree, but the front door bangs open and my mom lets out a loud whoop. By the time I make it to the hallway, she's closed the door and is shaking the rain off her jacket. "Wow, I thought I'd never get home." She puts the coat on a hanger and tucks it away in the hall closet before scanning the vicinity. "I was afraid the power would be out here, too. The traffic signals on the way home were all out. I'm glad you've already got some light in here. It must've taken forever to light all these candles."

Jodi catches my eye and winks as Mom brushes past us toward the kitchen. What's going on here? Jodi uses magic, but my mom doesn't know about it? At some point, maybe these differences from my old life will stop surprising me, but today is not that day.

Chapter Ten

We're in the middle of a candle-lit dinner of peanut butter and jelly sandwiches when a knock sounds at the front door. Jodi crams the last of her sandwich into her mouth before heading out into the hallway. Mom and I exchange a glance as the door creaks open.

"Seth?" Jodi's tone is more than a little surprised and, as Seth and Jodi move down the hall toward the dining room, I sit up straighter in my chair.

"My apologies," he says, pushing his sopping hair off his forehead and wiping his face with his hands. "When it seemed the whole of the town had lost its electricity, I grew worried. I hope it's not too great an intrusion. I wanted to be sure you and Kristyl were well."

My mom raises an eyebrows and I shrug, knowing it's his odd way of speaking that's taken her off guard. Besides his weird speech patterns and the fact I've had visions about him, Seth seems on the level, and I try to assure my mom of that with a tiny nod. The corner of her mouth quirks up and she folds her napkin and places it on the table before standing. "I assume this is the new employee you were talking about?"

"He's related to us," I blurt. When my mom turns, I add, "To the Barnettes, anyway."

She sighs, turning back to him. "Well, he's soaking wet. Kristyl, go up to my room and get a pair of sweats from the bottom drawer. They might fit him."

I'm dubious of her assertion as Seth is several inches taller than my mom, but I know better than to disagree. I do as I'm directed. By the time I get back downstairs, Seth is holed up in the hall bathroom. Jodi is standing by the door and takes the clothes from me, winking before she closes her eyes, her lips forming words that don't make it to my ears. She opens her eyes again and knocks on the door, which opens a crack before Seth's hand appears.

When he emerges from the bathroom a couple of minutes later, I'm shocked to see the gray sweatpants and blue sweatshirt actually cover him to the ankles and wrists. Jodi must have cast some kind of spell on them, because even if the clothes were baggy on my mom, there's no way they would fit Seth like this.

"Thank you for these," he says, stretching out his arms and legs, testing the length of the sweats. "And let me apologize again for arriving unannounced. I couldn't abide the idea of you here alone in the dark. I wanted to be sure you were all right."

"I'm more worried about you. With how cold it is out there, I won't be surprised if you get sick." Jodi squints. "Did you walk here? How did you even know where *here* is?"

Seth's mouth twitches, a shadow flickering across his face. Then he smiles, ducking his head. "Maggie at the bookstore. She was leaving when I arrived, and she told me where I could find you."

I study his face. There's something he's holding back, but I can't tell what it is.

Jodi doesn't seem to notice. She claps her hands together. "Since you're here, why don't we get some training out of the way? I'll show you around the greenhouse so you can start learning the herbs."

Seth nods eagerly and follows Jodi down the hall toward the greenhouse door. I go, too. Although I've learned a lot about the properties of the various plants Jodi sells at the shop, I don't know as much as I should if I've been around them for four years. With any luck, I can pick up some information while she teaches Seth.

The greenhouse is, of course, mostly glass, but it's so dark outside that the room is ensconced in shadow. Jodi clucks her tongue. "I'll go grab some candles from the dining room. Kristyl, I think there's one or two over there on the bench. Why don't you get those lit? I'll be right back."

Jodi leaves, closing the door behind her, and I cross the room to the far left corner where Jodi's workbench is positioned. She uses it when she's planting or re-potting, or when she's bundling herbs. There's a pair of pruning shears on the table, along with a spool of twine and a black Sharpie marker. But no candles.

"Perhaps the candles are in the box underneath?" Seth, who followed me over, bends down and slides the small cardboard box out from beneath the bench. He unfolds the top and grins, reaching in and pulling out a long white taper. I reach for it, but, in true guy style, he tosses it up, making it spin in mid-air. I bump it on its descent and it slips through his fingers, colliding with the edge of the tabletop before clattering onto the floor, broken cleanly in half with just the wick connecting the two sections.

"Good going," I grumble. I reach for it, but Seth is both closer and faster. He kneels down and closes his hand over the two broken edges of the candle. He's still for a moment before pressing himself to standing.

He holds his closed fist out to me, the candle jutting out on either side of his hand. "Here you are. No harm done."

I snort. "No harm done? Yeah, except now we've got two pieces instead of—"

Seth opens his hand. Resting on his upturned palm is an unbroken taper—just as unblemished as it was when he pulled it from the box.

I gape, brushing my fingers over the waxy surface. "It was broken."

The corners of his mouth turn down. "No, it—"

"Yes, it was. I saw it." I take the candle from him, examining it. There's no trace of the break.

He shakes his head. "You're mistaken. Perhaps the light—"

His alarm heats my skin. He's nervous—scared, even. He didn't think I saw it, and now I know. I know his secret. The realization washes over me like a wave and I close my fingers around the candle, rotating my wrist so the wick is upright. "Calm down. It's okay."

"I should go." He turns and strides toward the greenhouse door.

Panic rises. He can't leave—not right now. I need him to understand *why* what he did is okay. Closing my eyes, I take in a breath and connect with the energy around me. When I open them again, the wick of the candle is lit. "Wait."

Seth stops, spinning slowly on his heel. His green eyes widen at the sight of the flame. "How did you—?"

"I think you know." I take a few steps toward him. "This candle was broken. I saw it." His eyes flicker between my face and the flame. "I know what you did. I know what you *are*."

"Okay, this should be enough," Jodi says as she pushes through the door, a half dozen pillar candles tucked between her arms and torso. "Let's get these set up and let the training begin!"

Seth closes the distance between them and relieves her of the candles, following her directions about where to set them. He doesn't look at me.

I fight the urge to continue our conversation. Although Jodi knows about magic—and uses it in this reality—based on his reaction with me, I doubt Seth would want her to know he's a witch. I don't know why I'm surprised at all, really—after all, he *is* from the Barnette line. He knows the Barnettes helped found Clearwater, but does he know about the family's magical abilities?

As Jodi starts her herb tutorial, Seth makes every effort to keep his eyes from straying to me. My presence is making him nervous. I tamp down my desire to question him. We can talk when he's ready. Quietly, I slip out of the room.

***

Rain lashes against my bedroom windows, but it's not loud enough to drown out the shriek of sirens. My chest is tight. I spent some time trying to peer out the windows to see where the ambulances or fire trucks were headed, but it's impossible to see much outside. It's been over an hour since the storm started, and I still can't shake the feeling that a natural force doesn't propel it. The circle is behind it somehow—I can feel it. The question now is why it's *still* happening. The weather was affected—they've proven they can do it. But things are getting out of hand now and it doesn't look like the storm will break any time soon.

My stomach sinks. Maybe it hasn't broken because they can't

stop it. Like Bridget, who hurt Dana Crawford more than she anticipated, maybe this storm is worse than they planned.

The stairs creak. "Are you up here?" Seth calls softly.

I'm surprised to hear his voice. After what happened in the greenhouse—after his nervousness, his fear—I figured he'd ignore me the rest of the night. I sit up on my bed and scoot to the edge. "Yeah. Come on up."

He appears slowly, first the top of his head, then his face, his shoulders, his torso. Finally, he arrives at the top, taking a tentative step into the room. I motion for the desk chair and he hesitates before making a move to it. "About... About earlier..."

"We don't have to talk about it."

"I want to," he says quickly.

I smile. I understand exactly where he's coming from. For so long, I had the power within me, but I didn't know what it was. And once Jodi told me, she insisted I learn to keep it under control. But something that's so much a part of me isn't something I want to ignore. I want to be able to talk about it, to learn about it. From the look on his face, it's obvious Seth feels the same way. "How long have you known?"

He shrugs. "My whole life, it feels like. I always knew there was something within me. Once I realized what it was, I became obsessed with learning all I could about magic. My research is actually what led me here. I told you I study genealogy, but I only study it because I realized my abilities come from my family lines."

I lean forward, eager. This is the kind of conversation I've longed for. There wasn't enough time for it to happen in my other life before everything changed, and now I have to pretend like everything isn't brand new to me. But here, with Seth, it's perfect, because we're strangers. "I bet you know all kinds of spells."

"Know, yes. But the number of spells I can actually *do* is limited."

"Really? Why?"

"From what I can tell, there are many people in the world who possess the ability to wield magic. But most will never know they can. Some people are more in tune with their abilities than others. Some people can work spells without trying particularly hard, while others struggle to do even simple tasks." He holds his hands up. "I struggle."

This makes sense. The first time I did a spell with Crystal, she was shocked I was able to do it on my first try. She said it took Bridget countless attempts to do it, and even now, it was hit-or-miss. "Do you know other witches? Like—did you know some back in Massachusetts?"

His mouth twitches. "I had a circle, but we've since disbanded. You?"

I bite my lower lip. "I have a circle. I'm not sure they like me too much right now, but..."

His eyebrow furrows. "Why not?"

I hesitate. Should I tell him about the crystal? I suppose it doesn't really matter—it's not like he knows its history. And I don't have to tell him how we got it. "You know how certain things—like stones—can store energy? Well, we found a stone like that and they wanted to anchor the circle to it. I didn't."

"Did they do it?"

I nod. "And I tried to stop them. It didn't work."

A muscle in his jaw jumps. "That's unfortunate."

The wind howls against the house. "I think they're doing this. All day, they've been using magic, and this storm... It doesn't feel like a regular storm."

His eyebrows hitch upward. "They're using this stone to control the weather? That's powerful magic indeed."

"I don't trust it. I don't like that they're anchored to it. They think it's because I don't want them to be more powerful than I am, but that's not it. There's something... not right about the energy of the crystal."

He shrugs. "Why not sever their connection to it?"

"Is that even possible?"

"Why not? If it can be done, it can be undone."

My stomach flutters. Could it be that simple? Could I simply cut their tie to the crystal? "I don't even know where to look for a spell like that."

"Leave that to me. I'm rather good at research." He smiles.

I try to smile back, but it falls almost immediately. I look down into the smoky stone on my ring. In spells I've done before, it's been necessary to charge elements with power beforehand. What if that's similar to how the energy got into the crystal? "Couldn't we just... I dunno... *discharge* the energy or something?" I ask, pulling Seth into the middle of my thoughts. "Like, if it's not in the stone anymore, there's nothing left to be anchored to?"

Seth purses his lips, his eyebrows drawing together as he considers the idea. "I don't think it would work—not while they're linked to it." He offers another smile. "I'll add it to my list of research questions."

This time, I do manage to smile. It's good to have someone helping me with this.

Chapter Eleven

By morning, the sky is clear. The only indication of last night's storm is the damage it left in its wake. A survey out my third-floor windows reveals holes in roofs, broken windows, dented cars, and broken tree limbs.

Power was restored some time during the night, dashing my hopes of a day off school due to no electricity. Since Seth mentioned it last night, the only thing I can think of is the possibility of a spell to un-anchor the circle from the crystal. Especially after the conversation Fox and I have on the way to school.

"Did you lose power last night?" I ask as he pulls out of my driveway.

"Uh, no. You did?"

"Yeah. Here and at the shop."

He hums vaguely in response, discomfort radiating off him in waves.

"What'd you do last night?"

"Uh, you know. Homework."

Typically he glances at me when we talk on the way to school, but this morning, his eyes are on the road. "They were over last night, weren't they?"

He readjusts his grip on the steering wheel. "It's not like that. I mean, it wasn't an official meeting or anything. Everyone just ended up coming over. They wanted to do some spells and didn't want any adults interfering."

I cross my arms over my chest. "One of those spells wouldn't happen to have, I don't know, caused the storm, would it?"

He sighs. "Kristyl."

"I knew it."

He shakes his head. "It's not what you think. Crystal and Lexie and Bridget just wondered if they could do it. They didn't mean for it to get as crazy as it got—"

"That's exactly my point, Fox. There's too much power for them to control. Things are getting out of hand."

"No—it's not that. It's just... We need practice. I told you that. I think you've been so good at controlling it for so long you're forgetting what it was like when you were first learning to control your magic. You've just got to give us some time."

It's not time they need, but I don't tell Fox that. Instead, I let the subject drop. There's no need to fight over it. If Seth can find a spell to sever the circle from the crystal, I won't have to worry about their magic getting out of hand.

Like yesterday, Lexie does a glamor between every class to change her appearance. More people notice today and crowd around her to ask where she's getting all the fancy clothes. Bridget isn't around Crystal's locker nearly so much today. Any time I see her, she's with a tall, broad-shouldered guy with blond hair and a slightly dazed expression. He must Marcus, the guy Dana Crawford was talking about yesterday.

Like yesterday, the girls ignore me, but I don't mind. I've still got Fox to talk to, and for now, that's enough.

He's walking me to sixth hour when it happens. Crystal, Lexie, and Bridget stand at Crystal's locker, sipping from the same coffee cups they've carried all day—which have yet to run empty. Bria is walking down the hall, arms loaded with books. I catch the look in Lexie's eye just before Bria pitches forward, the books flinging out of her hands and clattering to the floor. The people in the hallway part like the Red Sea and a swell of laughter builds as Bria catches her balance.

"Why does she hate her so much?" I ask Fox.

The look he gives tells me I should know. "Come on. Lexie's pretty good at holding grudges."

That's an understatement. Bria stares daggers at Lexie as she reaches for her fallen belongings. Lexie just smirks before pivoting and heading down the hall, Crystal and Bridget beside her. The hairs on the back of my neck stand up and my skin prickles. A split second before it happens, a wave of energy courses through me.

As though the very air around them thickened into a wall, Lexie, Crystal, and Bridget come to a sudden stop, their coffees spilling down their fronts. An ear-piercing set of screams shrills through the hallway and everyone in the vicinity whips around to identify the source of the sound.

Everyone but me. This wasn't an accident—someone *made* them spill their drinks. Could it be another witch? I shake my head as soon as the thought occurs to me. Whatever just happened, it felt different than magic. But what could it have been?

The hallway is all motion now, with people rushing toward the girls—some to try to help, others just to get a better view. At least two people snap pictures with their phones. It's impossible for me to tell by looking who might have caused the spill, but maybe if I reach out with my abilities...

I focus the way I used to when I would share thoughts with Owen. In my mind's eye, I see a band of white energy trailing from the center of my chest down into my right arm, and out my fingers, spreading out around me like ripples on a pond.

Something resonates back to me. Someone is heading down the hall toward the sharp right turn by Mrs. Ortiz's room. Without waiting to figure out who the person could be, I take off at a quick pace in that direction, leaving Fox behind. I need to know who has abilities like that.

I'm fast, but not fast enough: By the time I arrive at the turn in the hallway, there's no one in sight. But there is someone ahead of me—where this hall joins another. Not wanting her to get away, I take off at a run.

Her. I know the person is a girl. And... familiar.

She's nearly to the next hallway when I catch a glimpse of black hair cut in a severe bob, and I take in a breath before calling her name. "Bria!"

Bria Tate turns toward me slowly, eyes wide and guilty. Her gaze darts behind me like she's expecting me to have backup. "Stay away from me," she says, her voice low.

I freeze, holding my hands up. "I'm not here to retaliate."

Bria's mouth twitches. "For what? I didn't do anything. Unless you're gonna try to blame me for your friends being clumsy bitches."

I take a slow step toward her, heartened by the fact she doesn't back away. "It wasn't clumsiness that made them spill their drinks, just like it wasn't clumsiness that made you drop your books." I step closer, keeping my eyes locked on hers. She's not a witch—her energy is different from that of anyone in the circle. But there's another explanation. "You're psychic, aren't you?"

Surprise flickers across her face, replaced immediately with fear. She snorts. "You're crazy."

"Am I?" I take another step. I'm barely more than an arm's-length away now. "I know more than you think I do."

She rolls her eyes and turns away, but I grab her arm, pushing a single thought from my mind as I make contact with her skin: *I'm one too.*

Bria closes her hand over mine as she turns back, eyes round. "You can't be. You're... you're..."

"A witch?" I supply.

"One of them." Her hand drops to her side.

I remove my hand from her arm but don't step away from her. "Things are more complicated than that—more complicated than I can even start to explain." I take in a breath, allowing the question that's been tugging at the back of my mind up to the surface. "Are there more like you. Like us?" I want to say his name—I want to ask if Owen knows who he is, what he is, in this reality, but I allow Bria the space to tell me what she knows.

"There are more. Two more that I know about. We meet up after school most days for at least a little while. We're still trying to figure out all we can do."

"Bring me."

Bria's eyes flicker to the ground. "I don't think that's a good idea."

"Why not?"

"Because they won't trust you. You're one of *them.*"

"Maybe that's been true in the past, but things are different now." I press my lips together, weighing my options. If I lie, she might be able to tell, so I choose my words carefully. "I've... changed a lot recently. I'm not the same person you've known for the last four years. I only found out recently about my psychic side, and I want to explore it."

She studies my face, eyes crinkling at the corners. "Fine. You can come today—but I'm not promising the guys'll like it. And if they don't want you there, it's majority rule."

Guys. My heart skips. Is Owen one of the guys? I want to ask, but doing so might set off red flags. So far as she knows, I have no reason to be so interested in Owen. "Okay. Where do you meet? When?"

She sighs like she's already regretting her decision. "Usually about half an hour after school at West Harmon's house. He lives on—"

"I know where he lives."

Bria arches an eyebrow and I bite the inside of my cheek. In my other reality, I've been to West's house. But I'm not that girl.

Before Bria can ask the question that's probably forming in her mind, I straighten. "I'll be there. See you after school."

Chapter Twelve

West's house looks just like I remember it from the other reality, which comforts me. I recognize Bria's mom's Camry in the driveway as I approach. Mom and Jodi are still at work and I walked here. I'm glad it's only a couple of blocks because my nose and ears are already frozen. I jog to the front door but pause before knocking, hoping to find Owen inside. Taking in a breath, I bring my knuckles down against the door.

"Who the hell knocks?" West's voice is muffled by the door, but still understandable. The curtain covering the front window flickers. "What's *she* doing here?"

"Open the door, West." Bria sounds farther away.

I bite my lower lip, waiting for something to happen. After a beat, the door swings open, revealing a thoroughly bewildered West. His brow is furrowed, making his eyes look even more deep-set than usual. "Can I help you?"

I scan the room—I can't help it—before looking at Bria. "You didn't tell him?"

She shrugs. "I didn't know for sure you were gonna show." She approaches West and gives him a gentle shove. "Let her in already."

I step inside, closing the door behind me. Besides West and Bria, the living room is empty. Unless the other guy Bria mentioned is in the kitchen, we three are the only ones here. "Hey, West."

"She says like she knows me." He crosses the room and sits on the armchair at the far side. "What are you doing here?"

I sit on the couch across from him—the same place I sat last time I was here, in my reality. "I bet you can figure it out."

He stares at me for a beat before looking at Bria, whose face remains impassive. When his gaze flicks back to me, he shakes his head. "Uh-uh. No way."

The doorknob twists and my heart picks up its pace. The last member of the group has arrived. I hold my breath as the door begins to swing open, just waiting for Owen's form to appear... But it's not Owen who enters.

"Felix?" I look at Bria, hoping maybe she'll be as surprised as I am, hoping he's not the person she was expecting either. But if she's surprised at all, it's at my reaction. Her eyebrows cinch together.

"Whoa—wait." Felix pauses, door still open. "Is this a dream?"

West snorts. "Nightmare?"

Bria crosses to Felix, pushing him into the house and closing the door. "Okay, clearly you two are wondering why she's here, even though the answer should be obvious."

Felix closes the distance between us and sits on the couch beside me. His brown hair tickles his shoulders as he bobs his head, appraising me. Although I've been sitting with him in health class, this is the first time I feel like he's accepting me and happiness rushes through me. Bria, West, Felix—three of my friends from my old timeline all here under one roof, all looking at me like I'm a person and not a thing? It's better than good—it's fantastic. The only thing that would make this moment better is if—

I bite the inside of my cheek, my eyes dropping to my lap. Owen's not here. And if he's not, could it be because he's not psychic in this reality? If he were, wouldn't Bria and the guys already know? They didn't know about me—but that was probably because our paths didn't often cross. But what about Owen? I scan my mental files from this week at school, trying to remember if I've seen Owen with Felix or West at all.

"I don't like it." West's voice cuts through my thoughts. His arms cross over his chest. "She's one of them."

His tone is so cold it makes me shiver. I've never heard West talk like this: The West I knew was quick to smile and laugh. But now, his deep-set eyes are fixed on me, his brow heavy and brooding. I square my shoulders. I figured this would come up—it was Bria's first reaction, too. "It's true. I'm a witch, and I'm part of Crystal Jamison's circle."

Beside me, Felix lets out a small, choked sound, pumping his fist. I glance at him, alarmed, but his eyes are fixed on West. "I *told* you. Dude, you totally owe me ten bucks." He sticks out his hand, wiggling his fingers. "Come on. I know you've got it."

Bria sighs, crossing and sitting on the couch adjacent to mine. "We've had our assumptions, but we didn't know for sure." She leans toward me. "What I don't understand is how you're *both*."

The fact that they didn't know about the witches, that I've let them in on a secret, should unsettle me, but it doesn't. I want their trust, and this might be the best way to earn it. "My dad's from a witch line. My mom's from a psychic one. Somehow, I'm both. That's all I know."

West settles down in the room's armchair after slapping a bill into Felix's hand. "And while that's fascinating and all, I'm more concerned with why you're here. Why aren't you hanging out with your circle or whatever you call it?"

I ignore the accusation in his voice. "I'm not here to *spy* if that's what you're thinking. I don't know if you've noticed, but I'm not exactly in Crystal's inner circle at the moment."

"So you think we want you?"

I open my mouth to defend my intentions, but Bria's faster.

"Stop being a dick, West. She's on the level."

Bria doesn't meet my eyes when I look at her. I'm not sure why she feels so confident about me. Did I share something more with her than I meant to? Or is she just able to sense more about me? I have no idea how much her abilities have developed, nor what she's capable of. An empty sensation gathers in the pit of my stomach. Maybe this was a mistake. What if she can sense the truth about me? Oddly, the idea doesn't send me into panic. It relieves me. I want her to know. Maybe if she knows who I really am, I can start putting my life back together. But would it be fair to her to learn about a life she isn't living, one that seems, in many ways, to be better than the one she has now? By changing things, I stripped her of her best friend, and turned Lexie into someone even I don't want to associate with. No, it's better that she go on thinking this is the way things are supposed to be, the way they've always been.

"If she's on the level, let her prove it." West holds his hands toward me, palms up. "Who's in this circle of yours?"

My mouth goes dry. I don't care so much about betraying Crystal's secret—and it's not like the witches are particularly stealthy about things, since, until recently, we all were in the same social group. The knot in my stomach is about Fox. By letting the psychics in on this information, I'm selling out Fox, and he doesn't deserve that. Then again, Bria doesn't deserve the abuse she endures from Lexie, and Fox hasn't stepped in to stop that. "Crystal, of course. She's kind of the leader."

"Surprise, surprise," Bria mutters.

"And Lexie. They get it from the Taylor line." I consider mentioning that our principal, who is also a Taylor, has magic, but I keep that to myself. They're just asking about the circle's members. "Bridget. Zane. Fox's older brother, Griffin. And..." I take a deep breath. "And Fox."

Felix gives a loud whoop, startling me. Bria rolls her eyes as he holds his hand toward West again. "And that's ten *more* dollars you owe me!"

West groans as he shifts to remove his wallet from his back pocket. "You don't have to be so excited about it."

I raise an eyebrow, confused. "Have you guys been betting on *everything* related to the circle?"

"Well, yeah," Felix says, relieving West of another bill. He pulls it apart at the corners, making it snap. "Excellent way to make a little extra spending money."

I smile, but his explanation doesn't answer my question. "No, I mean... You're *psychic*, right? Can't you figure this kind of stuff out without guessing?"

Felix cocks an eyebrow comically high. "Why, can you?"

"She figured out what I was," Bria says. There might even be a hint of admiration in her tone.

Felix apprises me for a moment before shrugging. "We're all

still kinda learning how to use our abilities."

"Yeah," West agrees. "And as much as it might surprise you, not everyone spends every waking moment obsessing over you and your friends."

The venom in his voice is more than I can take. I round on him. "Okay, enough. I come in peace. You want to know about the circle? I'll tell you. You want me to prove I'm psychic? I'll do it. Why are you being such an ass to me?"

Felix and Bria exchange glances and I know I'm missing something. Something alternate-me would know. West's face is tight and he examines me like I'm something unsavory he's found on the bottom of his shoe.

"You really don't remember, do you?" He snorts, shaking his head. "I don't even know why I'm surprised. It doesn't matter, not really. *I* remember what you did to Owen. So excuse me if I'm not your biggest fan."

The air rushes from my lungs. *Owen.* What did I do to him? My mind reels and I grip the arm of the couch. I want to know—desperately—what I did, but I don't think I can hear it. Is this why Owen looks through me? Did I do something that hurt him so badly he can't bear to look at me? Tears prickle my eyes. I can't cry—not here. How would I explain that reaction? Bria avoids my gaze and Felix is suddenly very interested in the dirt beneath his fingernails, but West's eyes bore a hole through me.

"I'm not that girl anymore," I manage finally. "Whatever you think you know about me, whoever you think I am, it's not me. I promise you that. Just... give me a chance. I'll prove it."

West leans back in his chair. "Pass."

"Okay, that's enough." Bria straightens, though her height is far from impressive. "Whether you like it or not, she's one of us."

"She's one of *them*," West grumbles.

"Which, if you think about it, is actually pretty cool," Felix says. "And it could be useful."

I shift, suddenly worried my scant knowledge of the circle might not be enough. "I'm not exactly one of them—not at the moment, anyway." I purse my lips when their eyes flicker to me. I press on quickly before I lose my nerve. "They did a spell the other day that increased their abilities. I thought it was a bad idea and tried to stop them. Now my membership in the circle is... tenuous."

Felix whistles. "Nice vocab word."

West crosses his arms over his chest. "Convenient."

Panic flares and I sit up straighter. "Still, I'll do anything I can do to help."

Bria smiles and my heart swells. Although we're meeting at West's house, I get the impression Bria is really the leader of this group. And if she wants me here, I don't think West will kick me out.

West sits up again. "Prove it."

"Sure. What do you wanna know? I already told you who's in the circle."

Felix leans forward, his knee brushing mine. "What do you guys do at your meetings? I mean, I assume you have meetings, right?"

I shrug. "Practice spells, mostly. What do you guys do?"

"The same thing, I guess," Bria says. "When we first started meeting, we'd do simple things—like try to figure out what each other was thinking or send thoughts. You know, the basics. But for a while now we've been working on some harder things."

"Like that invisible wall thing you did to Lexie and Crystal today?"

The curl in Bria's lips is all the confirmation I need.

"What else can you do?" Giddiness bubbles in my stomach like it did last night when I talked to Seth about magic. I have these abilities swirling inside, but I don't know what to do with them. I don't know what I'm capable of. The thought of being able to focus this power makes my skin tingle.

Bria's eyes light up. "Lately, I've been working on manipulating objects. You know, like making things levitate." A grin stretches across her face. "It's pretty cool, actually."

"West's been working on apportation—which is making something disappear and re-materialize somewhere else. He's lost more pencils and pennies than I can count. And I've been working on astral projection." Felix's eyes are alight. "I was actually able to do it for a hot second before it all went haywire."

Bria snorts. "You mean before you got so scared you almost crapped yourself."

"Hey, give me a break! Having an out-of-body experience is kind of freaky."

I lean in. "Out-of-body experience? Really?"

Felix nods, a smug smile on his face. "In theory, you can send your spirit out anywhere in the world. I'm aiming for the cheerleaders' locker room."

I shove his shoulder while Bria yells, "Gross!" Felix allows me to push him into the arm of the chair before righting himself.

"Astral projection is just step one. If I can get good at that, then I might be able to bilocate, which would be *epic*."

My eyebrows pull together. "Bilocate?"

He grins. "Be in two places at once. It's cooler than astral projection because you can actually interact with the place you're bi-locating to. And then, when you're done, you just—*pop*—disappear."

Everything sounds so amazing, I can't wait to start trying these things myself.

Over the next couple of hours, Bria and Felix take turns showing me the things they can do. They're disappointed that I don't know how to *do* more, but neither can hide how impressed they are with how quickly I pick up on how to levitate an object and apportate a newspaper from one side of the coffee table to the other. Since I already know how to direct my abilities to do magic, I'm able to channel my psychic powers with minimal direction.

West disappears soon after we start working—"Probably sulking," says Bria—and doesn't emerge until Felix, Bria, and I are about to leave. We're walking out the front door when he calls my name, asking me to hang back. Bria and I exchange glances, but I stay.

Felix pulls the door closed behind him, but West doesn't speak. I shift, uncomfortable. He asked me to stay, so he must want to say something. I consider reaching forward with my abilities to get a sense of what's on his mind but don't go through with it—not only is West a psychic and therefore possibly able to sense such an intrusion, I want to give him the respect and the space to say what's on his mind in his own time.

He surveys me with his deep-set eyes like he's trying to look inside me. After a minute, he shakes his head. "I bet you're happy right now. You think you've got them fooled—and you might. Just know that you don't fool me, Kristyl Barnette. Never forget I know who you really are." He pivots on his heel before heading toward the back hallway. "Now get out of my house."

Chapter Thirteen

West's words haunt me. *I know who you really are.*

But who is that exactly? Who does he think I am? There's no one who can answer that question for me. What am I supposed to do, go to Fox or Lexie or Zane and ask them to tell me about myself? Not an option.

I try to follow the thread of the conversation at dinner, but my mind wanders. There has to be a way to figure things out without being too obvious, without drawing attention to the fact that I don't remember my life here in Clearwater. There's the psychic angle: Maybe I can read someone's mind and get my answers that way? I dismiss the idea before it's fully formed. Even though using my psychic abilities is easier now that I know what they are, I'm still leaps and bounds from being able to scan a person's mind to find the information I want to know—if it's even possible. At best, I can get a sense of what people are feeling or thinking in the moment. I wouldn't know how to start digging through someone's memories.

I'm loading the dinner dishes into the dishwasher when the idea hits me. It's so obvious I can't believe it took me so long to think of it: my diary.

When I was younger, I kept a diary full of my innermost thoughts and feelings. When things got bad at the end of sixth grade, I quit—why would I want to record such terrible things? But my alternate-self lived a different life. Maybe once she moved here to Clearwater she started writing things down again. At the very least, it won't hurt to look.

I feel like a thief as I rifle through my dresser drawers.

Although I've been using the clothes in this room for days, sometimes it's still hard to believe all these things are mine. And even though I know alternate-me isn't going to come upstairs and catch me going through her things, I still feel like I'm doing something wrong.

The dresser drawers are void of anything helpful and I move to the closet. I poke around the shelves before an idea occurs to me: In my reality, there was a loose floorboard in the closet. That was where I found my dad's ring. I know the ring was never hidden there in this time, but maybe alternate-me found the loose board anyway. It would make the perfect place for hiding a diary.

My fingers pry at the board for a few second before it budges. I reach in the hole and my fingers brush against the soft leather binding of a book. I pull it out. It's brown and supple to the touch, with leather thongs tied and holding it closed. With trembling fingers, I undo the knot and open the book.

It's my handwriting. Of course it is—she would have the same handwriting as me—but for some reason it still strikes me as strange. The first entry is dated August, four years ago—right before I started seventh grade.

Tomorrow's my first day at Clearwater Middle School. I'm nervous. What if something happens? No one here knows about me, about what I did at Brittany's party. But I'm still afraid that somehow people will be able to tell. I had a dream last night—a nightmare—that I walked into my first class and everyone stopped and stared at me. Then they started pointing and whispering. The whispers got louder and louder and then someone started laughing. All of a sudden, Brittany was standing in the middle of the room, laughing and pointing at me and yelling, "There's the freak!"

I know there's no way that's going to happen. She doesn't know where I live now, and besides, there's no way her parents would drive her all the way down here on the first day of school, anyway. Still, every time I think about going to school tomorrow, my stomach twists and I feel like I'm gonna throw up.

I brush my fingers across the words. She sounds a lot like me the summer before I started seventh grade. Only I wasn't starting a new school. I hoped that Brittany and her friends would have forgotten about me over the summer, moved on to some other target. I wasn't that lucky, but *she* was.

I flip ahead a few pages.

School's going great. I guess everyone has basically known each other since birth, so they all want to be my friend. I'm new and exciting, not a freak. I like it.

A pang courses through me. My seventh grade experiences weren't nearly so pleasant and I can't help the surge of jealousy. I wish things had happened for me.

When we realized things were different, Crystal told me I should take the win, that I should be grateful for the changes. Is she right? We didn't actively affect the past, yet we came back to a different reality. Did we really reset things to the way they were meant to be? Is it possible I was never supposed to experience all the torment I did at my old school?

I leaf through a few more pages until a familiar name catches my eye. *Owen.*

That boy who sits behind me in math, who keeps kicking my foot? I finally got the nerve to tell him to stop today. I'm glad I did.

His name is Owen Marsh, and he apologized for kicking me. He said he didn't realize he was doing it. We talked a little and even worked on our homework together.

He's really cute. Like, really. Is it bad of me to think like that? Technically, Felix is my boyfriend—

I reread that part a couple times, thinking I've misread it. But, no, it doesn't say *Fox*, which I'd understand—it says *Felix*. The entry is dated November of my seventh grade year. A giggle bubbles inside me. He wasn't lying the other day in class. Felix Wolfe really was my first kiss.

Technically, Felix is my boyfriend, but Dana says it's okay to think someone else is cute, too. And Owen is. He's cute and nice, and I'm glad he was kicking my foot.

Dana? Were Dana Crawford and I friends in middle school? I scan several pages, searching for names. Who was alternate-me friends with when she first came to town?

I'm pretty sure Crystal Jamison hates me. It's not even fair. It's not my fault we have the same name. We don't even spell it the same...

She says she's not talking about me, but I know she is. Crystal and Lexie stop whispering whenever I come by, and they start giggling. It's exactly what Brittany did at the end of last year...

Today in history, I heard Crystal and Lexie whisper my name and I got all hot inside—like I was gonna explode. Just when I couldn't handle it anymore, the maps at the front of the room fell off their hooks and crashed on the floor and everyone jumped. Mr. McAllister grumbled about the custodian not putting them up right, but I don't think that's why they fell...

In science, Crystal was flicking little paper balls at me. I told her to stop, but she pretended like she didn't know what I was talking about. She just kept doing it. I swear, she hit me a hundred times. I got so. mad. The heat started in my stomach again and I tried to breathe through it like Jodi told me, but it didn't work and the projector caught fire. Mr. Holt had to get the fire extinguisher...

My body tenses. It had happened here, too—the uncontrolled bursts of magic. Jodi tried to help me control it, but did she tell me what I am? No, she can't have—information like that certainly would make it into the diary.

I flip back and forth through the pages, looking for something happier to focus on.

My first kiss occurred at a winter dance in seventh grade. I detailed the event with painstaking care as soon as I got home. Felix insisted the decoration above our heads was mistletoe. I smile. It's the kind of first kiss I'd imagined back in middle school, and I'm glad that in one reality, I got it.

Felix and I split up after the new year, but there isn't much detail surrounding it. It only mentions that Dana and I went to Millie's coffee shop after school that day and got coffee drinks and cookies. I can't tell if this was in celebration or commiseration.

My heart twists. I don't know Dana well, but apparently alternate-me *did*. She's mentioned more than just about anyone. I can't help wondering what happened between us, even though I have a sinking suspicion I already know. Crystal, Lexie, Bridget—they're all mentioned in passing, and it's clear from my references that we're not friends. But obviously, that changes. I assume Dana was a casualty of that transition.

As the seventh grade entries continue, there are more frequent mentions of Owen. *Owen walked me to class today, even though his next class is on the other side of the school... Owen and I met up at the coffee shop to study for Friday's test... Owen held my hand on the way to class today—just grabbed it like it was no big thing. My cheeks were on fire the whole way to English, and I couldn't look at him, but he didn't let go until we were outside Miss Stoker's class... Owen asked if he could give me a nickname, and I said yes, of course. Before when I thought about having a nickname, it was because Crystal Jamison wanted me to have one, so we wouldn't have the same name and so she would still be special. But this nickname is all about me, to make* me *special. He says from now on, he's gonna call me* Krissa.

My jaw drops. Darkness encroaches on my peripheral vision for a few seconds until I manage to take in a breath. Owen called me Krissa in this reality, too. Somehow the fact makes me happy and sad all at once. If that nickname was always meant to be mine, why does everyone call me by my full name? What was West talking about—what did I do to Owen? A weight settles in my stomach as I read on.

Owen. Just. Asked. Me. Out!!! I'm so excited I can't even think. We're going to the end-of-the-year dance together...

I don't know what to do. I just got back from dress shopping with Mom. She was chatting with Lexie Taylor's mom—she owns the store—when Lexie and Crystal cornered me. I thought they'd be mean to me—even though they've kinda cooled down on that at school. But they weren't mean. Well, not exactly. They called me a witch. At first, I thought they were trying to insult me, but they said they weren't, that they were witches, too. That it's magic—all those things that happen when I'm upset. Before I could ask them more, Mom came over and they were gone by the time I bought a dress...

I think I might know where this story is heading, but I have to read through to be sure. I turn a few more pages.

It's the day of the dance and my stomach is in knots. I was so excited when Owen asked me, but now... Now I'm just scared. I have to make a choice. Crystal promised she could teach me how to use my magic so it doesn't explode out of me—she's got a book of spells and everything. But she says she has to be able to trust me before she can share her secrets with me. If I want to be one of them—part of her circle—then I have to prove my loyalty.

The problem is I don't trust her. I don't like her—she's been mean to me almost since we met. But she's not lying about the magic—she showed me she could light a candle with her mind. It was incredible. Can I really do that? I tried to do it myself—down by the river so Mom and Jodi wouldn't see—and I did it, I lit the candle—but I was sitting on a log and it caught on fire, too. I had to splash water from the river onto it to put out the flames. I can't control it, and that scares me. She says she can help me control it, but I don't know if I can do what she wants me to do.

This doesn't make sense. Why didn't alternate-me just talk to Jodi about it? Clearly Jodi still practices. Is it possible she didn't know at that time? That has to be—otherwise why would she run to Crystal for help?

The next few pages are filled with more indecisive ramblings, but when I come to the entry for June tenth, my stomach clenches.

Owen Marsh will hate me forever, but I had to do it.

There's nothing more to the entry. I flip forward in vain—there are no details about what happened. Entries become infrequent, and the only people mentioned are members of the circle. By my fourteenth birthday in November of eighth grade, alternate-me was dating Fox and bragging about her magical abilities. Besides the entry on June tenth, there's nothing more about Owen, not even in passing. The one time Dana is mentioned, it's to comment on her outfit ("slutty"). Instead of the voice sounding familiar, by degrees, it feels like I'm reading entries penned by Crystal or Lexie.

That's it, then. West has every right to not trust me. My alternate-self chose magic over anything else. That's why Owen doesn't look at me. All these years later, whatever I did still hurts him.

But *I'm* not that person. And somehow, I'll have to prove it. This is my life now, and it's time I make it my own. I've already taken the first step by joining the psychics. Now I need to prove to West I'm not the person he thinks I am. And maybe there's some way I can apologize to Owen for whatever the old me did to him. Even if it takes years, I need to try. Reading the diary has solidified one fact in me more than anything else: Owen and I are connected—in every reality. Things got off track here, but they don't have to stay that way.

Guilt swells, but I push it down. Fox is sweet, but I didn't choose him. It's not fair for me to stay with him when my heart wants someone else.

I have to break up with Fox.

Chapter Fourteen

Fox's monster truck arrives in my driveway right on time the next morning and my stomach lurches.

I'm going to break up with him today.

It's the best thing to do—the only option, really. Or at least that's what I keep telling myself. It's not fair to him to be with me, not anymore. And once we're not together anymore, he can find someone who really wants to be with him—the person he's meant for. Because that person isn't me.

Although I've gone through every argument and assured myself I'm doing the right thing, I can't shake the guilt welling up inside. Poor Fox will be so blindsided. But it's the best thing, really. He doesn't deserve to be with someone who doesn't want to be with him. No one does.

I say goodbye to Mom and Jodi before heading out the door. They both wave, smiles playing about the corners of their mouths like they know something. Like they know I'm going to break up with Fox today. No, they can't. It's just my conscience.

Fox leans across the center console to hug me once I'm in the cab, placing a kiss on my cheek. I return his embrace as best I can, but when we separate, Fox's eyebrows pull together. "You feeling okay?"

I bite my lower lip, shaking my head. "I'm fine."

A smile curls the edge of his mouth as he puts the truck in gear. "Good."

I stare out the window beside me, eyes unfocused as the neighborhood slips by. I should do it now, like ripping off a band-aid. No—there's no reason to ruin his day so early. What if he has a test today? I don't want to be responsible for breaking his heart *and* making him fail a test. But to delay now is only to prolong the inevitable. Either way, he's going to be hurt, so I might as well get it over with right now.

So deep in this internal monologue am I that it takes several minutes before I realize I don't recognize our surroundings. The drive to school is barely ten minutes long—we've been on the road at least that and nothing around us looks the least bit familiar. I turn to Fox. "What's going on?"

He glances out the corner of his eye, grinning. "I'm kidnapping you."

My heartbeat accelerates. "No, for real?"

He laughs, his head tipping backward. "Don't worry—it's sanctioned. I was starting to think they told you, even though they promised they wouldn't."

"Who?"

"Your mom and Jodi, of course. It took a little bit of convincing, but they finally agreed."

I stare at his profile, waiting for him to go on. Agitation rises when he doesn't. "Agreed to *what*? Where are we going?"

He shakes his head. "It's a surprise. You just sit there and relax." He reaches into the back seat and grabs a paper bag. "Here."

I take the bag and peer inside dubiously. A sweet scent tickles my nose and I spy at least a dozen oatmeal cookies loaded with raisins, chocolate chunks, and walnuts. Although I've already eaten breakfast, my stomach rumbles and I have to stop myself from taking one. "You baked?"

He snorts. "You remember what happened last time we tried to bake something? No, I ordered these special from Treat Dreams."

A prickling sensation gathers in the corners of my eyes. "They're my favorite."

He gasps. "Really?"

My cheeks redden and I hit him in the arm. Of course he knows that about her—about *me*. He's been with my alternate self for so long, it would be a bigger surprise if he didn't know her favorite cookies.

I fall quiet. How am I supposed to break up with him now? I have no idea where we're going, and he's brought me a special present. My resolve wavers. If not now, then at the end of the day, for sure. I can't break up with him if I don't know where we are. What if he gets upset and drops me at the side of the road? No, I can't risk it.

Minutes tick by as Fox drives. He flips on his radio to a station I like and even hums along with the songs. He doesn't seem at all bothered that I'm not making conversation, so I don't let it bother me, either.

At the half hour mark, I get antsy. "Okay, for real, where are we going?"

Fox smiles. "Still a surprise."

I press my lips together. "Are you sure my mom actually okayed this? She's not gonna get a call from the school saying I'm skipping and be pissed when I get home, is she?"

He shakes his head. "Feel free to text her if you don't believe me."

I pinch my lower lip between my thumb and forefinger. After a moment's debate, I pull my cell from my back pocket and type out a text. Fox laughs quietly as I hit *send*. A minute elapses before my phone vibrates in my hand.

Jodi and I had a bet to see how long it would take before you contacted one of us. Looks like I win. Have a good time today.

When I look up, Fox is smiling. "Satisfied? Now, relax and eat a cookie. We're still a ways out."

Figuring I don't have many other options, I do as Fox suggests. We're on the freeway now and I watch as the scenery on the side of the road changes from field to small town. I'm reminded forcibly of when Jodi drove me from my home in the Detroit area out to Clearwater, after my mom's death. Are we heading in the same direction? I keep alert for signs that might indicate where we're going. After a few minutes of vigilance, I'm rewarded by a sign indicating how many miles away from Detroit we are. Is that where we're going? Back to my old house? But why would Fox be taking me there? In this reality, I haven't lived there in four years, and there would be no reason for Fox to have ever been there.

Maybe he's taking me to something *in* Detroit—the Detroit Institute of Arts or... or maybe Wayne State University. Are we going on a college tour? That would explain why my mom would be okay with me missing a day of school. But if that's where we're heading, why wouldn't *she* be the one taking us? Besides, college is still nearly two years away.

Different ideas chase themselves through my mind as we continue. I try to wheedle the information out of him a couple of times, but he quickly changes the thread of the conversation any time I get too close to asking about our destination. After a while, I give up entirely.

After nearly two hours pass, I suddenly know exactly where we are. I've been on this part of this freeway before. I scan the horizon to confirm my suspicions. When I see the water tower in the distance, I gasp. "Tell me we're going to the zoo."

Fox doesn't quite hide a smile. "It's still a secret."

But when he pulls off at the Woodward exit, I know I'm right. I haven't been to the Detroit Zoo since before my dad left—not that I haven't wanted to go since. But my mom worked full time and she claimed it would be too crowded to go on the weekends. Besides, there was the expense to consider; after my dad left, we didn't have a ton of extra money. I can count on one hand how many movies we saw in theaters once we were on our own.

As we approach the zoo's entrance, my skin tingles with barely-suppressed excitement. I wonder how much of it will be like I remember it and how much will be different. I also wonder what the reason could be for this impromptu trip. At two hours away, it's not like this is a quick jaunt.

Fox parks the truck and he shoves my cookies into a backpack before we climb out. I pull my jacket tight around my shoulders, glad I decided to wear it today. The day is cool, but not too cold, and the sun is out. It's warmer than it's been the last few days—a nice November day.

November... Could that be it? My birthday is just over a week from today. Is Fox taking me here as a birthday present? And if so, why is it just him, why not my mom and Jodi, too?

Fox takes my hand and leads me toward the ticket gates. There are a few people milling around—a couple of moms with strollers and a few couples in their fifties, but mostly the place is empty.

After paying for our tickets, Fox hands me the complimentary map. "Okay, where to?"

I turn to him. "Really?"

"Of course. You call the shots. I won't complain, even if you want to spend all day staring at the vultures."

I grin. "Or hanging out in the reptile house?"

He shivers. "As long as you protect me from all the venomous creatures, we'll be fine."

"I make no promises." My smile broadens and I catch myself. What am I doing? This morning, I was ready to break up with Fox, and now I'm grinning like an idiot because he kidnapped me and brought me to the zoo? But no matter how I try to tamp down my excitement, I can't do it. I don't dislike Fox—this would be much easier if I did. He's not a bad guy in this reality—not that he was exactly bad in my original timeline, anyway, just... misguided. He was kind to me then, and that side of him is intensified here.

I still need to break things off with him—it's the right thing to do. He deserves every happiness, and I'm not the one to give it to him. But it's clear he spent a lot of time planning this day—coordinating with my mom and Jodi, making arrangements to get my favorite cookies, packing provisions in a backpack. He doesn't deserve me to ruin this day for him.

I unfold the map and study it. To his credit, Fox doesn't rush me as I trace my finger along the different paths, reading which animals are where. After I'm done studying, I fold it back up and stuff it into a pocket of Fox's backpack. "Okay."

"Okay? Just, okay? What, do you have it memorized now or something?"

I start down the path to our right. "So what if I do?"

He follows, catching my hand with his. "No matter how long I know you, you're always finding new ways to amaze me."

My cheeks burn and I turn my face from him. Unfortunately, in doing so, I lock eyes with a girl in her late twenties who wears a shirt with the zoo's logo embroidered on the pocket and has a large camera strapped around her neck.

"Why don't you two get together for a picture?" The girl gestures at us with one hand, bringing the camera up with the other.

I shake my head, but Fox is already stopping, tugging me closer to him. He pulls me so my back is against his front, his chin brushing the top of my head.

"That's great," says the camerawoman. "Now smile!"

Like Pavlov's dog, I respond without thinking to her command. Her camera flashes and she hands Fox a ticket, telling us to check out our photo on the way out of the zoo. Fox thanks her before we continue.

We pass by the first set of animals, but I barely notice them. Is it fair for me to pretend with Fox, even for the day? Or will it just make it more difficult for him when I finally end things?

He tugs on my hand and I force myself to focus on the present. I can be horrible later, but not now. His gray eyes are bright; he's like a little kid, he's so excited. This trip today is as much for him as it is for me, and I want him to enjoy it; he deserves that much. He pulls me over to a huge fountain. The center fixture is held up by two brass polar bears while two smaller fixtures on either side look like otters, with water spitting out of their mouths. The inside of the fountain is littered with hundreds of coins. Fox digs into his pocket before pressing a dime into my palm.

"Make a wish."

My stomach twists. I wish things were the way they were supposed to be—that I was back in my own reality. But I also wish that my mom were still alive there. I wish Owen didn't look through me, and that the situation with Fox wasn't so complicated. I wish Lexie was the nice girl I got to know when I first moved here, and that Bria wasn't an outcast at school. I wish the circle hadn't anchored itself to the crystal.

Fox tosses a coin into the pool and I sigh and throw mine in, too.

I wish there was a simple solution.

We start at the reptile house, where Fox hides behind me when we get to the enclosures with the huge snakes. His fingers grip my shoulders so tightly I'm not sure whether he's pretending or not.

Outside, despite the cool temperatures—or perhaps because of them—many of the animals are active. The lion and lioness pace in front of the glass separating them from us. In the Arctic Ring of Life, the seals swim over the top of the tunnel that goes under their pool. Fox watches with wide eyes each time they pass over our heads, but it's not until the polar bear dives in the water that he gets downright giddy.

We eat lunch on a small hill overlooking the grizzly bears, who work hard to break the limbs off a large tree-sized branch that was clearly put there for their enjoyment. In addition to the cookies, Fox packed water, sandwiches, and chips.

About halfway through the meal, Fox passes his hand in front of my eyes and I blink. I haven't heard anything he's been saying— I heard his voice, but I wasn't paying attention to his words.

"Hey, earth to Kristyl," he says, wiggling his fingers.

On impulse, I grab his hand. I'm not breaking up with him today, I've already decided that, but it doesn't mean I can't take another step toward making this reality my own. "Fox, do you think you could do something for me?"

His eyebrows cinch together and he covers my hand with his free one. "Anything. You know that."

My chest tightens and I force myself to take a breath. I need to do this before I lose my nerve. "I'm... I'm tired of sharing a name with Crystal Jamison. I know you think she'll come around—that the circle will stop being mad at me for trying to stop the anchoring ceremony—and maybe they will. But whether they do or they don't, *I've* changed."

He nods. "Sure. I get it. Well, you know—kind of. Not like I've ever had to deal with another *Fox*, you know?" He grins, stroking the top of my hand with his fingertips. "What were you thinking of going by? Your middle name?"

I snort. "Agnes? I don't think so."

He laughs. "You sure? I bet you could pull it off."

"Oh, I'm sure." I take in a breath, readying myself. "I was thinking... Krissa."

My eyes drop to our hands when I say it, but I can feel Fox's gaze on me. "Krissa," he says, drawing out the name. "Isn't that..."

He stops, shaking his head. "It's nice."

I nod, making myself look at him. "I like it. I think... It suits me."

An expression I can't decipher flickers across his face, displaced almost immediately by a smile. "If you like it, I like it."

After finishing our lunch, we go to the kangaroo exhibit, where we can actually walk through the enclosure where the kangaroos and wallabies live. We take a ride on the carousel, admire the pink flamingos and peer into branches to catch a glimpse of the tree kangaroos. By the time we make our way back to the front entrance, I'm exhausted and delighted. Fox holds my hand and I don't feel guilty for letting him.

On our way to the parking lot, he stops by the photo booth and picks up a copy of the picture snapped of us upon our arrival.

As Fox pulls out of the parking lot and onto the freeway, I study the picture. His arm is around my waist, pulling me tight against his body, accentuating the difference in our heights. The smiles on our faces and lights in our eyes are identical—both kids in a candy shop, excited at the prospect of a day at the zoo. Looking at this picture, it's almost impossible to believe I woke up this morning with the resolve to break up with him. We appear to be the perfect couple.

And we did have fun today—I can't deny it. Fox is fun to be around. I honestly enjoy his company. And now, with the circle anchored to the crystal, I can't afford to lose him, to lose my only real connection to them. If I can find a way to separate them from the crystal, I'll need him on my side, not working against me.

As Fox hums along with the radio, I try to convince myself that I'm staying with him for his own sake, and for the sake of the circle—not because I like him. I try to convince myself, but I'm not entirely successful. Pictures, they say, are worth a thousand words, and the one in my hand speaks of too many possibilities for me to throw it away so quickly.

Chapter Fifteen

Someone jostles my shoulder and I blink a few times, trying to get my bearings. I'm in motion. No, not me. I'm in something moving. Fox's truck. I fell asleep somewhere along the highway. I shift in the passenger seat and shake my head before turning toward Fox.

He smiles. "Hey there, sleepy."

I rub my eyes. "How long was I out?" We're not on the freeway anymore. I'm not sure, but I think we passed this area on the way out this morning.

"About an hour and a half." He taps the clock on his dashboard. "Traffic wasn't as bad as I thought. You're not due home for another hour. We've got some time to kill." He waggles his eyebrows.

A shiver courses through me and I'm suddenly awake. Breaking up with Fox might be off the table for now, but does that mean I'm up for a make out session in the cab of his truck. I raise a wary eyebrow. "What are you thinking?"

He smiles and shakes his head. "Coffee. You in?"

My shoulders relax. "Coffee sounds great."

Five minutes later, Fox pulls up in front of the coffee shop on Main, down the street from Jodi's shop. Fox hops out of the cab and jogs around to meet me. When he takes my hand, it's so natural. It would almost be *more* awkward if we weren't holding hands.

There's a man in his mid-thirties in line ahead of us and I stare at the menu board, even though I'm pretty sure I know what I'll order. Jodi's friend Millie is working and smiles when she catches my eye. Once the man ahead of us moves off to the pickup counter,

Millie greets us.

"How was the big day?" Her eyes are wide and expectant.

Fox shakes his head. "I told Jodi not to tell."

Millie waves her hand dismissively. "You told her not to tell *Kristyl*. Come on, tell me. Did you have fun? How was the drive? I'm thinking of taking the kids there, now that they're a little older. Was it really busy there today? Probably not, right?"

She asks the questions so quickly I'm not sure which one to respond to first. Fox manages to get a word in and the two begin an easy banter.

A blast of chilly air hits me as the shop's door opens. Assuming it's just the other customer leaving, I don't turn. It's not until I hear poorly muffled murmurs that my ears tune into the voices behind me.

"What could *they* have been doing all day?"

"I'm surprised she can still walk."

Tittering laugher.

"Be nice, guys, be nice."

"She's not even *that* pretty."

An icy sensation prickles my neck as I recognize the voices. When I turn, Crystal, Lexie, and Bridget feign looks of embarrassment at having been overheard, but we all know their comments were meant for my ears. So, they're trying a different tack: Instead of ignoring me, they're going to try to get a rise out of me by talking about me? I click my tongue and roll my eyes as obviously as I can, eliciting curled lips from Lexie and Bridget.

At my old school, in my reality, I just took whatever abuse people piled on me. But I'm not the same girl here, and not just because I'm pretending. I've changed since arriving in Clearwater. Extricating my hand from Fox's I turn to face the girls fully, squaring my shoulders. Crystal's eyes flicker with surprise for the briefest moment as I approach.

"Look, enough already." I cross my arms over my chest and plant my feet. Although my stance is sure, my heart flutters in my chest. Adrenaline courses through my system and my body is coiled for fight or flight—but I'm hoping it doesn't come down to either. "You guys've made your point. But now it's time to grow up.

If we're not friends anymore, if you want me out—" I bite back the last words—of the circle—just in time. Millie is a witch and was in Jodi's circle when they were younger, but I have no idea how much she knows about me and the others. "Just tell me and move on. Stop acting like children."

Fox attempts, unsuccessfully, to hide a snort and Bridget's expression sours like she's smelling something rotten. Lexie's eyes flash and I'm pretty sure she's considering hitting me. The precarious balance between fight and flight begins shifting and I formulate an escape route.

Crystal, on the other hand, seems completely at ease. She gives a heavy, dramatic sigh. "I'll handle this," she says, taking a step toward me. "Can we talk outside?"

No, of course we can't. I want to say the words, but they stick in my throat. Without waiting for a response, Crystal pivots and sashays to the door. After a beat, I follow. People don't *sashay* when they're about to fight someone, and they certainly don't hold the door like Crystal is doing now. I glance back, giving Fox the briefest nod to let him know I'm okay.

The sidewalk outside is empty. Though it's not terribly late, the sun is nearly down and the chill in the air has turned to a bite. Two cars pass in opposite directions on the street. I wait until they're out of sight before facing Crystal. "What do you want to talk about?"

"For Fox's sake, I'm gonna tell the girls to knock it off with the hostility."

"For Fox's sake?"

"For him, yeah. And for circle unity. I mean, he hasn't said anything, but I know he's pissed with what's going on. I don't think he'll put up with it much longer. And now that we're anchored, it's not like he can just drop out of the circle."

Her words ring in my ear—*now that we're anchored*—and there's a slight emphasis on the word *he*. There's something I'm missing—something just below what she's saying. Tentatively, I reach out with my mind. The more deliberate I've been with focusing my abilities, the easier it's been to control them.

It takes a moment for the echo to build in my head, and a few more for me to decipher the thoughts behind it. When the sentiment clarifies, I gasp, my eyebrows pulling together. "I'm not part of the circle anymore?"

Surprise flits across Crystal's face. Her mouth twitches and her eyes dart to the street, to the storefront—anywhere but me. "I think you made it clear that you didn't *want* to be a part of the circle."

My mind spins. It's true, really—I never wanted to be friends with Crystal or Bridget or this alternate-Lexie. And after seeing the kinds of things they do with their power—like messing with Bria—I don't really want to be friends with them. But I *do* want to separate the circle from the crystal, and if they cut me off completely, I'm not sure I'll be able to do it. "You know why I didn't want to anchor—"

"Come on. It's not like you were ever really part of it anyway—not *you*. I thought you'd be happy—one less thing to pretend."

A black Dodge Charger turns onto Main from a side street over Crystal's shoulder, catching my attention as it eases toward us. The speed limit on this part of Main is only thirty miles per hour, but the car doesn't accelerate even that much. Something tugs at the back of my mind. This car is familiar somehow—it's like I'm seeing Fox's truck or Jodi's Focus—only I can't place where I know it. I squint as it nears, trying to get a glimpse of the driver, but the windows are tinted so dark I can't make out a face behind the glass. A shiver overtakes me as it passes, and I spin on the spot, keeping my eyes on it as it continues down the street.

The faraway tinkling of bells pulls my attention from the Charger. I'd know those bells anywhere: Someone is walking out of Jodi's shop. I'm only aware there's been a buildup of pressure in my chest when it ebbs as Seth steps out onto the sidewalk. My concern from a minute ago evaporates. So what if I'm out of the circle? I have Seth, and he and I can learn about magic together. He can teach me the spells he's found in his research, and maybe somehow I can help him tap into more magic—increase his abilities.

Seth catches my eye and waves, grinning. He checks both ways before loping across the street.

Crystal grabs my shoulder, turning me roughly toward her. "Do you *know* him?"

I'm taken aback by the intensity in her voice. I cover her hand with mine and pull hers from my shoulder. "Yeah. He works at Jodi's. We're actually related. Like distant cousins or something."

Crystal's eyes are wide and round as she follows Seth's progress toward us. She tugs on my arm. "Introduce me. But be cool about it."

I stare at her. She sounds almost starstruck. Maybe there's something to my visions of him in relation to her after all. Before I can put any of these ideas into words, Crystal pinches me and I turn to face Seth, who slows to a stop in front of me. He studies my face for a second, like he's making sure I haven't changed my mind about him since last we talked. He must see what he hopes to find because a moment later he pulls me into a brief hug.

"It's good to see you. I was hoping to talk, but Jodi said you wouldn't be in today. Something about a special trip?" His eyes stray over my shoulder, a look of polite curiosity on his face. "Who's your friend?"

Crystal pinches me again and I elbow her in the chest. "This is Crystal Jamison. Crystal, this is Seth White."

Seth offers his hand and Crystal takes it, but before she can shake it, he brings her knuckles to his lips, feathering a kiss there. "A pleasure."

Crystal giggles—a legitimate, all-out, school-girl giggle—but says nothing. Seth isn't fazed by her reaction. Instead, he releases her hand and refocuses his attention. "I can see you're occupied. We'll talk soon, though. Now, if you'll excuse me, I had better get Jodi her coffee." With a wink at me, he heads into the coffee shop.

The door swings closed behind him before Crystal exhales noisily. "Oh, wow. He is *gorgeous*."

"Um, okay." Seth's not ugly, but he's a little plain—far from gorgeous territory.

She rolls her eyes, exasperated. "Well, of course *you* don't think so. You're related."

I want to point out that before a few days ago, I'd never met him, and the two of us are so distantly related that it barely counts, but I figure my words will fall on deaf ears.

"Tell me everything you know about him."

The wind picks up and I shiver. We've been standing out here longer than I anticipated and I want to be back inside, sipping a hot drink. Has Fox ordered for me? Or is he waiting until I come back to get a drink? I squint, trying to peer through the glare of reflected streetlights. "I don't know. He's from Massachusetts. He's into genealogy." I bite my lower lip. I could tell her the reason he's interested in studying his ancestors—that his desire is spurred by his magical abilities. But it's not my secret to share.

Crystal turns, disappointment etched on her face. "You're holding out on me, I can tell."

I sigh. She's right. Besides him being a witch, there is something important I haven't told her—something that involves her. "Before everything..." I give her a look, spreading my hands out between us. "When I first got to Clearwater, I... Well, I was seeing... visions of him."

Her brow furrows and her eyes are focused for the first time since Seth walked out onto the street. "Visions?"

I nod, biting the inside of my cheek. While I had no qualms telling the psychics all about the witches, I don't feel the same about revealing the existence of psychics to Crystal. "Yeah. Jodi says it can happen sometimes—with family members," I lie.

Crystal nods, accepting the explanation. "Okay, so you saw visions. What were they about?"

"Nothing, really. Just his face—his eyes, mostly. And..." I hesitate, but I can't exactly stop now. I've already passed the big reveal—that I have visions. And the last part is the thing that concerns her. "And every time I saw those visions, they were around you—when I was touching you or touching something of yours."

Crystal's fingers trail across her neck, a small smile crossing her lips. I don't need to be psychic to know the kinds of things that are going through her mind: It's fate—the two of them have some sort of connection. I roll my eyes. "Look, it's freezing out here. I'm going in." Without waiting for her reaction, I head into the shop.

Fox stands from his spot at a table at the back of the shop. He's sitting alone, even though he knows Lexie and Bridget and the two of them don't seem to be mad at him at all, and I'm struck by his consideration. If they won't accept me socially, he won't accept them. Crystal was right about what she said—Fox isn't okay with how they're treating me. My heart twists. Would he walk away from the circle because of me? I don't want him to have to make that choice.

He holds a paper cup out toward me and I relieve him of it and take a sip, not caring what it is so long as it's hot. As the flavors collide on my tongue, my eyes close. Salted caramel. I've never seen this flavor on the menu, but I don't ask how he knew it's what I'd choose if I knew it were an option. After another sip, I follow his gaze across the shop. Crystal has installed herself with Lexie and Bridget at a table in the front window, and the three of them talk in low voices, their eyes fixed on Seth.

"Who's the guy?" Fox's tone is casual enough, but his eyes don't leave Seth, who converses easily with Millie as she makes drinks for him. There's the barest hint of tension in Fox's shoulders and I remember Seth hugged me. Is Fox... jealous?

And odd mix of pleasure and embarrassment courses through me. "That's Seth. He's new at the shop." Fox's posture doesn't relax and I push a bit further. "He's really nice. Super sweet. He's got this cute, proper way he talks." Fox's eyes narrow and I suppress a smile. "Oh, and did I mention he's my cousin?"

At the last word, Fox finally turns his attention from Seth. "Cousin?"

I grin, biting my lower lip. "Yeah. Cousin. Distant cousin, but we're still related."

He makes a face before taking a sip of his drink, his tension evaporated. "Crystal seems pretty interested in him."

I nod. "Apparently he's gorgeous." I roll my eyes for effect, and Fox smiles.

"We should head out." He stands, waiting for me to do the same.

Seth nods a goodbye as I pass, which I return. Fox calls goodbye to the girls and Crystal waves vaguely in response. Fox sighs as he pushes open the door. "Poor Tucker."

I gulp. I wasn't aware their relationship—if one could call it that—was common knowledge. "You know about them?"

"Um, yeah. They're not exactly stealthy. I mean, I know Crystal thinks they are, but Tucker... Well, let's just say he's indiscreet."

I shiver as he unlocks the truck. No, it doesn't surprise me that Tucker would brag about whatever he and Crystal do together. And I'm not sure if I believe that Crystal is unaware. She probably likes it. Back in our reality, she and Zane used to hook up. She clearly has a thing for bad boys. Still, I have to agree with Fox. After seeing Crystal's reaction to Seth, it's clear that her time with Tucker is limited. She's found a new target. I just hope Seth is up to the challenge.

Chapter Sixteen

Come Monday, Lexie and Bridget make good on Crystal's promise for an end to the hostility toward me, but that doesn't mean we're all friends again. While they're no longer talking behind my back or ignoring me, their greetings are tepid at best, and in health when Mrs. Stanton assigns a group project, Lexie quickly snags partners so there's no room for me in the group.

If I'm honest, I'm actually glad for Lexie's move. I'm sure she's only doing it to show me that we're still not friends, but I'm okay with that. I don't want to work with her because I don't *like* this Lexie. How can losing her as a friend hurt when I've already lost her as a person?

I lean across the table and tap on Felix's book. "You wanna work together?"

His brow furrows. "You mean that wasn't a given?"

I smile. I'm not sure if it's because of our history together or because I'm one of the psychics now—or just due to his easygoing personality—but I'm thankful for how readily Felix has accepted me. When he looks at me, sometimes I can forget that everything in my life is different.

"Felix, Kristyl? Are you working together?" Mrs. Stanton asks as she makes the rounds to be sure we've all followed her directions. When we nod her brow creases. "You should really have at least three for the skit," she says absently, scanning the vicinity. "Owen, do you have a group? Why don't you come work with these two?"

Owen picks up his notebook and pen and crosses to our table. He nods at Felix but barely glances at me; a muscle in his jaw jumps as he takes the empty chair beside me. Any illusions I had a moment ago are shattered: Things are different here, no matter how much I try to pretend they're not, no matter how many good things there are. Some things will never be the same.

Still, despite the fact that Owen's eyes are fixed resolutely on his notebook, my body tingles with electricity. I haven't been this close to Owen since before everything changed, and I forgot how he makes me feel. My fingertips tremble as I reach for my pencil. "So," I begin, but I clear my throat immediately. My voice is an octave higher than usual. Across the table, Felix raises an eyebrow. "So, um, what should our skit be about?"

Owen doesn't look up and after a moment, Felix clears his throat. "Maybe we should all be at a party?"

Felix launches into an idea involving a response to peer pressure and I try to pay attention, but Owen's presence distracts me. When it's clear Felix has taken control of the group, Owen engages him in conversation. Without my input, the two begin putting together our skit. The whole time, Owen doesn't say my name—he refers to me only with pronouns: *she, her.* When I make a suggestion, he pretends to look in my direction, but his gaze never actually reaches me.

I read the diary. I know my alternate-self hurt Owen somehow. But that was years ago. How can he still hate me so much? What could I possibly have done?

By the end of the hour, my stomach is in knots. I'm glad we're presenting the skits tomorrow, because there's no way I could do it today. Felix volunteers to take our skit up to the teacher to get it okayed, and as soon as he leaves I wish I'd gone—I don't want to be sitting here next to Owen, not when he's so thoroughly ignoring me. I'm too chicken to reach out with my psychic abilities to read what he's feeling—too afraid of what I might discover. One glance toward Mrs. Stanton's desk is all I need to know Felix probably won't be back to the table before the bell rings—there are too many people crowded around already, and a girl from Lexie's group is heatedly arguing a point, trying to convince Mrs. Stanton that something in their skit should stay. To distract myself, I pull out my Spanish homework and start scribbling in verb conjugations.

I'm writing in the last answer when an emotion radiates off Owen so intensely I can't help feeling it: surprise. I hazard a glance at him and my stomach swoops when our eyes lock. My heart rate increases. He has the most beautiful eyes.

I expect him to look away, but he doesn't. His mouth twitches like he's struggling over whether to say something or not. Finally, he clears his throat. "I haven't seen that name in a long time."

I stare, unsure what he's talking about. With another sigh, he taps my assignment paper, where I've written my name. When I look down, I'm surprised by what I see: I've written *Krissa Barnette*. I don't remember making a conscious decision to do it, but maybe telling Fox yesterday was enough to reset my nickname to automatic. Part of my real-self reclaimed. The curve of the letters is so familiar—in a way, even more familiar than the shape of my full name. This is who I am now—who I've been since I arrived in Clearwater. "It's time for a change."

Owen narrows his eyes. When he speaks, his voice is low and quiet. "Look, I don't know what you're trying to prove, but leave me out of it."

My mouth drops, and in response, he rolls his eyes. "You think I don't see it?" he presses. "You might be able to fool other people, but not me. Not anymore. I learned that lesson a long time ago. What? Are you bored with your friends? Or did they just finally see through you? Time to reinvent yourself—again." He shakes his head. "I kinda feel bad for him. Fox. How're you gonna rip his heart out? You got a plan already, or are you just gonna go off the cuff? If I'm honest, I'm surprised you've kept him around this long. Figured he would've bored you years ago."

I flinch. It would be better if Owen's words were full of venom, but they're not. His tone is cool and completely matter-of-fact, like he's explaining a math problem. There's no defense I can mount. I know enough from the diary entries to understand what he's saying. I could tell him he's wrong about me, but is he really? Isn't reinventing myself what I want to do? Just days ago, wasn't I ready to break up with Fox as a part of that plan? Despite this altered reality, Owen might know me better than I thought he could. But what does that say about the person I am—the person

I've always been?

The bell rings and Owen grabs his belongings and stalks toward the door. I can't move. Am I really the kind of person Owen thinks I am? I've been operating under the impression that my alternate self was different somehow, that I would have made different choices in her shoes. But the fact remains she is me. Maybe this is the way my life was supposed to play out—the way it would have played out if I had been the one making the decisions.

Warm hands clasp my shoulders and I blink heavily. Felix comes into focus. "Are you gonna barf?"

My stomach clenches and for a moment I'm afraid that's exactly what I'll do. It takes another second to realize I'm laughing. At first, it's silent, but then it overtakes me. My head tips back and my shoulders shake and I'm gasping for air. The sound escaping my mouth is desperate—almost a sob. Maybe I *am* crying. I can't tell, and I can't stop.

Felix pulls me to standing and wraps an arm around my shoulders, leading me out of the classroom and into the hall. My face is damp. Am I laughing so hard I'm crying or just crying?

I have no sense of where we're going, and Felix could be leading me down the hall or to another state, as aware of the time that's passed as I am. At some point, he pressed me into a chair, because, when I start to take in my surroundings, I'm sitting down.

The room comes to me by degrees. It's small—made smaller by racks full of boxes against two of the walls, two ladders against another, a small table by the door, and a small, stained basin on the floor. We're in a janitor's closet. The scent of soap and garbage fills my nostrils. Felix sits across from me, our knees nearly touching, holding my hands. His brow is creased with concern when I manage to fix my gaze on his face. He offers a tight-lipped smile and rubs the pads of his thumbs over the back of my hands.

"You wanna talk about it?"

Heat floods my body. I turn my head, looking for signs that the custodian might be back soon. "How did you get in here?"

He holds up his right hand, wiggling his fingers. "Telekinesis. Lock picking is one of the first things West and I practiced."

I smile, but it quickly turns to a grimace as my stomach twists.

West. He feels the same way about me that Owen does. I was so desperate to prove West was wrong about me, but what if he and Owen are right? Felix returns his right hand to my left and squeezes it. My eyes prickle. "Why are you being nice to me?"

"Why shouldn't I be?"

I blink and tears stream down my cheeks. "Because I'm a terrible person."

He squeezes my hands. "I don't believe that. Have you done some shitty things? Maybe. But that's the past, and there's nothing you can do to change it."

The irony of his words overwhelms me and I'm sobbing again. I curl forward, pulling my hands from his and pressing them to my face. I wouldn't be in this mess if the past hadn't been changed.

To his credit, Felix doesn't pull away. The legs of his chair scrape the floor as he repositions himself beside me. He rests a hand on my back, between my shoulder blades, patting gently. When the bulk of the tears have passed, he takes in a breath. "Maybe it's because of the psychic thing, or maybe it's because way back when we were actually pretty good friends, but I can tell there's something going on with you. And it's not just that your circle's kinda abandoned you—I noticed it before then. Last week, suddenly, you were... different. Not the same girl who's been stalking the halls with Crystal these last few years—more like..." He laughs. "More like the girl who was so nervous when I tried to kiss her that she almost gave me a black eye."

My eyes fill again. I read about that in the diary, but it's not the same as living it. I wish I could remember the event itself instead of the description of it. If I'm going to be held accountable for the bad things I did, I want, at least, to be able to remember the good. Messing with time has robbed me of my first kiss in two realities— one because I don't remember it, the other because Owen doesn't. My heart twists and I choke back another sob. "I'm not that girl, though. Not since... Owen. Not since I did... whatever I did to him."

Felix shifts, pressing his hand flat against the center of my back. Warmth radiates from his palm, coursing through my skin and sending jolts of electricity up my neck. It's not until he pulls away, scooting his chair so he can face me again, that I understand what he's done. He places his fingertips beneath my chin, pulling my face up so he can look into my eyes. "You really don't remember that, do you? How can you not remember?"

He scanned my memories. I've only ever picked up on conscious thoughts, but somehow Felix was able to see beyond that. "How did you do that?"

He presses his palms into his knees, exhaling and shaking his head. "Krissa..." He squeezes his eyes shut like the lights are suddenly too bright for him. "Even if you're not thinking about memories like that directly, when we're talking about them, they should be right below the surface. Bria and I figured that out months ago. But with you... I should've seen those things in your head—our first kiss, the seventh grade dance. But they weren't there. Why weren't they there?"

Thoughts swirl through my head. Lies. I could make something up to explain away the absence of the memories, but nothing seems plausible enough. Besides that, nothing would be fair. Felix is being a friend to me—a real friend. He doesn't deserve to be paid back with half-truths.

So instead, I give him the whole truth. As our knees brush each other's in the dank janitor's closet, I tell Felix everything.

Chapter Seventeen

I'm a thousand times lighter at the end of sixth hour when Felix and I finally emerge from the janitor's closet. Finally, someone besides Crystal knows my secrets—all of them. Although he's pale when we part ways, he promises to keep everything to himself, and I believe him.

A crowd has gathered by the time I make it to the hallway where my locker is, and I assume it's regular end-of-day traffic. But as I press forward through the bodies, a familiar voice rings out.

"Get away from me, Tucker."

Crystal's voice is icy. I push past a few more gawkers until I get to the interior of the circle. The center of the hallway is empty, but there are people standing two-deep against the lockers, and a mass of students continues to gather on either side of the hall. Bridget and Lexie stand back, but apart from the rest of the onlookers. Crystal and Tucker take center stage.

He takes a step forward, snatching her hand and tugging her. "Come on," he says, his voice low. "Let's talk about this somewhere else."

Crystal snorts, pulling her hand away. "Talk about what? As far as I'm concerned, we don't have anything left to say to each other."

Tucker sneers. "I was about done with you anyway." He turns and starts toward the side of the hall where I'm standing. People in the center start shifting, making a gap for him to pass through.

When he's only a few steps away from me, Crystal launches her final barb. "Not sure how we lasted this long anyway. I guess now you'll have to go back to getting girls drunk and taking advantage of them. That's typically how you get your action, isn't it?"

If he had just kept walking, her comment would've been written off as just another bitchy thing Crystal Jamison had to say. But there's a slight hesitation in Tucker's next step—just enough for everyone in the vicinity to notice, and a chorus of laughter swells around us. Tucker doesn't turn to snipe back—the damage has already been done—and when he shoves past me, the emotions radiating off him take my breath away. There's anger, yes, and a twinge of embarrassment, but also sadness and shame.

By the time the sensations ebb from my system, the hallway is in motion again. I swing by my locker before heading downstairs, my mind toying with the idea of trying to convince the secretary not to call home about my absence sixth hour. Is that something I can do as a psychic? Persuade people to do or not do something? Not keen on sitting through a lecture from my mom about skipping class, I figure it won't hurt to try. As I walk toward the office, I tap out a text to Fox, letting him know I'll meet him at his truck.

I'm halfway across the foyer when Crystal Taylor—I can't bring myself to think of her as *Mrs. Cole*—walks out of the front office. Her hair is pulled into a sleek chignon at the back of her neck and she wears a charcoal pencil skirt with a red button-down blouse. It's still strange to see her as an adult, because the image that always comes to mind when I think of her is as a teenager—just older than me—trying to cast a spell on the night she was supposed to die.

A guy in khakis and a polo follows her out and she smiles, holding a hand out for him to shake. It's not until he turns that I recognize him.

"Seth?" I cross the remaining distance separating us. Crystal Taylor smiles politely and nods, excusing herself back into the office. "What are you doing here?"

Seth offers a broad smile when he sees me, pulling me in for a quick hug. Apparently this is how we'll greet each other from now on, and I can't say I dislike it. It's sweet. "I was just talking to your principal about perhaps doing some volunteer work around the school. I mentioned to Jodi that I've always been interested in teaching, and she suggested I explore the possibility. I'm actually heading back to the shop now. Do you need a ride? You're working today, right?"

I grin. "No, thanks. My—" I stop short, the word *boyfriend* on my lips. It's technically true, but I've never referred to Fox that way. I roll my shoulders. "Fox usually gives me a ride. Since when do you have a car, anyway?"

"Jodi let me borrow hers." He glances at the clock protruding from the wall above us. "I should be getting back. I'll see you there soon."

The rapid clicking of high heels against the stone floor echoes through the sparsely populated foyer and before Seth has taken more than a few steps, Crystal Jamison is blocking his progress, her face flushed from rushing to his side. Bridget and Lexie follow at a distance, eying Seth with interest.

"Hi again," Crystal says, flashing her best smile.

A crease forms between Seth's eyebrows and I snort, covering my mouth in an attempt to pass it off as a cough when Lexie shoots me the evil eye. After a beat, Seth nods with recognition. "You're Kristyl's friend—from the coffee shop."

She grazes his arm with her fingertips. "That's right. I'm Crystal, too."

Seth nods, shifting away from her touch by a degree. "It seems to be a popular name here. I've just spoken with your principal, Crystal Cole—"

"Oh, she's my aunt," Crystal says quickly. Lexie clears her throat and Crystal adds, "And Lexie's aunt, too. We're cousins."

Seth nods again, his eyes straying to the clock again. "It was a pleasure to see you again, but I should really be getting back to work. Perhaps our paths will cross again sometime." He offers her a tight-lipped smile before waving at me and heading out the front door.

Crystal immediately groups up with Bridget and Lexie, probably to discuss the encounter. Rolling my eyes, I pass by them, heading out to the parking lot. It's not until I'm to the stairwell that the mingled scent of leather and cigarettes reaches my nose. Tucker. He leans in a doorway, his eyes locked on Crystal. When I'm even with him, he turns his attention to me.

"I hope he's worth it," he sneers.

I don't respond. Instead, I start off at a jog toward the parking lot.

***

An hour later, I'm restocking teas at the shop. My skin crawls whenever I think about Tucker, so I do my best not to think of him. Yeah, what Crystal did was pretty shitty, but I don't have it in me to feel bad for Tucker. Maybe I'm doing to him what Owen and West are doing to me—holding something against him that he doesn't remember doing. But something tells me that given the opportunity, Tucker would try to attack me again.

Seth walks into my aisle and leans against the shelves. "What's bothering you?"

I place the last bag on the shelf before closing the cabinet beneath. "I'm fine." Not making eye contact, I brush past him into the main area of the shop.

He follows. "It's about your friend, isn't it? The one so eager to talk to me?"

"I think *eager* is an understatement."

Seth's mouth twitches. "She is... a bit forward. More so than I'm accustomed to."

I study his face. "You're not... interested in her, are you?"

His eyes drop, the corners of his mouth turning down. "I'm afraid my heart belongs to another. It always will."

It's a sweet and romantic notion, but the sadness in his tone doesn't fit. Before I'm fully conscious of doing it, I've pressed forward into his mind and the echo of his thoughts fills my head. It's an emotion that clarifies first—pain—and I pull back, closing my eyes. "I'm sorry. I shouldn't pry—"

"Bess. She died." His voice is tight, quiet. He opens his mouth again but closes it quickly, shaking his head. After a beat, he forces a smile. "But that is, perhaps, a story for another day. Now. About your friend. Crystal, correct?"

I sigh, casting a glance toward the break room. Seth is still technically in training, and Jodi apparently doesn't trust the two of us alone in the store yet, so she's here for backup. So far, I've avoided bringing up circle drama around her or my mom since I'm not sure how either of them will respond—or how much they know. The look on Seth's face tells me he doesn't plan on dropping the subject. "You remember the night of the storm? When I mentioned my circle?"

He nods. "Ah. I take it things haven't improved? They're still upset with you."

"Yeah. The other day, Crystal basically told me I was out of the circle—all because I was trying to protect them." I run my hands through my hair. "Maybe I was wrong. Right after they anchored, they were using magic like crazy, but this week they've settled down—except Zane." I roll my eyes. "We *still* haven't gotten through a lesson in math."

His brow furrows. "Are you saying you no longer want to separate them from the crystal?"

I throw up my hands. "I don't know. Maybe I was wrong. Maybe I need to accept that it happened and move on."

An expression flits across Seth's face—a slight tightening around the eyes, a pursing of the mouth. "You have to do what you think is best."

A light bulb bursts above our heads and I jump, squealing. Jodi runs into the room, eyes wide, but by the time she gets to us, Seth and I are both laughing.

"It's nothing," I say, pointing up. "The light scared me, that's all."

Jodi presses her hand to her chest. "Please don't make that sound unless you're in mortal danger. Give me a heart attack." She points at Seth. "You, come with me. The extra light bulbs are up on a high shelf."

"Of course they are," I murmur as Seth follows her into the back room. I grab the broom and dustpan from behind the register and start sweeping up the broken glass.

The bells above the door tinkle and Crystal and Lexie enter the shop. They turn immediately toward the shelves holding different stones, but their muffled giggles reveal their true reason for stopping by. I don't bother concealing an eye roll as I go back to my task.

By the time Seth returns, I've swept all the shards. When he climbs the step stool to replace the bulb, Crystal stares unabashedly. Once he descends and throws away the broken bulb, she and Lexie cross to him.

"Hi, Seth," Crystal says brightly, bouncing on the balls of her feet.

His eyes dart to me before he gives a polite nod. "Hello, Crystal. And, Lexie, yes? What brings you to in today? Can I help you find something?"

"Actually," Crystal says, drawing out the word, "we were hoping we could help you. Kristyl told me you're interested in genealogy and you're related to her. I just happen to know a *ton* about the founding families of this town, and if Kristyl's from one of those families, you might be, too." She edges closer to him, smiling so broadly her cheeks must be hurting by now.

I'm surprised when Lexie turns, catching my gaze, her eyebrow raised. I'm right there with her: Crystal's behavior is bizarre. She's always so cool and collected. Even when I caught her with Tucker, she was calm and unruffled. But now she's acting strange. She's acting like I imagine I did while under the influence of Fox's attraction charm in the last reality. But Seth can't be casting a spell like that, can he? I take inventory of my own feelings, but I'm not drawn toward him. Perhaps it doesn't work on someone who's blood related? But it's not affecting Lexie either. I sniff, trying to detect a hint of lavender, but the nearby herbs make it impossible to tell whether he's got a sprig on him. No, maybe it's not an attraction spell. Besides, he just finished telling me his heart belongs to his dead girlfriend. This must be something else entirely.

Seth shifts backward a few inches. "As a matter of fact, I am from a founding family."

Crystal claps her hands together. "Great. I've got *tons* of information about them, and all kinds of stories about the town. If you like, I could tell you about it. Say, after you get off work? There's a restaurant down the street we could go to. It's cozy."

I roll my eyes. Can she be more transparent? And could it be any clearer that Seth is uncomfortable with her advances? A tinge of color rises in his cheeks. "Maybe another time," he says, retreating toward the register. "Perhaps we can bring Krissa and Lexie along."

Crystal's smile falters, but she regroups quickly, following him. Motion on the street catches my eye and I turn to the window. Across the street, Fox's languid movements draw my gaze and a smile curls my lips. He's a welcome distraction from the scene in the shop. I tamp down a swell of guilt as I head toward the front door. Besides Lexie and Crystal, there are no customers, and Jodi's in the back room to help if anyone does come in. Crystal can only throw herself at Seth for so long before she either gets the hint or runs out of material. Before I can talk myself out of it, I push open the door and check both ways before heading across the street.

Fox is nearly to the coffee shop when I reach him, tapping his shoulder. He turns, his harassed look melting into a smile. His hands cup my cheeks as he swoops down for a kiss.

For the first time, I kiss him back.

"Aren't you working?"

I slip my hand into his. "I am. But Crystal and Lexie came in." I roll my eyes for effect. "Does it make me a bad person because I left Seth alone in there with her?"

He shakes his head. "Nah. He's a big boy. He can take care of himself. Are you on break? We could go grab a slice real quick, if you want."

Although his gaze doesn't leave mine, he's distracted—I can sense it radiating off him. I reach forward with my psychic abilities—remembering the tips Bria and Felix gave when we met—and the echo of Fox's thoughts clarifies within seconds. "You're meeting Zane?"

His stormy eyes widen with surprise. "Yeah. How'd you know?"

My stomach drops. I don't know why I'm surprised he would ask such a simple question. If I were in his shoes, I certainly would. I open my mouth to explain it away—lucky guess or something like that—when the roar of a motorcycle's engine draws my attention to the road. Zane pulls his bike into a spot across the road, just past Jodi's shop. He pulls off his helmet and waves before dismounting.

"What are you guys up to?" I tug at his hand, hoping the question distracts Fox from the one I didn't answer.

The corners of his mouth quirk upward. "We're gonna head out to his grandma's place and do some target practice. And before you complain about what a guy thing that is to do, please remember that one of the reasons you like me so much is *because* I'm a guy, so you can't blame me for acting like one."

I can't help smiling. "I *definitely* appreciate that you're a guy. And it sounds fun. But if you're gonna go—I dunno—shoot things or whatever, what are you doing down here?"

"Last time we went out, we may have accidentally burned our target."

"Accidentally?"

He shrugs. "Well, maybe it wasn't an accident."

A horn cuts through the air and I turn toward the source of the sound. Zane is facing a blue sedan, his hands slammed down on the hood. The driver gesticulates wildly behind the wheel.

"I'm walking here!" Zane yells. "You better watch yourself, man!"

The driver, a mid-thirties man with a goatee, rolls down his window. "Damn kid! You're gonna get yourself killed not watching where you're going! I should've just hit you—teach you a lesson!"

Zane bangs on the hood of the car and flips the driver off before continuing across the street at a jog.

Fox laughs as he approaches. "Dude, you ass! Did you even look before you crossed in front of that guy?"

Zane shrugs as he comes to a stop in front of us. "No. Why should I? It's that guy who should watch himself." He turns his attention back to the sedan, which has resumed its course down the street. He narrows his eyes at it rolls past us, a smile curling the edges of his lips.

Smoke begins emanating from beneath the hood. I look from Zane to Fox, whose face is painted with amusement. Zane is doing something to the man's car. I grab his arm and jerk him. "Zane, knock it off."

He barely glances in my direction. "Why? The guy's a dick. He totally deserves it."

The car slows to a stop and the man rolls down his window and pokes his head out to get a better look at the situation.

"*He's* a dick?" I ask, tugging on his arm again. "Zane, *you're* a dick. The road's for cars, not for people. It's not his fault he was driving. Now, knock it off."

With a sigh, Zane fixes his gaze on me. "Fine. I'm stopping. Buzz kill."

Across the street, smoke still pours from under the car's hood. The driver pops the hood and gets out of the car.

"I thought you were stopping," I say. A sinking feeling creeps through my stomach.

"I did," Zane says, annoyed.

There's too much smoke for the fire to be out. Fox's face says he's noticed the same thing. Something bad is about to happen, and that man is far too close to his car for my comfort.

"Get back!" I yell, starting toward the man as he raises the hood. I get no more than a few feet before flames shoot up out of the engine, making the driver jump back, covering his face with his arms.

Fox's arms close around my middle and he pulls me backward, but I struggle against him, looking toward the car, toward the driver. I don't take in a breath until I'm satisfied he's unharmed, several feet from his car. I reach for Zane and punch him in the shoulder. "Put it out, Zane. I thought you said you stopped."

But the look on Zane's face isn't encouraging. His eyes are wide and they're darting all over the place. He's not in control of the fire anymore. He really did think he stopped it earlier. I pull on Fox's sleeve. "Put it out. Zane can't do it."

Fox gives a heavy sigh and closes his eyes. I watch the car, but the flames don't die down. On the contrary, they leap higher.

"Fox." I point toward the car. "Fox, it's not working."

He shakes his head. "I don't know... I can't..."

Panic flares. The fire has taken on a life of its own—just like the storm Crystal, Bridget, and Lexie started. The magic in the crystal is too much for them to handle.

What happens if the flames make contact with the gas tank?

I've seen enough movies to imagine a huge explosion. Would it be big enough to damage the stores on the block? Could a fire like that hurt someone? Seth and Jodi are in the shop, only a few doors down from where the car stopped. I need to warn them. I start across the street, but Fox's arms, which had loosened around my waist, tighten again, pulling me against his chest.

"Let me go! I have to warn Jodi—"

The door to the antique store two doors down from Jodi's opens and a balding man in his late fifties runs out, a fire extinguisher in his hands. He aims the nozzle at the engine and shoots a steady stream of white smoke until the flames disappear.

Relief swells in my chest and I take a deep breath for the first time in what feels like hours. Turning, I punch Zane in the arm, harder this time than before.

"Hey, what's that for?" he asks, rubbing where I made contact.

"You just lit that guy's car on fire and you're asking me why I'm punching you?" I wind up to punch again, but Fox catches my hand.

Zane snorts, all concern from moments before evaporating. "Dude had it coming. He shouldn't've messed with me."

I stare, incredulous. "Messed with you? You walked out in front of his car and he managed not to hit you. And to thank him, you light his car on fire? That's taking things a bit far, don't you think? He could've really gotten hurt if that guy didn't have an extinguisher."

He shrugs. "Who cares?"

"Who cares?" I turn to Fox, looking for assurance that I heard what I think I did, but Fox's eyes are averted. "Who cares? Zane, he's a human being—"

"Exactly. Just a regular person. He's not like us. He's *beneath* us. Do you care when you step on an ant? Then why should I care if I step on a guy like that?"

I can't believe what I'm hearing. Is he honestly comparing the man across the street to an insect? While I'll be the first to admit I don't really know Zane—either version—this seems an extreme stance. Is this really the kind of guy Fox would willingly hang out with? I understand that besides his brother, Zane is the only other guy in the circle, but that hardly means Fox *has* to be friends with him.

Zane shakes his head, pivoting and heading down the street. "Better check your woman, Fox," he calls over his shoulder. "I'll meet you at the hardware store."

I snort at his presumption—like Fox is going to hang out with him after this—but a look at Fox's face sends a shiver through me. Instead of looking appalled, he's sad, resigned almost. I cross my arms over my chest. "You're not seriously gonna go with him, are you?"

His hesitation is all the answer I need. I take a step backward but he reaches for me, brushing my arm with his fingertips. "Krissa, wait."

"Wait? You can't honestly tell me you think what Zane did is okay. You can't tell me you agree with him."

Fox's mouth twitches. "He has a point."

I push his hand away. "No, he doesn't."

His face hardens. "Well, there wouldn't've been a problem if that guy was like us, would there? If he was a witch, he could've stopped the fire."

I glare. "*He* could've stopped it? You and *Zane* couldn't stop it." I shake my head. "When the circle first anchored, you told me everyone would learn to control the magic, but you're wrong—it's too much for you. Even little spells are getting out of hand, aren't they?"

He throws up his hands. "Again with this. Listen, there's nothing wrong with the crystal. You're just jealous because now we've got more power than you do—that's what this is."

My breath catches. "You know that's not true."

"Do I? Because it seems to me you *liked* being the strongest one in the circle. Yeah, Crystal always thought she was the leader, but everyone knows you were really the one in charge. Since you were the best at magic, how could we *not* listen to you? But now that we've all got power—real power—you bail on us. You're not special anymore. You're barely better than all the ordinary people in this town."

His words stab through my heart. Is this really what he thinks?

No, I can't believe that—I would know if he felt that way about me. No one is that good an actor. I reach for his hand, but when my ring makes contact with his skin, a jolt of energy courses through me. The vision overtakes me so quickly I barely have time to gasp. I'm back in the low-ceilinged house. There's a cheerful fire crackling in the hearth, but despite it, the mood in the room is somber. The old man is once again seated in his chair, but the man standing before him isn't Eli. He's young, as Eli was, and he's dressed similarly in a billowing white shirt and simple breeches, but his hands are calloused and dirty—working man's hands. His blond hair brushes his shoulders, and the cut of his jaw is familiar, but I can't place where I've seen it before.

"His power increases by the day," the young man says. "And with it, his hatred."

The old man nods solemnly, his eyes downcast. "This news confirms what I have long suspected. Tucker, this is important. Has he harmed anyone?"

"Not yet. But I fear it is merely a matter of time. At every meeting of the circle, he makes fresh accusations against the newcomers—the *ordinary*, he calls them. He claims they are beneath us, that we must force them from our town by any means necessary."

The scene blacks out and I blink. Fox's gray eyes are narrowed with anger and my stomach twists. "This isn't you." The words come out a whisper and I'm afraid he didn't hear me. Tentatively, I touch his cheek. "Fox, you need to listen to me. I'm right about the crystal. There's something wrong with it, and I think it's changing you. Because this *isn't* you, Fox. Listen to yourself."

His fingers close around my wrist, pulling my hand from his face. "The only one who's changing is you. You used to be strong, powerful. But now that I'm the one with power, I can see you for what you really are. You're hardly a witch at all."

Tears prickle my eyes. "Fox." The hard set of his jaw is like a physical blow. This isn't him—not the person I knew in the other reality, and certainly not the one I've grown to care for in this one. "You have to stop using the crystal's magic. It's dark and it's making you dark, too. I'll prove it to you—just... stop, okay?"

He releases my wrist, flinging it from him. "You're so jealous, and you can't even see it, can you? Lexie was right about you from the start. To think, I *defended* you." He shakes his head. "No more. If you're drawing your line in the sand, don't expect me to cross to your side. I know where I stand, and it's not with you. Goodbye, Kristyl."

He turns his back, stalking away from me. I blink, sending two tears racing down my cheeks.

I was wrong to think the crystal is anything but evil. I have to find a way to separate the circle from its influence before it's too late.

Chapter Eighteen

Jodi drives me to school the next morning. By the end of first hour, it seems everyone in the school knows that Fox and I are no longer together. Or at least everyone in English class—thanks to Lexie, who will tell anyone who's listening about our fight. In her version—from what I overhear—I accused him, for the hundredth time, of cheating on me and he finally got sick of my insecurities and dumped me.

Eyes prickle the skin on the back of my neck in every class, and any time I dare to look up, someone hastily looks away.

At lunch, I make a beeline for the courtyard windows and sink to the ground beside Bria, who raises an artistically arched eyebrow.

"You sure that's the best idea?" she asks as I open my lunch bag. "Don't you think people have enough to say about you right now?"

"I don't give a crap what people have to say about me," I mutter, taking a bite of my peanut butter and jelly sandwich. It feels like sawdust in my mouth.

Bria sighs. "I stand corrected. You're in exactly the right place."

After lunch is math—the only class I have with Fox—and Bria does her best do distract me through it. Yet again, there is no lesson: Mrs. Hill continues her pattern of being forgetful and confused all hour. The class no longer gives even the pretense of paying attention. Even the good students who sit up front have given up trying to help her get the lesson started.

"One of them is doing it, aren't they?" Bria asks, raising her chin toward Zane and Fox. "It's a spell, right?"

I nod. "It's Zane. He thinks he's *so* clever."

"I wouldn't mind so much if it was just every once in a while. But, come on, this is getting a bit old." She sighs, resting her chin in the palms of her hands. Her eyebrows cinch together and she straightens her back, leaning across the desk toward me. "Do you think there's a way to stop it?"

"What? The spell?" My eyes go to the ceiling as I try to remember if I've ever overheard something about disrupting magic in progress. I come up empty, but that doesn't mean something like it doesn't exist. I'm sure there are places I could go to research magic. "Maybe? I mean, I don't know a spell for it off the top of my head, but—"

She shakes her head. "No, not a spell. I'm talking about, you know, *psychically*. Do you think we could, I dunno, disrupt their brain waves or something?"

My first instinct is to laugh, but I stop short. What if she's on to something? "That might not be a bad idea. We should try."

Her eyes widen. "What? Now?"

The corners of my mouth quirk upward—the first time I've smiled all day. "No, not now. Maybe later—after school? Do you think the guys could meet us?"

The idea that I might be able to keep the circle from using magic—and, more specifically, using the crystal's magic—puts me in a better mood. Maybe I could ask Seth about it. He mentioned before that he's good at research. I make a mental note to ask if he's made any progress finding a way to separate the circle from the crystal. If he has, maybe the psychics won't have to learn to block magic after all.

I pull out my phone, hiding it under my desk as I tap out a text to Jodi. *Is Seth working today?* When I hit "send," I feel silly for trying to be sneaky: Half the people in the room are on their phones, and Mrs. Hill doesn't notice. She sits on the stool in front of the room, staring vacantly across to the back wall.

My cell vibrates. *No. Why?*

I can't tell her the real reason—that I want to introduce him to my psychic friends so he can help us figure out how to stop witches from using magic—so I make something up. *Was wondering if he could pick me up from school. Would like to hang out.*

I bite the inside of my cheek as I wait for her response. She knows what happened with me and Fox—or near enough. Will she be upset that I'd rather be consoled by Seth, whom I barely know, rather than her? A full minute passes before she texts back. *I'll see what I can do.*

By the time I get to health class, I'm in much better spirits than I've been all day. When Owen sits down across from me, I give a warm smile. It's not until I look in his eyes that yesterday's exchange comes crashing down on me. Could it really only have been yesterday?

"I should've laid money down," he says, opening up his notebook to a blank page. "Especially after Crystal Jamison dumped Tucker Ingram. It was only a matter of time before you kicked Fox to the curb."

My stomach roils and I tamp down a wave of nausea. "He broke up with me." My voice is barely a whisper.

He snorts. "Not the way I hear it."

The legs of the chair beside me scrape against the linoleum as Felix pulls it backward with his foot. "Do you believe everything you hear?" he asks, taking a seat.

Owen's eyes flick between Felix and me. "Already got a replacement lined up, I see."

"Your mouth is talking, Owen. You might wanna see to that." Although Felix doesn't look at me, his support wraps around me like a blanket. After our conversation in the janitor's closet yesterday, he knows about my history with Owen—my *real* history.

Owen holds up his hands innocently. "Sorry. Didn't mean to offend your girlfriend."

Felix rolls his eyes. "Dude, get over yourself."

Owen leans back in his chair, crossing his arms over his chest. "The thing that I don't get is how eager you are to give her another chance. Didn't she break up with you once already? Have you just been waiting all these years for your next chance with her?"

Felix leans across the table. "Look, man. You've got your issues. I get that. But stop trying to project them onto everybody else. If anyone's hung up on Krissa, it's you."

Owen leans forward, jaw dropped. He sputters a few times

before managing to speak. "I'm not hung up on her. I know exactly what kind of person she is, and you couldn't pay me enough to ever want to be with her."

Heat builds in my core. "I'm sitting right here," I say through gritted teeth.

"It's a game to her, you know? It's all about power."

I breathe in through my nose, trying to cool the boiling sensation in my stomach. How can Owen say such hateful things about me when I'm just feet away? It's like he's trying to hurt me. And maybe he is. Maybe this is his way of getting back at me for what my alternate-self did to him so many years ago. My cheeks burn with the injustice of it. I'm not the one who hurt him, but I'm the one being made to suffer. He won't take an apology, won't listen when I tell him I'm not the same person—he wants to punish me. And he expects me to just take it.

The pressure building inside reaches critical mass, and before I can stop it, it bursts out. Owen's eyes widen in surprise as his chair crumples beneath him, sending him careening to the floor. Mrs. Stanton, who is at the front of the room taking attendance, stops what she's doing and rushes toward him, simultaneously asking if he's all right and admonishing him for destroying school property. Felix's eyes are wide, but they're not fixed on Owen—they're on me. I bite my lower lip and he stifles a smile.

***

After Owen gets a new chair, he ignores me for the rest of the hour, looking at me only briefly when we perform our skit for the class. When we walk out of the class, Felix insists I need to show him how to do what I did to Owen's chair, and I don't have the heart to tell him I have no idea how it happened. Even if I did, I'm not sure it was my psychic side. Although, if Felix can unlock a door with telekinesis, maybe he could break a chair, too.

I keep my head down in sixth hour, managing not to look at Crystal or Bridget once during the period. I just want this day to be over. I want to meet with the psychics and make a plan for combating the circle's use of magic.

When the bell rings at the end of the day, I hang back, making sure Crystal and Bridget are long gone by the time I leave the room. After a quick stop at my locker, I head for the main stairwell—the one I use every day—but something stops me, tugging me in the opposite direction. I hesitate for a moment before heading toward the back hallway—the one Crystal and Tucker used to use for their rendezvous. My stomach clenches as I approach, even though I'm sure I won't run into the two of them. But what if I run into Tucker with some other girl? The thought makes my stomach turn, but solidifies my resolve.

"Hey, there you are." Bria jogs to my side.

I glance at her but don't slow down. "What's up?"

She raises an eyebrow. "I could ask you the same thing. Why are you headed down here?"

We're two classrooms from the stairwell doors and the hall is nearly deserted. "Do you feel that?"

She stops and so do I. Her eyebrows bunch together and she purses her lips. "No. But if you think something's going on, let's check it out."

We start walking again and take no more than a few steps when a muffled female voice reaches us. Bria and I exchange glances before picking up our pace. As we push through the doors, a second female voice is talking—screaming, really. The sound reverberates off the walls and it takes a second for me to make out what's being said.

"I told you to stay away from him!" The voice is familiar, but I can't place it. "Marcus is with *me*."

Marcus. Suddenly it comes to me: Right after the circle anchored to the crystal, Dana Crawford accused Bridget of trying to steal her boyfriend. *That's* where I know the voice. There's no one on the second floor landing, so Bria and I glance down one set of stairs and up the other. Standing on the landing between the second and third floors are Bridget, Marcus, and Dana, whose broken nose is still in a splint.

"Oh, give it up," Bridget sing-songs. "Ask him who he wants to be with. Go ahead—just ask him."

Bria puts a foot on the stair but I stop her. It's not our place to get involved—not yet.

Dana is silent and Bridget lets out a laugh. "What? Afraid? You should be." She turns to the guy and runs a finger along his cheek. "Marcus, baby. Could you tell Dana which one of us you want to be with?"

Marcus blinks heavily, turning his gaze to Dana. "I want Bridget. She's the most beautiful girl I've ever seen. The most beautiful girl in all the world."

Although his words sound sincere, there's emptiness behind them. Bridget has him under an attraction charm all right—something much stronger than the one Fox used in the other reality. Now that she's got the power of the crystal behind her, Bridget could make any guy think he's in love with her.

Dana grabs Marcus by the shoulders, shaking him. "What's wrong with you?"

Bridget crosses her arms over her chest. "I think his only problem is you."

Dana spins, sticking a finger in Bridget's face. "You're doing this to him, aren't you? Somehow, you're messing with his head."

Bridget tips her head back, laughing. "You just don't get it, do you? He's mine now. And there's nothing you can do about it." She spins on her heel, starting toward the stairs leading to the third floor.

Dana launches herself at Bridget but doesn't get far. Marcus pounces on her, wrapping his arms around her middle. "You stay away from her," he growls. "You leave her alone, and you leave me alone. I'm with Bridget now. I don't want you anymore." He throws Dana toward the wall, which she clings to, chest heaving. Her eyes follow Marcus as he starts up the stairs after Bridget.

My heart twists. Although I was never friends with Dana, I know my alternate-self was. But even if that wasn't the case, I'd still feel badly for her in this moment. With her magic, Bridget could have any guy in the school. While it could be true that she's always liked this Marcus guy, I bet her reason for choosing him has more to do with messing with Dana than it does with true love.

Dana breathes deeply, her shoulders heaving. She's trying not to cry. I want to go to her, but I doubt my presence would make her feel better. We should leave her in peace. I raise my chin at the door we entered through and Bria nods. I've only gone a couple of steps when a current of energy thrums through me. Dana screams and a thudding sound comes from the stairwell. By the time I turn, Dana lies in a heap at the bottom of the stairs.

Bria gets to her first. Dana isn't moving, and my stomach lurches. Could she be...? But then she lets out a moan and I take in a breath, relieved. Bria kneels at her side. "Are you hurt? Tell me where."

Dana's leg is bent beneath her at an odd angle and blood gushes from a cut on her forehead. She wails but doesn't answer Bria's question.

"I'm gonna straighten out your leg," Bria says.

Heat surges through my body. "Are you sure that's a good idea?"

Bria doesn't look up. "My mom's a nurse."

It isn't exactly an answer, but Bria sounds sure of herself so I don't stop her. When she starts moving Dana's leg, Dana lets out a piercing shriek and I bend to her side and take up her hand. She squeezes my fingers so hard I gasp. Her face drains of color, the blood on her forehead a vivid contrast to the white of her skin.

"Bria, I think we should go get somebody. Is there a nurse? Or should I call nine-one-one?"

But Bria isn't paying attention to me. One hand grips Dana's leg above the knee, the other below. She closes her eyes, taking in a deep breath and releasing it slowly. Eyes prickle the back of my neck and I look to my left and right, but no one else is in the stairwell. I return my gaze to Dana, but the sensation doesn't go away. I tip my head backward. At the top of the stairs, peering over the concrete rail, is Bridget. A smile curls the edges of her mouth and her eyes are narrowed in triumph. A shiver courses through my body and I know for a fact she did this. And she likes it.

She blows a kiss before disappearing behind the rail. My stomach jolts and my legs strain to follow her, but Dana's grip on my hand keeps me in place. The color slowly returns to her cheeks and Bria pats her leg.

"Can you bend it?" she asks.

After a second, Dana attempts it and is able to move her leg without wincing. I watch Bria as she helps her to standing, but she avoids my gaze. She doesn't look at me the whole way down to the office to find the principal, but she doesn't have to look at me for me to know what happened: She healed Dana's broken leg. It's something I didn't even know was possible, yet Bria did it like it was nothing. I'm completely awed by the power she possesses.

By the time I make it out of the building, Seth is waiting for me in the parking lot. Despite the horror of the last fifteen minutes, I can't help smiling. If Bria is strong enough to mend a broken bone, I'm confident we'll be able to keep the circle from doing magic. We just need to figure out how.

Chapter Nineteen

West almost slams the door when I show up at his house with Seth half an hour later, but I'm ready for it and push it back into his face.

"West, let her in, for crying out loud," Bria calls from within. She lays sprawled across the couch, face buried in the crook of her arm.

"What, is it bring-a-friend day and nobody told me?" West doesn't try to close the door again, but he stands with his arms crossed over his chest, blocking us from entering.

I roll my eyes. Although I'm pretty sure I could use magic to shove him out of the way, I doubt it would help my case any. He already doesn't like me. "This is Seth. He's my cousin."

"He's cool," Felix says, dropping a hand onto West's shoulder. He smiles and I smile back, glad he's on my side.

After a beat, West backs up, grumbling. Seth nods politely as we pass him. I resist the urge to knock into him with my shoulder. I sit down at the end of the couch by Bria's feet. She still hasn't removed her arm from over her eyes. I pat her ankle. "What's wrong with you?"

Felix shrugs, taking a seat beside Seth on the love seat adjacent the couch. "Dunno. She's been like that since she got here."

"I believe I may have an explanation," Seth says, leaning forward and propping his elbows on his knees. "If what Krissa suspects is true, it's possible your friend has overtaxed her system."

West snorts as he sits down in the arm chair by Bria's head. "*Krissa.*"

Felix launches a throw pillow at him. "Overtaxed herself doing *what*?"

"She didn't tell you?" I shake Bria's foot and she mumbles incoherently in response. "Bridget Burke knocked Dana Crawford down a flight of stairs and broke her leg."

West leans forward, forgetting his air of irritation. "Dana's got a broken leg?"

I shake my head. "Not anymore." I glance significantly at Bria, who mumbles again.

Felix whistles. "Holy hell. I didn't know we could do that!"

"Wait—you said something about overtaxing herself?" West's deep-set eyes are fixed on Seth, his suspicion forgotten for the moment. "Is she gonna be okay?"

Seth nods. "How much do you know about the difference between witches and psychics?"

West's eyes flick to me. "Why? How much do you know?" His words are sharp, defensive.

"Quite a bit, actually," Seth says, unruffled by West's tone. "In addition to having quite the addiction to research, I also happen to be both a psychic and a witch."

This isn't the first time I've heard this, but my stomach still flutters. Of course, I already knew Seth was a witch, but when he told me he's also a psychic, it thrilled me. Once again, I'm thankful for his presence in my life. He's the one person who can understand me more fully than anyone else because he has the same abilities swirling around inside him.

Seth waits a beat before continuing. "As you may already know, there are certain things that both psychics and witches can do with their abilities. The main difference is where they draw their power. With witches, the power comes from nature—the elements, herbs, stones. They can connect with and channel the natural energy around them. Psychics, however, tap into an internal reservoir of sorts. Your abilities exist inside you. As such, both witches and psychics have their limitations. Witches need to be able to connect with something outside them to produce magic, so without proper concentration or ability to connect, the potency of their spells can be diminished. And while a psychic needn't connect with something external, the limitation is that you only possess so much energy inside you. Your friend Bria has used a good portion of that energy today, and it will take some time for it to replenish within her."

Felix's eyebrows pull together as Seth explains, his face scrunching at each odd turn of phrase. When he's done, I shrug. "It's just the way he talks. You'll get used to it."

West's posture relaxes. "Okay. So what? Is this why you brought him here? To give us a lesson on the differences between psychics and witches?" His tone is somewhat warmer than it had been when he spoke to me before, and I take comfort in this.

"Bria had an idea earlier. She wondered if there might be a way for us to somehow block the witches from using magic. I mean, it started because we were annoyed that Zane keeps confusing Mrs. Hill so we don't get through a lesson, but after what Bridget did..." I press my lips together, debating whether to share the next bit, afraid West might make a snide remark. But this is bigger than my own comfort, and I press on. "Yesterday, when Fox—" I take in a breath. "Zane was there and he lit some guy's car on fire. That's bad enough, but what's worse is he couldn't put it out afterward. We need to keep them from using magic that they can't control or using it to hurt people. And I figured having a second witch here could help us see if we can do it." I nod encouragingly at Seth, whose lips twitch in a smile.

"It is possible for a psychic to overwhelm a witch—to prevent him from connecting with a source of power and disrupt whatever spell he is attempting." His head cocks to the side. "In this case, it may take more than one psychic, as the circle isn't attempting to connect with nature in general but rather drawing their energy from a specific source."

Felix raises an eyebrow. "The crystal?"

Seth's eyes widen with surprise.

West raises his hand, like we're in school. "Excuse me—what crystal?"

I bite my lower lip. As much as I like sharing things with Seth— as much as I trust him implicitly—and as much as I want to be honest with the psychics, the prospect of telling everyone the whole truth about the stone makes my stomach twist. Felix already knows—I told him about it along with everything else. But when I finished explaining, he promised to keep everything to himself, to let me decide who should know and who shouldn't. A tiny nod from him now is all I need to know his oath still stands. I take in a breath and release it slowly. "Certain objects—herbs, stones—can be charged with energy, and it can be stored in them for use. Like a talisman. Like Seth said, instead of connecting to something like wind or water, a witch can connect with the stored energy. It's much easier to cast spells that way. And the circle found a quartz crystal—a *very* powerful one. And to focus their collective magic through it, they did a spell to anchor to the stone. Have you noticed they've been using magic more lately? And for bigger things? That's how they're doing it."

West nods, but his brow remains creased, like he doesn't entirely understand what I'm talking about. From her spot on the couch, Bria shifts until she's propped against the arm in an almost sitting position. "So," she says, her voice thick, "we have to keep them from connecting to magic they're already connected to? Awesome."

"It will most likely be exceedingly difficult," Seth says bracingly. "Indeed, I'm not sure whether you will be able to succeed at all. But Krissa says the circle is being reckless—endangering lives. That their control over the magic is tenuous at best. So, at the very least, we need to try."

West leans back in his chair, crossing his arms, his brow wrinkling in thought. "If this crystal thing is so dangerous for them to be connected to, why don't we just disconnect them?"

"Seth's been looking into that," I say quickly.

He nods. "Thus far, all I've located are spells for witches to cast, and all of those require an equal or greater number of witches trying to sever the connection than witches connected to the object."

"So, for now, all we can do is try to keep them from using the crystal's magic. Seth seems to think if we can overwhelm a witch's mind during a spell, we can stop it from happening." I clap my hands together and Bria jumps. "So, let's get started."

Training is slow and arduous, and to say the first tries were complete failures is being kind. Seth and I completed a series of simple spells—lighting birthday candles from West's junk drawer, changing the color of paper napkins from white to green or blue or purple, mending broken pencils—but neither West nor Felix succeeded in distracting us in the least. Bria naps on the couch while we practice, which Seth assures us is the best thing she could be doing at the moment.

After an hour of changing napkin colors, I move on to practicing glamors on my outfit, changing not only the color of my pants and shirt but the pattern and cut. Seth explains how to turn objects invisible and make them levitate, and soon magazines and remote controls are zooming through the air and Bria appears to be hovering in midair because I've used a glamor to make the couch disappear from sight.

Felix throws up his hands, sprawling across the love seat. "That's it. I give up. This is impossible."

The smile stretched across my face slips and the objects chasing each other around the room pause. "Oh, come on. You can't expect to get it your first try."

"Or my second or third or four hundredth. I'm glad you're having fun, because this is ridiculously frustrating for me."

I direct the magazines and remotes to rest on the coffee table as I cross to the love seat. I pick up Felix's legs and sit beside him, allowing his calves to settle across my thighs. "I'm sorry. It's just... I don't get to *do* magic much. I guess I'm getting a little carried away."

He shrugs. "It's not that. I mean, you *should* be doing crazy spells. But I was hoping to be able to stop you at least once."

A triumphant shout emanates from the kitchen and West bounds into the living room, fist punching the air. "I did it!"

On the couch, Bria stirs, blinking heavily. "Why's there shouting?"

West collapses onto the armchair, grinning broadly. "I did it. I kept him from lighting a candle."

Seth enters the room, nodding appreciatively as he leans against the wall. "That you did. Now, stop Krissa."

West leans forward, eyes wide and expectant. "Bring it."

I can't conceal a smile. There's a yellow birthday candle on the coffee table and I grab it. When I first learned this spell, it took concentration and visualization. Now it's as simple as breathing, and, in a blink, the wick is lit.

West's face falls. "What? But I—" He gapes, turning toward Seth. "I *just* did it."

Seth doesn't appear surprised by West's failed attempt. "My ability to connect with magic isn't particularly strong. At the moment, I'm a much more capable psychic than witch. Krissa, on the other hand, is quite strong. When she connects with an energy source, she fills with power easily. Yet even her abilities are pale compared to what the circle is capable of."

Felix shakes his head. "We're screwed."

"No," Seth says firmly. "You just need to practice. Indeed, I fear if you are unable to master this task, it will be impossible to disconnect the circle from the crystal at all."

Silence falls over the room as Seth's words sink in.

Felix swings his legs off mine, planting them on the floor and sitting up. "Okay. Let's try again."

West offers to order pizza half an hour later and I'm surprised by how dark it's gotten outside. "Won't your parents be home soon?"

He shakes his head. "Mom's out of town on business. Dad works second shift."

Felix snorts. "Why do you think we always meet over here?"

West points, shifting his finger between me and Seth. "Are either of you offended by pineapple?"

"I actually need to be going," Seth says, holding up his cell. "I promised Jodi I would have her car back to her by closing time, and it's nearly that."

"Oh." I bite my lower lip. It makes sense, of course—Jodi can't be expected to walk home from town, not with it as cold as it is. "I guess we can practice some more tomorrow, then."

I take a step to follow Seth, but Felix touches my arm. "Stay. I'll take you home. I'm not ready to stop practicing yet."

Bria lets out a breathy laugh from her spot on the couch. "You just want pizza."

He shrugs. "Maybe."

I hug Seth. "Thank you."

He smiles, his hand covering the doorknob. "Of course. Call if you need anything."

After he leaves, West places the pizza order while Felix attempts to keep me from levitating a throw pillow.

I've done more magic today than I've done ever, and with every spell I attempt, things get easier. The rush of energy that fills me each time I connect with an element no longer frightens me. I can direct the flow; I can control it.

We take a break when the pizza arrives. Bria manages to stay awake long enough to eat a piece, which I take as a good sign. After we eat our fill, Felix and West decide to pool their abilities to take me down rather than take turns. As I turn chunks of pineapple different colors, something tugs at the edges of my consciousness. It's not enough to keep the pineapple from turning blue, but it's enough to notice.

It's after eight when Bria's cell rings. She grumbles as she rolls off the couch, squinting at the display. "Yeah, Mom," she murmurs as she heads down the back hallway toward West's room.

I've moved on to turning the cheese green when my glamor fails, leaving it muddled and streaky. The boys whoop so loudly, slapping each other on the back, that I almost don't notice Bria when she reenters the room. She's pale, and the look on her face tells me it's not due to her spent energy. I put a hand on each boy's shoulder and the two become subdued, confused looks on their faces.

Bria shuffles toward us, a muscle in her jaw jumping. "That was my mom. She's at work—in the ER. She called because... she recognized him."

Felix and I exchange glances. She's not making sense, but I don't want to press her. I slip my arm around her shoulder and give her a squeeze, waiting for her to go on.

Bria draws in a shaky breath. "Dana Crawford's dad. He's dead."

Chapter Twenty

"I don't believe in coincidences."

West broods as he leans against his locker. It's been three days since Dana's dad died, and this is hardly the first time West has expressed this opinion. Still, my stomach clenches. Typically, I would agree with him, but I can't get my brain around the idea that the circle had something to do with the death of Dana's father.

According to Bria's mom, he was in a car accident, but it doesn't look like that's what killed him. The injuries he sustained when his SUV hit a tree weren't severe enough. His death is what caused the accident, not the other way around.

"How could they be behind it?" It's not the first time I've asked the question.

Felix sighs. "You said Bridget knocked Dana down the stairs without touching her. And that Zane lit an engine on fire. Is this really outside the realm of possibility?"

"I think the better question is *why*." Bria looks better today than she has since Tuesday: Her color is back and only the barest hint of dark circles hangs beneath her eyes. "I mean, knocking someone down a set of stairs is one thing. Murder? That's a pretty big escalation."

"I agree." I say the words, hoping doing so will make them true. But the fact is I'm not entirely convinced the circle is innocent, not with the crystal influencing them. I just don't *want* to believe they're capable of it. I don't want to believe Fox is. Despite the fact that he hasn't looked at me since our fight, I'm not angry with him. It wasn't him talking. It all comes back to the darkness they're anchored to.

"I really don't care about how or why," West says. "If you're right, Kris, then the only thing that matters is breaking their connection to the crystal. Seth still hasn't figured that out?"

Warmth bubbles in my chest. West's attitude toward me has done a complete one-eighty. Far from the venom he spewed the first time I showed up at his house, his demeanor is friendly, like the West from my reality. Yesterday was the first time he called me *Kris*, and although I prefer *Krissa*, I won't correct him. He's accepted me as one of them. "I talked with him yesterday. He says he found some resources that look promising, but he hasn't found anything concrete yet."

"Maybe we could help him look," Bria offers.

"Do you speak Latin? Because apparently that's what most of this stuff is in."

Bria pulls a face. "Seth speaks *Latin*?"

I shrug. "He's a man of many skills, apparently."

Felix claps his hands, rubbing them together. "In the meantime, we'll just have to settle for keeping the circle from doing spells."

I smile at his exuberance. While he and West had success working together to block my spell on Tuesday, it wasn't until last night that he was able to do it on his own. Although I'm not convinced this means he's strong enough to disrupt the tie of the anchoring spell, I'm eager for him to try.

The warning bell shrills overhead and the four of us start down the hall toward the cafeteria. Bria and I have stopped sitting by the windows at lunch and now share a table with the guys. It's funny that something so small can make me so happy. It's almost like old times—*almost*. Lexie, of course, still sits with the circle—not that I would want this version of her sitting with me anyway. The only other person missing from our group is Owen, who sits with friends from the track team. Since the chair fiasco, he hasn't made any rude comments. Yesterday, he came up to me in science to borrow a pencil, even though there are half a dozen people between us who could've lent him one. He looked in my eyes when I handed it to him and said *thank you*. Felix thinks Owen realizes he crossed a line and this is his way of saying sorry. I'm not sure how I feel about it. If he's actually sorry, he should say it.

"Hey—is that...?" Bria points as a girl emerges from the bathroom ahead of us.

"Dana." She hasn't been in school since her dad died—not that I blame her. I'm actually surprised to see her here today. "I'm gonna go talk to her."

Bria grabs my elbow as I start down the hall, tugging me backward. "Are you sure that's the best idea?"

"We used to be friends." I glance at Felix, who nods almost imperceptibly. "I'll meet you guys in the cafeteria."

Bria shakes her head as I jog to catch up with Dana, but I ignore her. It's not until I'm just steps away from her that my heart begins hammering in my chest. I only have guesses as to how our friendship ended. What if she brings up something I don't know about? And what if she asks about what happened on Tuesday in the stairwell? How much does she remember?

I could turn around now and she wouldn't even know I was here. But I can't do that. Of all the people in this school, I'm the one uniquely suited to understand her situation. I know the pain of a parent dying—the empty ache, the simultaneous desires both to remember every tiny detail and forget everything. And while the loss of her boyfriend must pale in comparison to her father's death, I can understand that hole, too. In fact, Dana and I might have more in common than any two people. And I owe it to her to offer any help I can.

"Hey," I say, falling into step beside her.

Dana jumps, hand pressing to her chest. When she gets over the initial shock, her lip curls. "What do you want?" Her voice is sharp, but quiet, like she can't muster enough energy to be as nasty to me as she'd like to be.

I press my lips together. Maybe this wasn't such a good idea. But I'm here now and I don't let myself walk away. "I just wanted to... I heard about your dad." I'm not sure what else to say. When my mom died, I wasn't in school—I'd been suspended, and Jodi pulled me anyway so she could take me here to Clearwater. I sat in a lot of sterile office rooms with men and women in suits while Jodi took care of the legal things, like claiming guardianship of me and dealing with my mother's estate. No one really spoke to me; I was like a piece of furniture during all the proceedings. And once I got here, no one knew. I have no idea what to say to her in this situation.

Dana stops and leans against the wall, staring. "Yeah, and?" She glances down the hall to her left and right. Besides a handful of underclassmen by the stairwell, we're alone.

"I'm sorry for hurting you." The words tumble out in a rush. If I'm going to comfort her now, I need to apologize for the past, even if I don't remember it. Dana's eyes go wide, but I don't give her a chance to speak. "We were friends, and I was terrible to you. You didn't deserve it, and I'm sorry... I'm sorry for my part in it. And if there's anything I can do for you... I'll do it."

Dana eyes me like she's not sure whether she can trust me.

The bell rings, signaling that we should be in the cafeteria already. I scan the emptying halls and a couple of teachers shoo us, eager to eat their own meals. I start walking and Dana falls into step beside me. "Do you really mean it? That if there's anything you can do, you'll do it?"

I nod, grateful for something to do. "Yeah. Anything."

She sniffles. "Would you let me copy your English homework? I'm, like, two weeks behind."

I laugh. "Sure. I'll go get it. Meet you in the cafeteria."

I head toward my locker and Dana stops, mouth open like she wants to say something, but after a second she closes it, shaking her head as she heads for the lunch room.

By the time I make it down, the cafeteria is buzzing with the voices of a couple hundred students. I locate Dana at a table in the back corner of the room. A group of guys—football players, I'd bet my life—sit at a nearby table, not quite veiling their glances in her direction. A group of girls sits toward the middle of the table Dana's at, but she's separated from them—though whether the separation is her doing or theirs, I'm not sure.

When I settle in the seat across from her, she looks up, startled. I slide my English notebook across the table and she laughs—tips-her-head-back-and-cackles kind of laughs. Heat rises in my cheeks, but I force myself to stay seated. So what if she's laughing at me? Her father just died. In those dark days after my mom's accident, I didn't laugh—I barely spoke. But when I met Owen and Lexie and Bria and West and got a taste of friendship for the first time in years, laughter was a healing balm. So if Dana wants to laugh now, I'll let her. She can laugh as much as she wants.

Dana's laughter subsides and she shakes her head as she digs through her purse, pulling out a pen and battered notebook. After opening to a blank page, she squints at my assignment for a minute before looking up at me. "This is legit."

Her surprised tone makes me shift in my seat. "Of course it is. Did you really think I'd take the time to scribble fake assignments before giving them to you?"

She pauses, her pen hovering centimeters above her notebook page. Her hazel eyes find mine. "It's not that, it's just—" She presses her lips together. "Thanks."

I nod and she returns to her work. I open my mouth and close it again quickly. I want to say something to her—something comforting, something to show I care—but I can't think of what that could be. I want to know if she'll be okay, to make sure she has someone to care for her now that her dad is gone. She had Marcus before Bridget cast a spell on him, but I'm not sure whether she has any other friends. We were friends once, before alternate-me chose the circle over everything else. But I'm not her. Dana could be part of the life I rebuild here. Maybe, like me, she just needs someone who can understand her, who can accept her for her, no background-check needed, no history weighing her down.

Dana spends the rest of the lunch period with her head down, alternately copying my work and taking bites of her lunch-line salad. I watch her as I eat my lunch, just waiting for the opportunity to say something more to her. I'm not sure exactly what it will be—an invitation out for coffee? Or is that too lame? Asking about plans for her father's funeral? Or is that too morbid?

I decide to lead in with another offer. If she's behind in English, maybe there's something else I can do to help her catch up.

The bell rings and she slides my notebook back across the table as she finishes writing the last answer. I tuck it into my backpack. When I turn back to Dana, she's smiling.

"Thanks," she says, her eyebrows pulling together. "You didn't have to do that. It was really... decent."

I nod, tamping down the wave of unease that rises within me. "Look, Dana. I wasn't kidding before. If there's anything else I can do for you, just say it. In fact, if you need—"

The rest of my words are cut off as Dana lets out a shriek. A hoarse cry escapes my lips, too, as flames erupt from her notebook and spread across the lunch table. The other girls who were sitting at the table have already vacated, but groups from the adjacent areas freeze, staring in our direction.

But my eyes aren't on the table. I search the room, my stomach sinking when my gaze finds the thing I was expecting: Crystal, Lexie, and Bridget. They stand along the wall of windows overlooking the courtyard, focus locked in my direction. They're doing this—they're causing this fire.

"Felix." I don't yell it—it's barely audible to me over the shrieks and murmurs of the gathering crowd. There's no way he can hear me, I know that, but he doesn't need to hear me. He knows. His consciousness tugs at the corners of mine and I allow my energy to link with his, the way I've done before during spells with the circle.

"You bitch!" Dana screams, pointing an accusing finger. "To think, I was actually falling for it!"

I hold up my hands, ready to defend myself, when a lunch lady runs forward, a fire extinguisher in her hands. She aims the nozzle, but before she can spray it, the flames dissipate, leaving behind only a wisp of smoke.

I rush around the table to face Dana. "Whatever you think I did, I didn't do it! I just wanted—"

Dana launches herself at me, cutting off the rest of my explanation. I jump backward, but the move is unnecessary: The arms of another lunch lady close around Dana's middle, holding her back. Losing my footing, I fall hard on my rear end, my palms slapping against the worn linoleum of the cafeteria floor. The woman detaining Dana pulls her backward, muttering something about a trip to the office, and I stand, ready to jump to Dana's defense, but arms close around my torso, keeping me from moving forward.

"Calm down, Kris."

I struggle against West's arms. "Calm down? *Calm down*? Did you see what they just did? I need to go tell Crystal Taylor—"

He releases me, looking down with cinched eyebrows. "Who?"

I shake my head. "Mrs. Cole. We have to tell her what really happened."

He snorts. "You really expect her to believe us?"

Felix and Bria arrive at West's side. "It's worth a try," Felix says.

As the four of us head to the office, I plot out in my head what to say. Does Crystal Taylor know her nieces have followed in her footsteps? Does she still practice magic, like Jodi does? I'm not sure how much to share and how much to keep back.

When we bustle into the office, I lead us straight back to the principal's door. The secretary stands, calling that we can't go in there, but I don't listen and push into the office.

Crystal Jamison, Lexie, and Bridget turn in their chairs, identical smirks curling their lips. Crystal Taylor stands, crossing her arms over her chest. "Excuse me, Miss Barnette, but you can't just barge into my office."

Relief flickers momentarily, replaced by dread. Dana's not here, which can only mean she's not in trouble. But that Crystal, Lexie, and Bridget are here isn't encouraging. "I'm sorry, Mrs. Cole. This can't wait."

She cocks her head, narrowing her eyes. "I'll decide what can and can't wait, thank you. Now, Kristyl, if you'll wait in the outer office, I'd like to talk with you in a minute. West, Bria, Felix—you can all go to class. Mrs. Davis will write you a pass."

Not one of us budges. Bria crosses her arms over her chest. "We're not leaving Krissa."

Affection for Bria swells and I can't help smiling. Lexie rolls her eyes.

After a beat, Crystal Taylor throws up her hands. "Okay, you want to get this over with here and now? Let's do it. Miss Barnette, since your school record is clean, I'm letting you off with a warning today, but if—"

"Wait—what?" I shake my head, sure I misheard her.

"A warning for what?" Felix asks.

It's Crystal Taylor's turn to look confused. "Arson is a very serious offense. According to the school code of conduct, I could issue a suspension—"

"Krissa didn't set that fire," West says.

Crystal Taylor's eyebrows hitch upward. "Are you saying Dana Crawford did it?"

"What? No," I say quickly. There's no way she deserves for this to come down on her. "Dana didn't do it. Your nieces and their friend did."

Crystal Jamison snorts. "We were all the way on the other side of the cafeteria. Ask anyone."

Anger boils in the pit of my stomach. I lunge toward her, desperate to smack the smirk off her face, but arms close around my abdomen as Crystal Taylor calls out in surprise.

"One more outburst like that and I'll change my mind about that suspension." Color blooms in her cheeks and she take s a deep breath before continuing. "Now, Felix, I recommend you get your friend out of here before she does something she regrets."

The arms tug me backward. "Let's go, Krissa," Felix murmurs. After a beat, I stop fighting and allow him to lead me out of the room. Crystal Jamison blows a kiss, wiggling her fingers as Bria pulls closed the door.

Chapter Twenty-One

Felix and I skip sixth hour again. I just can't face seeing Crystal and Bridget in history. Instead of hanging out in the janitor's closet again, we sneak out during hall passing time and sprint to his car. I'm more than a little surprised how easy it is.

"Should I take you to Jodi's shop now?" Felix asks as he pulls out of the parking lot. "Or will she be pissed you ditched?"

I shrug. "I honestly have no idea. I should, though, right?" I run my fingers through my hair, leaning back against the seat. "It's exhausting, you know? Pretending I know what's going on. Just when I think I've got things figured out, I realize there's something else I'm clueless about."

"Sucks." He reaches over and pats my knee. "I'm glad you told me, though. It... It means a lot that you'd share you freaky secrets with me."

"It means a lot that you don't think I'm insane."

"Pfft. I've known *that* for years."

Felix drives to the river just outside downtown and pulls into the parking lot beside the playground. It's too cold to get out and swing on the swings or sit on the bench overlooking the water, so we stay in the car, the engine running, and talk. When it's clear discussing the circle will only rile me up, he switches tacks, telling me stories about my history in Clearwater. I enjoy hearing my story through his eyes, even though I'm pretty sure he's holding back in places to spare me from the truth. But there are things I need to know.

"What happened with Owen? I looked through my old diary, but it didn't give details."

He winces. "Are you sure you wanna hear this? I mean, past is past. And it looks like Owen might finally be putting it behind him..."

I take in a breath. "I want to know."

Felix stares for a beat before shaking his head. "No one was surprised when Owen finally asked you out. You two were hanging out a lot and some people were convinced you were already a couple. I was at the dance with Heidi Holmes, and she's actually the one who pointed it out to me."

"What?"

"Your face. You were all... tight and nervous. Any time he reached out to touch you, you were jumpy. I remember thinking that was really weird because you were never like that with me." The corners of his mouth quirk upward. "Except, of course, the first time I tried to kiss you."

I don't return his smile. "What did I do?"

His shoulder sag. "Crystal and Lexie showed up late—on purpose, I'm sure, just to torture you. Once they got there, your whole demeanor changed. You looked relaxed for the first time all night. Heidi and I were on the dance floor and you pulled Owen out there—right next to us, right in the middle. And everything was fine until a slow song came on. One second, you guys were dancing, the next..." He squeezes his eyes shut. "You humiliated him, right there, in front of the whole school. Started going on about how pathetic he was, and how you only went out with him to win a bet. Started spilling all the secrets he ever told you—things West didn't even know, and he and West were real close back then. And when you were done, you stalked straight over to Crystal and Lexie and they both slapped money in your hand, like it really was all a bet. And he ran out of there crying."

My eyes prickle and my throat constricts. No wonder he still hates me. I kind of hate me.

Felix squeezes my shoulder. "Hey, it wasn't you."

Tears well and a blink sends them cascading over my cheeks. "It could've been." I wipe my eyes with the sleeves of my coat. I shouldn't get to cry about this. I wasn't the victim. After taking in a few deep breaths, I'm in control of my emotions again. "You should get me to the shop. My shift's about to start."

Felix's mouth twitches like he wants to say something, but the moment passes and he puts the car in gear. When we pull up in front of the shop, I check my reflection in the visor mirror before thanking him for the ride and hopping out.

Once I punch in, I throw myself into work. After restocking everything that is even remotely low, I find a feather duster in the break room and start dusting every shelf, grabbing a step stool for the high ones I can't reach. Jodi's eyes prickle my skin, but she says nothing. She's worried about me. She notices I'm different lately and although she's relieved I'm not hanging out with Crystal et al anymore, she likes Fox and is worried about how hard I'm taking the breakup.

I shake my head to rid my mind of her thoughts. She's itching to talk to me about it—to impart her wisdom, to make sure I'm okay. But the truth is I'm not. For so very many reasons, I'm not okay at all. And I can't tell her why. If I tell her why the circle shunned me, I'll have to tell her about the crystal, and if I tell her about the crystal, I'll have to tell her about what I had to do to find it—and why. And then she'll know I changed things. But she *can't* know that—because as bad as things are now, I don't know if I could survive if Jodi gave up on me.

A steady stream of customers keeps us both occupied for a good portion of my shift: It seems everyone in Clearwater is looking to boost their immune systems before winter hits. I lose myself in selling oils and supplements, books and teas, and manage to push all my other thoughts aside.

There's less than an hour left before closing time when the store empties, the stream switching to a drip. Emotions radiate off Jodi, brushing against my skin: She's steeling herself to come talk to me, but I can't face that. So before she approaches me, I turn, hitching on a smile. "You know what sounds great right now? Hot cocoa. You want? I could do a run."

An expression flickers across Jodi's face and for a moment I'm sure she'll say no, but then she returns my smile. "Sure. Grab some cash out of my purse."

I lose no time running back to the break room and grabbing my coat and some money. In less than a minute, I'm on the street, gulping down the frozen air. It chills my insides, firming a resolve I didn't realize I'd made. I have to talk to Jodi—she won't give up until we do—but I'll have to lie. I head across the street to the coffee shop, mind buzzing. Maybe I can text Felix, see if he can help me come up with a plausible fiction to spin.

When I step up onto the opposite curb, a tingle floods my body—like a hundred sets of eyes are on me, studying me. But the street is nearly empty. Besides a middle-aged man in a brown coat briskly walking his yellow lab and some pre-teen girls giggling as they spill out of a mini-van and into the bookstore, I'm the only one out here. There are cars on the road, but there always are. One in particular draws my eye—a black Charger with dark tinted windows. I've seen this car before. And as much as I try to convince myself it's no big thing, that in a town this small I'm bound to see the same car more than once, I can't shake the feeling that there's something special about this particular one.

The door to the coffee shop opens and a harassed-looking couple hurries onto the sidewalk, pulling their coats snugly against their bodies and muttering darkly as they head down the street. The Charger continues its route and I shake my head before jogging the remaining distance to the shop's door. There's a line inside. Millie's harassed voice calls to the employee behind the counter whose name badge reads *Elle*. "Try it again!"

"Nothing!" calls Elle.

The customers ahead of me shift and murmur in disgruntled tones. A few check their watches or phones for the time. I scan the room and my stomach clenches when I catch sight of Owen seated at a high-top table. I can't face him—not now, not when I finally understand the reason he treats me the way he does. But maybe facing him is exactly what I need to do. I should march right up to him and apologize for what I did that night, explain that I thought I had to. But the idea of doing so makes me want to run right out the door.

He catches my eye and my breath hitches. I'm sure I'll see there the same distaste that's rested there every time he's looked at me, but there's just mild surprise. His shoulders rise and fall as he takes in a breath.

Millie calls again from the back and the man in front of me nods apologetically as he pushes past me toward the door. A groaning, scraping sound reaches my ears. At first I think it's coming from behind the counter, but it's not. Owen is using his foot to push the chair opposite him away from the table. An invitation.

I leave the line and cross to him before I'm fully aware of having decided to do so. My earlier apprehensions are forgotten— or at least tamped down. This is Owen, and the two of us are simply having some coffee together, just like old times.

A text book and notes are scattered across the tabletop, along with an empty glass. He's studying, and he's been here awhile— maybe since right after school. I perch on the edge of the chair and nod toward the line. "What's going on here?"

"There's something wrong with the espresso machine, I guess. Millie's trying to flip the right breaker or something. They've been at it maybe ten minutes."

I lean toward him, dropping my voice. "You mean all these people have just been standing here for ten minutes?"

He nods. "Pretty much. It's pretty entertaining, actually. I'm trying to guess who can hold out the longest. The guy and the woman at the head of the line keep complaining that they're going to be late for something."

I make a face. "Then why don't they just leave?"

He snaps and points at me. "Exactly."

He's being nice to me—too nice, almost. His acting so much like my Owen, I actually pinch my leg to be sure I'm not imagining things. When the pain shoots through me and Owen remains, I blink and shake my head.

One corner of his mouth quirks up. "What?"

"You're being nice to me," I blurt.

His face tightens, but only momentarily. "Yeah. You know, Felix was right. I've been holding on to what happened for too long." He shakes his head. "I *have* noticed. That you're different. I haven't wanted to see it because I've *wanted* to be mad at you. But it's been years, and I can't keep all that anger. It's exhausting."

Tears prickle my eyes. "I'm so sorry," I blurt. "I'm sorry for what happened. I was awful—"

Owen covers my hand with his, just for a moment, but it's enough to cut me off. "Don't. I don't wanna talk about then. I wanna put it behind me—finally. What Felix said the other day... He was right." He offers a smile. "He's a good guy. Felix."

It takes a second for his meaning to sink in. Heat rises in my cheeks. "No—we're just friends. There's nothing between me and Felix."

"Oh."

The air between us changes, charges. There's a spark of possibility overshadowed by a wave of fear. I latch onto the first idea that strays into my mind. "So, which one do you think'll be the next to drop?"

Owen raises an eyebrow and I nod toward the line. His posture relaxes and he presses his lips together. "Hard to say. See, at this point, you've gotta imagine what's going through these people's heads. They're thinking about how long they've already waited and just how late they can be for their next engagement. And then there's the fear that you'll wait all this time and as soon as you walk out, everything's gonna start working again. I'm thinking the two up front are in it for the long haul. The woman in yoga pants? I bet she's next to go."

"I don't know. Yoga pants are pretty comfortable."

Owen snorts. "What does that have to do with anything?"

I shrug. "I don't know. Just, she probably won't care how long she has to stand there because her clothes aren't gonna start digging into her."

Owen shakes his head, smiling.

I return his smile. Maybe this can work, a friendship between us. Things won't ever be the way they were before, and maybe I don't want them to be. We don't have the same history. The Owen I knew, the one I was falling for, isn't the same as this one. But if he can move beyond this reality's history, I certainly can.

Behind the counter, Elle sighs. "Do you want me to try?"

"I think I can flip a switch by myself." Millie's tone is irritated. I can only see her arm from this angle, and I can hear the loud snaps as she flicks each breaker off and then on again. *Snap*. The overhead lights go out. A couple people call out in surprise. *Snap*. The lights are back on.

"I just want a coffee," calls the man stationed third in line. "Can I just get a cup?"

"Are you paying with cash?" Elle asks.

The man looks at her like she's crazy. "No."

She points at the register. "I can't ring any transactions right now. If you had cash..."

"Well, I have cash," calls yoga pants.

The employee looks at her expectantly. "And you'd like coffee?"

"No. I want a skinny half-caf vanilla latte."

"The espresso machine's still not working."

"Well, how do you know?" asks yoga pants. "You're not *testing* it."

The employee takes in a breath before responding. "There's a light that glows green when the machine is on—"

"Maybe it's broken," snaps yoga pants.

"Yikes," I murmur.

"Yeah, this is quickly dissolving into anarchy. How long do you think it'll be before they organize and storm the counter?"

I squint at the patrons. "I dunno. I think there might be a power struggle. Yoga Pants isn't going down without a fight."

Owen laughs and I bask in the sound of it. I've missed him—not in the romantic way I longed for him when I first entered this reality, just *him*—his humor, his friendship. I almost forgot how easy it's always been with him, how I've never felt like I need to pretend to be someone I'm not. My eyes prickle. I've missed having friends. When they associated with me, the circle didn't really fill that hole. And even with Bria, West, and Felix, the energy we have together is different than the easy playfulness we enjoyed before. But here, now, with Owen, it's like things are the same as they were before. I smile at him and as he turns his clear blue eyes on me, for the first time since I returned from the time-travel spell, I feel like I'm home.

"I give it two minutes before no-cash coffee guy steals a cup and gets his coffee," Owen says, grinning.

I smile back, but the expression quickly slips from my face as a sensation overtakes me. My whole body prickles as a current of energy thrums through me. I scan the coffee house, coming up empty before it dawns on me what I'm searching for: the circle. The charge in the air is so similar to what I felt just before Dana fell down the stairs.

The shop is plunged into semidarkness again, and yoga pants lets out a yelp. A few seconds slip by and the light doesn't return. The man at the head of the line begins grumbling about something, but his voice is drowned out by a scream. "Millie!"

I stand, suddenly on high alert. There's something wrong. It's not just the darkness: there's a scent in the air, like burning, or something charred. I edge toward the counter, dreading what I'll find there.

Lying on the ground below the breaker box is Millie, a wisp of smoke rising from her nose and mouth, catching the slanting light coming from the front window. Elle is bent over her, reaching toward her but not quite touching her.

"Call nine-one-one!" Owen calls.

No one moves.

Owen grabs my shoulder and shakes me. "Do you have your phone?"

I nod, numbly, my hand going to my back pocket.

"Mine's dead. Give me yours."

The man at the back of the line shoves forward. "I'm a nurse," he says, rushing behind the counter.

Elle lets out a wail as the man displaces her. Owen takes my phone and dials three numbers. "Hello? There's an emergency at Wide Awake Cafe on Main. I think... I think someone's been electrocuted."

Chapter Twenty-Two

Owen and I stand on the sidewalk, watching as the paramedics slide the stretcher into the back of the ambulance. The lights aren't flashing. There's no need. The white sheet covering Millie's face is final: She will not recover from what happened.

Died immediately, the nurse said when the paramedics arrived. The shock stopped her heart, and the nurse couldn't get it started again.

The paramedics close the back door before circling around to the cab of the ambulance. I stare until the vehicle has disappeared down Main Street.

Owen's hand closes over my shoulder. "Hey, let me walk you back to Jodi's shop."

I shake my head. "I can't... I can't..." I can't do it again, I want to say. I can't tell her that one of her good friends is dead, not again. I was the one to tell her that her friend Shelly was dead in my other reality, and I can't see that look on her face again.

"Okay," Owen says, even though I haven't made a coherent statement. "Okay. Walk down there with me. I'll tell her. You don't have to go in. I'll tell her and then I'll take you home."

I want to disagree with him. I should stay and Jodi should go. I should be the one to close down the store so Jodi can go home, but I know I can't do it. The aroma of burned flesh is still strong in my nostrils. I can't close the shop right now. I'm not entirely sure I can walk.

Owen leads me back down the street. It's not until we get to the front door of the shop that I realize I didn't get Jodi her drink. I reflect on how disappointed she'll be until I realize she won't care about her drink once Owen tells her what happened. She might never drink coffee again.

True to his word, Owen goes into the store without me. I stare off across the street, not wanting to catch even a glimpse of Jodi's face when she hears the news. My stomach twists. I should be in there, supporting her. But I can't. I just... I can't.

What was it I felt back there before it happened? Was it a premonition? Just my psychic senses hinting that something bad was about to happen? Or was it something else?

Owen is back at my side and I'm not sure how much time has passed. He places a tentative arm around my shoulder and leads me toward his car, which is parked at the end of the block.

"I should be in there. I should help her."

"No. Jodi wanted me to take you home." Owen's voice is firm, even if his hold on me isn't. Still, it's the closest the two of us have been in this new reality, and I'm forcibly reminded of all the other times he slung his arm around my shoulder or bumped my arm with his, the times he held my hand. It seems impossible to me that those things happened in a place where Owen will never be aware of them.

My stomach twists. How selfish am I? Someone just died, my aunt is probably a wreck, and here I am feeling sorry for myself because—what? I don't have a boyfriend?

Owen opens the passenger side of his white Grand Prix and lets me in. I slide into the familiar seat, my eyes scanning the dashboard for the little cracks and dings I remember from the last time I was in the car. Only some of them are there. After all, this car isn't exactly the same as the one I rode in before, just like this Owen isn't exactly the same as the one I rode in it with.

I don't ask Owen how he knows the way to my house, but he drives there without my input. When he pulls in the driveway, he cuts the ignition and comes around to my side to open the door. Ordinarily I would insist I could get the door myself, but these are not ordinary circumstances and I even need Owen's help getting out of the car. His arm is once again around me as he leads me up the porch stairs and to the front door.

"Thank you," I murmur when we reach the door. I'm not

entirely sure what I'm thanking him for, but the words seem appropriate. Thanks for walking me to the door? Thanks for telling Jodi her friend died so I wouldn't have to? Owen seems to accept that it's a cover-all and nods.

He shakes his head and runs his hand through his hair. "I just... I can't believe that happened. We were just sitting there and..." He rubs a hand over his face. "I'm an awful person."

His words jar me. "What?"

He sighs. "Someone was just electrocuted, and I'm thinking about how it ruined..." He turns, facing the driveway. "Felix was right. Completely right about me."

I grab his arm, tugging him until he faces me. "What are you talking about?"

"I've hated you. For the last three years, I've hated you, because it was easier to do that than to admit the truth. But these last couple weeks, you've been different. At first I tried to ignore it, tried to believe it wasn't really there, but... I see her there, inside you. The girl you were when you first came to Clearwater. I see Krissa when I look at you—not *Kristyl*, not the girl you changed into when you started spending time with *them*."

My heartbeat speeds up. "I can't explain it, Owen, but I *am* her—I *am* Krissa."

He blinks a few times, pressing his lips together. "We were friends—*good* friends. I've missed that. And then today, you show up and it was like old times, you know?" He reaches forward, caressing my cheek with his fingers. "It was going so well until..."

My breath catches, the force of a memory taking me by surprise. Owen stood on this porch once before—my Owen—and said those same words. And afterward, we kissed for the first time. I want so badly to kiss him right now, to relive that moment, to lose myself in it. But I can't—we're not the same people. I turn, heading toward the house. "I should get inside."

By the time I reach the front door, Owen is at my side. He places his hand over mine when I grab for the doorknob. "What's wrong?"

I don't look at him, afraid of what might happen if I do. "Nothing."

"Are you mad at me?" He removes his hand from mine. "Was it something I said?"

"Of course not." I don't turn to him and he puts one hand firmly on each of my shoulders, turning me so I'm facing him. The air outside is cold, but it's nothing compared to the icy sensation that engulfs me when my eyes lock on Owen's. The air is pressed from my lungs as memories of my life—my former life—flip through my consciousness like a movie on fast-forward. My first day at Clearwater High, when Crystal Jamison spilled her coffee over my clothes. Owen finding me in an empty stairwell and offering me his sweatshirt. His smile from across the lunch table. The first time he hugged me outside Spanish class. Our hands full of deep, rich compost when we helped the science teacher take care of the plants in the courtyard at school. The school dance when we slow danced in the corridor off the commons, the feel of his hand on the side of my face as he leaned forward... The panic in Owen's face and voice the morning after the dance when he admitted he'd foreseen an accident Felix was involved in. The confusion and elation at learning that he and I are the same—we both have psychic abilities. The rage that coursed through him the night Tucker tried to attack me, and the feel of his lips against mine when we kissed here on this porch.

Owen releases my shoulders, swaying slightly in his spot. His eyebrows cinch together and he shakes his head vaguely. "I should... go."

A shaky breath passes over my lips. Suddenly, I'm exhausted, my legs like jelly. I reach for the door to steady myself. "Thanks for the ride home."

He nods, his eyes slightly unfocused. "Yeah." He reaches for my face and leans toward me. My breath catches and my stomach flutters. Just when I'm sure he's going to kiss me, he straightens, taking a step back. His mouth twitches and he starts for the steps. "Bye, Krissa. See you tomorrow."

I watch as he crosses the lawn to the driveway, as he opens the door to his Grand Prix and climbs in, as he backs out of the driveway and heads off down the street.

What just happened? I know why this exchange was strange for me—because I remember the last time we spoke similar words in this very spot. But why would Owen suddenly start acting strange? And why did he almost kiss me?

Chapter Twenty-Three

I barely get a chance to catch my breath for the next few days. Mom insists Jodi take some time off work, which means Devin, Seth, and I have to pick up the slack. Come Monday, I convince Mom to let me work instead of going to school because Devin has a morning class and Seth can't handle things alone yet. She agrees, with the caveat that I have someone bring home all the work I miss so I don't get behind.

Millie's funeral is Tuesday.

Outside my bedroom window, the world is frosted. A light snow fell during the night, dusting rooftops and roadways with a powder that snakes in the light breeze. I stare at the clothes in my closet for a long time before deciding on black pants and a gray sweater. Because my hair is extra-staticky today, I pull it back, wrestling it into a strange clawed clip that's been hanging out on the counter in the bathroom.

By the time I make it downstairs, breakfast is ready. All weekend, Mom has been keeping up a steady stream of one-sided conversation, occasionally asking me questions about what's happening at the shop, just so we're not eating in silence. This morning, however, she elects to remain quiet.

Somber is the tone of the morning. Although the tone of the funeral is lighthearted, with people sharing stories about Millie and laughing, my eyes are consistently drawn to the two sets of small, shaking shoulders at the front of the room—Millie's children. No matter how many comical stories are shared, I can't get out of my head the fact that these two kids no longer have a mom.

We cut out right after the funeral to get me to school. Mom's plan is to drop me off and get back at the funeral home before the procession to the graveyard begins.

I walk to the front office in a daze, my mind still on Millie. For the past few days, I've kept myself busy—too busy to replay the afternoon she died. But now, in the silent hallway, the click of my boots against the stone floor, the memory floods back. There's nothing I could've done to stop it. It was an accident—something that gives me shivers each time my mom says it. Still, I had a feeling just before it happened. What could that sensation have meant? Was it a warning? Was I *supposed* to stop it?

"Signing in?"

I blink rapidly. I'm in the front office, standing in front of the secretary, but I don't remember arriving. She repeats her question and I manage to nod. When I sign in on the clipboard she indicates, shivering when I fill in the *reason* square, she directs me to lunch. The day is already half over.

Although I'm still wearing my coat, I don't bother stopping by my locker before heading to the cafeteria. It strikes me, as the buzz of voices reaches my ears, that I don't have a lunch, but I'm also not very hungry, so it doesn't really matter. I make my way through the commons and into the lunch room, weaving around clumps of people who are either slowly making their way to their table or stopped completely, chatting. When I plop down in my chair, Bria immediately wraps her arms around me, squeezing me so hard I can't draw breath until she releases me. Felix reaches across the table, covering my hand with his, and West pushes a cookie so it rests in front of me. For something to do, I start picking at the cookie, plopping chunks in my mouth and chewing. I don't taste it.

"So," Bria says after a minute, drawing out the word. "Do you have anything going on tonight? Working at the shop, or... other plans?"

I chew and swallow. "No. Shop's closed for the day. We were all at the funeral this morning and Jodi didn't want anyone to have to work afterward. Tonight, Jodi's going out with some people who came in from out of town for the funeral. Mom's going with her

because she's pretty sure Jodi's gonna drink her weight in rum."

"Does that mean you can come out, too?" Bria asks.

"Probably." I break off another piece of cookie but don't eat it. Instead, I work on breaking it half, and then half again, and again. "Why? You guys wanna practice blocking magic again?" I sigh, not sure I'm up for it. But being able to stop the circle from casting spells is more important than me sitting in my room, replaying whether or not I could have done something to keep Millie from dying. "Yeah, sure. We can do that."

Felix reaches across the table again, stilling my hands. The cookie is little more than crumbs on the napkin in front of me. "Not practice. We were thinking going out to eat, or watching a movie. You know—to celebrate."

The wheels in my mind turn, but something's off. There's something obvious I'm missing, but my brain won't land on it.

"You know," Felix says slowly, "for your birthday?"

I stare at him a moment. Something bubbles in the pit of my stomach, rising quickly toward my mouth. It's not until it escapes through my lips that I recognize it. Laughter. I tip my head backward and release a long cackle. The energy of the room changes as people at nearby tables turn to look, trying to discern what's funny, but it doesn't faze me. When the laughter has run its course, I return my head to center, wiping my eyes. The look on West's face—like he's afraid I've just lost my mind—almost pushes me back into a fit, but I tamp it down. "It's my birthday."

Felix nods matter-of-factly. "And we'd like to help you celebrate."

I take in a breath, connecting my gaze with each of them. "I'd like that."

West's eyes flick to the table. "Are you... gonna eat that?"

I push the napkin full of cookie crumbs toward him. "By all means. I appreciate the gesture, I'm just... not hungry."

West loses no time plucking up a few crumbs and popping them into his mouth. Bria vacates the spot beside me and edges Felix out of his place beside West, claiming her fair share of the treat. Instead of relocating to the next seat over, Felix comes around the table to sit in Bria's spot beside me. "Don't look now," he

murmurs, raising his chin.

Catching his meaning, I affect a long, slow stretch, linking my fingers behind my head and arching my back before pressing my connected hands above me. As I stretch, I look in the direction Felix indicated, sure of what I'll see. Crystal, Lexie, and Bridget, most likely, eyeing me and giggling. Or maybe it's Fox. He would know it's my birthday. Does he want to come say something?

But when my eyes finally land on the person Felix mentioned, I'm so surprised I look away immediately. From his spot across the room, Owen is watching me with unveiled curiosity. My head snaps back to Felix so quickly there's no way Owen couldn't figure out the purpose of my elaborate stretch.

"He asked about you yesterday when you weren't in school."

My heartbeat increases. "What'd he say?"

He shrugs. "Asked if I'd heard from you. Wanted to see how you were doing. Is it true? You and Owen were together when it happened?"

I nod and Felix raises an eyebrow. I smack his chest with the back of my hand. "Whatever's going on in that twisted little head of yours, you can knock it off right now."

Felix's expression rearranges into a mask of innocence. "I'm sure I have no idea what you're talking about. I'm just saying— you're a free agent now, and Owen's finally not acting like he hates you—"

I hit him again, heat rising in my cheeks. He has a point. Isn't it what I've wanted since everything changed? To be back with Owen? For things to be the way they were before? My eyes stray to the circle's table and to Fox. Things *are* over between the two of us—he hasn't so much as spoken to me since our fight. And the breakup wasn't for some fabricated reason I had to make up—it was *his* choice. My stomach twists. If anything was to blame for that fight, for our separation, it's the influence of the crystal. Does that mean that if we can separate the circle from it, that Fox will be back to his regular self, to the guy I could see myself with?

By the time lunch is over, the cookie has been devoured. West waves goodbye and splits off, headed toward his next class. Bria and I have been walking to our lockers together before math, and

today Felix joins us, throwing out ideas for the birthday celebration the whole time. Once we're done at our lockers and headed toward class, I assume Felix will split off, but he follows us into Mrs. Hill's room.

When he takes a seat next to me, I raise an eyebrow. "Shouldn't you go to your own class?"

He grins, holding up a blank square of yellow paper.

I exchange glances with Bria, who rolls her eyes. "So, what? You've got a blank piece of paper."

"Pfft. *This* is my all-access pass. It's not just paper. When someone else looks at it, they'll see what I *want* them to see. Get it? Psychic paper. Totally Dr. Who."

"Who?"

Felix's face drops and he stares blankly. "I don't know if we can be friends anymore."

I gape and Bria sighs, taking a few seconds to explain what Felix is talking about. When I get the basic idea, I shake my head. I fix my eyes on the yellow square, and even though I've never tried to do what Felix suggests, I give it a go anyway, projecting a message meant for his eyes onto the paper.

The warning bell rings and he reaches down for it, ready to present it to the teacher, but he stops short, snorting. "For real, Krissa? I can't believe I put up with this abuse." He winks as he stands, heading toward the front of the room.

"What?" Bria asks. "What did it say?"

I grin. "Nerd."

She gives me a high five and we share a giggle.

At the chalkboard, Felix is talking with Mrs. Hill. They're too far away and the buzz of the classroom is too loud for me to make out what they're saying. Mrs. Hill is as focused as she's been since the circle anchored and Zane's used magic to keep her from teaching the class. Her eyes are fixed on Felix, her eyebrows drawing together as she studies the yellow paper. Felix jumps slightly, rubbing the back of his head. I don't think anything of it until he does it again, this time rubbing his shoulder. I squint. There's a smudge of white on the dark blue of his tee-shirt. It happens two more times before I see what's happening: Pieces of chalk from the ledge are zooming from their position and striking Felix.

He and I come to the realization at the exact same moment. He turns from Mrs. Hill and finds Zane, lounging in his desk. Although Mrs. Hill is in the middle of a comment, Felix stalks away, approaching Zane. "Knock it off, Ross," he snaps, his voice low. "I know you think you're hilarious, but I'm not gonna put up with your bullshit."

Zane arranges his face into a look of polite bewilderment. "No idea what you're talking about."

"Yeah, right."

Another piece of chalk pelts Felix in the back and he lunges at Zane, who flinches.

"Felix!" I yell, although it's unnecessary. By the time the word passes my lips. Felix has already stopped and crossed his arms over his chest, grinning. He doesn't intend to fight Zane—he never did. He just wanted him to show weakness, and he did that. Now a titter of laugher rises up in the room, and Zane's face goes hard.

"Felix, I think it's best you head to your regular class now," Mrs. Hill says, clapping a hand down on Felix's shoulder.

Felix flashes a grin toward me and Bria before allowing himself to be led to the door. But before the door closes behind him, Zane is up and pushes past the teacher into the hallway. Mrs. Hill returns to her desk, apparently oblivious to the exit of her student.

My skin tingles. This can't be good. I tap Bria's shoulder. "We've gotta get out there."

She nods. "Already ahead of you." She slips out of her desk and weaves through desks toward the door. I follow her.

When I pass Fox's desk, he grabs my wrist. "Wait."

I pull my arm away from him. "Either help me keep Zane from doing something stupid, or let me go."

Indecision flickers across Fox's face and his mouth twitches. Shaking my head, I turn away, hurrying after Bria to the door.

"Believe me, you have no idea what I'm capable of." Zane's voice echoes off the corridor walls as Bria and I ease into the hallway.

"Pretty sure I do." Felix stand several yards away, facing Zane, whose back is to us. "It's not like you're exactly stealth about it, you know."

"You're gonna wanna be shutting up right about now." Zane's voice is low and the intent behind the word is clear: *Stop talking now or something bad's gonna happen to you.*

I step forward but Bria's hand catches the crook of my arm, yanking me backward. I turn and glare and she pushes a single thought into my mind: *Wait.*

"Look, I get it," Felix continues. "You got this shiny new power and a desire to show off. I'm just saying it's time for you to knock it off before someone gets hurt. Before *you* get hurt."

Zane chuckles. "The only one who's getting hurt here is you."

In a flash, Felix pinwheels backward as if some great force knocked him in the chest. He moves several feet before pitching forward like he's been hit from behind. The river of fluorescent lights overhead flicker.

The energy in the hallway changes. There's a restlessness now—curiosity and bodies in motion. "Bria, lock all the classroom doors."

Her eyebrows draw together, but she closes her eyes to do what I ask anyway. Down the hall, above Felix, one of the light bulbs blows, sending down a shower of sparks. The metal and plastic housing surrounding the bulb swings down as if on a hinge, colliding with the back of Felix's head, launching him forward again.

The vibration of doors in their door jambs is all I need to know Bria's successfully locked all the classrooms. The last thing we need here is collateral damage. We have to stop Zane, and soon. I haven't practiced stopping a witch from using magic, but it's been done enough to me that I understand the idea behind it. With a nod at Bria, the two of us step out into the hallway, eyes, minds, and energies locked on Zane.

He raises his hand toward Felix, who's on his hands and knees. Immediately, Felix's eyes bulge and his hands go to his neck. Zane is choking him. I have to distract Zane—I have no idea how long it will take to disrupt his connection to the crystal. I slip off my shoe and throw it, hitting him squarely between the shoulder blades. He turns, and at the other end of the hall, Felix takes in a deep breath.

Zane's eyes narrow when they land on me and Bria and relief wells in my chest. We haven't disconnected him from magic, but Felix can breathe, and I'll take that. But a smile curls the edges of Zane's mouth and I know I've miscalculated. Now he knows we're here.

An invisible pressure circles my chest, squeezing the air from my lungs. A glance is all it takes to know I'm not the only one he's doing it to—Bria and Felix are being affected too.

I tamp down the rising panic and try to clear my mind. The only thing that will help us now is stopping Zane's magic. My breath comes in shallow gasps, growing shallower by the second. I have to overwhelm Zane's mind—make it impossible for him to link to the crystal. But as the pressure around my torso increases, I can't think of a way to do it.

Mrs. Hill's door rattles on its hinge and a muffled shout passes into the hallway. Fox's stormy eyes are wide, terrified, as he pulls on the doorknob.

Help. I mouth the word because there's no breath left to make sound. Fox pounds at the glass upper half of the door, but it doesn't crack. His distress seeps into the hall, washing over me. It overwhelms my senses and I stop trying to distract Zane from his spell.

Overwhelms. As tiny explosions of light burst in my peripheral vision, the idea comes—so simple I'm surprised it's not the first thing I tried. Instead of clearing my mind of the surge of emotions inside, I push them out, directing them at Zane. I pull along Fox's anguish, and tug at Bria's and Felix's consciousness, urging them to do what I'm doing.

The smug smile on Zane's face flickers and the muscles in his jaw jump. Another second and he twitches, his hands going to the side of his head. The pressure around my middle subsides and I gulp in deep breaths. Bria pulls me into a tight hug, relieved laughter bubbling out of her. Down the hall, Felix grins, giving a thumbs up.

The *click-clack* of high heels against the floor deflates my bubbling relief immediately. I turn, expecting to see Crystal

Jamison or Lexie, but it's Crystal Taylor—Mrs. Cole—who approaches. The overhead lights no longer flicker, and in their harsh glare, the flush in the principal's cheeks is obvious. She points one red-tipped fingernail in our direction. "You four. My office. Now."

Chapter Twenty-Four

In the outer office, I sit between Bria and Felix on fabric-covered arm chairs whose cushioning has long since been squashed to nothingness. Crystal Taylor took Zane into her office first and gave strict instructions to her secretary that the three of us shouldn't be allowed to talk. Under the secretary's watchful, bespectacled eye, none of us has uttered a word. But it doesn't mean we're not communicating. To her, that I'm holding hands with both my friends probably appears to be out of nerves, but she doesn't know what we are, what we can do.

It takes a few minutes for them to get the hang of it. I guide them as best I can, relying on my experiences sharing thoughts with Owen as a blueprint for three-way communication.

Do you think Mrs. Cole knows about the circle? Felix presses the thought into my mind and I relay it to Bria. I expect her to offer a response, but a quirked eyebrow implies she assumes I'll have an answer.

I take a breath. When I told Felix everything, it included where the crystal came from; still, telling Bria about last generation's circle of witches gives me pause. Felix squeezes my fingers.

When she was in high school, she was part of a circle—so was her husband, and my aunt, and Miss Tanner. I gulp. *And Millie.*

Bria squeezes my hand when my sadness seeps through our link, but her curiosity is too strong. *She* was *part of a circle? You mean she's—what? Not a witch anymore?*

I shift on the uncomfortable seat. Here's the sticky part—the part I don't know much about. *Jodi still does small spells— lighting candles and such. But I don't think she's part of a circle now. There was... a falling out in their circle about twenty years ago. All I know for sure is that Crystal Jamison's circle is stronger than her aunt's ever was. Abilities grow through generations.*

Bria's follow-up question is lost as Crystal Taylor's office door swings open. Zane struts out, grinning as he passes us.

"Go right back to class, Zane," the principal says, a hint of warning in her voice as he wanders out into the hallway. When she levels her gaze on us, her eyes are cold, distant. "You three, in my office."

She turns on her heel and for the first time since we sat down, Felix, Bria, and I release each other's hands. By the time we enter Crystal Taylor's office, she's already seated in the black leather chair behind the desk. I sit opposite her, once again between Felix and Bria.

"As I understand it," says Crystal Taylor, straightening a pile of papers, "you three were in an altercation with Zane Ross?"

Felix leans forward. "I don't know if 'altercation' is really the—"

"Answer yes or no, please." Crystal Taylor's eyes jerk upward but don't quite reach Felix's face. Her fingers move to the leather-covered cup containing a half-dozen pens and pencils.

Felix gives me side-eye before answering. "Yes...?"

Crystal Taylor's fingers graze the pencil erasers before straying to a stack of yellow sticky notes. "And, Felix, you were in Mrs. Hill's class, even though you're not scheduled with her this hour?"

"I had a pass—"

"Then you accused Zane of doing something to you, and when he denied it, you behaved aggressively toward him?"

In my old life, I've been on this side of the conversation too often to not know where things are going. Crystal Taylor's mind is already made up. She's just going through the formalities now.

Felix picks up on this too. Slouching in his chair, he crosses his arms over his chest. "This is ridiculous."

"Yes. It is." For the first time since we sat down, Crystal Taylor looks each of us in the eye. "It is completely ridiculous that three students should gang up on another for no apparent reason. Kristyl, I know you and Zane used to be friends—"

I snort.

"—but just because a friendship ends, you don't have the right to antagonize people."

Bria throws up her hands. "Since when is getting the breath squeezed out of you antagonistic? Zane could've killed us."

Crystal Taylor's eyebrows hitch upward. "You're saying Zane was strangling all three of you at the same time? How? He only has two hands."

Bria's mouth drops. "But... You *know* how. Magic."

Crystal Taylor sighs, shaking her head. "Flights of fancy aside, the only wrongdoing I see perpetrated here is by you three. My secretary is contacting your parents now. You're all suspended. You can return to school Friday."

"Suspended?" Felix asks, incredulous. "For what?"

"Is Zane suspended too?" Bria asks at the same time.

The principal merely stands, gesturing toward the door. "If your parents have questions, they can contact me. I'll be happy to answer their questions."

"But not ours?" Felix snaps.

I stand, tugging at his arm. This is a fight we're not going to win, and he's only going to make it worse by arguing. It's not until Bria pulls at his other arm that he stands, muttering darkly as the three of us exit the office. "Let's just go," I murmur. "It's not worth the fight."

"Oh, it's worth a fight, all right," Bria says. "But Mrs. Cole isn't the target."

***

Felix drops me off at home and my foot barely touches the front step before the door springs open, revealing Jodi. Her eyes are red-rimmed from crying, but it's not sadness that laces her features now, it's anger.

"You get in here right this instant," Jodi says through clenched teeth.

I hurry into the house, afraid to make her angrier by dawdling. I pull off my coat, laying it across the chest beside the closet, figuring she won't take kindly to me taking the time to hang it up right now. I peer into the living room. It's empty. "Where's Mom?"

"I made her go to work," Jodi says, walking into the living room. "No use both of us staying home. She called me right after the school called her. I told her I'd handle this." She nods toward the armchair and I sit in it. She remains standing, pacing in front of the couch. "So, you're suspended."

I wait for her to go on, but she doesn't. I take a breath. She knows about my magic—she has to. At the very least, she knows magic herself, and that's a good enough starting point. Without preamble, I launch into the story of what happened today, leaving nothing out—except, of course, exactly *how* the circle got its hands on the crystal in the first place. As I talk, Jodi stops pacing and sinks down to the couch. I watch for a reaction when I reveal the part about the psychics—about me being one—but Jodi doesn't seem surprised.

When I'm done talking, Jodi sits up straighter, squaring her shoulders. "I'll take care of this. I'm gonna call the school right now and set up an appointment to talk with Crystal and we'll get this straight." She stands, heading toward the dining room.

I stand, too. "What about..." I stop, afraid to reveal I don't know something key about my own life. But curiosity gets the better of me. "What about Mom?"

Jodi's shoulders drop. "I'll tell her. Don't worry. I'll... I'll make her understand. It'll be okay."

My stomach clenches. So my mom doesn't know about me—about what I am. Deep down, I hoped she did already—that she'd known about it for years and already accepted it. Not knowing how she'll react to this information makes my insides roil.

Jodi crosses the room, pulling me into her arms. "It's okay. She loves you. Knowing this won't change that." She holds me at arm's length, a watery smile on her lips. "I can cancel dinner tonight and—"

"Don't you dare," I say, squeezing her hands. "You go out and drink all the rum."

After a beat, she sighs. "I do love rum." She bites her lower lip. "I'll tell her." She stands, heading for the dining room. "But now, I've gotta make an appointment with your principal."

***

Mom brings a cake when she gets home from work. Her face is tight when she hugs me and wishes me a happy birthday—she's upset about my suspension. Jodi assured me she convinced Mom—without getting into specifics—that my punishment is unjust, but it's clear Mom's waiting to make that determination for herself when she gets all the details.

Despite the chilly temperatures outside, my cake is an ice cream cake, as it's been every year in my memory. I'm glad some things haven't changed.

As we dig into the cake at the dining room table, I share my birthday plans: Bria, Felix, West, and I are going to the movie theater two towns over, and probably out to eat as well. When my mom mentions a curfew, Jodi snorts. "What? It's not like she's gotta be up early for school tomorrow."

I bite the corners of my mouth to keep from smiling at the look on Mom's face.

We're just finishing our cake when there's a knock at the door. "Am I the first one here?" West asks as I let him in, followed almost immediately by, "Is that ice cream cake?"

West is in the middle of the slice Jodi cut for him when Bria arrives. Her fingers find the bare skin of my wrist and she presses a thought into my head: *I need to tell you something. It's important.*

She doesn't need to tell me her news isn't for adult ears. I don't bother suggesting we wait until Felix gets here—if she thought we could wait, she wouldn't bother sending me the thought now. "You wanted to see the greenhouse, didn't you?" It's the first private place that pops into my mind—besides my bedroom, and I'm sure Mom wouldn't be thrilled with me bringing West up there. "Jodi, would you mind if I showed it to them?"

West whines, indicating his remaining cake. I raise my eyebrows and he sighs, taking up his plate and following us down the hall.

Bria waits until the greenhouse door closes behind us before speaking. "What you told me earlier, about Jodi's old circle and Millie and Mrs. Cole and Miss Tanner being witches—it got me thinking."

West chokes on his cake. "What?"

Bria rolls her eyes, holding a hand up to his face. "Old news. Catch up."

He sputters, but Bria ignores him.

"The Taylors, the Tanners—they're from founding families. The Barnettes, of course. The Burkes."

I nod. It isn't news to me that the founding families had abilities.

"I did a little digging, though," Bria continues. "You know who else is from a founding family? Alec Crawford."

My eyebrows scrunch. "Who?"

"Dana Crawford's dad. They're descended from the Hills. And Millie? Her maiden name was Yates—*another* founding family." Bria's eyes are wide and round. "You see what this means, don't you?"

Goosebumps prickle my skin. "You think there's a connection between the deaths? That someone's targeting members of founding families?"

West swallows the last of his cake. "Those deaths were accidents. Krissa was there when Millie died, she can tell you."

I purse my lips. "I felt something. Before it happened, I felt something strange in the air. I've been thinking maybe it was just—you know—a premonition or something. But if you're right..."

"If she's right, what? You think there's a psychic killer out there targeting people from founding families?"

"Or a magic one."

My words hang in the air. It can't really be true, can it? These deaths could just be coincidences—after all, neither one exactly screams *murder*.

West breaks the silence. "Well. Guess it's a good thing I'm not from a founding family."

Bria smacks his chest. "*West.*"

"What? Neither are you."

"But Krissa is. And Felix."

I pull my cell from my back pocket and check the time. "Speaking of Felix, where is he? I thought we were supposed to leave here by quarter till?"

Bria huffs. "I knew I should've picked him up on my way over. West, you text him. I swear, if he's not ready when we get to his house, I'm gonna kill him."

We emerge from the greenhouse and I say goodbye to my mom and Jodi before heading out into the quickly darkening evening. The three of us pile into Bria's mom's Camry and she takes off. West sends a text but there's no response. Not that there's much time. In less than five minutes, Bria pulls up in front of Felix's house. "That's his car," she says, pointing. "He's still here. Surprise, surprise."

I suppress a smile. "Maybe he's got a legitimate reason for running late," I offer as we climb out of the car.

Bria grumbles under her breath as we approach the house. I catch West's eye and the two of us exchange a smile.

Bria is the first to the front door. She knocks and waits, but Felix doesn't appear. With a sigh, she presses the doorbell. Another beat passes and there's still no answer.

Something in the air changes. The lighthearted silliness of a minute ago is gone, replaced by a heaviness whose source I can't identify. There's something charged around us. I look at West to see if he senses it. His eyebrows are cinched together above his deep-set eyes.

"Something's wrong," he murmurs.

Bria knocks on the door again, and when that doesn't get a response, she starts pounding. "Felix!"

"Do you smell that?" A heady scent invades my nostrils, followed by a sharp, acrid sting. It's familiar, but it takes me a second to place it. There's one time I've smelled something similar—when I was in the past, leaving Crystal Taylor's house. "Fire," I say quietly as the realization dawns on me. "It's a fire. The house is on fire!"

"What?" Bria asks. She jiggles the doorknob, but the door doesn't open.

West moves to the nearest window and starts banging against it with his elbow. "Felix!"

West's elbow is making no impact on the window, so I scramble off the porch in search of something harder. Rocks the size of my fists put together line the flowerbed in front of the porch and I pry one up from the ground. "Try this!"

West leans over the railing and grabs the rock from my hand. From barely a foot away from the window, he launches it at the glass. I expect it to shatter, but the rock merely bounces off the pane causing West to jump backward to avoid it hitting him in the foot. "What the—?"

I struggle to swallow as a thrum of energy courses through me. I've felt this before. "It's a spell," I say. "It's a spell!" I repeat, louder, when it's clear West and Bria haven't heard me. It takes a second before they stop pounding on the house and look at me. "Someone's using magic. I felt the same thing at the coffee house when Millie died." I didn't recognize it for what it was at the time, but now the signature of a spell is unmistakable.

"Oh, my god," Bria murmurs. "Felix is from a founding family." She starts pounding against the door again.

"Stop!" I run up the porch stairs and tug on her arm, making her face me. "If this is magic, then it doesn't matter how much you pound. You've got to use your abilities. If it's a spell, maybe we can disrupt it."

It's all the convincing Bria needs. Her eyes close and her face slackens; she's visualizing something, trying to focus her psychic abilities. Behind me, West is doing the same thing. I allow my eyelids to drop, but instead of clearing my mind, I allow my fear, my panic, to fill me before pushing the emotions out, seeking the thread of energy connecting the magic to whoever's casting the spell. Felix's face dances in my mind's eye as I link to the connection.

The crash of breaking glass cuts through my concentration. The window West attempted to break earlier is shattered, like the pane had some sort of delayed reaction to the impact of the rock. I stare, dumbfounded, but West rushes forward, kicking out the remaining glass before climbing through. Moments later, the front door swings open.

Bria loses no time. She pushes past me, running into the house, yelling Felix's name.

"I'll check upstairs," West says.

I step over the threshold tentatively. Whatever presence was here only moments ago appears to have disappeared, but I don't want to take any chances. It was magic, all right—something deep and dark. But it was more than that. I just don't know how much more.

"He's here!" Bria's voice shrills from the back of the house. West's footsteps thunder down the stairs and he and I make it to the kitchen at the same time. My eyes take in the scene: It looks like the fire started on the stove. The tile backsplash is covered in a thick black layer of soot, and the ceiling is scorched. The blackened remains of a towel and an oven mitt smoke ominously on the counter. Felix is laid out on his back in the center of the kitchen floor, his eyes closed. Bria's face is close to his. When she looks at me, her eyes are shining. "He's not breathing."

My breath catches. Before I can do anything, Bria works to position his head the way we were taught in health class. She pinches his nose closed before leaning down and pressing her mouth over his. Felix's chest rises and falls as Bria forces air into his lungs.

Beside me, West dials his phone and presses it to his ear. "Yeah, I need an ambulance," he says. "My friend—there was a fire and he's not breathing."

Bria continues breathing for Felix and my vision blurs. It was magic that did this, and I think I know who was behind it. And things have gone far enough. I have to stop the circle before it can hurt anyone else.

Bria blows more air into Felix's mouth and when she pulls back, he sucks in a noisy breath. I drop to my knees beside Bria, who smooths strands of hair from Felix's forehead. I place my hand on his chest, reassured by the shallow rise and fall. But his eyes don't open and Bria releases a shallow sob.

"No—no, he's breathing now," West says, still speaking into the phone. "But he's unconscious..."

My skin prickles. I don't want to leave Felix's side, but I have to. I have to tell the circle I know what they're doing. I have to stop them. While Bria is distracted, I reach into her coat pocket and pull out the car keys. Without a word, I run out of the house and aim the car toward Fox's house.

Rage bubbles as I drive, every nerve ending in my skin burning. It's not enough for Zane to try to kill Felix once today. I can imagine Crystal and the others sitting around in the Holloways' basement, laughing as they plan another murder. Do they know I know? Do they know I'm coming for them?

Fox's driveway and the street in front of his house are filled with cars. Good. The circle hasn't left yet. Muffled laughter reaches my ears as I push open the front door. So they think what they've done is *funny*? I stalk across the floor toward the basement stairs. If they think fire is so funny, what I'm planning should be *hilarious*.

Before I hit the bottom step, I focus all the pent-up fear and rage into the center of the room. A fireball explodes in midair, hanging there like a sun. Screams and shouts of surprise rise up, but instead of causing the hot sphere to lessen, their fright pushes me to expand it. By the time my foot hits the basement floor, the glowing ball is at least five feet in diameter. The heat is incredible, but I feel it only peripherally—like sunshine through a window. Holding my hand out in front of me, I squeeze my fingers, sucking the room's oxygen into the fire.

Griffin is pressed against the floor, covering his head with his arms. Crystal, Lexie, and Bridget cower against the couch cushions. Fox scrambles over the chair he's in, backing as far away from the heat as possible. Zane gapes, frozen in his place on his usual armchair. His chest heaves, struggling to draw breath. I curl my fingers again, claiming more oxygen.

"You think it's funny?" I scream. "Flames burning your skin, black smoke filling your lungs? You think it's okay to leave someone gasping for air? Tell me now! Is it funny? Do you *like* it?"

Fox stumbles forward, heading for me while keeping as much distance between himself and the fireball as possible. His hand clutches his neck as he takes clumsy, labored steps. "Krissa, stop it!" he gasps, placing himself between me and the rest of the circle.

"Get back, Fox," I snap. "You're one of them. You made your choice. I'm not gonna feel guilty on account of a bunch of murderers."

"What are you talking about?" Lexie squeals.

Crystal and Bridget murmur a counter-spell from their spot on the couch and I feel a flickering in my control on the fireball in the center of the room. Any other day, the two of them working together coupled with the fact that they're anchored to the crystal would make them stronger than me. But today is not any other day. My fear and rage feed into my natural abilities and instead of the flame dimming, it expands, causing the girls to shriek and the guys to call out. Fox's eyes go wide and he takes my hands, pulling them until I'm looking at him.

"Krissa, talk to me! What is going on?"

"Don't pretend like you don't know!" I point at Zane. "He almost killed Felix tonight!"

"Wait—what?" Fox pulls my face around, forcing me to look at him again. "What happened to Felix?" His stormy eyes are wide, afraid—like they were earlier today during the incident with Zane. His confusion, shock, and fear hit me square in the heart. He has no idea what I'm talking about.

The rage within me fizzles, replaced by the image of Felix's still body on the floor of his charred kitchen. The fireball disappears in the blink of an eye, leaving the room feeling twenty degrees cooler in its absence. I fall to my knees, covering my face with my hands. "There was a fire at Felix's house, and it was magic—I felt it. Someone tried to kill him with magic."

Fox crouches beside me. "It wasn't us."

Tears prickle my eyes and I rub at them. "You expect me to believe you?"

He presses his hands to my cheeks. "Of course you can believe me. Krissa, you know me."

His emotions radiate off him, but I do my best to ignore them, too angry to allow myself to feel bad about what I just did. I push his hands away. "I thought I did, but I'm not so sure anymore. The crystal's changed you, Fox. It's changed you all."

Lexie snorts, her earlier loss of composure forgotten. "This again? Really?"

I press myself to standing, backing away from Fox. "Even if it wasn't you who attacked Felix, it doesn't change the fact that Zane tried to strangle me and Felix and Bria at school today. Fox, you *saw* it. And Bridget knocked Dana Crawford down a flight of stairs last week. Zane lit a guy's car on fire." I connect with each set of eyes, but, save Fox, no one looks the least bit abashed. "You can't even see it, can you? You're all just embracing the darkness? Well, you'd better pay attention to this: I'm going to stop you. No matter how strong or powerful you are, I'll find a way to stop you."

Chapter Twenty-Five

Instead of seeing a movie, Bria, West, and I spend the majority of the night at the hospital, where Felix is treated for smoke inhalation. His mother, who sits in the waiting room with us, is beside herself. She and Felix fought earlier about his suspension, and she'd been so angry she had to leave the house to cool off. She keeps murmuring things about how "if only she'd been there" this wouldn't have happened. The three of us try to comfort her as best we can, but all I can think is that if she'd been there, she may have been hurt, too.

Bria's mom is working and, even though it's against the rules, she lets us in to see Felix before shooing us home. His complexion is ashy and his eyes are red and irritated, but he smiles when he sees us. The three of us were split about whether or not to tell Felix our suspicions, but West and I outvoted Bria and we told him about the fire having been produced by a spell.

"Zane?" he asks, his voice hoarse.

I shake my head. "That was my first thought, too. But Fox honestly seemed to have no idea what I was talking about when I confronted them."

"They could've been lying."

West laughs. "I think they were too busy crapping themselves to lie."

I'm torn between smiling and vomiting at the memory of the fireball I conjured. I'm still not sure how far I was willing to go before Fox got me to stop. It's Fox's face that swims in my vision, giving me pause. He was terrified this afternoon when Zane was attacking us. He wanted to stop Zane then, but he couldn't. And when I accused the circle of hurting Felix, he looked legitimately bewildered. "I'm not saying I think they're entirely innocent. I'm just saying we can't take for granted it's them."

At this, we all fall silent. As much as I want to believe that the circle hasn't escalated its violence to the level of murder, I don't like the idea that there's an unknown entity out there.

That night, I barely sleep, and when I do, my dreams fill with flames. If it's not the circle doing it, then who? And why? Is Bria right—is the connection that the victims all have been from founding families? If so, does that make me a target? Or my mom or Jodi?

At five in the morning, I send a text to Seth asking about his progress finding a spell to disconnect the circle from the crystal. Even if they're not behind what's been happening, I still don't like the idea of them being anchored to the stone any longer than necessary. Whether or not they're behind the magic that's killing founding family members, there's still darkness in their spells, and I don't want to give it the chance to escalate any further.

I doze after that, slipping into a dreamless sleep. When I open my eyes, my room is filled with sunlight and I blink a few times before I can focus on the time on my phone. Eight seventeen. Panic flares—I'm late for school—before I remember I'm suspended.

The house is quiet—Mom and Jodi are already at work. Mom left a note on the refrigerator informing me about our meeting with Crystal Taylor after school.

Seth texts back around nine. *I've had no luck yet, but I may be on to something. Believe me, if this crystal is what you say it is, I want nothing more than to find this spell.*

No sooner do I read this text than another arrives: *When the time comes, I hope you're ready.*

His words resound in my brain. Am I ready? Whatever this spell is, it'll probably be complex and difficult. Will I be able to do it? I can do simple spells now without much effort, but since I've been spending time with the psychics, I've been mostly neglecting developing my magic. Last night's fireball was the biggest thing I've ever done, and I'm not sure I could repeat it on demand.

With nothing else on my agenda today, I spend the time practicing. Simple glamors come as easily as breathing now, but I haven't been able to repeat a complete makeover that sticks since the day I used the crystal. I'm still in my pajamas and use magic to change the look of my clothes. It sticks until I try conjuring a palm-sized fireball, so I try again.

When I run out of ideas to try, I scour the internet for suggestions, laughing at some of the more fanciful—turning into a crow—and trying others. I spend some time in the greenhouse, managing to make a basil plant double in size. I find some palm-sized quartz crystals in a box in the corner and practice charging a chunk of rose quartz with energy. Since Seth's ability to use magic is limited, maybe I can give him a stone to help focus his power.

I sit on the couch, reading different articles about storing energy in crystals and practicing charging the rose quartz with magic before discharging it again. By the time I hear a car door slam in the driveway, I feel accomplished, like I've learned more today than I have all year at school.

Mom pushes open the front door and a gust of cold air follows her in. My stomach clenches. By the time I got back from the hospital, she was in bed, but Jodi said she told her everything. I pressed her for Mom's reaction to learning her daughter's a psychic witch, but Jodi claimed she couldn't get a read. Now I watch Mom's face for a hint about what she's thinking. I could try to pick up on her emotions, but I'm afraid of what I might sense.

Mom uses a hand to straighten her ruffled hair, pausing to smile when she catches my eye. I relax, smiling back, until her expression flickers, her eyebrows pulling together. "Where'd you get that outfit?"

"Oh." After practicing, holding onto a glamor without thinking about it became easier. Right now, I'm in a pair of high-waisted, wide-leg cream pants and a green blouse with puffy sleeves—something I saw in one of Jodi's magazines on the coffee table. I exhale and the glamor falls, leaving me in a plain tee-shirt and jeans.

Mom gasps, her hand flying to her mouth and my muscles tense, my mind spinning. Why did I do that? Am I *trying* to freak her out? I open my mouth, ready to apologize, but mom lets out a short laugh. "Wow. That was pretty much the coolest thing I've ever seen."

I smile, too, but the expression slips almost instantly and I'm crying, my knees buckling. Before I fall, Mom is beside me, her arms around me, holding me up. She ushers me toward the couch and we both sink down onto it. She holds me close, rubbing my back with one hand and patting my hair with the other.

When my tears subside, she asks, "What's wrong, honey?"

I wipe my eyes. "I was afraid you'd think I'm a freak."

She puts her hands on my shoulders, holding me out so she can look at my face. "Oh, hon. Let's be honest. I always knew you were a freak." After a beat, she grins and I swat at her.

"Not cool, Mom." My eyes prickle again, but it's a laugh, not a sob, that rises in my throat.

She strokes my cheek, her face serious. "You're my daughter. There's nothing you could do or be that would make me love you any less." Her mouth twitches, like she's holding something back.

I scan her thoughts without making a conscious effort to do so, pulling back only when I brush against the thing that's keeping her silent. "What about Dad?"

Her eyes widen with surprise before she sighs, shaking her head. "Before he left, he told me you were different. Special. He didn't explain what that meant, but he told me to move you here, that Jodi would be a good influence."

My mind struggles to file this information. Did Dad tell her this in the other reality, too? I can't imagine he did—otherwise, why did we stay in Fraser? But what's different here that would've made him tell us to move? Does my father know what Jodi is— what I am? If so, how is that different from before? Except that now, Jodi still practices magic; in the other timeline, she didn't.

"That being said," Mom continues, "I think we need to lay some ground rules about you mind-reading me or whatever it is you do."

I bite my lower lip. "Yeah, sorry about that. Sometimes it just happens. I'll try not to."

She sighs. "Some moms worry about their kids doing drugs. I worry about mine scanning my thoughts."

We laugh and she pulls me into a hug. I lean into her, breathing in the scent of her shampoo—vanilla. I close my eyes, slipping my arms around her back and pulling her close. I love her so much. No matter what complications there are now from bringing the crystal back, they're all worth it just for this. I have my mom, a fact I'll never take for granted again. I've regretted going to the past for the crystal so many times since we did the spell, but this one moment eclipses all those others.

The front door opens and Mom and I separate. "I'm here!" Jodi calls. "Let's go or we'll be late."

On the way to the school, Jodi insists she should be the one to talk to Crystal Taylor. "I've known her the longest. I might be able to reason with her."

The parking lot is less than half-full when we arrive. Most students have already cleared out for the day, leaving teachers and students sticking around for tutoring or clubs. Jodi parks in one of the spots up front reserved for guests and we head for the main office.

Crystal Taylor is waiting for us. Her eyes narrow momentarily when she sees Jodi, but the expression passes quickly and she offers a warm smile, shaking hands with Mom and Jodi in turn. I only know Jodi's history with Crystal Taylor up until the night of the fire—the night Crystal Jamison and I went back in time. They were part of the same circle, but Jodi was against her friend's quest for more magic and refused to take part in the spell that ultimately caused the fire. A pang shoots through me as I sit down, realizing my relationship with my circle, with Crystal Jamison, is an echo of that past.

Crystal Taylor settles in her chair, her eyes on my mom. "I understand you have some questions about Kristyl's suspension."

"Yeah," Jodi says, drawing the principal's attention. "We were wondering exactly what she's suspended *for*."

"Aggressive behavior." She says it as if it should be obvious.

Jodi crosses her arms over her chest. "What *behavior*, exactly?"

The corners of Crystal Taylor's mouth downturn. "She and two friends were ganging up on another student. Luckily, I arrived before they could attack him."

Jodi doesn't disguise a snort. "Attack? From what I understand, it was Zane Ross doing the attacking."

The principal sighs. "You honestly believe their story? That Zane was choking all three of them at once? He wasn't even anywhere near them—"

"You can stop pretending," Jodi snaps. "I know you know. We *all* know."

"Jodi, please—"

"Please what? Ignore the fact that you've got a problem of a magical variety going on here? Look, I wasn't there. Maybe Krissa and her friends *did* do something to piss Zane off. Not that I believe that, but let's just go with that for argument's sake. Nothing—*nothing*—gives him the right to strangle people."

Crystal Taylor shakes her head. "Sometimes kids do stupid things. They don't always think."

"And that's an excuse? Tell me, Crystal—did you suspend Zane?"

Her eyes flicker down to the desktop. A confession. "I told him on no uncertain terms that misuse of magic like that won't be tolerated."

The injustice of the situation rankles and I can't keep quiet. "But you *are* tolerating it. You're punishing me and my friends when all we did was stop ourselves from getting killed!"

"Please, don't be dramatic. I highly doubt—"

"You weren't there. It was like a giant snake was squeezing the air out of my lungs. Zane wasn't going to stop."

Jodi leans forward. "You, of all people, know what that kind of power can do to your mind. You tore our circle apart—you burned down your house, for crying out loud!"

Crystal Taylor rolls her shoulders, her expression tightening. "I'm not interested in discussing the past. You came here to talk about your niece's suspension. We've talked. She and her friends can return to school on Friday." She stands, extending an arm toward the door. "If there's nothing else—"

"Like hell," Jodi growls, also rising. "We're not being dismissed here. Kristyl's suspension stands? Fine. Bullshit, but fine. But when she gets back, you'd better make sure certain students understand this building is, on no uncertain terms, a magic-free zone. If you don't—if anything happens to her—there will be hell to pay, Crystal. Bet on it." Jodi nods at Mom and me and we take her cue to leave.

Jodi seethes on the way to the car and Mom insists Jodi hand over the keys, that she's far too upset to drive. Jodi doesn't fight, and the whole way home, her anger radiates off her in waves. There's no doubt in my mind her threat was serious, and I can't help wondering what kind of hell she plans to unleash if Crystal Taylor can't meet her demands.

Chapter Twenty-Six

I'm in my room after dinner when Mom's voice drifts upstairs. "Krissa, there's someone at the door for you."

Before I get to the bottom stair, I know it's Fox standing on my front porch. I hesitate. What could he be doing here? Is this about last night? Does he have a message for me from the circle? I cross to the door and nod, a tacit invitation for Fox to enter the house. As Mom closes the door behind him, I incline my head toward the stairs. After a beat, she nods and I lead the way up to my room. I perch on the edge of my bed and Fox grabs the desk chair, setting it three feet in front of me.

"Hey," I say as he sits.

He exhales noisily, running both hands through his hair. "Krissa," he breathes, propping his elbows on his thighs.

I wait, but he doesn't continue. I press forward with my abilities just enough to get a sense of his emotions and am surprised when it's guilt and shame that rush to the forefront. Was he lying last night when he said he didn't know what happened to Felix? "Fox, what's going on?"

He covers his face with his hands for a beat before seeking my eyes. "You were right. I'm so sorry I didn't believe you before."

Panic flares. "About what? The circle? Fox, did they hurt Felix?"

His mouth twitches at the sound of Felix's name. "No. It's not about last night. I was telling the truth—none of us are behind the fire at his house. It's about everything—since the night we anchored to the crystal. You were right—the whole time. I just couldn't see it. I don't think I wanted to." He takes in a breath. "I want to apologize."

My skin prickles. "For what?"

The corners of his mouth quirk up. "Too many things. But specifically what happened the other day with Zane. He was hurting you and... I didn't do anything to help." He squeezes his eyes closed, the pang of guilt that courses through him spreading to me.

I force his emotions out. I don't want to feel what he's feeling. I don't want to feel sorry for him. I square my shoulders. "We handled it. I'm fine."

He squeezes closed his eyes. "I wanted to help you, and I need you to understand why I didn't. It's not because I thought Zane was right for what he was doing. I punched him in the face after school." He smiles grimly at this. "I just couldn't do anything to stop him. I don't have the power to—not on my own."

My ears perk up. "On your own?"

He nods. "Since we broke—" He presses his lips together in a tight line. "Since we fought—after it sank in what I said, what I did—I haven't used the crystal to do magic. Unless it's a spell I can do with my own abilities, I don't do it. And it's crazy—it's like my head is clearer, somehow. And now when I'm listening to the circle talk, I hear what I must've sounded like to you that day. When I punched Zane, you know what he did? He laughed. He couldn't understand why I was getting so worked up over you—how you weren't even a real witch and so you weren't worth my time."

Heat prickles my skin. I'm not sure how to respond to this. Is this how the whole circle is thinking? If so, maybe it's not such a stretch to imagine them stepping up their violence—even on people from founding families.

Fox reaches across the void separating us and takes up my hands. "I can't tell you how much I regret how I acted the day we fought. I've replayed it a million times in my head, and I can't even remember why I got so mad or why I said the things I did. All I can think is you were right and there's something wrong with the crystal. And I can't help that I'm anchored to it now, but I'm not using it—and it's not using me." He presses his lips together, squeezing my fingers. "Now, I understand if you don't want to give me a second chance. I understand if you've moved on. I've seen you with Felix—"

I sigh, cutting him off. "He's my *friend*, Fox. I'm not... We're not *together*."

The tension in his shoulders fades, relief spreading across his face. He scoots forward on his chair, closing the gap between us. Our knees are nearly touching. "Thank god," he breathes. He brings my hand to his mouth, brushing his lips against my knuckles. "Are we okay?"

He's not asking if I'm mad at him, if we can still be friends. I don't have to be psychic to know that. His question is deeper; he wants to know if we can go back to before—before he said those hateful things, before the crystal clouded his mind. Although he choked over the words earlier, it doesn't make our current status any less real: We're broken up. Two separate entities. No longer Kristyl-and-Fox, the unit we've been for years.

It's what I've wanted since I found myself in this reality—not to be tethered to Fox, to end things without hurting him. He says he'll understand if I've moved on, and I know he'll honor my decision if it's the path I choose.

I've given up the fantasy of being with Owen again. There's too much history—bad history—between us to think we can ever move past it completely. There was a moment, the day Millie died, when we were on the front porch that I thought there was a possibility, but Owen pulled back. Maybe we can be friends, but we'll never be more than that. But it's not a fear of being alone that concerns me: It's the fear of missing out on what I could have with Fox. Despite my best efforts, I can't pretend I don't have feelings for him. At first, I didn't understand why alternate-me would be with him, but I see it now. Fox is sweet, considerate, and supportive—and he wears his feelings for me on his sleeve. He loves me. The thought sends a pang through my core, but it's obviously the truth. He loves me enough to trust me, to give up addictive, powerful magic—enough to risk being shunned by his core group of friends for standing with me.

It would be easier to make a clean break—then I wouldn't have to pretend like I remember a relationship I've only recently been inserted into. But I'm increasingly realizing that *easier* doesn't translate to *better*.

Are we okay? A simple question without any simple answers.

I tug my hand from his lips, brushing my fingertips over his jaw line. "I don't know."

Fox's face falls. It clearly isn't the answer he was hoping for. I reach forward and slide my fingers through the hair above his ear. "I'm sorry, Fox. It's just—"

He shakes his head. "You don't have to explain. I hurt you. I get that. And I'm still connected with the crystal, so it's not like I can guarantee it won't happen again. I'll just have to prove it, again and again, every day until you believe it."

My heart lurches. Part of me is still mad about the hurtful things he said the day of the fight, still upset that he didn't do more to stop Zane from hurting me and my friends, but a larger part is just sad that things have to be so complicated. But he's right: So long as he's anchored to the crystal, I can't trust that it won't cloud his thoughts and emotions.

Fox stands, heading for the stairs. I follow, reaching him just before he starts down. I tug on his arm and he spins to face me. He waits for me to say something, but no words come. There's nothing I can say right now to lessen his disappointment. I can't tell him what he wants to hear. But I don't want him to leave without knowing that this isn't an easy decision for me. I wish he were psychic so I could share my swirling emotions with him, but that would make things too easy. On impulse, I push up on my tiptoes and press a quick kiss on his lips. When I sink back to my heels, his gray eyes cloud, but he isn't angry.

"Walk me out?"

I nod and Fox takes my hand. I hesitate as we start down the stairs, but he didn't misinterpret my kiss. His relief laps over me gently: He's glad I haven't written him off entirely, grateful for an opportunity to prove himself to me.

We pause at the front door. "I'll see you tomorrow?"

I pull a face. "Still suspended."

He presses his lips into a tight line. "It's such bullshit. Zane's the one—"

"I know." I squeeze his fingers and release his hand. "I'll see you Friday."

He nods, leaning forward and planting a soft kiss on my cheek.

"Bye, Fox," Mom calls when he opens the door. He gives a sheepish smile, waving, before ducking out into the night. Mom waits until the door closes before clearing her throat. "So, back with Fox, huh?"

Heat rises in my cheeks. It's not a ridiculous conclusion. "No. It's... complicated."

She raises an eyebrow. "Well, then. Let's expand the no-boyfriends-in-the-bedroom rule to a no-boyfriends-or-complicated-boy-relationships-in-the-bedroom rule, okay?" She winks before heading back into the living room.

I go back upstairs and grab the picture of Fox and me from the zoo off my dresser before lying on my bed. I trace our faces with my fingertip, trying to convince myself I made the right decision.

I must drift off, because when pounding assails my ears, I jolt, feeling groggy. I can't quite pry my eyes open. Where's the noise coming from? It sounds nearby, and it's growing nearer. Something like wood and anger. It's familiar, but I can't place it.

My body jostles and hands clamp down around my shoulders. My eyelids flutter open as fingernails dig into my flesh and shake me. "What did you do?"

I blink against the harsh artificial light from the overhead fixture. It's still night. It takes several moments before I focus on the face before me: Crystal Jamison's eyes are red-rimmed, her cheeks blotchy, her hair wild. I grab her wrists, trying to pry her off me. "What's going on?"

"Don't pretend like you don't know!" She releases me, shoving me back toward my pillow. She stands and begins pacing beside my bed, pointing an accusing finger. "She's dead, and you're behind it—I know you are!"

I sit up straight, all traces of grogginess gone. "Dead? Who's dead? What are you talking—"

"Don't pretend like you don't know!" Crystal screams, rounding on me, eyes wild. "This is revenge—revenge for something I didn't even *do*!"

My mom's head appears in the stairwell. "Hon, is everything

okay?"

Crystal's entire body tenses, her face going red. Despite this, I nod. "It's fine, Mom. I've got this. You can go back downstairs."

Mom's lips press together in a tight line, but after a beat she nods, descending.

I stand, crossing to Crystal. "Now, you wanna calm down and tell me what you're talking about before my mom calls the cops or something?"

She snorts. "Your mom. She's not even supposed to be here! Your mom is *supposed* to be dead!"

My chest constricts, pressing the air out. "You think I don't know that?"

Crystal's gaze wavers for an instant before burning into mine once more. "There was a fire, earlier tonight. Uncle David came home and there were fire trucks and ambulances outside the house. He said they told him the fire just wouldn't go out—no matter what they did..."

My stomach twists. "Oh, god..."

"Aunt Crystal—she's... she's..." Crystal sniffs, knees buckling. I wrap my arms around her and ease her down so she's sitting on my bed. "It's not supposed to be like this. I had her back and she was supposed to help me and teach me. But now she's gone." Two fat tears slide down her cheeks.

A pang courses through me. "I get it. I do. When we got back and my mom was alive, it was like a gift. It *is* a gift. And your time with your aunt was a gift." I rub her back, trying to comfort her. "You were able to meet her—to get to know her. I mean, that's something, right? You were never supposed to know her."

"Yes, I was," she snaps. "I made sure of it! She's supposed to be here now. Why do you get your mom when you didn't even want her back? You didn't do anything to *get* her back. But I wanted my aunt, I saw a way, and I took it. But it's *you* who has everything she wants—of course it is—"

I stare at her, processing her words. She can't mean what I think she does, can she? I shake my head, standing. "Crystal, you can't mean—"

"I *saved* her! I pulled her out of the fire and I saved her. And for what? Now she's gone!"

"You changed things? Crystal—you *changed* things? I thought you said it was just because we took the crystal. You never said your aunt was alive because you *pulled her out of the house!*"

"Why are you so upset?" she asks, standing. "You got what you wanted, didn't you? Your whole perfect family back together. Your mom's still alive, you're living here with Jodi. You have your new friends worshiping at your altar. So what, you aren't with Owen? Don't think I don't know Fox is still in love with you. I gave you this life—don't you forget it. Your mom's the one who deserved to die, not my aunt!"

I shake my head. "What have you done? We're not supposed to mess with time. We went back for the crystal, that's it. You weren't supposed to—"

"But I did! I saw a chance to save my aunt and I took it. Are you telling me that if you had the same opportunity, you wouldn't have done it? If we'd gone back to the day your mom died, you wouldn't have found a way to keep it from happening?"

I don't know how to respond. Would I have had the willpower to allow things to take their original course if I had the power to stop it? Part of me wants to say yes, I would have been strong enough not to interfere with the way things were supposed to happen. Then again, if that were entirely true, I wouldn't have agreed to go back in time in the first place, to acquire a crystal that was supposed to burn up in a fire in order to save Jodi's life.

"We can't change anything now," I say quietly. "What's done is done."

Crystal shakes her head. "No. I can fix it—I know I can."

I grab her shoulders and force her to look at me. "Some things can't be fixed. And even if they can, they *shouldn't.*" Her eyes dart downward and I position myself so I'm in her line of sight. "Do you understand me?"

She takes in a shaky breath, nodding almost imperceptibly.

"Good. Because there's a bigger problem we're facing. Dana's dad, Millie, Felix, your aunt—do you realize what they all have in common?"

She blinks, her expression blank.

"They're all descended from founding families. It can't be a coincidence—all these things happening so close together. And if I'm right, it means neither one of us is safe. We need to find out who's doing this."

She snorts. "Yesterday you were convinced the circle tried to kill Felix."

"And I'm willing to admit I was wrong. I think all these attacks are connected, and there's no way you or Lexie would hurt your aunt." I take in a breath. "Is there some kind of spell you can do to figure out if there's anyone in town practicing magic?"

She squints. "Not sure. Maybe."

"Will you look into it?"

After a beat, she nods.

I perch on the bed beside her. "We're on the same side now. We have to figure out who's doing this and stop them." Crystal's lower lip trembles and I slide my arm around her shoulders. "Is there anything I can do for you?"

She shakes her head. "No. I should... I should get home. My mom..." She squeezes her eyes closed.

"I understand. Look—call if you need anything. I know that we're not exactly... But I know what you're going through. So, if you need me, I'm here."

Crystal nods once before standing and heading for the stairs. She doesn't look back.

Chapter Twenty-Seven

Despite the fact I thought Crystal and I were on the same page about things when she left my house Wednesday night, she ignores me completely when I return to school on Friday. Surprisingly, I'm fine with this. Although I know in my head the best way to find whoever's behind the attacks is to work *with* the circle, my heart can't help feeling betrayed by her lie. All this time, I've been operating under the assumption that the change in our reality couldn't have been helped, it was simply the price to pay in order to bring the crystal back, to save Jodi's life. But things are different now that I know Crystal actively influenced the change. She pretended to be surprised when she told me her aunt was alive, but she wasn't. She *knew* Crystal Taylor didn't die in that fire and she lied to me. She might still be mad at me for something I had no hand in, but I'm equally as mad at her for something she *did* have a hand in.

Or at least, sometimes I am. But, as indignant and holier-than-thou I feel about her disregarding our promise not to affect anything while in the past, I can't pretend I haven't benefited from her choice. For some reason, the act of saving her aunt from that fire rippled out and saved my mother. And, if I'm being entirely honest, it saved me, too. In my reality, I spent four years in a hell of my own making, my abilities causing problems and making the people in my life avoid me—or worse, torment me. But alternate-me never went through that. Instead, having spent the last four years here in Clearwater, she was accepted and popular. *I* was accepted and popular. So, as mad as I'd like to be, I'm conflicted.

Also avoiding me at school is Owen. I'd write it off as being due to Fox hanging around, but he's late to school Friday, arriving about ten minutes into our shared second period class. I smile and wave as he moves up the aisle to his seat, but he averts his eyes immediately. I try not to be too disappointed, even though I was really hoping the two of us could be friends.

Crystal Taylor's funeral is Saturday. As I expected, the parking lot is nearly packed when we arrive. Most of the community seems to have turned up for the funeral. Mom and Jodi gravitate toward Shelly Tanner and Lexie's mom as soon as we walk in the building. I see Lexie almost immediately and my breath catches: She's wearing the exact outfit she wore to our principal's funeral in my other reality—a simple black dress with a chunky turquoise necklace. I almost go to her to hug her and offer words of comfort, but I stop short. She's not the same Lexie here. She dabs her eyes with a tissue and Bridget rests a hand on her shoulder. Crystal Jamison is nearby, standing between Griffin and Fox. Her eyes narrow when they land on me and I press my lips together, unsure how to read her.

Fingers graze my elbow and I jump, clutching my chest. I turn and Seth offers an apologetic smile.

"I said your name a couple times," he says quietly, nodding down the hall toward a less populated area.

"Sorry," I murmur, following. "Didn't expect to see you here."

He shrugs. "I met with your principal a few times—discussing volunteering at the school. She was kind to me, and I wanted to show my respect."

We stop beside a half-empty coat rack toward the far end of the hall. "Have you found something?"

He shakes his head. "Nothing concrete."

"Do you have a lead, at least?"

Seth shifts his weight from one foot to the other. "Maybe. But I need to get a better sense of exactly what kind of energy is in the stone."

I nod. "No problem. If you want, I could probably get Fox to come over and—"

"Actually, I was hoping to talk with Crystal. From what you've told me, she seems to be the most emotionally connected to it, and

I believe that will help."

"Okay. Well, you're on your own there. I don't know how she's feeling about me at the moment."

"That's fine. She seems comfortable around me. I think if I go over to offer my condolences I might be able to steal a few minutes with her."

People start moving toward the open door at the end of the hallway and Seth and I follow suit. Jodi and my mom are sitting toward the back and Seth and I settle down beside them.

During the service, emotions swirl so quickly through my mind that it's hard for me to follow what the funeral director is saying. Though she's sitting a few chairs away from me, being here reminds me of the time when my mother was gone. I'm still afraid that if I blink, she'll be gone again.

Halfway through the service, Crystal Jamison lets out a wail and hurries from the room. My heart twists; when I did this in our other reality, it was Crystal who followed me outside and tried to comfort me. I shift in my seat, prepared to be the one to comfort her, but Seth beats me to it. I watch him leave the room, unsure whether this is the right time for him to corner her with questions about the crystal. Minutes tick by and I keep expecting Seth to reenter the room, but by the time the service is over, he still hasn't returned. Mom and Jodi don't exit the room right away, instead, taking time to offer condolences. People begin milling around, and though the volume isn't extreme, it's enough to make me feel hemmed in. I need to get out of here. I could just go outside—it's unseasonably warm today, which might be Crystal and Lexie's doing—but what I really want is to leave this place. Unfortunately, Jodi and my mom know too many people here and appear to be in no hurry to take off.

Without looking, I turn and start for the door. I make it no more than a few steps before colliding with someone. "I'm sorry," I say, keeping my eyes down. But the hands of the person I collided with remain on my upper arms and I look up to see who they belong to. My breath catches when I find myself looking into Owen's clear blue eyes.

"I'm sorry," he says quickly, releasing me. "Do you think...

Could we talk for a minute? Alone?"

My skin prickles. "Alone?"

He nods. "It's... It's kind of important."

After a moment's hesitation, I agree. Owen reaches down and grabs my hand. Gasping, I allow him to pull me out of the room, past knots of tearful people, and down an empty hallway at the other side of the funeral home.

By the time we come to a stop, his grip on my hand is painful. I extricate it, rubbing it against my upper thigh. "Okay, what's going on? Yesterday you ignore me, now you're desperate to talk?"

He takes a step toward me, invading my space, his eyes clasped on mine. "What did you do to me?"

I lean back. "What? Nothing."

"Yes, you did." He presses a hand to his eyes. "I can't explain it, but ever since we were at your house... I remember things." He runs the hand through his hair, letting it come to a rest on the back of his neck. "I remember *us*."

My eyebrows draw together. "What about us? What? From back in seventh grade?"

He shakes his head and points. "No. I remember... Seeing *Planet of the Apes* at the bookstore, and Tucker coming after you. I remember... kissing you on your front porch. We didn't know each other in seventh grade. You moved here a month ago." He squints, his eyes flitting over my face. "I'm not crazy—I knew it. You remember those things, too, don't you?"

My jaw drops and I gape. "How do you...?"

He shrugs, the corners of his mouth twitching. "At first... At first it was like remembering pieces of a dream, you know? All disconnected—nothing was making sense. It started on your porch. I... I could feel what it was like kissing you."

My heartbeat increases, thudding in my veins. "Owen..."

"And then more things started popping into my head—like helping Mrs. Bates out in the courtyard—or dancing together at the harvest dance." He releases a noisy breath. "Being psychic. And since I remembered that—remembered having a vision about Felix, remembered sitting at your dining room table while Jodi explained everything to us—it's like someone flipped on switch in

my head. On your birthday, I had this bad feeling about Felix—
nothing specific—but then I find out he was in a fire. How did I
sense that, Krissa? How do I know any of this?"

I open my mouth, but no words come out. I don't know how to
answer him.

"And why?" he continues. "*Why* did it happen two different
ways?" He takes up my hands, squeezing them with gentle
pressure.

I press my lips together. I have to tell him, don't I? If he's
remembering the other timeline, I have to tell him why things are
different. I already told Felix, after all, and my reason for sharing
with him was so much less pressing than the reason Owen wants
to know. But as I open my mouth to begin explaining, my palms
begin to tingle and I realize why Owen took my hands to begin
with. I pull away from him, glaring. "What the hell, Owen! You
can't just reach into my head like that!"

"You went back in time?" He murmurs it so quietly I'm not sure
he realizes he said it out loud. He takes in a breath. "You weren't
even gonna tell me."

"Of course I wasn't," I snap.

"But I deserved to know—"

"If I told you right after it happened, you wouldn't've listened to
me. Or worse, if you did, you would've thought I was insane!" I
pause, waiting for him to disagree, but he doesn't.

After a second, he averts his eyes. "You're right. But I know
now—and that's what's important." He takes a step toward me,
cupping the side of my face with his hand. He swoops down so
quickly I don't have time to do anything but react when his lips
touch mine. It's what I've longed for since before the time-travel
spell, and for a moment, I kiss back. But then warning bells and
sirens sound in my head—I *can't* kiss him, not now. I have to
figure out what's happening, and I can't let my desire to kiss him
get in the way. Placing my hands on his chest, I push him away.
His blue eyes are confused. "What's wrong?"

"Owen, stop. We have to figure this out."

His lips curl in a smile. "Figure what out? I feel like everything's
finally making sense. Now that I remember, we can be together."

He tucks a loose strand of hair behind my ear. "I want this, Krissa. Don't you?"

My hands go to the sides of his face and I fight the urge to pull his lips to mine. I *do* want this. "What if it goes away?" Just saying the words makes my stomach clench. "I have no idea why you remember these things. What if you start forgetting them and you go back to the Owen you were a week ago? What if you wake up tomorrow and go back to hating me? I couldn't handle that." My eyes fill and when I blink, two tears stream down my cheeks.

"Hey." Owen catches the droplets with his fingers, wiping them away. "That won't happen. Even if I forget these memories, I won't go back to hating you. Remember at the coffee shop? We were getting along just fine—and that was before I started remembering this other life. I could never get over you, Krissa, and now I know why. We're supposed to be together." He leans in, pressing his lips to mine. As I kiss him back, my heart swells. He's right. *We're* right. But if that's true, why is my stomach so unsettled?

I push him back gently, breaking our kiss. "Owen, stop. We can't—not right now."

He nods, glancing at the surrounding hallway. "Yeah, I guess a funeral's not really the right atmosphere."

I shake my head. "It's not that. It's... complicated."

His expression clouds and his eyebrows scrunch. "It's Fox, isn't it? But..." He squints like he's trying hard to recall something. "You two aren't together, right? You... were... but you broke up?"

I grip his shoulders, peering into his eyes. "That happened last week. Don't you remember?"

He blinks heavily, the corners of his mouth quirking upward. "Yeah. Yeah, of course I remember."

But I can tell he's not convinced. I slide my fingers to his cheeks and use the contact point to push into his thoughts. His mind is a confused jumble and I reel back from it. "Owen—what's happening to you?"

A muscle in his jaw jumps and he can't quite force a smile. "Since that day on your porch... Since I started remembering the other life... It's like there's not enough room in my head for both. The more I can remember from the other reality, the more this one slips away."

I step backward, dropping my hands. "You're forgetting your life?"

He shakes his head, reaching for me. "No, Krissa—I'm *remembering* it."

I turn, running my hand through my hair. How is this happening? This isn't my Owen, yet now, somehow, he's remembering a life he didn't live. I *wanted* this, I wanted him to be the person I was falling for. Is it possible I'm somehow doing this *to* him? Am I casting a spell or using my psychic ability without knowing it? I take stock of my powers, my energy, but I can't identify anything within me that could be causing this. But if it's not me, what could be doing it?

Owen's hand grazes my shoulder. "Krissa. If I didn't know any better, I'd think you weren't exactly happy about this."

I bite my lower lip, turning but not meeting his gaze. How can I explain that I *am* happy about this—but I'm also terrified because I don't know what's causing it, or how long it will last? "Maybe we should take things slow. Make sure you don't have any... complications."

His eyes darken. "Take it slow? No. That's what I was doing before and then suddenly I'm living a different life. Look, I know how I feel about you, and I know how you feel about me. I don't see why we can't just pick up where we left off."

My heart twists. There's nothing I want more than that, but still there's hesitation within me. The memories flooding Owen's mind are turning him into the guy I knew a month ago, but I'm not the same girl I was then. The last few weeks have changed me, but have they changed my heart, too? When Fox came to my house the other night, I had the opportunity to make a clean break, but I didn't take it. In the days immediately following the time-travel spell, I would have jumped at the chance to sever ties with Fox; that I didn't when he gave me the option speaks volumes.

Owen stiffens, his shoulders drawing backward. "Oh. I see."

Panic flares. Has he been scanning my thoughts? "It's not what you think."

He snorts. "It's not what I think? When I kissed you on Jodi's porch, you remember the last thing I said to you?"

"Owen—"

"I told you not to change your mind. And you smiled and said 'no way,' like it wasn't even a possibility. But here we are a couple weeks later—"

"A couple weeks?" I laugh. "A couple weeks? Owen, this is an entirely different reality! One where you, until a few days ago, didn't want anything to do with me. So stop acting like I betrayed you or something, because I haven't."

"Then why does it feel like you have?"

I open my mouth to respond, but Owen doesn't give me the chance. He pivots and stalks down the hallway, back to the main corridor. I take off after him but slow as the buzzing of voices grows louder. What could I say? I don't even know how to explain my swirling emotions to myself. I want to be with him, but I can't pretend I haven't developed feelings for Fox—I'm just not sure what those feelings mean. I need to sort everything out before I can make a decision. I don't want to hurt either of them.

By the time I make it to the main hall, Owen has disappeared into the crowd. In addition to the people milling about the main hallway, there are several groups heading toward their cars. An official-looking man in a black suit is directing people inside; the procession must be about to begin. I scan the crowd for my mom and Jodi but don't see either of them. I pull my phone from my back pocket. There's a text from my mom from a minute ago saying she and Jodi are at the car and will be leaving in five minutes, with or without me.

Just outside the main door stands Owen, distractedly listening as one of his track buddies chats at him. I start for him, but before I've taken more than a couple of steps, someone hooks me by my elbow, urging me to a stop. Fox's stormy eyes fix on me when I turn.

"Hey, there you are. I was wondering if you might wanna go grab a bite." The corner of his mouth upturns in a boyish half-smile.

Owen's gaze prickles the back of my neck and I can't help turning.

Fox looks, too. "Why's Owen staring at you like that?"

"Like what?" I ask, too quickly.

His expression clouds as he presses his lips into a tight line. "Like he's jealous." He blows out a breath. "That's why you didn't want to get back together, isn't it?"

Heat floods my cheeks, even though his suspicion isn't correct. I want to tell him he's wrong, but my groping mind can't come up with a plausible reason for Owen to look so upset right now. I can't exactly tell Fox the truth.

Fox takes a step back, holding his hands up. "I just don't get why you didn't tell me the other night. I gave you the out, but you didn't take it. What, are you just stringing me along in case things don't work out with him?"

"*No.*" I take a step toward him, reaching out my hand. "It's not what you think. What I said the other night—it's true. I don't know what I want or how I'm feeling about any of this. But I don't want to hurt you. Even if we're not together, I want us to be—"

"*Don't* tell me you want to be friends." He closes his eyes, taking in a deep breath and releasing it before opening them again. "After what we had, I can't be *just* your friend."

I open my mouth to say something, but nothing comes. After a beat, Fox turns, heading off into the parking lot. I start to follow when my cell vibrates. It's my mom again, informing me the engine is running. Cursing, I head into the parking lot.

I haven't gone far when someone catches my eye. Crystal Jamison stands around the side of the building, propped up against the sandy bricks, looking a little disoriented. Seth is nowhere in sight. I start toward her, hesitating only briefly when I consider what her reaction to me might be.

"Crystal?" I ask as I approach.

Her movements are slow, like she's in water. Her mouth twitches when her eyes land on me. "Krissa. Hey."

I tense. I expected her to be a little more hostile toward me, based on the look she gave me earlier. Maybe grief has taken away her venom. "You okay? You seem a little out of it."

She presses her lips together, a crease forming between her eyebrows. "I just... Need a minute."

I nod. There's something off about her, but I can't place what. I consider reaching out with my abilities to scan her, but out of the corner of my eye, I see Bridget approaching. Not wanting to deal with her, I jog toward my mom's car. Crystal will be fine—Bridget will get her.

Is this another side effect of the crystal or something else entirely? As I pull open the car door and slide into my seat, I make a mental note to check with Seth to see if she was weird when they were talking.

Chapter Twenty-Eight

When we finally arrive home, Felix's car is parked out front. My heart swells and my eyes prickle. I jump out of my mom's Cruze and run to him, almost knocking him over with the force of my hug.

He pats my back a few times. "I had a feeling you'd be happy to see me."

I pull away, studying his face. "I really, really am. I need to talk."

Once Felix and I are settled in my bedroom, I explain what happened with Owen at the funeral. By the time I'm done, Felix is rubbing his forehead with his thumb and forefingers.

"Is it because he's psychic?" he asks after a beat.

"Is what because he's psychic?"

He waves his hand in the air, wiggling his fingers. "You know, this whole mind-meld thing you two have going on. You guys had a pretty intense history. Couple that with psychic stuff and, bam!" He claps his hands for emphasis.

I shrug. "Maybe?"

"Does he know about the rest of us?"

"No. You guys weren't psychic in the other timeline—or at least you didn't know you were."

Felix purses his lips. "You know what I'm gonna say, don't you?"

I sigh. "You want to tell him."

"He deserves to know. He should be a part of our group—learn to use his abilities. And before you start about how tense and awkward that'll be, let me remind you of your first meeting with us." He reaches forward, giving my hand a brief squeeze. "Maybe he won't want to—if things are really that bad between the two of you. But maybe he'll be able to put it aside—and let's face it, that wouldn't be a bad thing."

He's right, and I know he is. Before I can do more than nod in agreement, my phone buzzes. "It's Seth," I say as I pick it up. "He wants all the psychics to meet at his apartment." My heartbeat kicks up a notch as I read the next part. "He thinks he knows how to separate the circle from the crystal."

Felix rubs his hands together, grinning. "Awesome. Hey—I'll drop you by there."

I squint. "Drop me? You're coming too, right?"

He stands, heading toward the stairs. "He said *all* of us."

My stomach sinks as I follow. "You really think now's the time to tell Owen?"

"No time like the present. I mean, who knows when someone's gonna travel back in time and mess everything up?"

***

Felix drops me off on Main and I circle around the bookstore. There's a metal staircase leading up to a plain white door. Seth pokes his head out as soon as my foot touches the bottom step, and I take them two at a time until I'm in his apartment.

The space is small but open. A small kitchen is directly to the left and straight ahead is a bank of windows overlooking Main Street. Two folding chairs and a rickety card table covered in haphazard stacks of paper are shoved against the right wall, but that's all there is in the way of furniture. Several paper bags piled in the far left corner is the room's only other adornment.

Seth throws an apologetic smile over his shoulder as we walk into the space. "Sorry for the mess. I don't exactly entertain often." He makes a sweeping motion toward the card table and I settle across from him.

"How'd the talk with Crystal go? Good, I'm guessing, since you want to see us all."

He presses his lips into a tight line. "The talk was... interesting. It confirmed some suspicions."

"What suspicions?" I glance around the room. "Do you wanna wait until everyone else is here before—"

He shakes his head. "I think it's best to tell you before they're here. I fear the others might find this a bit disconcerting."

I lean forward, my stomach twisting. "Okay. Tell me."

He takes in a deep breath. "After you told me descendants of the founding families might be the target for the attacks we've been seeing, it put me to thinking."

I hold a hand out toward him. "Wait—this is about the attacks? Not that that's a bad thing, I just thought maybe this was about the crystal?"

He nods grimly. "I believe it is."

My mind starts racing, but I ignore the thoughts chasing themselves around. There's no point in me theorizing before Seth says his piece.

He shifts a couple stacks of paper before picking up a smoky quartz crystal. "You're aware that stones are good for channeling energy."

I nod. "Of course. Channeling, directing—"

"Storing."

"Yeah. Storing." I've practiced charging stones before, so this isn't news to me.

Seth's fingers traced he edges of the smoky quartz he holds. "Well, what if you could store a person's energy? Their magic?"

My skin prickles. "Why would you want to do that?"

He shrugs. "Any number of reasons, I imagine, but the one that makes most sense here would be to use it. You told me that the crystal your friends anchored themselves to was particularly powerful, didn't you? Where do you think the energy comes from?"

"I don't know—nature?"

"Sure. Nature." His eyes lock on mine. "Or there's the alternative."

I stare at him, trying to understand his meaning. "Are you saying that the crystal could be filled with energy from *people*?"

"Perhaps. You said you felt something when you interacted with it, didn't you? Typically, something that is purely from nature wouldn't fill you with the kind of dread you described."

I cycle through the meaning of Seth's words. The energy in the crystal isn't from nature; instead, it's energy stored from people—but what people? My stomach twists. "Wait—are you saying what I think you're saying?"

Seth's fingers curl around the quartz. "Think about it. Think about the targets. Millie and your principal were witches. Felix is psychic. If I were to guess, I would say that the first victim also had abilities of some kind."

I clutch my stomach, curling forward as I sort through this information. I assumed the link between the victims was that they descended from founding families, but what if it's both more and less than that? Were they all targeted because they have abilities of some kind? "So you think someone's killing these people and storing their powers in the crystal? Who's behind it? I mean, the crystal can't be doing it itself, right? So someone, some *person*, has to be doing it?"

Seth averts his eyes. "It's possible that something more than abilities was stored. If a person's essence—a soul—were within, it could, perhaps, influence those around it. Especially if those around it were tethered to it."

My stomach lurches with a wave of nausea. I grab onto the sides of the table. "You think there's someone's consciousness trapped in the crystal and it's killing people to get more energy? And you think... the circle..."

He reaches toward me. "If I'm correct, they probably aren't even aware they're doing it."

My mind reels and my breath comes in shallow gasps. Is it possible that the circle has really been behind the attacks—the *deaths*? Fox insisted they weren't, but if Seth's right, they could be completely unaware. I was right—there *is* something dark and evil within the crystal. Could it be forcing the circle to do dark and evil things on its behalf?

If what Seth's saying is true, it's not the circle's fault at all—it's mine. If it hadn't been for me, they never would have located the crystal. They needed a psychic to access time. But I *had* to help them. If I hadn't, the curse afflicting Jodi would have killed her.

And my mom would still be dead. Even knowing what I know now, if I could go back and change my decision, I'm not sure I would. And it's that fact that hurts most of all.

I push aside my swirling emotions. I press my hands to my face and take in a breath before fixing my gaze on Seth. "Okay, so, this isn't all, right? Otherwise, why would you want all the psychics?" I square my shoulders. "You figured out how to do it, didn't you? How to break the anchoring spell?"

The corners of his mouth quirk upward. "I think I may have."

Chapter Twenty-Nine

While we wait for everyone to arrive, Seth and I begin preparing for the spell. The paper bags in the corner are mostly from Jodi's shop, and Seth directs me where to place candles and stones. As he fills a stainless steel bowl with different herbs, I use several boxes of sea salt to outline a circle in the middle of the floor.

Bria and West arrive and watch our progress with arched eyebrows. Once Seth is done giving me orders, I can't keep myself from glancing toward the door every few seconds, both looking forward to and dreading Felix's arrival.

When the door finally opens, my breath catches. Following Felix into the apartment is Owen, his eyes downcast.

Bria glances at me. "Wait—what?"

Seth turns his attention from the bowl of herbs, his brow furrowed. "Felix?"

Felix's eyes flick to me momentarily. "Long story short? Owen recently discovered he's also a psychic. And since Seth wanted all of us..." He shrugs.

Owen lifts his head, offering a smile and nod to Seth, Bria, and West in turn. When I think he's going to ignore me completely, he surprises me by crossing to my side. "Felix explained about the crystal. If it's really affecting them like you think..." He closes his eyes momentarily. "I know she's not my friend, but I want to help her."

West and Bria exchanged confused glances, but I understand: Lexie. They were best friends in the other reality, and since Owen remembers it now, he remembers that, too.

Seth clears his throat. "Since we're all here, we can begin." He scoots to a spot just inside the edge of the salt circle and spreads his arms wide, inviting us to do the same.

I settle down on the floor across from him and he spreads out a handful scanned pages from handwritten books and printouts from websites.

"This is all the information I could find about anchoring ceremonies and how to break an anchoring spell. Now, I can lead you through it, but I'm afraid I won't be much help. Krissa, you will have to take control of the magic. You're the strong one, and there's only a little I can add to the process."

Bria raises her hand to half-mast. "I'm hearing a lot of talk about *spells* and *magic*. Where do we come in?"

Seth nods like he expected this question. "At the funeral today, I spoke with Crystal Jamison." He bites his lower lip. "Perhaps *hypnotized* is a more accurate description. What I learned is that while it is a spell that bound them to the stone, because of the unique quality of the energy contained inside it, a psychic link has also been forged."

Hypnotized. That explains why Crystal seemed off when I saw her in the parking lot.

"Because of this," he continues, "it necessitates magical and psychic ability to sever the tie."

"But if Krissa's both, why do you need us?" West asks.

"She needs her magic to connect with the crystal, but it's psychic ability that will combat the anchoring spell. If she does it alone, she may exhaust herself before it's done. But if she can draw from the four of you, she should be able to accomplish the task." He surveys the group but is met with only blank stares. With a sigh, he continues. "If you're all focused on the same goal, putting your energy toward it, you can accomplish more together than one of you could do alone."

"So, we're linking together?" Bria asks.

"Informally," Seth says. "There are certain spells—binding spells—that can link you formally, so that members can draw on each other's abilities at will. If a binding spell includes psychics, then thoughts and emotions can be passed with little effort. But there's no need to perform a binding spell today. Your united focus will suffice. Any more questions?"

"Just one," Owen says. When all eyes flick on him, he offers a small smile. "I know I'm the new guy here, so maybe you've already talked about this, but... what do we do once the circle's not anchored to the crystal anymore? I mean, what's to keep them from just doing it again? Are we gonna destroy it somehow? Or..." He shrugs.

"Discharge the energy?" I suggest. "I mean, once they're not connected to it anymore, we can just discharge the energy, right?"

A muscle in Seth's jaw jumps. "Yes. Once the circle's no longer anchored, we'll remove the energy from it."

"Okay. Let's do it." I take in a breath and twist my father's ring around on my finger. "It's not—it's not going to hurt them, is it?"

Seth leans forward, catching my gaze. "It's not their magic to begin with. And whatever's inside that crystal is making them do things they wouldn't ordinarily do. Being anchored to it is what's hurting them."

It's not lost on me that he didn't exactly answer my question. A flutter of unease builds in my stomach, but I tamp it down. Seth's right: Being anchored to the crystal is the real danger. "Let's do it."

All at once, the candles around the circle spring to life, causing Owen and West to jump. Felix's mouth twitches as he tries to conceal a smile. Bria rolls her eyes, mouthing, *Boys*. I offer a smile, even though I was startled by the candles as well. I didn't think Seth could light so many at once like that.

Seth waits until everyone stills before moving to the next phase. He holds his hands out toward the bowl, nodding at me so I do the same. He murmurs an incantation under his breath, and after a few times through, I start chanting with him. A few times more and I'm chanting on my own. Power wells inside me and I allow it to fill me up. My palms tingle, and when I focus on that spot, a jolt of energy leaves me, lighting the herbs in the bowl on fire. Seth smiles, nodding encouragingly.

"Now, locate the crystal. Seek out its energy."

I press my lips together, unsure how to begin doing that. An echo builds in my head as Felix sends me a thought. *Astral projection*. It's something he mentioned at my first psychic training session, but I've never tried sending my spirit out somewhere. Before I can tell him I don't know how, the knowledge fills my head. Felix gives me his experience and it's like my own. I understand the process, and I know to expect a disconcerting separating feeling when my spirit leaves my body, so I'm not scared when it happens. Suddenly, I'm looking down on the scene—the six of us sitting around the salt circle in the center of Seth's apartment. But I can't waste time marveling—I need to find the crystal.

I know the feel of it, and I search for that feeling. It's a simple shift of attention—like looking for a pair of sunglasses in a cluttered pile. But instead of knowing the look and shape of it, I know the sensation of it.

And suddenly, it's in front of me. I stand in an unfamiliar bedroom, and although the crystal is hidden at the bottom of a wooden chest, I know it's there.

Seth's voice reaches me, as if from a great distance. "Connect with it."

I stretch my hand forward, toward where I know the crystal lays. The heavy wood of the chest doesn't impede the motion and my fingertips slide through it. For a moment, I hesitate. How is this possible? The answer inserts itself into the corner of my mind—Bria's thoughts: As an astral projection, I'm just energy. If I were bilocating—taking form in two places at once—then I could interact with the things around me.

Seth's voice echoes again. "Connect with it."

My hand is still halfway through the wood of the chest. I press forward until my fingers slip into the center of the quartz.

And I'm back in Seth's apartment, in my body once more. But now I'm linked to the crystal—a fine, shimmering thread connecting it to me.

"Find the circle," Seth murmurs, his voice louder than before. "Use the psychics."

Their energy joins with mine effortlessly and together we travel along the connective thread, back to the crystal. Now I sense six silver cords extending out from it. These are the links anchoring the circle's members to the stone. Instead of being equal in size, some are thicker than others. I choose the thickest of the lot.

Seth begins chanting again and I allow the phrase to repeat before joining him. Each time I say the words, a thrum of energy emanates from my core, shooting out like a shock wave toward the thick cord. Each time I say the words, the link weakens.

It's working. We're really going to do it. We're going to separate the circle from the influence of the crystal. No one else will die.

A wind rips through Seth's living room, blowing my hair back, catching my shirt. But when I look around, the candles' flames are unaffected. I continue chanting. The first cord is nearly severed now.

The wind swirls around me again, this time bringing with it a searing agony in my stomach. I fall backward, twitching on the floor, clutching my middle.

When I'm aware of my surroundings again, Owen is crouched over me, his blue eyes wide and terrified. His hands on my shoulders, he eases me to sitting. "Krissa, are you okay?

Seth's eyes blaze when he looks at me. "What happened? You were so close—"

"I—I don't know." I take in a deep breath. All traces of the pain have vanished. "Something was wrong—like, bad wrong. Couldn't you feel it?"

Bria and West shake their heads and Felix frowns.

Seth crosses his arms over his chest. "How do you know it's not the crystal, protecting itself? Did you think of that?"

I press my lips together. The thought hadn't crossed my mind—in the moment, nothing did, just the pain. But the crystal isn't sentient enough to do something like that, is it? Or maybe I'm not giving the abilities trapped within enough credit. If the power within the crystal is aware enough to cause those anchored to it to provide it with more energy, then why couldn't it work to keep me from doing what needs to be done to cut off its supply chain?

"We have to continue," Seth says, his posture relaxing. "We were so close before—if you just go a little further, you can break the anchor and your friends will be free."

I exchange glances with Felix. The look he gives me echoes what I'm thinking. Seth is right. We can't stop now, not when we're so close. If I don't do this, someone else could die. I cup the sides of Owen's face and nod. He takes my meaning and settles back in his spot from before. I take a breath when my phone rings, startling me.

Seth curses and I offer an apologetic smile. I pull the phone from my back pocket, ready to put it on silent, but when I see Fox's name, I can't dismiss the call. After how things left off between us at the funeral, he must have a good reason for calling. Ignoring Seth's impatient glare, I accept the call, stand, and exit the circle.

"Hey," I say when the call connects. "Fox, I—"

"Krissa—it's... it's happening again, I think." Fox's voice holds and edge of panic that puts me on alert.

"What's happening? Fox? Where are you?"

"It's Zane—oh, god—we were just standing here and then he fell down—" Sirens wail in the background.

Icy dread fills my core. "Fox, slow down. What's going on with Zane?"

"It's just like you said," he continues, and I'm sure he's not really hearing what I'm saying. "I felt it—I *felt* the magic. One minute he was standing here, and the next second he was on the ground, shaking and I tried—I tried everything I could—"

The sirens' volume increases, and it takes a moment for me to realize the sound isn't coming only from the phone. "Fox," I say, trying to keep my tone even. "Where are you right now?"

"I'm on Main—near Jodi's shop. The ambulance is here now..."

I rush to the bank of windows and survey the street below. An ambulance is parked one store down from Jodi's, and two paramedics are crouched beside a crumpled form on the sidewalk. Zane. Fox stands off to the side, phone pressed to his ear.

"Oh, god. I don't know... Krissa, I think it's bad—"

I turn to Seth, eyes wide. This can't be a coincidence, Zane collapsing right when I'm about to sever a link to the crystal. I want to leave the apartment right now, to run down to Fox and wrap him in my arms—but I want to know what's happening first.

"It'll be okay, Fox," I say, trying to keep my voice calm. "Zane's gonna be fine."

"They're taking him to the hospital. I'm gonna go with him."

Muffled voices filter through the phone. They're urgent but not unkind.

"I've gotta hang up. Krissa, I..."

"I'm coming, Fox, okay? I'm coming."

The call ends and I shove the phone back into my pocket before stalking toward Seth. "You *said* it wouldn't hurt them! The ambulance outside tells a different story."

Seth avoids my eyes. "I was afraid of this."

Heat floods my body. "What? Afraid of *what*, Seth?"

He steps backward, eyes still downcast. "Since the circle anchored itself, has he been using magic very often?"

I nod. "Yeah—all the time, actually. He's always doing spells in school so we wouldn't have to do anything in class, probably a hundred other stupid things, just because he can."

"Is it safe to say he was using magic more than the others?"

My stomach twists. "Well, I don't know for sure, but if I had to guess, yeah. Why?"

He runs a hand through his hair. "I saw mention of this in my research, but I thought it would take longer to affect them, that's why I didn't say anything. But if they're using the magic this liberally... They're becoming dependent on it, and the magic in the crystal is infusing their systems." He says everything quickly, almost under his breath, like he's talking to himself and not me.

I take him by the shoulders, giving him a shake. "Seth."

When he meets my gaze, his eyes are hard. "If we don't separate them soon, it will be impossible to do it at all."

"But we can't do it now—look what happened to Zane!"

"We'll take precautions—"

I throw up my hands. "I can't do this right now. I have to get to the hospital."

"You *need* to finish the spell—"

"*You* need to figure out how to sever the connection without hurting anyone!" I pivot and head for the door. "I'll be back in an hour."

Seth calls something behind me but I'm on the stairs. When I'm halfway down, I hear footfalls behind me.

"Owen?"

"Do you even know where the hospital *is*?" Without waiting for an answer, he holds up a set of keys. "I'll take you."

Chapter Thirty

Owen parks in the lot closest to the emergency room and cuts the ignition. When his hand goes to the belt buckle, I cover it with mine. "I should go in alone. You coming in... It'll just make things complicated. Fox is already upset enough."

Owen's jaw clenches but he nods.

Guilt swells, but I tamp it down, opening the door and climbing out of the car. I run through the parking lot to the emergency room entrance. If Zane arrived by ambulance, that's where he'll be. And if he's not, I'll figure that out when I get inside.

From all the movies and television shows I've ever seen, I expect the ER waiting room to be bustling and full of energy. The reality couldn't be further from the truth: A dozen seats in the waiting area are full of people in varying states of lethargy and boredom. The nurse behind the main desk looks harassed but not frenzied. Neither Zane nor Fox are anywhere in sight. I cross to the nurse, a woman in her late forties with her frosted blonde hair pushed into a high pouf on the top of her head, and hover, not sure the best way to attract her attention. Her eyes remain on the computer screen before her as she clicks deliberately on her mouse.

I clear my throat. "Excuse me?"

She arches an eyebrow and turns her face incrementally toward me, but her eyes don't shift. "With you in a sec."

I count to ten, my agitation growing. Fox sounded so panicked on the phone. He has to be out of his mind with worry. "I'm just looking for someone. A boy—seventeen? He would have come in on an—"

"In a sec," she repeats.

Irritation flares and I dig my fingernails into the palms of my hands. Anger rises from the pit of my stomach. In the past, such uncontrolled emotions would be cause of concern, but now I understand what's happening, and I know how to direct the energy building. I focus on the computer monitor and release a pulse of power, a wave of satisfaction overtaking me when the monitor buzzes and the nurse's eyes go wide, her face bathed in the glow of the dreaded blue screen. Her gaze flicks to me just as I hear a familiar voice coming from the hallway behind her. Without a second thought, I take off around the corner, not caring if I'm allowed to or not.

Fox stands at the end of the long corridor, gesticulating wildly at a man in a lab coat who looks both concerned and nervous. The man holds an allaying hand toward Fox, but the gesture seems to have the opposite of its intended affect.

"Young man, if you don't calm down, I'm going to have to ask some orderlies to come remove you—"

"Just tell me what's going on!" Fox's voice is strained. "They just wheeled him in there—I just want to know—"

"Fox?" I'm still several feet away, but I want him to know I'm here, I came.

He turns and the lab-coat-clad man takes the opportunity to disappear through the double doors behind him. Fox's face is splotchy and red, his eyes wide. His mouth opens but he doesn't say anything. Instead, in two steps, he's closed the distance between us, wrapping me up in his arms. His breath is hot and labored against my neck and I return his embrace, stroking his hair. Fox's shoulders shake and I squeeze him tighter. "Sh. It's okay. It'll be okay."

We stand like that for several minutes. Occasionally, someone walks in or out of the double doors, but no one gives us a second glance. A display like ours must be commonplace here. Finally, Fox straightens, taking a step away from me. I feel the absence of his warmth and resist the urge to pull him close again.

"We were headed to Jodi's shop," he says, his voice small and distant. "He said he needed supplies for a spell. I asked him what he needed and he pulled a list out of his pocket and—it got caught in the wind and I started to chase after it, but he said he'd get it. The wind picked up in the other direction and the paper started coming back toward him and... he just dropped."

I freeze. *Wind.* Wind ripped through Seth's apartment when I was trying to break the anchoring spell. It must have been Zane's cord I was severing—that's why I felt his spell. I grab Fox's arm and squeeze it. "It's gonna be okay, Fox."

Voices rise at the far end of the corridor, drawing our attention. Crystal, Bridget, and Lexie turn the corner and take off at a shuffling run toward us. Lexie displaces me unceremoniously, fixing me with a withering stare. "You can go now."

She reaches for Fox and I bristle. Is she honestly using this moment to make a move on him? I grab her by the elbow and spin her around. She has a couple of inches on me, even without her heels, and glares down. "What? Why are you even here?"

I open my mouth to respond but am cut off by a male voice calling my name. Owen. When I turn, he's heading up the hall toward us.

"Dammit, Owen," I say through clenched teeth. "I said wait in the car—"

Fox tenses, his jaw clenching.

My stomach sinks. Fox is already upset and worried about Zane—the last thing I wanted was to bring more drama. "I didn't have my car. He just gave me a ride."

The tension drains from Fox's body and he rubs a hand over his face. "You were together?"

"I told you," Lexie says fiercely, tugging Fox's arm so he faces her. "I told you not to trust her. Since she's not the best at magic anymore, she's gotta get her power trip somewhere. Looks like she's collecting guys so she can—"

My hand connects with Lexie's cheek, the resounding *smack* satisfying. She reels back, bringing her hand to cover the red mark blossoming, her eyes murderous. She steadies herself before starting for me, but I'm ready and launch myself at her before she gets any forward momentum. She pinwheels backward and slams against the wall behind her, pressing her palms against it to keep from falling. I draw my arm back, aiming a punch at her chin, but a force pulls me backward. At first I figure Bridget or Crystal have pulled me back, but I don't knock against anyone's body. Instead, I rocket backward until I'm pinned against the wall opposite Lexie. She presses herself to standing and grins maliciously before taking a step toward me. I fight against the invisible barrier holding me in place, but can't budge it.

Lexie is halfway across the hall when she buckles, her hands going to her head as she crumples to the ground. The force holding me in place dissipates but I'm too dumbfounded to do anything. Fox, Crystal, and Bridget moan, their postures copies of Lexie's. I open my mouth to call for help, but no sound comes out. I cross to Fox, crouching so I can peer into his face.

"I'm okay," he murmurs, pushing me away. He's pale, but his movements are sure as he presses himself to standing again.

"No, you're not." I reach for his face, but he pulls back. "Fox, what was that? That wasn't normal. Why did you all fall?"

Fox takes a step back and Lexie snorts. She's standing again, too, her hair mussed and her complexion ashen, but looking otherwise normal. "Take a hint. He doesn't want you here."

I ignore her. "Fox?"

His eyes flicker to Owen. "Maybe she's right. You should go."

I grab his hands before he can pull back farther. "I'm not leaving until I figure out what happened just now. The four of you just collapsed in unison—*clearly* something's wrong."

Lexie crosses her arms over her chest. "Like you care if something happens to us."

I turn, catching her gaze. "Honestly, I don't care if something happens to *you*." My eyes flick to Owen, whose face is tight. "Except that I do. I care more than you can understand."

Lexie's expression clouds, her lips parting.

Fox curses quietly as his cell buzzes. Pulling his hands from mine, he reaches into his back pocket and swipes at the screen. His eyes narrow. "It's Griffin. He says, *What the hell was that?*"

A thrill of dread courses through me. "You mean—did *he* feel whatever happened to you guys a second ago?"

Fox shrugs. "Maybe. Why? What—"

I shake my head, backing down the hall. It can't be a coincidence. Zane was doing magic and collapsed when I was trying to work the de-anchoring spell, then everyone collapsed when Lexie used magic to pin me against the wall. Whatever I did is having effects for the circle. I need to get back to Seth, to figure out what's going on. "I have to go," I say, my eyes on Fox. "Promise me you won't do magic until you hear back from me."

Lexie presses her hands to her hips. "I'm sorry, but since when does he take orders from you?"

I point at her. "You either. And text Griffin. Don't do any magic."

Crystal's eyebrows lower, her expression pinched. "What's going on?"

Before I can answer, the double doors behind them open to reveal a female doctor in her forties, her brown hair streaked with gray at the temples. I figure she's just passing through, but her eyes fix on Fox. "You came in with Mr. Ross?"

Fox nods. "Yeah. I've been trying to get someone to tell me what's—"

She holds up her hand and a cold wave rushes over me. Before she forms the words, I know what she's going to say. And when the news breaks and Fox's face crumples, I know the cause—or near enough. Zane was tapped into the crystal when I tried to sever his connection to it. And although I didn't finish the spell, I did something to alter the circle's relationship to the energy.

When Lexie used magic just now, it affected all the other circle members, including Zane. But he was already weak from before, and whatever affected them all was too much for him. Whatever was happening to him, he wasn't strong enough to survive it.

And it's my fault.

Chapter Thirty-One

I don't speak to Owen the whole drive back to Seth's apartment. It's not until he makes a move to follow me in that I break my silence. "You should go."

His face tightens. "You'll probably need me for whatever the next spell is. I want to help."

I shake my head. "You've helped enough. I asked you to do one thing, Owen. *One* thing. Stay in the car. But no." I gulp down a breath. "If you hadn't come in, Lexie wouldn't've started in on me. She wouldn't've used magic and Zane..." I clamp my hand over my mouth, not allowing the building sob to rise and escape.

He closes the distance between us, pulling me into his arms. My body instinctively relaxes into his embrace for a moment before my mind demands I pull away. Owen presses his lips together, his eyes wounded. "I didn't mean for anything bad to happen. I planned on waiting in the car, but I felt how upset you were. I just wanted to make sure you were all right."

My emotions swirl so quickly I'm not sure how to feel. I want to be mad at him, to blame him for what happened to Zane, because doing so relieves some of my own guilt. But that's not fair to him. I want to fold myself in his arms, to allow him to hold and comfort me, to make me forget the last hour of my life—hell, the last few weeks. But that's not fair to him either.

"I need to tell Seth what happened. I'll text you if we need you."

Owen's shoulders droop at the brush-off. "I want to help."

A pang of guilt shoots through me. I should let him come upstairs with me, but I can't. My mind keeps conjuring the look on Fox's face when he showed up, Lexie's words, the resounding *smack* when my hand hit her cheek. I should be with Fox right now. I should be the one comforting him—not Lexie. But it's more important for me to figure out how to fix whatever my spell did to the circle's connection to the crystal before someone does magic and hurts the rest of them.

Owen's face tightens and he nods, even though I haven't said anything. He gets back into his car and takes off.

The sun is low on the horizon and the darkness brings with it a sharp wind that lashes against my exposed parts—my ears, my fingers, my neck. My feet pound against the metal stairs, which shake with every footfall. I bring my fist down on the aluminum door, hoping Seth's figured out a way to fix things. I want the circle to be severed from the crystal, but not this way. There has to be something else we can do.

The door swings open and my fist continues on its trajectory. Seth catches me around my wrist and smiles. "Eager to get back to work?"

I press past him into the sparse apartment. The candles and circle still stand in the center of the room, like I never left, but besides Seth, the room space is empty. "Where is everyone?"

He closes the door. "They ran out to get something to eat. They'll be back soon." He cocks his head to the side. "What's the matter? Is Zane all right?"

A dam bursts inside me, unleashing a heavy wave of emotions. Everything I've been tamping down since the hospital bubbles to the surface. My eyes fill with tears so quickly that my attempts to blink them back only result in sending them over my cheeks. I double over, my hands clenching into fists as I bring my arms across my chest. Seth crosses the room and takes me into his arms. I try to push away—I don't deserve comfort, not after what I've done—but he's too strong. I stop trying to choke back the sobs rising up in my throat and let them out, my body collapsing against his. He holds me up, making soothing sounds, but I barely hear him.

"He's *dead*. I did it." I gulp, the words piercing my heart. "It was the spell. I did something and... I *killed* Zane."

Abruptly, Seth grabs my shoulders, holding me at arm's length.

His face is drawn, inscrutable, and the intensity burning in his eyes quiets my cries. "He *died*?"

I nod. "And now every time one of them does magic, they all... collapse. I'm afraid... I'm afraid something bad's gonna happen to them all."

Seth's eyes glaze and he looks through me rather than at me. He runs his hand through his hair again absently. His gaze drops to the floor and his tongue wets his lips. "This changes things. I wasn't prepared for this development."

I open my mouth to ask what he means, but he's already turned, heading for the center of the circle drawn on his floor. He flips open a book and leafs through its pages. I edge closer. "Is there a way to undo it?"

Seth gives no indication he hears me. His fingertips skim the text for a moment before he stands, crossing to a folding chair and grabbing a paper bag from Jodi's shop. After pulling out a few bunches of herbs and sniffing them, he selects two and adds them to the bowl from earlier. He murmurs under his breath as he works.

My phone vibrates in my back pocket and I pull it out. There's a text from Owen. *I've got a bad feeling. Are you okay?*

I stuff the phone back into my pants. I should text back, but I can't bring myself to. But we might need all the psychics back for whatever Seth has planned. "Should I text the others? Tell them to get back here?"

Seth stirs the herb mixture in the bowl with his hand a few times before lifting it so it's level with his chest. In a swift motion, he stands, turning toward me. "That won't be necessary."

My skin prickles. If the psychics were necessary for the spell that caused this problem, why wouldn't they be just as integral to undo the damage? A wave of unease courses through me. We *can* undo the damage, can't we? Otherwise, what spell is Seth preparing?

The corners of his mouth turn up as though he's heard my unspoken question. Flames erupt from the bowl and I jump back, yelping. The flames of the candles around us leap and dance rhythmically. I choke on the thick smoke emanating from the bowl.

"What's going on?" I step back, meaning to leave the confines of the circle, but the candle flames are too large, too erratic. I stare at Seth. He's a witch—I *know* that—but I also know the limitations of his magic. He's told me, yes, but I've felt the energy within him. The magic filling this room is more than he should be capable of. It swirls around, pressing in on all sides. It's like he's channeling it from somewhere, like I was doing with the psychics earlier—except he shouldn't be capable of that kind of spell work.

I need to get out of the circle of fire. I wait for an opportunity and leap between two candles, but the bottom of my long sweater catches as it passes through. The rote knowledge that I should stop, drop, and roll is overcome by a more primal urge. If the elements are working against me, I must subdue the elements. Magic wells in my chest and fills me to my head, fingertips, and toes. "Flame *out*."

Not only the flames on my sweater, but the red-gold firelight of all the candles disappears immediately, leaving behind so many puffs of smoke. Seth's lip curls. Gone is the kind young man, the friendly distant relative, the mentor I've grown to know, replaced by a sneering stranger.

"You shouldn't have done that."

Blackness encroaches on my peripheral vision. I'm careening toward the floor and I can't stop it. As the darkness overtakes me, Seth's green eyes are the last thing I see.

Chapter Thirty-Two

My eyelids feel glued together. Try as I might to open them, they won't separate. I need to rub the sleep away.

Ropes cutting into my wrists restrict the movements of my hands. With an almighty effort, I wrench my eyes open, only to close them immediately against the harsh glare of a bonfire several feet in front of me. Now that I've seen it, I can't believe I couldn't feel the heat on my skin. Warm air caresses my face, my neck, presses against the fabric of my sweater and pants.

I passed out. No, I've passed out before, and this was different. Instead of coming from within me, this was done *to* me. A spell.

Seth.

I open my eyes again. The fire is at least five feet wide at its base, with flames leaping up nearly twice that into the black night sky. I'm lying on my side on the cool night grass, arms and legs bound.

I scan the area for others—the psychics, Seth—but I see no one. I struggle to right myself, jamming my hand and elbow into the cold grass. My head pounds against my skull. Whatever Seth did to knock me unconscious, it was a doozy. And where could he be now? Why knock me out, bring me here, light a fire, and leave? The fire, surrounded in a circle of large white rocks, doesn't seem to be set to spread to the nearby woods.

Woods. I squint into the darkness on all sides. Trees are visible to my right and beyond the firelight, but I can't see what's to my left. I strain my ears. Am I by the river? If so, I can follow it to town. Of course, I can't do it tied up. The rope around my ankles is intricately tied—twisted and looped back around itself. I can't even locate the ends. My heart thuds in my chest.

I take in a breath. I'm ignoring the obvious solution—*magic*. It can't be much different than lighting a candle. With my mind focused on what I want to happen—the knots to unravel—I try to call up the energy inside me. But nothing happens. I close my eyes, searching for the surge of magic.

A chuckle sounds behind me and I twist. Seth emerges from the darkness, a smile playing about the corners of his mouth. "Try all you like. You'll not be able to access your magic."

I pull against the ropes, but that only makes them dig into my flesh. He's right. The spark within me is there, but muted, like it's behind translucent glass. I can't connect with it. "What are you doing to me?"

He shrugs as he positions himself between the fire and me. "A simple channeling spell." He points at a ring on his pinky finger and my stomach clenches. It's my ring. "Since your friend died while you attempted the spell earlier, I was fairly certain you'd be reluctant to assist me in finishing the work. I knew I would have to take matters into my own hands. I didn't want it to come to this, but it has. I need the circle separated from the crystal. They have no right to use the energy trapped within it. It was never meant for them."

I can't believe what I'm hearing. His voice doesn't even sound like the man I've grown to know—it's rougher, colder. "And what? You think it's meant for you?"

"Meant for me? In a way, yes, but not the way you think. The magic inside that crystal *belongs* to me. I was separated from it the night you and Crystal returned from your foray into the past. *Yes*, I know about that." A smile curls the edges of his mouth. "It was, after all, my idea."

His words clang and clash in my mind. "What? You didn't even come to town until after—"

"On the contrary—I've been in this town for more years than I care to count. Suffice it to say, I was here before your parents and their parents and their parents before them."

I stare at him. There's no way he's telling the truth. How can he be that old? He's barely older than I am. But another thought tugs at my consciousness. I had visions of him before he ever showed up in my life—visions Jodi brushed off as simple foreshadowing of his arrival, that Crystal believed meant they were destined for each other. But what if they were more than that? I attributed my visions to being around Crystal, but that's not entirely accurate. The visions occurred when I was around the pendant she wore—a shard from the quartz the circle anchored itself to. What if my visions had nothing to do with Crystal at all, but with the pendant? And the visions I've had since coming to this reality—the ones I thought meant there was something wrong with the crystal? Stones can channel energy, yes, but they can also store it. There's no reason a stone would be inherently *evil*—it would have to be imbued with something dark.

Or someone.

"I never did thank you. Although, truly, I'm not thankful to be in such a pitiable state, it is preferable to what I experienced in your reality. For a brief moment when you rescued the stone from poor Crystal Taylor's fire, I reconnected with the full extent of my abilities. And while it would have been preferable for Crystal Jamison to release me from the stone with my abilities intact, I'm not entirely sure she possesses the power to have completed the spell, and I'm unsure what would have become of me had she died midway through. So, in a way, I suppose I do owe you a debt of gratitude for intervening. When you redirected the crystal's magic—*my* magic—you freed me from my prison." He holds his arms out, wiggling his fingers. "It is wonderful to have corporeal form again. Still, it is unacceptable to be cut off from my power. Your circle anchoring itself is a complication that needs to be sorted out."

"That's been your plan all along, hasn't it? To kill them—like you've been killing other people in town?" I bite the inside of my cheeks, watching his face, wanting to be wrong. But the flicker in his eye is all the confirmation I need. "*Why*? Why would you kill them? Millie has young *kids*—"

"I'm simply putting things right—punishing the children of those who betrayed me all those years ago. Alec Crawford? He's from the line of Joseph Hill, who was instrumental in casting the spell that entrapped me. The delightful Millie? Her ancestors, the Yates family, provided the crystal."

I can't believe what I'm hearing—he's *admitting* to murder, right here in front of me. There's only one reason he'd be doing that: He doesn't expect I'll ever be able to tell anyone. I've figured him out, and once he's finished his spell, I'll outlive my usefulness. I have to get out of here, but I have no idea how. He's blocked me from my magic, and I can't see or feel enough to undo the ropes without it.

"And your friend *Felix*." He sneers at the name. "Tucker Wolfe was the one who betrayed me to the town elders to begin with. Felix is the last of his line to possess abilities. That he still draws breath is a thorn in my side."

Felix. The psychics. That's it. Seth is tapping into my magic, but maybe he's not touching my psychic side. I've moved things with my mind before—maybe I can move the ropes now. It might be a long shot, but if I can catch Seth off guard, it might be my only hope of getting out of here—and of saving my friends.

I need to distract him. "If you want Felix dead so badly, why haven't you killed him yet?" Hope flashes. Maybe there's something about Felix that Seth didn't account for. "After we stopped the spell, why didn't you just try something else?"

He snorts. "My own abilities are pitifully limited, so I needed help. Crystal Taylor and I have a long history—after all, she possessed my stone back when she ran her own circle. When I had my form again, it was a simple matter of reminding her of our connection. While my connection to magic was woefully limited, my psychic abilities have remained stronger. It took little persuasion to make her do my bidding. She didn't even know she was doing it. But that changed when the target was Felix. Her consciousness fought back when she realized he was a child."

I shiver, despite the heat of the fire. When Crystal Taylor died the day after the attack on Felix, I knew there had to be a connection, but I never considered this. She wasn't just the next victim on a list—she was being punished for failing.

Seth turns toward the fire. With a wave of his hand, a bunch of herbs to my right lifts off the ground and flies into the flames, which devour them instantly. I'm struck again by the ease with which he's wielding magic. He shouldn't be able to do much of what he's doing. "If your magic's trapped in the crystal, how are you doing all this?"

He grins over his shoulder. "Do you know the best way to lie? It's to tell things that are partially true. Abilities can be stored in quartz, it's true, but they can also be directed into a willing host. My powers have increased with each death. Alec Crawford, Millie, Crystal Taylor—their energy now courses within me." He shakes his head, sighing. "Unfortunately, this magic is merely a hollow echo of what resides in the crystal. Not nearly enough power to do what needs to be done."

I take in a breath, calling on my psychic side. I need to keep him distracted. "And what needs to be done?"

"The town needs to be cleansed. It's spent too many generations under the control of the ordinary and the unbeliever. When I control my magic again, Clearwater will return to its roots as a haven for people with abilities."

I fight the urge to close my eyes in concentration. I don't want Seth to suspect I'm up to anything. In my mind's eye, I call up an image of a knot binding my wrists. I reach forward with my mind, willing the ropes to loosen. "If your goal is to reclaim the town for magic, why are you killing all the people with abilities? If you separate the circle from the crystal, won't they all die?" I sink my teeth into my lower lip, wanting him to disagree, to share a loophole in the end result I foresee.

He glances back momentarily before returning his attention to the fire. "It's lamentable, to be sure, but it's unavoidable, really."

My breath catches and my stomach clenches. *Fox.* I have to do something—I can't just sit here while Seth uses *my* magic to kill someone I care about. I twist against the ropes, my heartbeat kicking up when I detect more wiggle room than before. *It's working.*

"It is a shame about your friend Crystal. She looks so like my beloved Bess. She was from the Taylor line, too, you know." He sighs. "Ah, well. It's a minor problem—especially once I have my abilities back."

A rope scratches against the inside of my wrist as it slides through the loops confining it. I tense as a burning sensation radiates up my arm. Seth turns, squinting, and I say the first thing that pops to mind to distract him from what I'm doing: "So, what? Crystal is some distant relative of your dead girlfriend and you were going to...? What? Dress Crystal up in old-timey clothes and convince her that her name's Bess?"

His face hardens and a hard, sharp force connects with the right side of my face, sending me reeling backward. Unable to break my fall with my hands, I land face-first in the cold grass.

"You will *not* speak of my Bess with such disrespect. As if I could ever be satisfied with such a hollow imitation of my love."

I roll onto my back, afraid he might notice the knots are looser than they were when he tied them, but the look on his face makes it clear he's not seeing such details. His features are contorted in a mask of rage. Reflected firelight dances in his eyes, making him look entirely deranged. "I'm sorry," I say quickly, struggling to push myself back to a sitting position.

Seth gives no indication he hears me. "Bess was the gentlest soul that has ever walked this earth. In the end, it was that gentleness, that goodness that was her undoing. She sought to keep her younger brother safe from a gang of ordinary who wanted to entrap him in a barn. But it was she who became ensnared when a lantern caught some hay alight." His eyes squeeze closed. "But she and I will be reunited—and we'll be together as we were always meant to be."

So focused am I on the gentle tugging of ropes against ropes, the incremental slackening of my bindings, that I almost miss Seth's words—and their implications. "You can't mean what I think you mean. You're going to bring her *back*?"

His lip curls. "That's hardly your concern." He tips back his head and I follow his gaze. The waning moon is high, almost aligned with the bonfire. "Not long now."

His words send a wave of nausea through my stomach. If I'm going to get away, I have to do it *now*. If I can get the knots undone and catch him at the right moment, maybe I can get to the tree line. Abandoned is my earlier idea of following the river to civilization: Hiding in the woods is probably my best option now. But will physical distance be enough to block him from channeling my magic? I have no idea. I don't know how to break his connection to me, any more than I know how to break the circle's connection to the crystal without killing them all.

The ropes around my wrist go slack and fall silently to the ground behind me. Seth's back is to me, his eyes still on the moon. I bring my hands around to the front of my body and my fingers dig into the knots at my ankles. Seth lifts his hands and my stomach clenches as the ember of my magic flickers to life. Whatever he's doing, he's starting now. My pointer finger wiggles into the center of a knot and I pull at the rope, slipping the ends over and through each other until it, too, falls. My eyes dart to the trees to my right and I take in a breath. It's now or never. The power is beginning to well within me, and I don't know what will happen once he begins the spell properly.

Heart hammering, I push myself to my feet and take off for the woods. I'm maybe twenty yards away. If I can make it, I might be able to hide somewhere. Ten yards. I hazard a glance over my shoulder. Seth still faces the fire. I might actually make it. I pump my arms and gulp in the cold night air. Five yards. I'm almost there—almost free.

Although my path is clear, I stumble, tumbling forward. With my right hand I reach down to break my fall; my left reaches for the tree trunk less than a foot before me. My fingers don't even skim the bark. My body thuds against the ground and my legs straighten behind me, pulled irresistibly backward.

"No you don't." Seth's arm stretches toward me, his fingers splayed. My father's ring glints on his pinky. My body bumps against the ground as an invisible force reels me back toward him. He raises his eyebrows, his expression dripping condescension. "Did you honestly think you could get away so easily?" He closes his fist and my muscles tense and lock, my body going rigid as a board. He smiles, his eyes flicking to the sky. "It seems that, like the moon, my hold on your magic is at its zenith. It's time to begin." He crouches to my side, brushing a strand of hair off my forehead. "I do hope you said goodbye to your dear Fox."

Chapter Thirty-Three

Seth begins chanting words I don't understand in a low, rhythmic tone.

This is it. Game over. I've lost. My eyes fill with tears and I blink to clear them—thankful that my eyes and eyelids still function. The rest of my muscles are still frozen. I can't even open my mouth to release the sob that builds in my chest.

I didn't say goodbye to Fox. *Why* didn't I? I take a tiny bit of solace in the fact that I probably won't outlive him by much. Once Seth has his power back, he'll have no more need for me.

The flicker of magic in my core flares, filling my abdomen. If only I could tap into that energy! To think, just weeks ago, that power scared me so much I wanted to tamp it down, to ignore it. Now I'd give anything to use it.

Tears streak from the corners of my eyes, across my temples, and into my hair. The cold night air freezes the damp trails. I'd shiver, I'm sure, if I could move.

Seth's voice rises in volume and I stop trying to watch him, allowing my gaze to relax and stare straight up instead. The moon hovers above me and I fix on it. If I'm going to die, I at least want my final moments to be filled with beauty. I try to block out Seth's chanting, but it fills my ears. Tears well up in my eyes so quickly I don't bother blinking them away. The moon blurs to a smear of light against blackness.

A shadow crosses my vision, followed by a low grunt. Seth's rhythmic chant ceases and hands clamp down on my upper arms. I blink rapidly and a face comes into focus.

Owen.

I want to scream, to wrap my arms around him, to smile—but I can't. He pulls at my arms, trying to help me to my feet, but my muscles are unyielding. I cast my eyes in all directions, trying to see around him. Seth hasn't pulled Owen away yet, and he hasn't started chanting again, so there must be someone else here.

Two figures struggle against each other in front of the fire. One silhouette is clearly Seth, but I can't immediately place the second. It's not until he straightens to his full height that my heart twists with recognition: Fox.

"Krissa, what's wrong?" Owen's fingers dig into my arms.

I can't answer with my words, so I try sending an impression telepathically. A slight widening of Owen's eyes tells me he understands.

Fox lets out a low cry before crumpling to the ground near my feet. Seth straightens, wiping a smear of blood from the corner of his mouth. His lips begin moving in a murmured chant and I send another thought to Owen: *Get my ring.*

Owen nods and launches himself over my body, straight at Seth. Seth throws him off easily and Owen lands on the ground just inches in front of the bonfire. I wait for him to spring back up to his feet, but he doesn't. Seth raises his arms toward the moon again, his volume increasing. My father's ring catches the light and I stare at it. A jolt courses through me and I know this was Owen's plan—he wants Seth to *think* he's won. I reach my mind out to connect with Owen's and then focus on the one thing that might stop Seth: removing my ring from his finger. Slowly, the ring slips upward, toward Seth's first knuckle. His chanting reaches a fever pitch and Fox moans. With every fiber of my being, I will the ring to slide off Seth's finger, but it doesn't move. Fox's moan turns into a wail and my skin prickles. If Fox—who used the crystal's power least of all the circle—is in this much pain, what must be happening to the rest of them?

Fox's body convulses against my legs. I'm losing him, and there's nothing I can do about it. The ring still hasn't cleared Seth's knuckle. So long as he has it, he controls my magic.

Fox's movements still and adrenaline washes through my body. I have to get to him. I *have* to. Abandoning my focus on the ring entirely, I turn my will inward. Seth may have my magic, but he doesn't have all my abilities. Like using my mind to undo the ropes that bound me earlier, I see in my mind's eye the result I want: the free and unrestricted motion of my body.

Fox moans and my right pointer finger twitches.

It's working.

I imagine a pulse of energy shooting from my finger up my arm, coursing through the rest of my body, waking it. My muscles relax and I know it's working. One glance at Seth shows he is unaware his spell's effect is dissipating—he's too focused on the magic he's wielding now. I wiggle my toes before pulling myself up into a crouch. Owen's eyes widen but I shake my head. I need the element of surprise. Seth stands a yard away, his face skyward. Fixing my eyes on his ring finger, I launch myself at him, knocking him off center. He stumbles, releasing a surprised holler. I grab around his wrist with one hand and yank my ring off his finger with the other. It slides off the tip as he collides with the ground. I curl my fingers around the ring, relishing its weight in the palm of my hand. The barrier between me and the spark of magic inside evaporates. I don't wait for Seth to react, rushing instead to Fox. Owen is already crouched at his side, his fingers pressed against Fox's neck. My blood runs cold as I lock eyes with Owen, terrified of what he will reveal. It seems a geologic age passes before Owen nods, a tight, pained smile almost imperceptibly tugging the corners of his mouth. My pent-up breath rushes past my lips in a relieved sigh. *He's still alive.* And he'll be okay now—Seth can't complete the spell.

"Help me, Owen." I hook my arms under Fox's armpits and tug at him, but his body barely budges. He's heavier than he looks. I glance back at Seth, but he hasn't moved from where he landed on the ground.

Owen displaces me, imitates my posture, and hoists Fox to a sitting position. "We should go check on the others," he says, grunting. "They all dropped on the way here."

"The others?" Had the rest of the circle come to help, too? I peer through the black night but can't make out their forms against the ground.

A low chuckle builds behind me, causing the hairs on the back of my neck to stand at attention. I turn to see Seth, reclining easily on one arm, like he's relaxing on a day at the beach. He clucks his tongue. "You think you've beaten me, but I assure you, you're already too late. The spell is complete." He inhales deeply, his chest expanding. "With every moment that passes, the energy from the crystal—*my* energy—is making it back to me."

My muscles coil and my jaw clenches. I rush at Seth, wanting to rip the smug expression from his face, but with a wave of his hand he sends me careening to the ground. My hand opens when it slams down, the ring bouncing out into the grass. I groan as I press myself to my hands and knees, skimming my fingers over the blades of grass and twigs in the vicinity, searching in the darkness for the familiar circular shape.

"Zane's death was an unfortunate loss—one I don't intend to repeat."

I stiffen, peering at Seth. "You mean the spell won't kill them?"

He draws his knees to his chest, resting his arms casually around them. "You misunderstand. They shall all still die. With Zane, I was unprepared. I could have absorbed his abilities before they melted back into nature—as I did with Alec Crawford and Millie and Crystal Taylor."

Seth doesn't need to spell out what this means. I've already sensed the power within the crystal. That alone is a formidable amount of ability. Add that to the magic contained within the members of the circle and he'll be too powerful to challenge. Unstoppable.

My fingers brush against metal and I pick up the ring, slipping it onto my finger. Immediately, my muscles lock up again. Has Seth cast the immobilization spell again? He didn't even move. But unlike last time, my body doesn't freeze. Instead, it is as though someone else is controlling my movements. Stiffly, my body stands up from the ground, and my arms lift to the sky, like Seth's had earlier. Out the corner of my eye, I see Owen imitating my posture, his limbs moving with the same jerky quality. Slowly, like an inexpertly controlled puppet, Fox rises to his feet, his head bobbing lifelessly, his chin to his chest, as his arms reach heavenward.

I'm sure Seth is doing this to us, but that idea is shattered when his face twists into a mask of fury. He stands, his mouth moving, but I don't hear his words. My mind fills with voices murmuring words I don't understand. They repeat the same phrase over and over, an echo building in my skull with each recitation. There are male and female voices and there's something familiar about them, but I can't place what.

Heat radiates from my ring, burning against my skin. Whatever is happening isn't Seth's doing—it's emanating from the ring. I allow my body to relax into it, to let the words in my head wash over me. This ring was my father's and his before him. It's been passed down in my family for generations. I imagine the combined power of all those ancestors filling me, coming to assist me in this moment of need. In the past, Levi and his grandfather from my visions joined together to rid their town of a person with evil in his heart. They joined together to overcome *Seth*. Maybe they're reaching out across time to help fight against him again.

The kernel of magic in my core flares, filling me with fire and ice, whipping through me like wind and supporting me like the earth beneath my feet. My consciousness rips open, images pouring into my mind, flipping by so quickly I can't discern more than colors and forms. Fear clouds my head, punctuated by flares of hope, elation, and anger, before giving way to peace, like a tranquil lake winking in the summer sunshine.

My arms drop to my sides, the voices disappearing from my head. Seth's eyes are wide and wild, panicked. His gaze darts between me and Owen—Fox has dropped back to the ground in a heap. Every cell in my body vibrates, like I'm in tune with every bit of energy in the world. I feel a cool, rough pressure in my left palm and look down. There's nothing there, but the phantom feeling remains. *The crystal.* I'm not sure how I know it, but it's nearby. Crystal Jamison is clutching it. I turn to Owen, who is looking at his left hand in confusion. "Go get it!"

His eyes lock on mine for an instant before he takes off toward the river's edge, heading upstream along its bank. Seth raises his arm—he's going to pull him back like he did when I tried to escape.

Instinctively, I raise my hand, wanting to knock Seth over, to distract him from the spell he's casting. Owen stumbles once before Seth falls flat on his back, grunting as the air rushes from his lungs. He pushes against the ground with his elbows but I reach my hand out, pressing him against the earth with an invisible force.

"What did you do?" Seth thrashes futilely against the ground. "Your magic isn't this strong!"

He's right, the abilities I'm displaying are beyond me. It feels similar to when I channeled the psychics' energy earlier during the spell in Seth's apartment, but it's more than that. I'm not exactly sure what happened, but I accept the power now. I need it to fight him.

He struggles again, attempting to curl his body upward to sitting. The pressure of his movements reverberates through the air into my palm, like the movements of a fly transmitted through a spider's web.

"You're still too late." He grunts, pressing his forearms into the ground beneath him and forcing his torso into the air. The movement echoes through my hand and through my body. "Each moment, I grow stronger. Do you hope to use the crystal's magic against me? You *can't*." He plants his palms on the ground and manages to sit. The force of his motion knocks me back a step.

"I'll stop you. I'll find away."

He grunts with exertion. "Your ancestors thought the same thing, but, as you can see, they were unsuccessful. What makes you think you'll be able to accomplish what they could not?" Slowly, laboriously, he drags his legs toward him. My hold on him is weakening—either that, or he's growing stronger with each passing second. "Unless you plan to kill me." His upper lip curls and he narrows his eyes. "After all, you've killed once already."

His words are like a physical blow, knocking the breath from my lungs. My tenuous control over him slips and he stands in one swift movement. *You've killed once already.* The truth of the statement stabs my heart. Zane is gone, his fate sealed the moment I started the spell to break the circle's connection to the crystal.

But it was never my intent to hurt him—to hurt anyone. It was all Seth, all his desire to regain his power. Rage bubbles through my veins. *He's* the one who's ultimately responsible. How dare he accuse me of murder? If there's one person who deserves to die as a result of all this, it's *him.*

The fire in my body connects to the flames of the bonfire. I focus all the heat, the hate, on Seth, and the fire shoots up like a pillar before twisting down like a snake. Seth's eyes lock on mine, wide with surprise, as the serpentine figure strikes out toward his body, encircling him.

"Krissa!" Owen's heavy footfalls draw my attention. He holds the crystal toward me limply, his eyes full of reflected firelight.

I open my mouth to explain, but when I turn back, the fiery snake disappears in the blink of an eye, leaving emptiness where Seth stood. I scan the vicinity, but there's no trace of him—his body—anywhere.

"He just disappeared," Owen murmurs, bumping my arm with the crystal.

The only other time I've heard of someone winking out of existence before was at West's house with the psychics. Felix mentioned it my first day there. "Bilocation." I shake my head. Of course. Seth wouldn't chance someone being able to capture him. By bilocating, he could keep his physical self safe from harm while conducting the spell here.

The spell.

I turn, grabbing the crystal from Owen's hand. Although physically it feels the same as it always has, the energy of it is off—less intense. Still, I can sense a tremendous amount of magic still trapped within it. And I know what I need to do—what I should have done the first time I thought about it. "We have to discharge the energy from the crystal."

"Wait—what?" Owen closes his hands over mine, covering the crystal. He looks down at Fox who remains in a motionless heap. "What about...? Will what happened to...?"

"Zane..." My throat constricts. "He was using magic when I tried to separate the circle from the crystal. Seth said separation was best because it would cut them off from the magic in it. But of *course* he wouldn't want to discharge all the magic—he wanted it back for himself. If we push the magic out of here, it'll just go back out into nature, where anyone can use it. He won't be able to absorb it into himself because it won't be *his*."

Owen's face is tight. "And the circle?"

I squeeze my eyes closed. In truth, I don't know what will happen to them. I have to believe they'll be okay—after all, they won't be cut off from the energy, it'll just be stored somewhere else. Seth can't be allowed to absorb all this power—who knows how many more lives he'll take in the name of "cleansing" the town. I open my eyes, covering Owen's hands with my free one. "It's our only shot."

After a beat, he nods. "What do we do?"

I take in a breath. "I'm not sure if you can help—you're not a witch. But... can you feel the energy inside the crystal?"

He nods. "I—I think so."

"Okay. Connect yourself to the energy and push it *out*—into the world around us."

"What—that's it?"

The energy inside the crystal shifts. Seth is still drawing on it. "It's the best explanation I can give. Just—follow my lead." I don't wait for him to respond. Closing my eyes, I focus on the power stored in the stone resting in my hand. I just have to force the energy out.

Jolts of energy shoot through my palm and up my arm. My instinct is to drop the stone, but I resist, squeezing it tighter. Heat radiates off the crystal, searing my skin. I bite my lower lip to keep from crying out. It's as if the quartz has a mind of its own and is fighting against my efforts to rid it of its energy. Pain spreads through my arm, cresting over my shoulder and filling my chest. My body shakes violently in protest, my grip loosening.

"No!" I squeeze my fist, crying out in pain when Owen crushes his hands over mine. The power of the crystal is trying to overwhelm me, but I can't let it—I have to push it back. I have to succeed for the circle.

For Fox.

An icy chill builds in my center, flowing outward, combating the heat invading my body. The cold pushes it back, out of my chest, over my shoulder, past my elbow, into my hand. I take a deep breath, calling up all the energy within me, all the power of the raging bonfire, of the rushing river, of the night breeze, of the earth beneath my feet. *"Get out!"*

A flash like lightning shoots out of the crystal, connecting with the ground beneath it. I scream as the pain of a thousand knives rips through my hand. I lose my grip on the crystal and fly backward; Owen's hands slips from mine as he is launched in the opposite direction. I land on my back several feet away, the air knocked from my lungs by the impact. I struggle to draw breath, unable even to take in a shallow gulp for what feels like minutes. Finally the dam breaks and cool night air rushes in. I inhale and exhale deeply several times before sitting up. Owen is still flat on his back and I struggle to his side, crawling with the help of only my left hand, my right in too much pain to place weight on. Panic rises with every inch nearer I move.

He groans when I shake his shoulder, opening his eyes and squinting against the firelight. "Did we do it?"

The crystal rests in the center of a scorched patch of earth several feet away. We crawl to it and I pick it up in my left hand. "It's... it's just a stone. There's nothing left in it."

A smile breaks across Owen's face, but my elation is trampled by another thought. "Fox." I scramble to his side and pull him so he's flat on his back. My fingers tremble as I reach for his neck, afraid of what I'll find. What if there's no pulse? What if he's—

Owen places a hand on my shoulder. The gesture gives me the strength I need to touch my fingers to Fox's skin. Nothing. A sob rises in my chest as I move my fingers to the hollow spot just below his jaw, pressing my fingers more firmly to his flesh. *Oh, god, what have I done...*

A slow, rhythmic thud pulses beneath my fingertips and another sob claws its way out of my mouth—this one of relief. I bury my face in Fox's chest, tears overfilling my eyes and dripping onto his shirt.

"He's alive."

Chapter Thirty-Four

I stay with Fox while Owen checks on the other members of the circle. I should go with him, I know I should, but I can't bring myself to leave Fox's side. Owen's hurt—his jealousy—flares through me as he leaves us, but I can't allow myself to dwell on it. My feelings for Fox are real, and although they hurt Owen, they're not something I can just turn off. Sorting out my feelings toward Owen versus my feelings toward Fox is a problem for another day.

I remain pressed against Fox's chest until after my tears stop flowing. I come back to myself by degrees—first aware of the night air nipping against my exposed skin, then the fatigue of my muscles, and finally of the searing pain in my right hand. When I investigate my palm, I immediately wish I hadn't—the skin is shiny with angry red blisters. A small price to pay for Fox's life.

Fox moans and I pull away, giving him space to move from side to side. After a few seconds, he opens his eyes a slit, curling his body toward a sitting position but stopping before he's even halfway upright. "Krissa? What happened?"

I can't suppress a smile as I reach for his face with my left hand. "Later," I choke, my throat constricting as fresh tears spring to my eyes. I wipe at them with the back of my right hand, wincing. "Can you stand?"

With much effort and assistance, Fox manages to get to his feet. I pull his arm over my shoulders and help him shuffle in the direction he and Owen first arrived from. He's brimming with questions, but he keeps them to himself, giving me the space to tell him what happened in my own time. I'm struck by the clarity with which I know the things going on in his mind. I'm not even trying to use my psychic side. Maybe I'm still amped up from everything with Seth?

Murmured voices float through the darkness as we follow the bend in the river. My heart swells: Voices mean people. Voices mean the other members of the circle are okay, too.

Slowly, Fox and I make our way to where the others are gathered, in a small clearing just beyond the river's bend. A wave of irritation washes over me when Owen catches a glimpse of the two of us and my cheeks burn.

Fox stiffens and our shuffling progress halts. "Are you... embarrassed?"

I press my hand to my cheek automatically, even though there's no way Fox can see my blush. In addition to the fact that the light of the waning moon is unlikely to reveal the color in my cheeks, Fox is much taller than I am and completely unable to see my face from his angle. "How do you know that?"

He shakes his head. "I don't know. I just... feel it."

It's my turn to freeze. If this comment came from Owen, I wouldn't give it a second thought, but Fox isn't a psychic. He shouldn't be able to sense my emotions.

"Krissa!" Crystal's voice cuts into my thoughts and I turn to her, glad for the distraction. She hobbles unsteadily toward me, launching herself into my arms when she's close enough. I return her hug as best I can, trying not to throw off Fox's balance. She squeezes me tightly before holding me at arm's length, her eyes burning into mine. A dozen emotions play out over her face and her mouth twitches like she's trying to come up with the right thing to say. Finally, she settles on, "I should've listened to you."

Anger, irritation, and regret all swirl through me. The urge to punch her face is strong, tempered only by the equally strong urge to pull her in for another hug. Moonlight catches the tears filling her eyes and I sigh. "Let's go home."

I end up supporting both Fox and Crystal on the trek back to the riverside park. Owen assists Lexie and Bridget. Griffin trudges slowly behind the rest of us, stubbornly refusing any help.

My teeth are chattering by the time the playground is in sight and I wonder what time it is. My mom and Jodi are probably worried that I'm not home. I have no idea how I'll explain where I've been and what I've been doing. Jodi might understand, but what am I going to tell my mom? She seems to be adjusting well to the fact that I have abilities, but how will she react if I tell her the truth? "Sorry I'm late, I was defeating a centuries-old super-magical psychic dude who's been posing as a harmless employee at Jodi's shop." Yeah, that'll go over well.

The silhouette of Fox's monster truck stands out in the parking lot beyond the playground, but that's not what draws my attention. There are people milling about the lot, leaning against other parked cars. Did my mom send out a search party when I didn't come home? It can't be *that* late, can it? But as soon as this thought enters my mind, it's dispelled by another thought—no, a certainty. Before I can make out their figures, I know who the three figures are: the psychics.

Bria, West, and Felix take off at a run toward us and my heart swells at the sight of them. They're okay. I've been so focused on keeping the circle alive and keeping Seth from reabsorbing all his magic that I haven't spared a thought for them in too long. They slow as they near us, Bria giving Lexie major side-eye as she passes her to get to me. I smile as she approaches, but Bria doesn't smile back. Instead, she extends her greeting by punching me hard in the shoulder.

"Hey! Ow!" I take a step back in case she intends to hit me again.

"Bria, what the hell?" Fox asks, shifting so he's in front of me.

Bria stares at him incredulously. "That's what you should be asking *her*." She peers around Fox, locking her eyes on mine. "What did you *do*?"

"Whoa, calm down, psycho," Crystal snaps. "What? Are you pissed we're all still alive?"

Bria holds a hand up to silence her, eyes still fixed on mine. "Someone tell bitch-face I'm not talking to her. I want to know what you did. Something's different—I can feel it. So can West and Felix."

I shake my head. "I didn't *do* anything—"

"The chanting," Owen murmurs. Leaving Lexie and Bridget

with Felix and West, he approaches. "After you got your ring back—there was chanting in my head. You heard it too, didn't you?"

The sense memory of being unable to control the movements of my body makes me roll my shoulders. "Yeah. I heard it. But I didn't *do* it. I put my ring on and it just *happened*."

Griffin edges up beside his brother. "I think she-psychic's on to something. I haven't felt right since I woke up."

"Maybe because you almost *died*, genius," Owen says dryly.

Griffin arches an eyebrow in his direction but doesn't respond. Instead, he looks past Owen to West, who sighs.

"He's got a point," West calls. "I didn't really understand till everyone got here. I mean, it's been a pretty crazy day, what, with being sneak-attacked with knockout gas at Seth's house and all. But since we woke up in his room, I've been feeling... more. Emotions I was pretty sure weren't mine. At first, I figured they were coming from Bria and Felix—or you, Krissa, or Owen."

The look on Owen's face tells me he has no clearer idea what West is getting at than I do.

"And then there's the fact we're *here*," Felix adds.

Owen takes in a sharp breath and I know I'm missing something. "What?"

"After I dropped you at Seth's place, I went to Fox's house to check on him." His mouth twitches. "You wouldn't let me help *you*, and I knew you wanted to make sure he was okay."

Fox runs a hand through his hair. "He convinced me not to slam the door in his face and then started telling me about the spell you guys were trying. But before he got too far, he started freaking out about how something bad was happening to you—how he could feel it." He presses his lips together in a tight line.

"We went to Seth's place, but you weren't there. I couldn't figure out where you were. I could sense you, but I couldn't pinpoint your location."

"So I called the circle and we did a locater spell," Fox says quietly. "That's how we figured out where you were."

I look back and forth between them. Besides the fact that they worked together to find me, I'm not seeing the significance. "So?"

"Don't you see?" Owen asks. "I'm psychic, and I couldn't find you. I needed a witch to help. If all the witches were here, how did the rest of the psychics find us?"

I shake my head. "I don't... I don't know." I survey Felix and West before my gaze lands on Bria.

"It's like we were drawn here," Bria says. "We woke up and we just *knew* we had to come here—to come to you. But not just you, Krissa. It's like we were drawn to *all* of you. Or each of you." She bites her lower lip, shifting from foot to foot as her gaze flicks to Lexie.

"Oh, my..." Lexie presses her hand to her mouth. She blinks rapidly, pressing her lips together. "Bria, stop it—*please*."

Bria squeezes her eyes closed. "I'm sorry," she murmurs. "I just had to see if I was right."

"Right about *what*? What's happening?" I take a few steps toward Lexie but Bria catches me by the elbow.

"I just shared a memory with Lexie. I shouldn't be able to *do* that because she's not psychic." Bria rubs her hand over her face. "Don't you feel it? It's like... It's like my abilities are on hyperdrive, but mostly with Lexie. Like I'm—I don't know. Like I'm linked to her or something."

Crystal sucks in a breath, pressing a hand to her mouth. "I think I know what's going on. The chanting you and Owen heard in your heads—is there any chance it was a binding spell?"

Chapter Thirty-Five

A binding spell. In a way, it makes perfect sense. Crystal told me about binding spells before the circle anchored to the crystal. She said they're a way to pool abilities so a person can draw on them. Seth said basically the same thing earlier tonight. The swell of power I felt after the chanting ended? I was drawing on the collective energy of all the witches and all the psychics, as most of them were in no position to be using it themselves. But how could it have happened? And what are we going to do about it?

After a few minutes' debate, the consensus is to deal with the implications of having bound the circle and the psychics tomorrow, after we've all been able to rest. As most of the witches are having trouble standing on their own, it's the only logical suggestion—even if we figure out how to fix things, it's unlikely we'll be able to do anything tonight.

The psychics, being in better shape than the witches, volunteer to take people home. Owen offers to drive me but I refuse in favor of getting a ride with Bria. I don't need to be a psychic to interpret the look on Fox's face when Owen suggested I ride with him. Although I have a heightened awareness of the thoughts and emotions of all the witches and psychics, I'm most in tune with Fox and Owen, and I'm not sure why. Is it because of my feelings for both of them? Or is there another reason?

Bria is quiet when she drives to my house, murmuring a goodbye when I get out of the car. I'm so distracted by the night's events that I'm almost to the porch before I notice the car parked in front of the house: It's the black Charger with tinted windows I've seen around town. I shiver and my heartbeat picks up. There's a black Honda parked across the street, behind red Mazda. I sigh. Maybe a neighbor is entertaining and the car in front of our house belongs to some party guest. Jodi's car is in the driveway, but my mom's isn't. Where could my mom be at this time of night? Guilt stabs at me: What if she's out looking for me?

I've come to a stop at the base of the stairs. I shake my head before starting up onto the porch. There's only one way to know what's going on, and that's go get into the house. I cross to the front door and pause when my hand touches the knob. I can hear muffled voices inside. What could be going on?

I open the door and cross the threshold. The voices silence immediately. I peer into the living room just as Jodi stands, relief washing over her features. She crosses to me, taking me into her arms. As she hugs me, I glance over her shoulder. Sitting on either end of the couch are Shelly Tanner and David Cole, her alternate-reality husband. I tense. In my timeline, the last time David Cole was here, it was on magic-related business. In her youth, Shelly was also part of Jodi's circle. I push Jodi from me gently, studying her face. "The chanting—the spell. Was it you?"

Jodi's expression clouds. "Before we get into that there's something we need to talk about."

I cross my arms over my chest. The last thing I need right now is a lecture. If she wants to have a discussion about what happened tonight, she'll have to wait until tomorrow. "Look, I'm really tired. Can this wait until morning?" Without waiting for a response, I turn toward the stairs. I don't make it two steps before she hooks my elbow, spinning me back around.

"No, it can't wait. There's something you need to know—"

I yank my arm away. "What? That you bound the witches and the psychics together? Because I already know that. You wouldn't happen to know how to undo it, would you? Because no one's really super happy about it."

Jodi opens her mouth, but it's not her voice that fills my ears. "It was the only way to save your friends." The voice is masculine, but doesn't belong to David Cole—I know that immediately. Besides the fact it doesn't sound the way I remember his voice sounding, it's coming from the dining room on my right, not the living room on my left. I turn toward the person who spoke and immediately reach for Jodi to keep from falling over. The man standing in the archway between the hall and dining room is tall, with broad shoulders and sandy brown hair. There is more gray in his hair now, and there are more wrinkles around his eyes than I remember, but he hasn't changed enough that I don't recognize him.

"Dad?"

My father nods, his face tightening. In two steps, he's crossed to me and pulled me roughly into his arms. He even smells the same as I remember—Old Spice with a subtle note of sweetness under the surface. My eyes prickle and I can't swallow. After a beat, my arms wrap around his back and he releases a shaky breath.

How long we stand like that, I'm not sure, and before he finally releases me, he kisses the top of my head just like he used to when I was younger. His eyes glisten and his mouth twitches as he studies my face. "Honey, I've missed you so much. Not a day went by that I didn't think about you." He pauses, swallowing. "And as much as I've been looking forward to the day I'd be able to see you again, I'm afraid my being here isn't good news."

I glance at Jodi, wondering if she has any idea what he's talking about. "You're here. How could that be a bad thing?"

The corners of his mouth droop as he smooths the hair on the sides of my head. "I need you to understand I didn't leave you and your mother because I wanted to—I left because I had to. And I'm back now because the thing I've been preparing for—the thing I've been fearing—is beginning. This thing with Seth isn't over."

My muscles tense and my skin prickles. "Wait—what do you know about Seth?"

"More than you, I'd wager. And I know that him coming back is just the beginning." He squeezes my shoulders, pursing his lips. "Others will follow. And we need to be prepared."

ALSO BY MADELINE FREEMAN

Clearwater Witches Series
Crystal Magic
Wild Magic
Circle Magic
Moon Magic
Cursed Magic
Dark Magic

Fate Bound Trilogy
Fate Bound
Death Marked
Soul Cursed

The Naturals Trilogy
Awaking
Seeking
Becoming

Shifted Series
Shifted
Tangled
Twisted

ABOUT THE AUTHOR

Madeline Freeman lives in the metro-Detroit area with her husband, her daughter, and her cats. In the time she should spend doing housework, she rewatches *Fringe*. She also loves anything to do with astronomy, outer space, plate tectonics, and dinosaurs, and secretly hopes her daughter will become an astronomer or a paleontologist.

Connect with Madeline online:
http://www.madelinefreeman.net
http://twitter.com/writer_maddie
http://facebook.com/madelinefreemanbooks

CPSIA information can be obtained
at www.ICGtesting.com
Printed in the USA
LVOW11s2318250417
532191LV00001B/191/P